And Again

Tales of Destiny

Book Two

M. Kari Barr

HeartString Publishing

a Division of Stone Creek Farms

P.O. Box 734

Airway Heights, WA 99022

First Edition: January 2020

Printed in the United States of America

ISBN: 13: 978-1-7321401-4-1

*To my family
for accepting me as I am*

With gratitude

to those who helped me edit and

refine my story. Your contributions are invaluable.

Contents

Once Again

"So I can't accidentally get lost, or stuck in anything like a wall?" Mara asked.

"No, the light is not really slicing through anything, it is simply creating a portal if you will, and it can only be created to put you in a place you have been before. You can take others with you, but they must be within reach, yet they do not need to be touching. Usually, we as Fairies prefer to Travel by air anyway, so we often pop out of a place into the air above the place we wish to be. It takes far more practice say—to move a car and have it land safely on a tiny ledge." Aerrvin offered a crooked smile of mischief. "Go on, try to get into the car," he urged.

Mara thought about being in the driver's seat, but it would not appear, so she thought about the passenger's seat and a window of light opened. She stepped through and found she was indeed sitting in the soft leather seat. Suddenly the car was on a highway. Mara turned to say, "I did it!" to Aerrvin.

Only Aerrvin was not in the driver's seat, Morvayne was. "Yes, you did, My Buttercup."

And Again

1
Captured

Mara felt a scream building in her chest. Panic made her hands tremble as she tried to open the car door. When that failed, she remembered to think of being elsewhere—like back on the ledge, but nothing happened. Frustrated, she smacked the window.

"Let me go!"

Morvayne simply pressed the pedal down further. "Now why would I want to do that? This is such a sweet car, don't you like going for rides?" He slowed and turned off the highway into a small settlement.

Mara recognized the village. *We are in Italy! I flew over this very village with Hannah and the others just two days ago.* It was after having visited the cave of Meriel to get a Dragon shed for Aerrvin's Birth Day gift.

Mara tried to picture Meriel's cave, but nothing appeared. Summoning all her mystical Light, she fairly burst with it, but it stayed close as though a forcefield were around her.

"What have you done? Release me!"

"Come, Mara," Morvayne said, having parked and exited the car. She startled when he opened her door from outside. "I have something to show you."

Mara refused to move. She felt herself lifted into the air and floated into Morvayne's arms. "I don't want to see anything of yours, Morvayne!"

An invisible gag stopped all sounds from her. "I do prefer you silent, if you cannot keep your tone musical. Mara, you have such a pretty voice, you must learn to moderate your tone." Morvayne set her down on a beautiful sofa in the sitting room of a palazzo.

"I designed this home with you in mind; I do hope you like it. Pity I do not know all your favorite colors, but I think I have come close. Are you thirsty?" He waved at someone behind her and a servant arrived with ice water on a silver tray. She set it on the side table and left. Morvayne took a glass and sat next to Mara.

"Mara, Mara, I had hoped to have gone about this differently, but your little Fairy friend forced my hand. I could not get in to the Prince's Birth Day Bash myself, nor could my followers. But having announced his presence, I could not help but know his intentions of stealing you away from me. I had trusted him too!"

Morvayne moved his eyes slowly over her. His eyes grew wide before squinting shrewdly. "So. He has brave friends too, giving you Dragon sheds to wear. Have no fear, my dear, I do not intend to harm you. I have hundreds of years to win you over. You *shall* be my wife, and you *will* enjoy it."

Snapping his fingers, the gag lifted and he called the servant to show Mara to her rooms.

***

"Mara!" Aerrvin called—at first exasperated that he did not know where she had popped off to, before realizing a figure sat in the driver's seat. "NO! Morvayne! Seamus, are you here?"

Hannah materialized, with Jasmine, Elwood and Ivan. "Seamus, Clay, and Daisy were in the car," Hannah soothed with authority, "Let us return to your house to counsel."

Arriving in the house, Aerrvin roused his family and Nest Mates, sending someone to call on Ironwood, Brand and the rest. Once assembled, he asked Hannah, "Can you contact Clay?"

"Not until he stops to enter the Void, as you well know. We will have to wait until we receive a message. Jasmine go make yourself comfortable and wait in your Dream for Clay." Hannah expelled her own exasperated sigh. "That is the best we can do. Ironwood, what do you suggest?"

"We have followed him to three different locations over the years. His residence on Vashon Island, a palazzo in Italy, and a sea cave off the cliffs in Greece."

The great Ogre, Morthe, spoke up, "I will check the residence on Vashon if I can get a contingent to come with me."

Gareth assigned a company of fifty to him.

Aerrvin had been glaring at everyone, but saw he must wait, so he held his head in his hands instead. He felt justified in his pain and depression. *This is all my fault.*

Two of Lorelei's cousins arrived, volunteering to spy on the two other locations as they had been doing so for years. Gareth assigned battalions to attend them as well. All three groups left.

"I should never have left the property," Aerrvin moaned.

"Now, Aerrvin, it was not your fault. He could have taken her while she was at school, or riding the bus," Ironwood replied. "Remember, I told her to continue on. I did not think he would make his move before her Birth Day. I thought he would do it *on* her Birth Day, which is why I wanted her at my home for the occasion. Really, Aerrvin, there is nothing you could have done."

"I am going to wait for her Dream-self in the Void," Aerrvin said, "Come find me if you learn anything." Aerrvin left to climb into the nest with the kittens; they were more rambunctious since their eyes had opened, but not too much: he still had a few weeks with them before it would be too hard to rest in their box.

***

An older woman who barely spoke English showed Mara to her rooms. Mara did not think she was a Brownie, *surely all Brownies can speak English. Can't they?* She doubted a Brownie would wish to serve Morvayne, as slimy as he was. She went willingly to her room; at least it was away from Morvayne and she had her dignity to maintain. It would not do to be dragged everywhere he wanted her to go, especially if it took days to be rescued. Mara refused to believe it would take years, let alone decades.

"Of course, they still haven't found Daddy," she murmured to herself as the maid shut the door.

Mara did not hear a click signaling being locked in, but she doubted she could go anywhere unnoticed. She did not want to be walked in on, so she locked the door from the inside. Knowing it did little good, but at least it let who ever entered know that she wanted privacy.

She threw herself onto the pale lavender bed. Obviously, the antique dealer had told Morvayne her favorite colors based on her living room. Mara picked up one of the deep purple pillows and threw it across the room. Angrily she made herself comfortable on the rest of the pillows and tried to think. *Where was Seamus? He always comes with us, but allows some privacy. He must have been in the car. I don't know that he has much power, but he might be able to contact Aerrvin. That is my best hope.*

Thoughts of hope, anger and despair warred within her mind as she gradually drifted off. Once asleep, she realized she was being watched and suddenly rejoiced as she remembered she could talk to Aerrvin herself. Slipping into the Void, she found his Dream and walked in to find him sleeping fitfully with the kittens, who were nursing contentedly. Aerrvin rolled over and leapt into the air.

"Mara!" He held her close. "I did not know how much control he would have over you. Are you unharmed?"

Her Dream-self looked fine, but she could be knocked out for all he knew.

Mara clung to Aerrvin as tightly he clung to her. "I am. Morvayne took me to Italy, but that is all I know. It is one of the villages Hannah took me to, near the seashore."

Aerrvin interrupted her, "Shh! That's fine, we know where it is. Ironwood has had the place watched for years. Did you see Seamus, Clay, or Daisy?"

"Were they all in the car too?" Mara hoped, her eyes alight with the prospect of a quick delivery.

"They were. Hannah and the rest will be there soon. Let's go tell Jasmine; she awaits in the Land of Dreams for Clay." Aerrvin opened the way into the Void and located Jasmine's signature star.

Quickly they confirmed where Mara was and left to allow Jasmine to wake and report.

Mara asked, "What happens if Jasmine wakes up while we are in her Dream?"

Aerrvin hugged Mara, quickly suppressing a smile. "Ever seeking knowledge, Mara! Nothing happens. We would simply be returned to the Void to find our way to our own Dreams whithersoever we will."

"Please don't leave me, Aerrvin." Mara clung to him. "Let's

just lay down with the kittens. I know he is going to come and get me soon, probably wants me to dine with him."

The sweet orange tiger-striped kitten, Growly, stopped nursing and was trying to find a comfy spot to lay down to sleep since he got pushed out of his place by Fluffy. Aerrvin scratched behind Growly's ears, the kitten sprawled down next to its mother allowing Mara and Aerrvin to cuddle up against his downy softness. "This is just my Dream, Mara, but Growly really does love you." Then changing the topic he said, "Tell me about the interior of the house."

Mara explained that the car was driven into a gated drive. Then they walked through, or rather she was carried, through an interior courtyard, very richly planted. Inside was the grand foyer with a large sitting-gathering room to the right, and on the left large sweeping stairs lead up to an airy landing. Most likely the kitchen went deeper into the house as a servant came from a door to the rear of the great room. Mara explained that she had been led up the stairs, and had passed two doors—one to the left and one to the right, before being placed in a suite of rooms at the back of the house. In front was a sitting room and in back was a moderately sized bedroom with a large bathroom. The bedroom had a balcony facing the sea.

"Mara, you can show me instead of telling me."

Mara kept forgetting they were in a Dream, not the new nightmare that was reality.

Instantly, Aerrvin found himself "in" her new surroundings searching everything she had seen downstairs and then going up to see the view from her balcony. He could not actually step out onto it, because she had not been out there yet. But he recognized the beach anyway. "I know this beach, Mara! I am going to come closer to you and will meet you again soon. It is nearly dinner time in Italy, so I will say goodbye now, rather than have you ripped from me." Aerrvin looked somberly into her eyes. "I couldn't bear it. I love you, Mara. Take courage; he cannot cause any permanent harm as long as you wear that armor, keep yourself covered . . ."

***

Mara had been ripped from his arms. Aerrvin cried out in anguish as he woke, "No! Not again." Aerrvin collected the new weapons, which he had received as gifts. Strapping them on, he retrieved his bow and quiver as well. He left his bedroom suite to tell Ironwood where he was going.

"Has Morthe returned yet?" Aerrvin nearly barked as he entered the music room where Ironwood waited. A young Brownie missed a note before continuing on.

Ironwood winked at the Brownie and replied, "Yes, he just stopped by the kitchen to have some food. Traveling makes him hungry. I assumed Gareth would be going with you, so I sent him to get Mara's gift of Dragon armor; she told me she left it in her room. I want him to wear it while he is out, since I will not be able to participate in the rescue. I have allowed my body to get too old before Choosing. I intend to take the vows tonight, so I will be strengthened for what lies ahead." Ironwood was stiff with grief, yet ever graceful with his limber, yet aged, body.

Aerrvin bowed to the royal heir and progenitor. "Welcome to the Way." Ironwood nodded solemnly in return.

Aerrvin then went to say his goodbyes to his mother and father. "Surely you understand my need, Mother?" he asked.

"Yes, I do. But I have no need to enjoy it. Remember to use your intellect before using your strength. Learn his wards and spells, perchance you can untie them. Surely Mara can free herself; her abilities will exceed any Power seen in a thousand years and maybe more. I know Morvayne desires to control her, but she has a strong will, almost equal to Harmony's," the Queen smiled at her daughter who returned a small smile of her own. "She will hold out against him for decades if need be."

"He will not have her longer than a week if I can help it!"

In the garden room stood three companies of fifty trained guardians. It was a large number of Fairies, considering only five hundred thousand Fairies were scattered throughout the world. Yet having seen Morvayne's Ring at the zoo, Aerrvin knew there were probably equal numbers on Morvayne's side.

Aerrvin could count on all the Blues, battle and honor being their passions. Also most of the Whites, despite their preference to be alone, they could always see reason and truth. Greens were wild and could not be counted on, but if they arrived, they would be an asset. Very few Purples would be usable he knew, and Reds had passion, but preferred to write about it, not participate in it. The Yellows and Oranges mostly went to Morvayne. The few Yellows he could count on would be from Harmony's group of friends in Ireland and England.

Morvayne had not been to Ireland but once in the last 200 years. Harmony's friends her own age would not be tainted. But Aerrvin did not know what use they would be anyway, being the scholars that they were. Aerrvin sighed.

Finally, Gareth returned. "Sorry, it took awhile to get someone to let me in. Jill was in the shower and the Brownies were in bed. Sylvie finally let me in through Mara's window. She is spitting mad and wants to be taken to Mara. I told her we will have to see how things go first."

With a nod, Aerrvin explained the location. Morthe and Gareth had both been there before, so each, with command of one company, opened Traveling Windows to file through. The position Aerrvin chose was actually a mile away from the palazzo; large rocks and a small cave led to an exclusive Water Sprite colony, in essence a spa community for Fairies visiting the seashore.

Morthe led his company to another location near the cliffs where a shadowed entrance to a much larger cavern could be discerned, within which a friend of his lived. He surmised she could be an ally if she felt she could gain by it. An Ogress is far more rare than an Ogre, which is why they were dwindling in numbers, not to mention as a species they are loners by nature. Morthe told his company leader to stay put while he went inside.

***

The cave was dark and comforting to the Ogres' sensibilities. Morthe smiled, thinking about Zara. She wore her long dark bangs down so they nearly fell into her eyes, which were so big and brown—like mud. She normally kept her hair in a large braid which hung down to the middle of her back, but Morthe had seen it once undone on May Day many years back, and it had been lovely.

He was just standing there daydreaming, when he heard a voice like a babbling brook speak. "Well, are you going to ask to come in, or are you going to stand there all day with that goofy smile above your chin?"

"Oh, pardon me, uh Zara, it's me Morthe, and I come to make a request." He stood up straight, trying to look more formal.

"Speak your request and learn your fate, make it your best or land in my plate," she replied with equal formality.

Morthe knew he was poor at this; he should have stopped to think before entering the cave. Drawing in a breath, he said, "The future Queen of all the Realms has been stolen and taken away, my men are here to save the dear, and we are willing to pay," he ended, looking expectantly in her direction.

Zara smirked, "O Morthe, dear Morthe, you need some help. Lucky for you I can give it. You can stay as long as you pay, and favor me with your visit." She smiled invitingly.

Morthe followed her into her main cave. "Thank you, Zara, it has been a long time, I know. I have fifty Fairies outside with no place to stay."

"Why don't they stay at the colony?" Zara asked.

"Prince Aerrvin has another one hundred with him, and he is already checking to see how much space they can give him," Morthe replied. His eyes scanned the room, noticing how neat she kept her place. *Books actually on the shelf!* Unlike his place with books everywhere.

"Why so many? It sounds like you are gearing up for a war. Is Morvayne really trying to harm the Future Queen?" Zara asked.

"Have you not heard the news? Queen Gwennara has been kidnapped, and hidden below the sea. Where, we know not. But we have some ideas, at least Ironwood does. Morvayne has Mara in his palazzo down the road. Does he ever talk to you, or does he have you under surveillance, do you know?" Morthe asked.

"No, I had not received that message yet. They are slow to deliver things my way. I do not think I am being kept in the dark on purpose though, and I am not being guarded. I would know if there were Fair Ones within one hundred paces of me. I felt you and your fifty when you arrived. I even knew it was you," she smiled shyly and turned back to the entrance to invite the Fairies in.

***

Aerrvin went to the main counter, though it wasn't a counter at all, but it was where the Head Water Sprite sat to check guests in. "I invoke the name of the Rose Crown as I request refuge for one hundred and three Fairies."

The Sprite nearly choked on the kelp she was eating. "What! We only have twelve rooms left. I guess you woodland

10

Fairies are better at cozying up though; you can have the rooms, but I don't think we can feed all of you, I mean from the kitchens. We can create whatever—you know what I mean. Be that as it may—"

She rang a bell and asked a cute blue and green Water Sprite show them to their rooms. Sprites rarely wear clothes at all, being that they are in the water so much. Instead, they wear their skin in fantastic color combinations. This one started out with intense blue feet gradually turning green until she ended with her face and hair a pale watery green. Aerrvin knew she would look stunning in the water with her hair swirling in the currents.

He chose the nicest of the rooms for himself, as was proper. Then he selected the ten unit leaders to stay with him in his room as well, along with Gareth and Bronwyn. The room was sufficiently large and would not be very crowded since Aerrvin intended to send units of twenty out on patrols every twelve hours. Besides, sleep was not needed, nor possible for Aerrvin. He would rest while contacting Mara when she slept.

They just needed a staging area out of sight. Aerrvin was sure that Morvayne knew about the resort, but he doubted he would think they would dare to stay so close. Two of his unit leaders were Yellows who were actually double agents. They attended Morvayne's Fairy Ring Councils in the zoo and told Gareth everything that was done. Gareth trusted them, so Aerrvin did too.

2
Waiting

Speaking to the Yellow Fairy named Orrin, Aerrvin asked, "Did Morvayne give any hints that he was about to do this?"

Orrin looked at Pauli, "No, but Pauli here, heard some of the higher up Orange Fairies bragging about how much they have improved their battle skills."

Pauli added, "Actually not just with sword and bow, but with positive and negative ions. Morvayne has been teaching new techniques to the smarter Oranges. It would be wise to study the protective wards on the property."

Aerrvin grimaced, "Yes, Queen Laurel said much the same thing. Very well, let us set to."

Aerrvin and Pauli's unit left to study the spells, while Gareth took a unit to survey the area. They split into pairs to visit the locals.

***

Mara awakened from her Dreamstate by a knock at her door. "Oh, Aerrvin! I'm so sorry."

Louder she called, "Hang on."

Mara was disheveled as she had slept restlessly. She opened the door to find Morvayne there.

He looked at her as though she were a hopeless puppy.

"Dear Mara, I'm so sorry to have awakened you. I forgot you were on Seattle time. It is a bit late, even over there, for you to be sleeping. As for where we are, it is nearly 4:30. I came to invite you to dinner and to give to you time to freshen up. We will eat at 5:30. Do ask if you need anything. Tessa, here, is very capable; she can fix your hair and dress you, should you need help. We tend to dine formally, so choose something appropriate from your closet. Tessa will wait in your front room. Until dinner, then." Morvayne bowed.

Mara felt it a mockery to whom she had become. She was thankful he left as she flared Brighter than ever. Even so, it never left a confined halo about her person. Tessa did not seem to notice.

Mara did not care what she wore, so before going into the bathroom she instructed Tessa, "Just find anything, I'm not particular." Tessa bowed and hastened to the closet.

Mara entered the luxurious bathroom. It had a giant jetted tub with a shower right over the middle of it. The tub was so large there were no worries of splashing water onto the floor from the shower. Mara allowed the dress she had created to disappear and was surprised that it obeyed her desire. She did not think she had any Power left. So she experimented, trying to learn what her new limits were. Stepping under the rainfall-like shower, she allowed the water to pelt her harshly. There was a button to the side where she could change the flow and she had chosen the massaging one, even though it stung somewhat. She felt numb anyway.

She tried to call forth the shampoo, but it would not come until she was within six inches of it. "So six inches is my limit. Let me try this."

Mara tried to place a protective shell over her to prevent

the water from getting her wet. At first, she saw no change, but slowly less and less water hit her until she had a complete barrier all around her. The line was just within the barrier which surrounded her, the same barrier that kept her light from extending to its fullest.

"So I cannot affect anything beyond six inches, yet I can control what comes at me. I don't think I can be killed and I certainly can't be molested. Not with this armor on." Mara rinsed her hair and applied conditioner.

"So, I might as well relax and accept this as an educational experience. If Morvayne thinks I am coming around, he might even relax the security. Though he plans on waiting a hundred years. Humph! I guess he really does not intend to kill me."

Mara plugged the tub and turned on the jets. Filling the tub as full as it could, she floated in the bubbles, enjoying the scented oils she had poured in. "I'll say one thing, the Fair Ones really know how to live."

Mara thought about her mother; why she would want to deny such awesomeness was beyond her. "I could have had such fun as a child." Then she frowned thinking that had she been raised as an Elf she would still be considered a baby. *Dad must have had a plan to explain it.* Her brain scattered as her thoughts jumped about. *Morvayne is terribly old. Don't they have rules about such old people going after babies? Mom is right; he is just plain smarmy.* Mara practiced changing the shape of her Dragon shed. She even made it into boots.

Could I divide it into two and still have one? If so the amount of armor I could share might be near limitless, unless it has a defined number on how many times it can be divided.

Mara started to remove one of the boots, when Tessa knocked and entered. "My Lady, it is nearly 5:30 you must get dried and dressed. Morvayne is quite punctual."

The boots were under water and Mara did not think Tessa saw them, so she turned the skin back into a delicate knotted belt. Tessa held a towel out, so Mara stood and allowed Tessa to wrap her up in its rich softness. Mara smiled as she thought about how much Aerrvin would love the soft towel. "Thank you, Tessa, I will be out momentarily."

Mara toweled herself dry and brushed out the tangles from her hair. She fashioned her armor to look like a slip, happy that it complied, and went to see what ghastly fashions Morvayne preferred.

***

Tessa felt her eyes widen at the slip, she had not seen any additional clothing in the bathroom, and for that matter had never seen clothes that swirled. She had seen odd things since she started working at the Palazzo de Maurice, but this was unexpected.

She kept her mouth shut though, as Master Maurice paid well, and he rarely stayed for more than a month at a time. He only came by maybe three or four times a year, almost always with a guest or two. This girl was different though, she did not seem so excited to be here. She was afraid of the Master, and she talked to herself.

"My Lady, Master Maurice has a dinner theme and tonight it is King Arthur's Court. The only things in your closet are items related to that time period. He always changes the entire wardrobe in the closets when he changes his theme, so I chose what I thought matched your coloring. If you do not like it you may select something else."

"No, I am sure what you have chosen is fine," Mara replied without interest. Mara was grateful that this younger servant spoke English, even if it was with a heavy accent.

First Tessa fitted her with an under dress in a pale creamy

cotton, it was very full and looked like a nightgown though very low in front. Then she had Mara raise her arms as she pulled a skirt over her head, as it was easier to put on that way rather than step into it and have to tuck in the voluminous under dress.

The skirt was a deep midnight blue, almost teal in the highlights as it reflected the light on its silky surface. Finally the maid helped Mara into an overdress with a tight fitted bodice which laced up the front.

It was a deep royal red and the sleeves fit somewhat snugly from the shoulder to the elbow, and then had a slit allowing the cream sleeve beneath to blouse out in rich puffs. The wrists were held tight with diamond encrusted cuffs.

Tessa had been instructed to remove the necklace Mara wore and replace it with a diamond choker. It was a bit odd, but the Master had required others to dress as he demanded before.

"Turn around, let me remove this, it does not match as well as this choker." Tessa instructed. She tried the clasp, but it would not come undone.

Mara moved away. "That's alright Tessa, I don't want to wear the choker."

***

Tessa dropped her eyes, she had failed, but did not want to press. She had never had to force a guest to comply before. In all the years she had worked for Maurice, she had never met any guest over the age of twenty-five, but she doubted this Mara was even twenty. She seemed so young and innocent. Maurice was surely fifty even though he looked thirty.

He had owned the place since before Tessa was born and she was thirty-two. She felt privileged that he had hired her the very day she had submitted her application.

Tessa lived in the servants' quarters behind the house, in

the back corner of the property. It was hidden behind a screen of trees so as not to be seen by visitors. Gianni the gardener lived there as well, with his wife Isadora, the housekeeper and cook. The three of them maintained the property, keeping it ready for whenever Master Maurice decided to show up.

Since Mara did not want to wear the necklace, Tessa set about doing Mara's hair. She did not have much time because Mara had taken so long in the bath. Tessa decided to leave most of it down and just took a twist of hair on each side, arranging it to look like a crown of hair, clasping each twist at the back of her head with a ruby and diamond clip. Mara was stunning.

"Mara, you look beautiful! Look in the mirror, see? Maybe you should have been born in the days of kings and queens. Yes?"

Mara looked; she did look quite authentic. *Morvayne probably knew Guinevere, and had tried to steal her away from Arthur along with Lancelot,* Mara thought sourly. She tried to moderate her surly appearance. No sense in looking pouty, and Tessa did not seem to be any kind of magical being.

Mara spoke up finally, "Thank you Tessa, I do look lovely. How long have you worked for Mor…" Mara did not know what name he went by.

"Maurice. I have worked for Master Maurice for ten years, almost eleven." Tessa wanted to ask how long she had known him, but that, of course, was not her place, nor business. "Come, he waits."

3

Dining With the Enemy

Mara felt shocked to see Morvayne wearing a kilt. She was expecting a doublet and hose, or even a tunic and leggings, but not a Scottish kilt! He did look impressive, if arrogant.

"Ah, Mara, you look resplendent. Red suits you. I see you are surprised at the Scottish attire. Surely, you knew Arthur grew up in and ruled from the lower part of Scotland? He often hosted members from the Wallace and Stewart clans almost exclusively.

"You should be quite aware that you hail from the Wallace clan."

He paused to look her over from head to toe. Nodding in approval, he continued. "Back then, long before Arthur's time really, Elves and Humans lived more harmoniously than they have since Christianity took hold over Europe. It might interest you to know; the Scots got most of their surnames from the Fair Ones, not the other way around. I am, of course, a descendant of the Stewart clan."

He flourished his elegant hands down his person, drawing attention to the traditional red and green over white plaid. With a practiced grace, he jerked his head to the side to clear his blond hair from his cloudy blue eyes. He kept his hair trimmed just past his ears, leaving the bangs fashionably long, which he swept to the side.

18

A knock at the door diverted their thoughts. "Ah! Our guests have arrived. See them in Gianni."

The servants had more than one job when Maurice hosted a party. A limo pulled to the front and disgorged five couples, all dressed in period costume. Gianni held the door.

"Welcome! Friends, please come in. Dinner is ready. But first, say hello to my special guest, Mara." Morvayne oozed with charm.

They were Fairies, and they were not even trying to hide their Light. Only one of the males was Yellow, but all the girls were. The rest were Orange.

Morvayne lead the way to the formal dining room, which was open and spacious, with a small stage and a dancing area. Morvayne took Mara's hand, and tucked it into the crook of his arm familiarly.

Unable to resist, Mara asked softly, "Don't you have any Elven friends?"

Morvayne laughed as though she had told a marvelous joke, garnering looks from the others in the room. "Mara, Mara, you have spirit—that you do!" He chuckled again. "Of course, I realize that Fairies are not as eloquent and interesting as Elves are, but I thought you enjoyed Fairies and wanted you to be comfortable with our guests. I will introduce you to my Elven friends in due time."

He stopped to admire her from head to toe again. "You look as though you stepped right out of a painting; you look just like her." He raised her hand to kiss it and she quickly covered her hand with the Dragon skin. He kissed it regardless, but narrowed his eyes. "I see you have mastered its use. Mara, one day you will relish my attention. It is quite exquisite to the touch though, I shall enjoy the sensual nature of it as well."

Mara contained her glow, but flushed in anger anyway, spilling sparkles upon her person only.

"I shall need to find a way to collect your Dust. Perhaps when you change. I will send one of the little Yellows. Yes, you probably need a second personal assistant. Tessa is wonderful, but I need, I mean you need *more*—owing to your status and all."

Mara said nothing in response.

Mara was starving. Dinner was not Italian, as one would expect in Italy. It was old English and Scottish, including a traditional haggis. She dared not even taste it. No red meats were served, besides the goat. Fortunately, there was roasted chicken and spring potatoes, crusty bread and a cheese and fruit platter.

Mara ate far more than one would think a tiny person could consume, especially extra meat and fruit. Morvayne had, of course observed the flight she had taken before he captured her and insinuated the cause of her hunger. "That Purple was foolish, teaching you to fly like that! You are lucky to have a more accomplished teacher now."

He made to pat her hand, but stopped when she flinched.

Dessert was a plum pudding. Mara found it passable, but she would have preferred more sugar. Morvayne and the Fairies appeared to love the entire meal.

Once the dishes were cleared away, the musicians (who had arrived half way through the meal) began to play some of the same music Mara had heard Balmoral play. Morvayne required her to dance song after song.

"Mara, I do believe your gracefulness on the floor has improved already. Perhaps that Purple did have some use after all. Although, I did hear the reports, that not only is he the Prince, but that he has acquired Blue wings as well. Hah! He will always be the little Purple to me. How about you, Mara, did you really think a Fairy was worthy of you?”

Blinking back the tears of anger, she asked to be excused. Morvayne allowed it; sendingh a sleek, red-haired Fairy as an escort.

***

Tessa observed the tension the entire evening as she set out dishes and cleared them away, or stood waiting to be of service. No, this was not the usual guest. Never had a guest been afraid of Maurice, always they were fawning all over him trying to curry his favor. The Master himself was as graceful as ever, but Tessa could see a sense of anxiety about him as well. She started to follow Mara to her room when he stopped her.

“Tessa, wait a moment, allow her to collect herself; she has learned of a loss. Kiera will watch over her.”

Tessa bobbed a curtsy and went back to the wall. *How long to wait?* She had barely met the girl, but already she felt great compassion for her. If the girl was sorrowing, she wanted to be there. Tessa watched as Morvayne drank his second bottle of wine while flirting with the remaining guests. Now that Mara was gone, the party began to appear as they always had. Tessa assumed the rich always behaved this way; she’d witnessed numerous guests at Morvayne’s palazzo. Always the parties ended in wild dancing, laughter, and drunkenness.

Tessa went up and found Mara in bed. Kiera sat in the waiting room, looking glum. “I will watch her if you would like to return to the party,” Tessa offered. Kiera jumped up, not needing a second urging.

“I may be back, if that is what he wants, but thank you.”

Kiera seemed to fly out the door. Tessa shut it and went to turn off the lights in Mara’s room. Mara stirred and then sat up.

“Signorina, can I get you anything?” Tessa surveyed her

ruddy face and puffy eyes.

"Is there headache medicine in here?" Mara asked.

"No, please forgive me, let me get some for you." Tessa went to the bathroom and wet a cloth first and brought it to Mara. "Here this will soothe you."

A linen closet down the hall contained a shelf for first aid and medicines, so Tessa did not take long. Mara had a small bar in her waiting room, where Tessa got a glass for the water. Mara looked better already as Tessa handed her the pills.

"The Master says you have suffered a loss, I am so sorry. Please know; I am here for you. Would you like me to stay in the front room? I can rest on the couch if it pleases you?"

***

Mara studied Tessa, she seemed innocent and sincere, unlike Kiera. *If I must have a guard, I would prefer Tessa.*

"Yes, I would like that." Earlier, Mara had jumped into bed as soon as the dress was off with only her dragon slip. "Please, could you find me a night gown?"

Tessa felt ashamed that Mara needed to ask. "Oh, forgive me, I did not realize."

Mara looked at the poor servant and felt her own compassion. *What must it be like to have to work for the Master of Smarm?* When Tessa returned from the wardrobe with a satin nightie Mara sighed, but said kindly, "Tessa, please call me Mara when we are alone."

"Yes, Mara. Thank you, I can do that," Tessa replied, while disconcerted at the shifting slip Mara wore. It was no longer a slip at all, but a tight fitting tank top and boy shorts. Still it swirled in beautiful, almost oily glittering specks of ever-changing rainbows.

Mara realized it was totally new to her, since she herself

had only seen it for the first time the day before. *Was it really only yesterday?*

"Tessa, I do not know how much you know, but I can tell you are amazed at my armor."

"Armor, Signor–Mara?" Tessa stumbled.

"Yes," Mara answered as she pulled the slinky gown over her head. It barely covered the armor.

"It is magic, as is my necklace; they cannot be removed." Mara sank back onto the bed waiting to see Tessa's reaction.

Tessa crossed herself and offered prayers in Italian. Wide-eyed she asked, "And the Master he knows this, yes?"

"He knows magic, yes, but he holds me prisoner and hopes to use me somehow. I know you cannot release me. I am not asking you to do that. I just wanted you to be aware, because I will not be removing either item, nor will I remove this ring."

Mara had not had a chance to take a look at it closely until her bath. Aerrvin had indeed given her a lavender gray diamond, with a rose carved within it, no less!

She looked at it and felt her lips form a bittersweet smile.

"My fiancé gave it to me last night. He will rescue me, but I don't know how long it will take." She hiccuped and lay her head on her drawn up knees.

***

Tessa sat next to her and soothed her back. She had no words to say. *Was the poor girl delusional? Maybe her grief—but no, I see the 'armor' swirling, it really is moving right before my eyes. Magic would explain a lot of things I have thought I have seen for years. Do Gianni and Isadora know? They have worked for him longer, ten years longer at least.*

A knock at the door sounded and Morvayne came in with

Kiera, not waiting to be invited.

"Poor Mara, you should be sleeping. Tessa you may retire for the night."

Tessa had never done this before, but she requested permission to stay. "Mara, she said she would like it if I would sleep on the couch, Signore." Tessa bowed and awaited his decision.

"Mara, I know you are lonely, but it is not fair to Tessa; she has been up all day working. Kiera has just had a long nap and will gladly sit on your couch, awaiting to serve you." Noticing the cloth and glass, he tsked in pity. "Did you have a headache too, I am so sorry. It must be the jet lag. Coming across the ocean and finding yourself in a different time zone can do that to you. No, Tessa, perhaps another time when you have rested better. I will sit with Mara until she sleeps, and then I will leave Kiera to watch through the night. Run along."

Tessa took one last compassionate look at Mara; witnessing as the young woman hung her head on her knees again. "Good night, Signorina. Signore." She refrained from looking at Kiera and left.

Tessa could think of nothing to help the poor girl so she went to her cottage at the edge of the property, contemplating whether to approach Isadora or not. She decided to sleep on it.

Mara lay down hoping Morvayne would go away. He approached the bed and sat at the foot. Mara grew her armor, covering herself up to her neck and fingertips.

"Mara, you should know I mean you no harm. Are you even aware of who you are? You will be the Queen of all the Realms! Imagine the possibilities! You will see I have much in the way to offer. I can begin by reciting our history from the beginning; every Elf needs to be fully educated. I do not know why Ironwood kept putting it off. But no matter, we have time and time again. Relax, take your ease, Mara. I will speak and you will remember, whether you sleep or not."

Mara shut her eyes and tried to block Morvayne out, but she did hear and remember everything he told her. Some of his lessons were stories her father had told her, the same stories in *Enchanted Lives*. Others were new, or had different points of view as to why, or how a thing had occurred. It was an important lesson, she realized. But she would not feel gratitude, she was sure Ironwood would have taught those lessons soon.

***

Aerrvin sat outside the palazzo all afternoon, studying the wards on the gate. A limo arrived at 5:30, activating the wards. Aerrvin watched with interest as the space between the columns of the arch transferred from negative to positive, while a new element was added allowing the limo to pass through the portal. One of his Blues tried to ride the bumper through, but he got knocked off as the car drove past the barrier.

"Interesting. I think you have to be inside the car. I have to believe that Seamus and the others are inside. I don't think I can solve this particular ward. I think there should be an easier opening near the back. Let's just see who is getting out of the limo." Aerrvin was already cloaked as a dragonfly, as was Pauli, so they flew up to get a better view.

The driver opened the door and ten Fairies exited, dressed in traditional old English wear. Elves love costume parties with themes; Fairies are more carefree.

I cannot fathom what these Fairies are hoping to gain by all this!

"Pauli, are these the more talented Fairies you were talking about, the ones learning new skills?"

"Not the maidens; they come for the prestige and power. But yes, the rest are his most trusted from the Ring at the zoo."

Just then, Aerrvin saw a squirrel run around to the back of the house. *That might be Daisy or Clay,* he thought. He was unable to enter the airspace above the grounds, so he flew around the perimeter hoping to catch sight of it again. There! Aerrvin swooped down to rest on a rock at the edge of the property where a small grove of trees surrounded a couple of cottages. For the servants he assumed.

He became a squirrel as well. He chattered a hello, to see if he could get a response. He did; one was an actual squirrel who wished he would go away, and the other was Daisy.

She came to the edge and stopped. "I cannot find a way to leave the property and can't enter the house either; it has an invitation spell on it. If Mara learns that we are here, she can eventually invite us in. But Clay thinks it best if we take our time. He recognizes some of the wards and says they are not new; rather they are old and have not been used much in the last 400 years. Some of them have nasty surprises attached and it would be best to not trigger them, especially the front gate and the ones on the windows and doors. So, really, our best chance is when Mara starts coming outside. Morvayne has to allow her to get sunshine eventually." Daisy snatched up a seed and stuffed it into her mouth, garnering a chastisement from the wild squirrel.

"Then where are Clay and Seamus? I need Clay's advice and want to give some to Seamus."

"Clay left Seamus as is, he thought he would look more suspicious to the local Brownies if he looked like he was skulking. He is looking for any local Brownies. There were none at all beneath the palazzo; now he is checking the cottages and the garden house."

"Good, that is what I wanted to tell him. Well good. Then I will wait here for Clay; when you see him ask him to let me know what can be done."

"Okay, but the squirrel here is overprotective. You should probably switch to a lizard or something, and do it out of sight, there are at least ten Oranges patrolling the perimeter, and two are in the trees above us." She chattered angrily at him advising him to leave. Daisy made a challenging hop at him, which caused Aerrvin to chuckle at her show. Chattering happily he scampered away.

Once he was well hidden in a shadow, he became a sleek blue skink. Then he returned to sit in the shade of the rock.

Pauli continued to flit about as a dragonfly. An hour went by before Seamus and Clay emerged from the shrubbery closest to the rock where Aerrvin hid. Clay was a full inch and a half taller than the little Brownie, each wore colors to match the vegetation.

"Well, what news?" Aerrvin asked anxiously.

Clay answered for both of them. "Seamus found that the cottages do have Brownies, and they can get off the property, but the tunnel is deep and takes days to traverse. None can Travel. Also, one of Morvayne's guards patrols the exit. He is lax though, as he has been at it for twenty years. He has never had anyone try to enter who had not received a pass at leaving. The Brownies do not know of any traps or wards set on their opening, so they think it is safe. They rarely leave as they have no need, but if they do, the Orange Fairy takes their name and has them sign a ledger. He allows them back in when they complete their errand."

"I see," said Aerrvin. "So if we ambush this entrance we have to completely remove the Fairy to make sure he does not warn Morvayne. But what if he is the trap? What if Morvayne is attuned to him? And if he dies, or Travels elsewhere, Morvayne knows immediately. Then we have ruined what little chance we thought we had."

Aerrvin's form slithered back and forth across the rock. It

was dark now, he could probably resume his Fairy self. He zipped back and forth a few more times and then stopped in the shadows of the night, there was no moon which helped. Though the Fair Ones can see as well as any night owl. Best to stay motionless he thought.

Clay allowed the prince to settle into his own skin and then responded, "I think we should send Seamus out of the tunnel. He is young enough to have never left home before. The Fairy will not have records of who lives here, so Seamus can just say he is setting out to find his bride. He may be able to enter and leave several times without comment, a fellow has to come home to sleep sometime right?" Clay clapped Seamus on the back.

Evidently everyone knew about Sylvie. Seamus grinned stupidly. Aerrvin smiled briefly, but stayed on track. "So what will that accomplish?"

Clay explained, "Once he has built up a friendship, he can offer presents for more frequent passage and then perhaps we can drug the Orange Fairy, he will still be on duty, but incapacitated enough so as not to be able to sound an alarm."

"Okay. Why not try drugging him sooner?" Seamus asked.

"If you offer something right off you look suspicious; it will have to take time. Maybe two weeks. I know that is so very close to Midsummer, but that is all I can see from that angle. I have another avenue I can try as well. I have secretly maintained a friendship with Morvayne," Clay confessed.

"What?" Aerrvin exclaimed. "You are sworn to Mara's protection! How could you be a friend to Morvayne?"

"He is my brother," Clay replied simply. "I am fifty years older and grew up with Tigerlily and her sisters, Arianna and Daffodil. Morvayne knows that I loved those three princesses as much as he did. I too was upset when Tigerlily chose Humanity. I could not understand her choice. Eventually I accepted it and made my peace with Tigerlily. She respected me, and chose to honor me with the charge to protect Mara. Morvayne has never learned of this assignment."

Aerrvin was shocked, but saw a small glimmer of hope. "I see. What do you think you can do?"

"I am still considering. Forget about trying to break or undo the wards. It is far too dangerous. Proceed with the plans to send Seamus out. I will see if I can get Morvayne to meet me at his place in Vashon. Maybe while he is gone, you will be able to sneak Mara out. Remember this will take two weeks to accomplish. So hold your peace. Speak to Mara in her Dreams and let her know it will take time."

Aerrvin deferred to Clay's nine hundred years of experience. "All right, but let me know when there are any changes."

He returned to the spa and allowed the cute Blue Water Sprite to give him a mud bath and massage. Then he took a quick swim in the sea.

Mentally exhausted, he went to his room to sleep. Only two others were sleeping as well, the rest of those assigned to his room had free time and decided to take advantage of the amenities.

Aerrvin could see Mara's Dream, but it was too weak, she was somehow still tethered to the waking world. He could not open it even to see what was occupying her thoughts. Frustrated, he dreamt that she was with him anyway, reliving the whole of last night. Until he came to the point of her capture and he woke with a start. It was morning again. He had nothing to do, so he went back into the Land of Dreams.

4

Accepting the Here and Now

Mara never really went to sleep, so she missed getting to meet with Aerrvin. She didn't know if that was Morvayne's plan, or if he really wanted her educated. She climbed out of her bed and found Kiera and Morvayne cuddled up on the couch in the front room. She padded back to her room, shut the door and locked it. She took a long, hot shower and then came out to find Kiera standing ready to serve as her maid.

"I do know how to dress myself; I have been doing it all by myself for years now. You can go out and tell the kitchen help that I am ready for breakfast, and I would like bacon and eggs along with a muffin and some fresh fruit. Go on! That is what servants do, now get!"

Kiera looked at her smugly and sauntered out of the room.

Mara watched her go and then pronounced, "Hah, like I care what she thinks!"

She surveyed closet. It held pretty white summer dresses, fit for walking on the beach. The freestanding wardrobe held more of the same in blues and greens. She looked in the drawer, all it had was swim-wear.

"Doesn't this guy believe in jeans?" Going back to the closet, she chose a skirt and blouse combo that reminded her of the one Aerrvin had created. *I look nice in white.* Her hair was still wet, but she didn't care, she went down for breakfast.

Morvayne sat in the front room, waiting to greet her as she came down the stairs. "Morning, Mara, I trust you are feeling better? We will have breakfast on the veranda. Come this way."

The property was certainly large and well-manicured. "How do you keep everything so nice? I don't see evidence of Brownies."

"No, I do not allow them in the house; they are like vermin. Elves do not need to keep Brownies in order to maintain their homes. Yes, I admit they do fine work and all, but I have my Humans and they do well enough; what they miss can be fixed with a flick of the wrist." He motioned disdainfully. "Really, Mara, you will learn all things in order. I realize, of course, that you have acquired more power than you know how to handle; that is the reason for the safety capsule I have placed around you. You are far too pretty to lose again—"

He sat in a stupor, momentarily lost in his own thoughts. Mara wondered how old he was. *He must be close to losing his mind.* She noticed he was having wine with his fruit and cheese. *He really is poisoning himself! He must drink all day long. Granted it does not have the same effect on him as it does Humans. He's not drunk, but he is not in his right mind. Oh, Light, save me, I've been taken not only by a lecherous Elf grieving the loss of his true love, but he is totally mad as well!* She wiped her brow before taking the glass of orange juice offered by Tessa.

"Yes, it does tend to heat up by late morning. We can go down to the beach today. Do you like swimming, Mara?" Morvayne asked solicitously.

"Why, yes I do, Maurice. That would be lovely." She loaded her plate and ate it all. She didn't know if more calories gave her strength or made her sluggish, but she felt hungry so she ate.

"Perhaps I should begin creating some of your meals.

Since you like to eat so much, as Fair Ones tend to do, you must learn to create your own meals. They have half the calories and more of the nutrients we need for our quick metabolism."

Morvayne proceeded to teach the mechanics in a very dry and boring way, not at all like Aerrvin's playful style. Mara kept that thought very tight and close to her heart and soul. Morvayne relaxed the 'capsule', as he called it, to allow her to practice. She feigned ignorance by failing to produce a meal.

Scrunching up her face in effort, Mara lied, "I don't think I can do it."

She thrilled at lying, it was not something she had ever needed to do. Not counting lying to herself all her life about the truth she saw around her. While she was free, she wrote a note on a leaf and dropped it with a breeze near the squirrel she saw, which actually was not a squirrel at all. Mara was pleased that her power extended that far. Then the shield clamped down and she was once again captive.

"That is alright, Mara, it takes practice and time. Pity your father had not been around to help you. He was a fine man, Brentwood was, truly a remarkable man. Did I ever tell you about the project we were working on? No, I guess I didn't; you were just a wee lass then."

Morvayne went on to tell her about her father's search for the Lost City of Atlantis. "Of course, it was never really lost, the Mermaids, and the Sea Dragons have always known where it is. That was part of his research though, he would talk to the Mermaids and gather clues. They have hidden it well. They do not want us land creatures to know where it is, as they have collected thousands of years' worth of treasure, which they keep there. But, with my help, he found the final clues. Pity I say, that he never got to see that glorious city." He smirked and took another sip of his wine.

Mara did not interrupt because he might realize he was telling her something important, but she also wanted to know more. "How can land creatures see something which, surely, must be so deep beneath the ocean?"

"What? Oh, we Fair Ones can do anything with the right spells or desires. Why, Mara, with your Dragon skin, you could fashion gills and swim wherever you please. No need for an oxygen transfer device, which is what your Father and I use. Or we *became* Water Sprites. Those kind of skills are decades away for you, I fear."

Morvayne patted her hand. "I have some business I need to attend to today, you may visit the gardens and talk with Tessa; she will be a suitable companion after all. Kiera really did not know how to serve properly. She has been sent away. I will take you to the beach after lunch." He lifted her hand and kissed it, ignoring the Dragon skin.

As soon as he was gone, Mara went to the small grove and sat down beneath one of the trees. The squirrel who was not a squirrel spoke to her. "Mar, it's me, Daisy. I cannot get inside the house unless someone inside invites me in. I can be on your balcony tonight and you can let me in. Okay?"

"Okay. But what is being done to get me out?" Mara asked. Daisy explained all the details of their situation including Clay's revelation. Which was no surprise to Daisy, of course. "They are so different, how could Clay still want to even talk to him?" Mara exclaimed, quietly, having been warned about the patrols.

"Well, he has had six hundred and fifty years of good times and only two hundred, or so, of bad. He's family. Clay thinks maybe he can still help his brother. Clay is that kind of guy. At least that's my theory," Daisy declaimed.

***

Tessa cleared the table; Maurice asked her to be Mara's

33

companion for the day. Happily, that meant no dishes for her. She noticed Mara talking to herself, again. *She really is a troubled girl.* Tessa joined Mara under the trees.

"Mara, would you like to see the gardens now?" Tessa asked.

Mara's intense focus as she pondered what she just learned about Clay, including his age, caused her to startle when Tessa spoke.

"What? Oh, yes, Tessa. I would love to." Mara got to her feet, noticing Daisy had run up a tree. "Do you help tend the gardens? They are very well groomed."

"Sometimes, but mostly Gianni takes care of them. He knows all the names and what they need. Of course, he knows very little English, and I know very little translations for plants," Tessa replied apologetically.

"That's okay, I recognize most of them. Your English is lovely."

They went towards the rose garden first. Gianni was a master gardener, and the blooms were full and fragrant. Mara stopped to enjoy the scent of a sweet yellow and pink bloom, which reminded her of the bouquet of the Rose Elixir from Aerrvin's homeland. She breathed it in deeply, closing her eyes with a sigh. Opening them, Mara saw Tessa looking at her and smiled. "They smell heavenly."

Tessa agreed and made a mental note to place some in Mara's room. Next, she showed her the vegetable and herb gardens. "Fresh is preferred. We rarely go to market because this garden provides so well."

Mara noticed the orange and lemon trees, as well as a small arbor covered in grape vines. The sun had heated up the morning, so she sat inside the arbor for respite from the glare and heat.

"This is nice. Thank you, Tessa, for showing me these gardens. Do you live in one of the cottages in the far corner?" Mara waved to the southern corner.

"Yes, I do. It is a humble place, but I have enjoyed working for Master Maurice these past ten years. He rarely comes here and when he does, he entertains for a few weeks and then leaves. It is usually quite peaceful here."

Mara saw a slight movement in the vines. Tessa did not seem to notice at all. "Tessa, would you mind bringing me a glass of water? I am not used to so much sun."

"Of course, signorina," Tessa replied leaving in haste. Maurice was generous, but he did get angry when his guests were not served well.

Once Tessa was gone, Mara spoke to the Brownie huddling behind a group of grape leaves. "You may come out now. I would like to speak to you." The Brownie was a well-groomed little fellow dressed in cream-colored shorts and nothing else. His hair was neatly combed to the side and he sported a small line of whiskers along his chin. Mara smiled at the sight. "My name is Mara. Do you live in this arbor?"

"No, I live beneath the garden house, but I tend this arbor," he replied in perfectly good English—touched with a slight Italian accent. "And my name is Cord."

"Cord, does Maurice know you live here?" Mara asked.

"Yes, he does. He does not allow us near the main house, but we are permitted to tend the gardens and the cottages. He pays no attention to us, as long as we stay out of sight. I would normally be to bed right now, but this particular vine is having a little heat stress and I wanted to help extend its roots to provide access to the stream beneath us here."

"Did you see my friend, Seamus?" Mara asked, assured that

the Brownie would not betray her.

"That I did not, but my son is one of his escorts. He will take two days to get to the exit and two days back. There will be no trouble in the tunnels themselves; they are quite safe. Rest assured, we will be giving you the best help we can provide. Are you truly the next High Queen of all the Realms?" Cord asked with a slight hesitation.

"Do you need proof?" Mara asked shocked that he did not take Seamus and Daisy's word on it.

"My Lady, I mean no disrespect. We do not receive news quickly here because of our isolation. I am one who needs— reassurances, shall we say. Truly, we would offer our help even if you were a simple Fairy being held captive. Maurice is the only Elf I have ever met. I have only left this property once and that was to find my bride. That is, I never saw another Elf until Daisy arrived and now you. If I could glimpse your Glory once it will last me a lifetime and beyond."

Mara felt compassion for the awkward Brownie. "Very well, but you must swear allegiance to me when you are satisfied that I am who I say I am." Mara opened three of her pockets, knowing the fourth was completely unnecessary in this situation. Her glow completely filled the tiny six inches of freedom the barrier around her afforded, yet that glow still brightened the shady arbor. The Glory awed and bowed the Brownie's face to the dirt. Mara was becoming used to the reaction, still she hastened to call him to his feet. Tucking the light away she commanded, "Rise, Cord, and swear allegiance."

Cord rose, beaming as though he had witnessed Heaven itself. "Your Highness, I swear all my soul and posterity to serve you for eternity and a day."

Mara smiled at his word choice. "Thank you, Cord, that will do."

Tessa had been quick, as she had gone to the garden house rather than the palazzo. Returning, she heard Mara talking. She stepped softly to listen in; it sounded as though she were talking to someone named Cord.

Cord ventured a further question before departing. "My Lady, do you know the maker of your necklace?"

Mara grasped her locket. "No, I do not. Do you?"

"Aye, I have seen the same work before. My wife's own father is a Master Jeweler. I saw many samples of his work all those years ago when I met with him to plead my case. I am positive that he is the one. It has many layers of magic in it, too fine for me to see. You will need to meet with him to learn all of its properties, unless you have been taught them already, My Lady." He bowed deeply awaiting her response.

"No, no there was no time. My Aunt died before she could teach me." Mara sighed her next statement, "She wasn't even my Aunt; she was Princess Tigerlily herself and I never knew it. Now Morvayne, or Maurice, or whatever he wants to call himself, wants me to be his wife—since Tigerlily refused him. I won't do it! Cord, do you think you could contact your father-in-law, and have him come here to teach me?"

"As you wish, My Lady, my son is only eight hours into his journey. I can send my daughter, Swallowtail; she is rightly named and can to catch up with them in another six hours. By your leave, Your Highness?"

Mara replied, "I am not Her Highness yet. Please, My Lady will do. And yes, by all means, go!"

Cord stood, bowed again and ran toward the garden house, leaving Mara with a bemused expression when Tessa arrived with the water. It even had ice. "Thank you, Tessa! That was quick."

"We keep a small kitchen with a refrigerator in the garden

house, Gianni works there most days for many hours and does not like to leave for lunch," Tessa replied, wondering at the one sided conversation she had heard Mara having.

"Mara, the master does not keep a television or phones in his palazzo, but we have them in our cottages. If you would like, when he leaves, I can bring you over. Or is there someone you would like me to call for you? If you are really being held captive I could call the authorities, yes?"

Mara considered, "Thank you, Tessa, I forgot to even think of calling anyone. My friends who are planning to rescue me already know where I am. Hmmm—I think if I called the police, Morvayne, or Maurice, as you know him, would simply hide me or whisk me away to somewhere else and then my friends would have to try to find me again." Mara rubbed her brow and sighed.

"I don't think I should alarm Mother, just yet, but I should call Grandpa when I get the chance. I guess you could call Jill and Jaera for me. Tell Jill that Morvayne has taken me to Italy, and that she can ask Jaera about it. Wait! Call Jaera first and ask her to attend classes for me, my schedule is in my notebook. She can talk to Jill about it. I guess that is all I can do about that. Thank you, really, Tessa, I had not even thought about missing school next week. I am supposed to graduate on June 5th; I worked so hard to earn that privilege.

My mother will be coming for that, so I hope to be rescued before then. I don't think Jaera can fool my mother into thinking she is me."

Mara looked at the ground forlornly, then she took the pen and scrap of paper Tessa had taken from her pocket for Mara to write their numbers on.

***

Tessa still did not know how stable Mara was, but she knew that Mara believed what she was saying. She leaned in to pat her and was surprised when Mara hugged her and wept on her shoulder briefly.

Mara collected her reserves and said, "Tessa, I know this is all bewildering to you. Thank you for being so understanding. It is all new to me too, magic I mean. I've barely learned about it in the past two weeks myself. Let's see the orchard and your little corner of the property; then I will return to my rooms."

The orchard was small as orchards go, but it had variety; including plum trees, apricots, peaches, and apples as well as the citrus trees. Best of all, in the far corner stood a gloriously old olive tree. Mara's fingers itched for her camera, but she didn't think to call it to her.

She could also see two Orange Fairies sitting in the upper reaches of its branches. One feigned disinterest, while the other waved and watched intently with a little smirk on his face as she turned away. Her skill at ignoring annoying creatures remained intact.

They walked along the fence defining the property line. Mara looked out on the sea as it crashed upon the rocky shore. There were sandy beaches, but they were farther east and west. Once again beneath the woods which sheltered the two cottages, Mara spotted a seagull standing on a nice big rock. She stopped to look and realized it was Aerrvin, she walked forward and was seized by a strangling sensation upon her body. It felt as though the 'capsule' binding her had constricted upon her. She fell helplessly to the ground.

"Mara, what happened? Are you okay?" Tessa asked in alarm.

At the same time Mara heard Aerrvin saying, "Mara, you need to stay away from the fence; when you come near it, the bindings will constrict."

Mara sat up and scooted away feeling the release

immediately. "Okay, I'm fine. I just need to keep my distance. I guess when I leave with Morvayne, to visit the beach, he will ensure that I can cross the boundary safely."

Aerrvin understood and replied seemingly in her ear only, "Mara just play along. I cannot enter the property. Have you talked to Daisy yet?" Seeing her nod he continued, "Great, so you know that it will take some time to put together a rescue. I can meet you here at this time daily if you can arrange it. The Fairies guard the corners mostly and flit across only twice, once at noon and then again at dusk. How much do you trust your maidservant?"

"Tessa is . . ." Mara began and then realizing how she sounded changed her tack. "Tessa, you are such a trustworthy friend, please do not tell Maurice of this incident."

"Of course not, Mara," Tessa replied. "It is of no consequence. Nothing to tell, really. Do you wish to lean against this tree?" Tessa motioned to the large tree which hung its branches over the fence, and asked, "Do you not have much sun where you live?"

Mara smiled as she sat beneath the tree. Aerrvin squawked at another seagull and then stabbed his beak at a beetle; snatching it neatly, he held it jauntily a moment then he turned sideways to wink at Mara before gulping it whole. She smiled, knowing he would be sporting a mischievous smirk were he himself. She did not know how she knew, but she was certain that he was not using a glamour as a disguise, that he had actually changed his form. *That surely takes far more skill than I could learn in a few days.*

"Sun? Oh, we get sun, but only occasionally until summer. Even then it rains a little, not quite daily and often it's more of a misty drizzle. As a result, Seattle is very moist and generally cool. We get up into the 90s in the summer, but an average is 72, I guess. It must be over 75 degrees right now. Sorry, I don't know Celsius. Really, besides the heat, I guess Italy is similar in moisture content. The air feels about the same. I love being on the ocean."

"Me too," both Aerrvin and Tessa replied in unison, bringing a smile to Mara's face.

"Mara," Aerrvin said urgently, "I could not reach you in your Dream. What happened?"

"Last night Morvayne stayed in my room explaining the History of the Realms. I think he told me all of it in its entirety. It is all in my head now. I guess it was not a bad thing, though I would rather have learned it from another." Mara tossed a seed to the seagull, he snatched it, nibbled at it, and then dropped it.

Tessa replied. "I do not know what that history was, but you must not have slept well. Would you care to return and nap before lunch?"

Before Mara could answer, a dragonfly came and smacked the seagull on his head and then the two flew off together. Morvayne strolled up, "Ah, there you are. A little ways from the gardens, are we not?"

"Yes, we are, but the heat was bothering me and I wanted to watch the waves in the shade," Mara replied smoothly.

Morvayne surveyed the rocky shore and then nodded. "Yes, well about going to the beach. I am afraid I need to go into town first, but I should be back by 1:00 p.m. I would feel better about leaving if I knew you were safe inside. It is air-conditioned and you should be able to find things to entertain you should you have need. Tessa, please show her the conservatory when she feels up to it."

Morvayne held his hand out to Mara and she begrudgingly allowed him to help her up from her leaning position against the tree. He held her arm in his as they strolled back to the palazzo. Tessa stayed a respectful distance behind.

Morvayne murmured to Mara, "You look lovely today. I

can see you are covered in Dust. Were you practicing your powers? In front of the Human?"

"No, I did not do anything in front of her. I was thirsty, she left to fetch me a drink. I tried to fetch my own while she was gone. It still did not work, but I can open myself to the—the glow is that what you call it?" Mara asked trying to sound timid, which was not too hard with her breathy voice.

"Mara, maybe you should try something easier. We call it the Light or the Power; we sometimes refer to it as a Brightness. We could say for instance that Mara is very Bright, and we are not talking about academics. It means you have a significant portion of Light and Power. Let me see you to your room and I will give you a simpler lesson to work on."

Morvayne did indeed see her to her bedroom, shutting the door on Tessa as she entered the sitting room.

Morvayne released the restraints on Mara. "Now, let me show you a simple trick my mother taught me when I was just a wee babe." Morvayne sat Mara down on the bench at the foot of her bed.

"Now close your eyes and imagine your power is a blanket. Can you see the Light?"

Mara nodded, only her hankie was out, but he would not know. "I see it, do you want me to wad it up?"

"What? No! I want you to spread the blanket around your shoulders like a cape; make yourself all comfy cozy." Mara complied easily thinning her hankie and stretching it out to make a cape of Power, she clasped it with a silver pin.

"Mara!" He interrupted her thoughts. "I can see you are not using all of your power, you were burning far brighter when you were angry with me. Now you must collect *all* of your light. It must be laying there in front of you; now pick it all up."

He had been harsh, but now tried to moderate to a soothing tone again; the lessons do require calm serenity to work well. "Now, Mara, collect your Light and wrap yourself in it. Good that is better. Yes, now I can see your Brightness. That's a good girl," he crooned with satisfaction.

Mara had released the two front pockets while placing extra restraints on the other two, she did not want him ever knowing how much Power and Light she really held. She smiled, pleased with herself.

Morvayne felt like he was finally getting somewhere. "Very well, Mara, now that you are cloaked in Light you should be able wish to be very small. I know you have imagined yourself tiny before. I saw you within that buttercup in your Dream. Just imagine you are tiny. You can even add wings, if you like; it is fun to pretend to be a Fairy when you are young."

Mara decided that she had to show some progress at learning or he would become angry and suspect her of not trying. She remembered being that tiny girl and thought about being tiny. Opening her eyes she felt herself being lifted by those elegant hands she detested. Sitting in his palm, she looked up at his beautiful face as he whispered, "Well done, my little Buttercup. Now flit about the room; you will not tire when you are this size."

Mara leapt from his hand and flew gratefully away from him, only to find he had joined her in her miniature bumblebee size. Being this small, Mara could see that there was indeed dust, which a Brownie would have never missed.

"Very good. Now land on the bed or chair, somewhere safe. I want you to try returning to your natural state while I put the restraints on you." She felt her power being tamped down again; a sickening pressure which threatened to cause her to release her other two pockets of power. But looking at her imaginary neighbor Fairy, she was reminded of Aerrvin, as he was an exact likeness, and she tempered her desire to lash out. *I must wait for his rescue.* She knew using the Light on her own person was possible, so she returned to her full size."

Morvayne returned to his former nature and, having seen her success, reached out to hug her. Mara endured it stiffly. "You may not appreciate me now, but once I have taught you everything I can, you will thank me. I have a brother who is a fine teacher. He has offered to assist me, so I am going to go meet with him now to ascertain his sincerity. You did say you would prefer to meet more Elves. I will see who is available for dinner tonight. You would do well to nap until I return." Taking her hand, which was immediately sheathed in oily swirls, he kissed it and said, "Until 1:00 then. Sweet dreams, Buttercup."

As soon as she was sure he was completely off the premises, she put herself into her Dream and waited for Aerrvin. She did not need to wait long.

Embracing, she exclaimed, "Aerrvin, good news, I think. He says he is going to let his brother be my teacher. That should be Clay, right?"

Releasing her so he could look at her Aerrvin said, "I do not believe he has another brother. It is rare to have more than three children. Two is the most common among Elves. Did he try to harm you?"

"No. Why?" Mara asked.

"Because you are covered head to toe in your armor." Aerrvin said looking her in the eyes, while he produced a mirror. Mara turned and gasped.

"I didn't know it could do that! I had been thinking about what I was going to do should he try to really kiss me. I guess this should work."

She laughed as she studied her form in the mirror. The skin did indeed engulf her entirely. Her face and hair were fascinating, she looked like a lizard woman from outer space.

Her nails were elongated into claws and she even had short toenails that scraped the floor lightly as she moved closer to the mirror. She had the Dragon's double eyelid and her hair formed spikes, not unlike Gareth's punk look, only it was entirely rainbow sparkles in oily swirls.

Aerrvin tried it too. He stood next to Mara looking just as out of this world as she did. Mara burst out laughing. Calming down to speak she gasped, "That is the funniest thing I have seen in ages!" Aerrvin had not spiked his hair in a crest; instead, it went out in every direction. He amended the look and matched her cocks comb spike down the center of the head.

"It may look funny, but this will come in handy while searching the ocean floor. We could stay under for days before needing to surface."

Something tickled Mara's memory, but she could not quite recall what it was. "What do the Mermaids do to help you stay under water with them?"

"Well, for the Fair Ones, they don't need to do anything for short visits because we can devise our own breathing apparatus which we just place over our heads. It collects oxygen from the water and allows us to breathe and speak normally. If we want to stay longer, as I did when I went to learn from the Mermaid Academy, then they have a conversion spell they can bestow with a necklace. Then again, some of us can transform completely. Mara you were so brave to have visited a Dragon, and I do love the softness." Aerrvin pulled her lizard body to him in a caressing embrace.

A sigh escaped Mara's lips, but then she gasped in another fit of laughter as she changed her appearance to jeans and a peasant blouse. "Sorry, I just can't kiss a lizard; you'll have to change."

Aerrvin changed to his normal Fairy attire of leggings and a tunic, belted, with the addition of a sword. Mara also noted he had a pair of boots with knife handles peeking from the tops of each as well as a third belted opposite the sword.

"I don't know, Mara, you felt pretty nice covered in dragon skin." He looked at her now from head to toe and smiled rakishly. "But I guess you do look a sight better this way." Then he continued from where he left off, pulling her close once more.

5
Mental Anguish

It was late Sunday and Mara had still not come home. Jill was getting perturbed, at whom she did not know. Calling the mansion on Saturday, she had been told that Aerrvin had taken Mara to Colorado and that the birthday party was canceled. "How could he cancel his own birthday party!" she wondered out loud.

The phone rang just as she was reaching for it. "If that's Mara . . ." she fumed. "Hello."

"Hello, is this Jill?" asked a foreign voice.

"Yes."

"Jill, my name is Tessa. Mara has asked me to call you—"

"Wait a minute, did she get married to that guy or is she hurt? Because if she's not hurt I'm going to kill her," Jill exclaimed.

Tessa paused momentarily trying to make sense of the fast-talking American. "No, not married. She asked me to tell you that Morvayne has taken her to Italy and to talk to Jaera about it."

"What!" Jill screamed. "That slimy Morris took her! Why didn't anyone tell me sooner? Where is Aerrvin? Who are you?"

"I do not know a person named Aerrvin. I am a servant for Maurice or, as Mara calls him, Morvayne. I have been given the task of being Mara's maid and companion. She does not have a phone, so I am calling from my house. Please, I do not know much, she says her friends have a plan to rescue her and for you to talk to Jaera. I must go now." She hung up leaving Jill feeling anxious.

Fuming, Jill dialed the number she had for the O'Shea Mansion.

Button answered. "Hello—"

"Hello, is Jaera there?" Jill demanded.

"No, she just left, Jill. She should be there shortly." Button replied as the doorbell chimed.

"Okay, got it, thanks." Jill hung up and ran for the door.

Opening it she exclaimed, "Would you care to fill me in? What happened, and why didn't anyone tell me yesterday?" She let Jill in as well as Dougie, who obviously knew. "And how come Dougie knew before me?"

Jaera hugged Jill trying to calm her. "Shhh! Jill, we were trying to find her first. Then we wanted to come up with a plan." Jaera raised her hand to stop the flow of questions. "Her Grandfather knows, and we have everyone, especially her Attendants, working on freeing her."

Jaera went on to explain everything that she knew so far. "So anyway, she wants me to assume her life until she returns. I won't look like her while in the house, but when I leave I will, so that I can go to class for her. Aerrvin and Clay are hoping to have her back in time for her graduation. It's the best we can do." Jaera shrugged her tiny shoulders and gave Jill's hand another squeeze.

"You forgot to say why Dougie knew before me." Jill said, looking at Dougie who sat silently on the sofa.

Dougie replied for himself. "I was still in the house when

the news arrived that she had been taken."

"Wait a minute, still in the house? You were invited to the midnight party? Why?" As she said it, a conclusion dawned and she looked at him with new eyes.

"Yes, it is a part of my world." Dougie responded shyly. "I am a Brownie. I have been stuck in this Human size ever since my master, Brentwood, disappeared. Only Brentwood can return me to my proper size."

"So you've been watching over Mara like a big brother all these years?" Jill said with a sense of relief. "Here I thought you had a crush on her, always coming by to say hello, and she was too sweet to send you away."

Dougie replied, "Yes, her safety has been my constant concern since she moved in. But her six Attendants have kept me informed of her safety. I truly enjoy coming over. You throw great parties, Jill." He smiled openly, surprising Jill with the revelation. *He likes me?*

Changing topics, Jill said, "Okay, Jaera, so you are moving in. This means that the attack on the house has ceased, right?" Receiving nods from both of them, she continued. "Good, but I would still like to move into my apartments as soon as possible. Can you have my place ready by Tuesday?"

"Of course, we can finish most of it up today if Dougie can come and help. What do you say?"

Dougie replied, "I usually go sailing, but I can make over an apartment for a change, as long as I get to install a mondo sound system!" He grinned. His weathered face made both Jill and Jaera laugh.

***

Mara was exploring the conservatory when Morvayne returned.

"Ah, I see you are taking advantage of the amenities. I realize you prefer photography, but you can learn to draw and paint just as well as the finest artists. Indeed, many of the renowned artists in history are truly Fair Ones themselves. I shall let you discover who they are in the years to come. Bene vieni; our picnic is ready." Morvayne looked her over and directed her back to her room. "You will want to change; we are going in for a swim."

Mara found that he did not provide any one-piece swimsuits. She was not going to wear a string bikini for him, so she decided to see if she could morph a suit while she held it. It worked. It was still a two-piece, but she had transformed a pink top into a tankini and the bottoms became boy shorts. She left her arms and shoulders bare, as she did not know if the armor prevented tanning. *I do want to tan if I am going to be in the sun!* She found a sundress for a cover up and selected a pair of flip-flops and went down for lunch. She was starving again.

Morvayne drove a golf-cart down the little path behind the house to the secluded beach. He laid out the picnic with great care as though he thought they were on a date. It made Mara feel very uncomfortable, so she watched the waves as they receded. It was low tide and they were pulling away from the shore, exposing thousands of gasping clacking forms of sea life on the few rocks this part of the shore held. She walked toward a tide pool and marveled, as always, at the wonders of starfish and sea anemones. Realizing that one of the starfish was Aerrvin, she stroked his nubby surface and left before Morvayne approached. She did not know what powers of perception he might have and did not want to expose Aerrvin. She returned just as Morvayne popped a bottle open. "Mara will you join me in a glass?"

"You know I do not drink, Morvayne," Mara replied as she sat down, taking a few grapes to eat.

"Ah, but this is Elven made Honeysuckle Dew. My own

private collection is quite expansive; this particular bottle was harvested the year you were born. I have not tried it yet and it would please me to share this bottle with you," Morvayne plied.

Mara hated this, but she played along. "Very well, if it is safe. I am trusting my health to your hands, Morvayne."

Morvayne smiled languidly as he stretched out on the blanket, propping himself up with the large pillows he had produced from thin air. "You can trust me, Mara. I assure you, with you in my hands, we will rule the world; bringing it back to its former glory. Mankind will once again revel in our power and we will live in peace and prosperity with them. No more hiding who and what we are. You would have known everything about yourself had we lived in a time of openness and peace. Humans are to blame. Not that there is anything wrong with you for having Human blood. Believe me, I understand the genetic need to incorporate variety. I simply believe the overall proportion has gone too far toward the Human side. We will work together you and I. We will bring back the proper balance of magic to this poor, blighted world."

Mara's mind reeled at the information he was laying on her. It was horrifying, but she fought to maintain control. She sipped the Honeysuckle Dew—it was delicate and very sweet; she wanted to gulp it down in fact, but she fought that too.

Instead, she said, "This is delicious. What are its properties? I mean, does it affect Elves in any particular way?"

Morvayne looked at her as though he had forgotten she was there. "Hmmm? Oh, no it does nothing except delight the senses; it should be tantalizing you to gulp it down. You are doing well to resist, which is proper; its ability to delight lasts proportionately to how long you can resist its allure. Within the hout., at any rate.

"Every minute you resist another sip gives you about ten

minutes of heightened sensual perception. Now try eating another grape; you will find that your tongue can separate each little explosion of sweetness apart from the sour, also texture will be heightened. Go on—enjoy the meal. I have ordered a variety of textures and flavors; this should be an experience to last a lifetime for you." Morvayne took his second sip and collapsed on his pillows to enjoy a few shrimp in detail.

I, Bronwyn, must interject my narration here. Obviously, I was unable to witness much of Mara's terrible entrapment, but I conducted interviews later, once her life was stable. I myself have never been given the opportunity to drink Honeysuckle Dew, what with the Elves being very tight with it and all.

It is purported to be quite potent; it allows the consumer to taste and feel with precision. Aerrvin managed to get a bottle of it in his youth, when he first chose to explore texture. He vouches that it is a mind reeling experience, and one worth having. Truth to tell, Aerrvin had planned to share the experience with Mara himself as a wedding gift. His hatred for Morvayne violating this desire burns within him to this day, though he has mellowed and lives in peace.

Mara found herself enjoying the meal despite the company. Every bite was a taste sensation and even lounging on the pillows enticed her as she enjoyed the texture of the sand beneath the blanket, the blanket itself, and the softness of the cotton-covered pillows. Finishing the meal, Morvayne took her to explore the beach. He encouraged her to miniaturize and go swimming in one of the tide pools. Aerrvin was no longer there, for which Mara was thankful. The sensation of touching sea life was incredible and she could not help laughing in delight at the experience. Then they went into the ocean itself and explored the depths, after Morvayne fashioned breathing devices. Though for Mara it was unnecessary, because as soon as she entered the water she extended her armor completely.

Mara enjoyed her increased senses from wearing Sea

Dragon armor. Surprise caught her when she saw a Water Sprite, having never seen one before, so she chased it around for a while. Morvayne pulled her this way and that, showing her items of interest, allowing her to touch and feel to get the best benefit of having sipped the Honeysuckle Dew.

The flaxen haired Elf pulled her to him and kissed her. With her heightened senses, it felt delicate and wonderful, before she exploded in a shockwave of energy as she realized what she was doing. Bursting on the surface, she realized that the 'capsule' binding her powers had been replaced. She swam to the shore, hastened to the cart to get a towel, and quickly dressed herself. Seeing that a few others were arriving on the beach, she ensured that she no longer looked like a lizard lady, but maintained the armor everywhere else, not caring if she appeared to be made of moving tattoos. Morvayne walked handsomely out of the water as Mara sat in the passenger seat waiting to be taken home. She seethed, but sat helplessly, knowing that had she tried to go farther, her bindings would have clamped down further, squeezing the air out of her.

Morvayne had no wordy quips, he simply maintained a cocky smile, packed up the picnic, and drove back to the palazzo. Mara stomach cramped. *Did Aerrvin see; was he a fish swimming nearby? Even if he wasn't there, he probably had a number of his battalion in the water; surely, someone saw and will report it.* Yes, she was definitely sick. She barely made it to the guest bathroom before she emptied her stomach.

Morvayne was the epitome of solicitousness. "Tessa, I fear it was still too much sun for Mara; please see her to her room and tend to her needs."

Then to Mara he said, "Mara, forgive me for keeping you out so long; your pleasure on the beach was mine as well. I blame myself for your condition. I will be up later to see how well you have recovered."

***

Tessa worriedly helped Mara to her room. She had seen tourists visit often enough, and they rarely ever had problems with the sun. No, this poor girl was seriously troubled. *One minute she is pleasantly sound; the next she is crying and speaking of magic—and she always is talking to herself.*

Mara wanted a cool bath, so Tessa ran the water for the distraught woman as she removed her clothes. Mara had the rainbow swirls still and there was no accounting for that. Tessa crossed herself again as chills ran up her spine. *Is there good magic?* she thought. *Surely, this good girl is not evil. Maurice could be; his party habits surely are.*

"Mara, I called your friends for you. Jaera said she will take care of everything." Tessa said as she handed Mara a washcloth.

Mara teared up at the thought of her friends and her shame. *What would they think of me if they knew?* Speaking weakly she said, "Thank you, Tessa. I would like to soak a while. You may find me something to wear and wait in the front room." Tessa nodded and closed the bathroom door. Mara felt constrained from crying aloud as she would have liked, so she simply sobbed, mingling her tears with the rose-scented water.

***

The shock of seeing Mara linger at the kiss before exploding to the surface pounded through Aerrvin's entire being. He felt conflicted anger, but more of his wrath was aimed at Morvayne than Mara. For Fair Ones, kissing could be meaningless fun, or it could be powerful magic. In his heart he knew Mara had not kissed with the least intention of bestowing gifts or favor on Morvayne, and yet he knew that she had been raised Human, not Faire, and Humans did not go about kissing indiscriminately once they were engaged. *She had been laughing and having fun!* Aerrvin seethed with emotions and did not know what to do with his jealousy. So he swam.

***

Mara tried reaching Aerrvin in the Land of Dreams, but he was not there. *Why did I enjoy the kiss? Morvayne is smarmy, reprehensible, disgusting. I could list a thousand synonyms, and yet . . .* she could still feel the softness of his lips.

She thought she would sick up again and lurched out of the tub to be racked with dry heaves, bereft within—physically as empty as she felt emotionally. She had no more tears.

Tessa dressed her silently since Mara was too numb to respond.

Once dressed she tried lying down, but there was no need for sleep and the Land of Dreams held no comfort. It took her hours to realize that it was the Honeysuckle Dew that Morvayne had given her which heightened her senses; as did the armor. She had felt the tenderness of Morvayne's love for Tigerlily. "Not me! It is not me he loves. Remember that, Mara, he is a sick, twisted, vile…" Mara cut off as the door to the outer room opened.

"Tessa," Morvayne said smoothly, "Has Mara recovered?"

"She is awake," Tessa replied.

"Good, please tell her we will have only two guests for dinner. It will be a peaceful night and she can choose her own attire. We will eat in half an hour."

Tessa found Mara sitting frightfully still. "Did you hear?"

"I did," Mara replied quietly. *It must be Clay. How can I face him?* She knew she was being silly. *How would he know unless Morvayne boasted?* Clay would pretend to meet Mara for the first time. He was going to help train her for Morvayne. *Had Aunt Lily intended for Clay to be one of my teachers anyway?*

55

Taking a deep breath, Mara looked in the mirror to see what she was wearing. Tessa had dressed her in a sundress. Mara decided to see what was in the closets now, since the clothing in it always changed. Most of the clothes remained, but a few dresses and a pantsuit had been added. Mara thought the pantsuit was too old lady fuddy-duddy looking, so she bypassed it; choosing a simple black evening dress instead. The scooped neck showcased her pendant prominently and the high-waist caused the skirt to swing away gracefully to her knees. She had no desire for dancing, but it would have swirled beautifully had she wanted it to.

She had mussed her hair in all her tossing and turning, so Tessa put it into a thick braid to hang down to the middle of her shoulder blades. She chose no make-up nor perfume. Reluctantly, she admitted she was hungry. Tessa hugged her silently before going down to help with the service.

Silencing all her fears, Mara walked resolutely down the stairs. The guests had already arrived, but were facing away from her. Clay was there, with his almost broad shoulders clothed in a white cotton shirt with the sleeves rolled up, revealing his sleek wiry form. He was so thin, yet every muscle was defined. He had tied his hair with a leather thong. And he held a single rose. His companion was not one of her Attendants as she had hoped. She was a dark-haired Elf with perfect white teeth that flashed at each of the men as Morvayne completed a witty comment. Morvayne turned then and said, "Ah! Our guest of honor has arrived. Mara I want to introduce you to two of my very dear companions, Breeze and Clay."

Mara nodded with a slight smile as she choked up, unable to speak. Breeze could have been a twin to Aunt Lily, she looked so similar.

Morvayne flashed a knowing smile. "I see you have noticed a similarity. Breeze is a second cousin to Princess Tigerlily; I have known her since we were younglings. And, of course, Clay is my older brother. I told you I would be meeting with him. Shall we dine?"

Morvayne took Breeze by the arm, to Mara's relief, allowing Mara to take Clay's proffered arm. He handed her the fragrant rose; she inhaled it briefly and bowed her head in thanks. She clung tightly to his arm until he loosened her fingers, as her nails were digging into his bare flesh. He gave her hand a squeeze before dropping his opposite hand to his side again.

They ate outside near the pool, beneath a covered patio. A light breeze wafted in from the sea, cleansing Mara's unease for a moment. *Aerrvin knows I love him, he won't leave me, and Clay has sworn to protect me. I am safer now.* She sat up straight in her seat; determined not to show weakness. *How many times have I made that resolve?*

Shaking her head violently enough to swing her braid she banished all negativity and sat waiting to bend with the breeze. She smiled at the pun, looking pleasant when Tessa arrived. The servant looked rather weary as she placed salads before each diner.

Morvayne had wine already opened, so pouring each a glass he offered a toast. "To old friends and new, may we find the treasures in life that we seek."

Glasses tinkled and three pretended to drink while one downed half the glass. Clay took water, and poured it in each of the three glasses and then proffered his own toast, "To Family, Honor, and Virtue." Three drank and Mara alone pretended. She knew she could partake. Aerrvin and Clay did, but it was still poison, she could not force herself to do it. From now on she wanted nothing from a bottle. She requested the cranberry juice, which she saw on the cart. Removing the wine, Tessa replaced it with the juice, offering Mara a smile of encouragement.

Breeze waited until Tessa retreated and then offered her

own toast. "To life everlasting; may we seek it in glory." So far, Mara had not heard anything to disagree with, not that she would do so openly. Yet she could not tell from the toast offered by Breeze whether she was a friend of Clay's, and knew his position, or whether she meant to help Morvayne in his Quest to reduce the Human population.

Mara supposed they would be expecting something from her, so she raised her glass and said, "It bears repeating: To Family, Honor, and Virtue." Her voice was whispery, yet steady.

During the meal, Mara remained silent, except when asked a direct question. Most of the conversation was reminiscing from their childhood. Mara was content to consume as many servings as were offered. She really was curious as to why she was so hungry all the time. The others seemed satisfied with one serving. *Is it my age or something else?* She did not wish to look the fool in front of Breeze, so she decided to wait until she could ask Clay. Looking out to the shore, she watched the seagulls, absently wondering if one might be Aerrvin, until one did a backward loop de loop, which could only be him. She was grateful that Morvayne was not facing the shore, keeping her smile hidden as she took a drink; her eyes nevertheless sparkled with relief.

The sun was not quite set, but it had cooled as the breeze picked up. Mara ventured to be bold. "Would you mind if I had my dessert later? I guess I ate too much dinner. It was delicious by the way; please tell your cook. But I was wondering if I could walk closer to the shore to feel the breeze?"

Morvayne was in the middle of a bottle of wine, as well as a story so he waved to Clay, "Would you be willing to walk her to the property line, there is no need to get closer than that to feel the breeze."

He winked at Breeze, causing her to offer a delicate giggle. "Enjoy the flower garden along the way, it smells divine at eventide." Turning back to his wine and his story, he excused them.

Grateful to be away, Mara allowed Clay to walk her through the rose garden first. "Clay, will you be able to help me?" Mara asked, unsure of wanting to hear his answer.

Clay was so refined and well composed, he never ceased to amaze her. He took her hand causing her to face him. "Your Highness, I know you are not yet crowned, but I have sworn to protect you all the days of my life. I cannot fail. My honor will not allow it."

Mara searched his face and knew he meant it. "But you toasted Family and Virtue as well; how can you turn your back on your brother to help me?"

Clay kept her hand and pulled it onto his arm as he walked along the path toward the orchard. She thought perhaps she still had a residue of the Honeysuckle Dew within her, because his smooth muscled bicep felt so pleasant to the touch. *Not proper*, she thought, but he kept her hand firmly in place when she shifted.

"I can be true to Morvayne, because I intend to help him free himself from his wicked designs. He is not in his right mind, as surely you have ascertained by now." He waited for her nod and continued. "He is my brother and I love him. I loved Tigerlily every bit as much as he did. I have not made the same choices he has. As a result, I was blessed to spend more time with her than he did and I came to understand the choice she made."

Mara was afraid to ask, but she really wanted to know, so she pressed forward, "What does virtue have to do with anything?"

They neared the place by the woods where Mara had spoken to Aerrvin, though she knew he would not be near because the Orange Fairies patrolled more carefully at dusk. Mara sat on the chair that Clay created as he sat in its twin. "Virtue has everything to do with it. Have you never read of Sir Galahad?"

"Yes, but those were just tales to me. I never supposed they were true. How true are the stories we have today?" Mara asked.

"They are changed, of course, but the essence is accurate. Galahad was seeking for truth represented by the Holy Grail, the grail or cup did, or rather, does not exist. Truth and Light, those exist, and it takes virtue to attain them to their fullest."

"Hmmm, so what is your definition of virtue?"

Clay responded in kind, "Tell me your understanding first. Then I will clarify."

Mara smiled at his teaching technique, definitely an improvement. "Well, it is generally thought to be connected with virgins as in the Galahad story. But I don't see how that can be correct. My pastor is married and I believe he is virtuous. So I think it has more to do with how you think. Does that make sense?"

Clay smiled at her, "Yes, that makes perfect sense. You are correct; virtue means to have moral excellence. In other words, one filled with virtue has high moral standards, integrity, honesty and the like."

"Okay," Mara said getting into the process of dissecting meanings. "Well then, what are morals? I have been learning they are relative. What is moral to one might not be moral to another."

Clay noted the many Fairies flitting about, the Oranges crossed at mid-point from corner to corner saluting Clay as they passed. Morvayne had introduced him to them earlier in the day. Out over the beach soared several of Aerrvin's Blues passing as seagulls. Clay knew that if he could tell they were Fairies, Morvayne could as well. He doubted the Fairies guarding the perimeter could tell though; they really were not very bright. Oranges never were. The Yellows on the other hand would be quite astute, but they were not being used for patrols. Daisy ventured near as the evening darkened and the patrols were again at their corner posts. She was still a squirrel.

"Hello, Daisy. What took so long?" Clay asked, instead of answering Mara's question.

"I have been learning about the Oranges here. Four are on duty at all times while two get to sleep or play, as they want. They maintain their stations two to each corner. Pretty much the same as they did in Mara's back yard. They don't seem to have much initiative to come up with new routines or patterns." Daisy scratched her fuzzy ear daintily, drawing a smile from Mara.

"No they don't, and my brother is losing more of his sense of reality. He does not appear to have time to teach them any new tricks, so that is something. I am hoping to learn more about the position of Gwennara before he loses himself completely."

"Precisely. So what is it I should be doing?" Daisy asked. "Do you want me to stay put in the tree, or would you like me to enter the house, as a mouse perhaps, and keep Mara company?"

"I think you should keep an eye on the yard. While I am here, I can stay with Mara inside if need be. You can continue to keep Aerrvin notified as events occur. I realize he is getting anxious, but really, there is nothing to be done as yet. Here he is now. Aerrvin." Clay nodded as the Seagull approached and sat atop the rock.

Mara leaned forward. "Aerrvin, I have missed you! I tried to contact you in your Dreams, but you weren't sleeping. I don't think Morvayne will keep me awake tonight. Will you meet with me?" Mara asked tremulously.

Her tremor gained a sharpened look from Daisy and Clay. Aerrvin replied stiffly, "I was swimming all day, trying to think things through. I would like to meet with you, but it might be late. I will come to you when I am ready."

He paused and then asked Clay, "So, you will stay in the house then, and will he be leaving soon?"

Clay ignored the stiffness between Mara and the prince. "Yes, Morvayne has no reason to suspect. He has agreed that I am a better teacher than he is. I will teach Mara everything she needs to know. I believe he has business to attend to; probably going to the sea prison. After he departs, I will try to reason out where the portal leads, but it is very tricky and must be done within minutes. I may not have enough skill. I have only been correct five times out of the hundreds of times I have tried. Although, I always get the correct latitude; that will be something, anyway."

"Very well. Until we meet, Mara." That was all he said; he flew away, ripping Mara apart. *He saw the kiss. I knew it!*

Clay stood, taking Mara's hand, he said, "Come along then, we do not want to let that dessert go to waste."

Returning to the table, Mara was startled when the outside patio lights came on, as well as the ones for the pool, which made sparkling lights shimmer and dance against the columns of the patio. She was not really surprised that the lights were being turned on, but she had allowed a tear or two escape on the quiet walk back. She quickly wiped her face, trying to appear casual.

Morvayne noticed though, as did everyone else. "Making her cry as well, Clay? You said you would be better than me?"

Breeze responded quickly, shaking a finger at Morvayne, "Shame on you, Morvayne, and you too, Clay! What is this all about? Making young maidens cry!" She wrapped her arm around Mara protectively.

"We will take our dessert in her room." She turned Mara around and marched her up the stairs.

Tessa brought apple turnovers with a generous scoop of

ice cream. "Would you like me to stay, signorina?" Tessa said as she bobbed to Mara.

Mara was back in control, yet bewildered. Breeze felt safe.

"No, Tessa, you look so tired, go sleep in your own bed and sleep well. Thank you for being here for me; I truly appreciate it. Breeze will keep me company, and I trust Clay. I will be fine. Again, thank you."

Mara stood and hugged Tessa in appreciation. She had never made friends so fast in her life. She sat on the couch and picked at her turnover. *What is Breeze up to?* She waited for her to speak first.

"So, you are a descendant of Tigerlily's I take it," Breeze said.

Mara nodded, but then decided she should not be so rude. "Yes, she was my great-great grandmother. Brentwood is my father; do you know him?"

"No, I am afraid I have been in the Land of Dreams these past one hundred years. I only returned as a favor to Morvayne; he said he had urgent need of a woman's touch. He did not specify and I assumed he meant something else; yet I can see, if he has a young Elven maiden to train, he definitely has need of help. If you don't mind my asking, where are Tigerlily's children and your parents? Why have they neglected to teach you?"

Mara became fierce, which she much preferred to weepy, "Goldenrod chose Humanity along with Tigerlily. My grandfather is at home and was all set to teach me, when Morvayne scooped me up and brought me here. My father has been missing for ten years and Morvayne knows what happened to cause his disappearance! I did not ask to be here, and I do not know if I can trust you or not! Morvayne is drinking three bottles of wine a day, and I don't think he has a sane brain cell left!" Mara was at a loss for words so she screamed, "Ahhh! I can hardly stand it anymore!"

She slammed her dessert onto the coffee table and held her face in her hands. Steaming, she watched sparks pool within her capsule at her feet.

"Well, that would explain all the detailed wards he has, as well as the field around you, holding your Power at bay." Breeze said dryly. "You said you trust Clay. Why? He says he has agreed to teach you, he is helping Morvayne. Why would you trust one and not the other?"

Mara considered before answering. Picking up her dessert, because she was feeling hungry again, she took a bite.

"Clay generates a different vibe. Don't you feel it?"

"Yes, I do. I just wanted to know your reasoning. I noticed too that there are Orange Fairies in the trees and Blue ones masquerading as a variety of birds and wildlife all around the property. You have seen them I assume?"

"Yes, the Oranges are Morvayne's followers and the Blues are mine and Aerrvin's."

"Aerrvin, the Prince of the Rose Crown?" Breeze asked with sincere surprise.

"Yes, he is my fiancé." Mara held up her hand with the large diamond. Breeze took her hand to look at the ring closely.

"Yes, that ring was made by Laurel ap Rose," Breeze confirmed. "She made me a few things many years gone by. I love her skill. Speaking of jewelry, I recognize the necklace as well. It was a gift to Tigerlily from her mother. Did she give it to you, or did you take it?"

It seemed significant the way she asked so Mara gave Breeze the truth, telling about having put it on without permission and Aunt Lily's subsequent bestowal. "So would it have been more significant had I never put it on without permission?"

"Perceptive. If you had waited for her to give it to you, it would never have locked up on you. Now, every time you put it on, it will take a month before its powers will work. Then you will be able to either remove it, or use its remarkable properties." Breeze finished her dessert and placed the dish on the table.

"Do you know what those powers might be?" Mara asked hopefully.

"No, not really. I do know that it works only for a blood relative. It should work for me. I am not a descendant, but I have the same ancestors as the Queen. Maybe Morvayne wants me to wear the necklace. Can you take it off?"

Mara liked Breeze, but she did not want her to have the necklace, obviously, so she did not tell that she had been wearing it for a week. "No, I just put it on. Why am I so hungry? Ever since I got here I have been starving!"

"Oh, sweetheart, it's the barrier he has on you. The energy he uses to maintain it drains power from you. Shame on him for not telling you!" Breeze created a meal of fruit and cheese and set it on the table. "Here eat this, it should help. I am going to go have a talk with those lads; they should know better than to treat a Royal Heir this way. What would Gwennara say about this?"

"Breeze, how long ago did Morvayne wake you?" Mara asked.

"Yesterday. He has visited me once or twice in the past fifty years, but only briefly; just to play or dance really," Breeze answered. "Why?"

"So you really don't know?" Mara asked incredulously. "All of Gwennara's daughters are dead or missing. Gwennara has been taken captive and is being held prisoner at the bottom of the sea.

An announcement went out this week to all the Realms. I am the Future Queen, Gwennara transferred her Power to me. I am sure Morvayne knows this; in fact, my Grandpa Ironwood believes he is behind all of the disappearances. My kidnapping only makes the theory more likely. Breeze, I don't know if you support Morvayne or not, so I can't tell you much more than that."

Breeze stared at Mara, contemplating. By rights, Elves have allowed themselves days and weeks to make conclusions, so truly it was amazing that she judged so quickly or at least appeared to. "All right, I will take you at your word for now. You do have the necklace and I feel compassion for you. If I were to ask for proof, you would have to expend your power, which would make you hungry all over again." She smiled approvingly as Mara ate a hunk of cheese. "Have you not learned to create food yet?"

Mara replied truthfully, "Yes, I can, but I did not want Morvayne teaching me, nor knowing my abilities, so I pretended to have difficulties learning. I do not know if the food I create has extra nutrients, but I was told it has half the calories. Do I need to think the extra nutrients in, or is it a byproduct of the creation?"

"You do think things through; how old are you anyway?"

"I will be twenty-one on Midsummer's day. Well?" Mara prodded for an answer.

"Oh! Yes, it is a byproduct of the creation. You need to get some rest, but one last question. What did Clay do to make you cry?"

Mara had nearly forgotten and hated the reminder. "Nothing. It was something we were talking about: Virtue and morals, I was just upset about a choice I made, nothing to do with Clay really."

Breeze knew she would get nothing more from her, but she found it intriguing that Mara would open up so fast. Being willing to talk to Clay about deep subjects and now discussing important matters with another stranger, namely herself. Breeze thought, *She is just a babe, not even sworn to the Light yet.* She fought the urge to roll her eyes, so she merely lowered her lashes a touch longer than needed for a blink.

"Very well, sweet child, I will see you in the morning."

Breeze showed no surprise when she opened the door to find both Morvayne and Clay waiting. Morvayne entered first, followed by Clay. Breeze watched from the door.

"Mara, dear, I hope you feel better soon. I had such a delightful time this afternoon with you on the beach; it will be a memory I will treasure—always. I hope to have many more such memories with you. I just want to tell you; I will be gone before you rise tomorrow. I may be two days, or three. Clay and Breeze will take care of you and see to your instruction. Sleep well, My Lady."

She had given up resisting his kisses as she automatically sheathed her hand moments before he touched her. She was not aware that she sheathed herself entirely. It became quite evident that Morvayne found lizard ladies attractive because he smiled appreciatively and stroked her cheek. Sauntering out he instructed Clay, "Teach her the Rights and Privileges of the Crystal Throne before you retire." Placing an arm around Breeze he said, "Breeze would you care for a late night swim?"

6
Lessons Learned

Before Clay shut the door, Mara heard Breeze ask, "She owns a Dragon skin?"

Blinking her eyes, Mara realized what she had done. She returned to wearing the armor as a belt, causing all the tears she had held back to tumble down her face. Clay came to her on the couch and held her as she sobbed. "Mara, I know you are having difficulties with Aerrvin. What is it?"

Haltingly she told about the picnic and the joy of feeling every little sensation and finally Morvayne's kiss, and her shameful response. Clay stiffened as she came to that point, though he knew it was coming; he had hoped it would not.

"Mara, do not blame yourself. Aerrvin will not hold you accountable either. That drink is used all the time by sweethearts to bind them together; it is traditionally a wedding gift and rarely ever drunk by persons unwilling to share their sense of wonder in the world. Opening your eyes to the senses is not bad, in and of itself. Violating your personal space was. If you had been given any, it should have been a single sip. Not an entire glass. Did you have more than that?"

She shook her head.

Clay shifted her onto his lap, holding her like a baby. Her scent was intoxicating; she had no idea how powerful her Fairy

Dust was. Even encapsulated it was strong. Inhaling and sighing deeply, he stood and carried her to bed.

"You should wait to meet Aerrvin in your Dream. I will join you and teach you there. That way you will not miss him when he arrives, and I will still have taught you."

He left her in her room and retired to her couch, easily making the transition to her Dream.

"Mara!" Clay called looking around for her, before spying her sitting on top of her dresser as a Fairy sized being. Minimizing to match he said, "Sorry, I could not see you at first. Your Dream is so spacious. I keep my Dreams small and tightly controlled. You did not place a ward! I was able to walk right in without asking; may I ask why?"

"I knew you were coming and did not expect Morvayne to be spying on me since he is in the pool."

"I see, but you should get in the habit of warding your Dream always. You can create openings for specific persons like Aerrvin or me; that way we can come in, but you can keep all others out unless you grant permission."

He quickly taught her a symbol to draw while speaking the name of the individual she would grant access to. Then he settled down on the jewelry box, while she leaned upon her toy tiger, and proceeded to teach her about the Rights and Privileges of the Crystal Throne. It took two hours to tell and Aerrvin never arrived. Clay could see her melancholy growing by the minute.

"Mara, I will explain everything to him if he does not show up. Surely, whoever reported it also saw the picnic. I do not see why he would be upset anyway; Fairies are more flirtatious than Elves. I am sure he will kiss far more maids than you will ever know."

Clay was not getting anywhere with her, in fact she began

to weep. "Mara, please don't, it hurts me to see you cry."

He still ached to hold her, but in her Dream she no longer had the Fairy Dust to pull him in. He knew it was not really Mara he wanted. Like Morvayne, he suffered from unrequited love. He loved Tigerlily and had sought her love once, but more than that, he loved her sister, Arianna. She had rejected him more thoroughly than Tigerlily ever had. Mara resembled Tigerlily, but she smelled like Arianna. Clay prided himself on having done so well during the past one hundred years, putting Arianna out of his mind (for the most part), while serving Tigerlily so faithfully. Now, Mara was growing into her Power and her alluring scent was truly intoxicating to him, just like Arianna's.

Clay recalled having fallen for Arianna on the first day that she had arrived at school; she had shown up a few days after the first day of that quarter. He was always prompt, to the point of being early and she was always late. Remembering caused him to smile. Being in a Dream he inadvetantly recreated Arianna as she had been then. She flitted about teasing him with her sparks. He nearly flew after her, until he saw Mara looking askance. With a bemused expression, he allowed "Arianna" to fade away.

"Sorry, I am prone to flights of fancy when in the Land of Dreams."

Mara waved at the air. "She looked like Arianna, you know from Grandpa's drawings?"

Clay sighed, "Yes, you found me out. She is the Elven Maiden of my Dreams. I miss her."

"How long ago did she go missing?" Mara felt her compassion rising for Clay, he looked so miserable compared to his normally cool, calm exterior.

"She disappeared about eight years ago, but she stopped seeing me some three hundred years back. It was a harsh break up. I know this might sound cruel, but we, my friends and Hold

Mates, all agreed Humans were too prolific and destructive. Arianna wanted to interact with the Humans; influencing the artists and musicians; she stayed and encouraged better health and productivity among Mankind. While it is a noble thing to do, we felt it was unwise, as it increased the Human population. And— there were other extenuating circumstances, of no import. When Tigerlily changed her views, it was almost more than I could stand and certainly, it put Morvayne over the edge. As you know, I eventually learned to accept Tigerlily's decision." Concluding his sad tale, he sat staring bleakly at the tiger Mara was sitting on.

Mara rose to offer him comfort and was surprised by the strength of his returning hug. He held her tightly for a minute and then loosened his hold, looking down into her face. He kissed her on her head and said, "Mara, I need to go. Try to get some real sleep for a change. You will need your strength to practice with your restraints on. I need to find out Morvayne's itinerary, so I can check his Travelers' Shadow for clues."

"But, will you please stay in the front room? Or get Daisy? I don't want to be left alone, please." She grabbed at him, truly afraid of Morvayne encroaching on her.

"Peace, Mara. I said I will keep you safe and I mean it. Go to sleep. I will remain in the front room until Morvayne leaves." Clay gave her hand a squeeze and left her Dream.

Remaining in her Dream, Mara returned to her full size, clothed in her cotton nightgown, she took Growly and climbed into her bed in Aunt Lily's house. Taking comfort in the familiar surroundings, she hummed herself to sleep. Trying to empty her mind, she felt a familiar presence as she drifted off.

***

Aerrvin felt out of sorts all day. He had been told about the Honeysuckle Dew and knew that Mara had been given an entire glass to drink. Aerrvin wanted to kill Morvayne and hurt

Mara.

Why would I want to hurt Mara? He could not understand it; it was not her fault. Yet, he was hurt and wanted to lash out. He tried to be civil when he went near her, but the pain was so raw he could barely stand to speak to Clay. She invited him to her Dream; he knew she would like to explain, but he did not want to hear it. Any explanation would be wrong anyway; she was not at fault. He knew he was thinking in circles, but he simply could not stop.

He went swimming with the Water Sprites. Although they were playful, and the blue Sprite with the pale green hair offered another massage, he did not feel up to it. He was in a White mood and wanted to be alone. Bronwyn had arrived and waited in his rooms at the spa, so Aerrvin did not want to go there. Finding an empty shell on the floor of the sea, he climbed inside and sulked.

Mara was such an innocent, he longed to hold her and comfort her. Yet he was helpless. She was in Clay's hands; *he* had *all* the power. *It is so frustrating!* Sighing, he decide to check in on her Dream. Clay was teaching her the Rights and Privileges lesson. Aerrvin watched from the closet. Wincing when the conversation turned to his flirtatious nature, Aerrvin considered leaving, but stayed anyway. Mara cried, and.Clay just sat there not offering comfort; Aerrvin almost went in. But he stopped when Mara stopped to watch a miniaturized Elf flit about the room. This was interesting news to hear. All Fairies love listening in on private conversations, so Aerrvin stayed put. Clay then left Mara's Dream. Mara resumed her normal size and climbed into her bed, looking exactly as she had on the first night that Aerrvin had visited her.

Dreams have layers and this simple Dream was on the outside edge of the Land of Dreams. Mara sank deeper, so Aerrvin carefully stole near and replaced the toy with himself, snuggling up beneath her neck.

***

Mara awoke feeling surprisingly refreshed. She had not slept well for days. Now she had finally gotten some deep REM sleep, not even remembering her Dreams. She checked to see if Clay was still there. He was not, so she assumed Morvayne had left.

"Good! Now I can finally enjoy my stay in Italy."

Humming the lullaby she had gone to sleep with, she showered and primped, coming out to find that Tessa had laid out some clothes for her. A pretty aqua sundress, embellished with ruffles, with white and melon embroidery, it was paired with a cute, cropped jacket in white cotton, which Mara pulled on as she headed down the stairs. Not knowing where breakfast would be she went to the kitchen. She had not been in it yet. She thought of Jill when she saw the bright morning light shining in on the spacious room. It was like the one at Ironwood Estates, Mara could not imagine ever needing such a kitchen.

Upon seeing her enter, Isadora began saying something in Italian with a lot of, "No, no, no," mixed in. Tessa came from the pantry and hustled over to Mara. "My Lady! I am sorry I thought you would be longer at your bath. Come."

She guided her to the patio in the sun where they had breakfasted the day before. "Isadora does not like people in her kitchen. She is particular. Would you like some tea? Breakfast will be a few minutes still." Tessa bobbed a curtsy by way of apology.

"Yes, please. Do you have mint?" Mara asked.

Breeze and Clay arrived together and requested tea as well.

Breeze said airily, "Mara, you look refreshed."

"Thank you, I feel refreshed. Is Morvayne gone?"

Clay replied, "Yes, he had an early departure. I will tell you about his plans later." Not knowing how Breeze was leaning, he did not wish to reveal too much.

"Good!" said Breeze. "Then we can play today! Who says lessons have to be boring? Right, Clay?" Breeze lifted her slim finger to point at him. "Do you remember that time…"

Breeze filled the morning with stories of her youth at the Academy in Scotland, where she went to school, before going to the one in Ireland, mingling in embarrassing stories of Clay and his other Hold Mates.

Clay was so smooth and self-assured, it was really hard to imagine him playing pranks and being disrespectful to his instructors. Mara smiled at the last example Breeze told, revealing Clay's fear of Elephants. "Elephants! Clay why would elephants be so frightening?"

"Breeze doesn't have the whole story. Before I even went off to school, when I was fifteen, my parents took me on a tour of Asia down through India. We had minimized ourselves to sit with the birds: One day with the wrens, the next with the herons. As it was, I was sitting in a nest with two adorable newly hatched snipe, when suddenly a herd of Elephants came charging up to the water, scattering the nest and killing the poor hatchlings and breaking my arm. My father healed it right away, but the pain was real while it lasted; believe me it is not something you would want to repeat," Clay finished by flicking his wadded up paper napkin at Breeze.

Tessa arrived to clear the table. She was pleased to see Mara feeling better.

Clay excused himself. "I have a few things I need to attend to. I will see you in an hour or so." He looked out at the shore to ensure plenty of Blue Fairies were flitting about; his mirth rose as he could see both Hannah and Ivan dive bombing the waves, catching fish for their breakfast.

They would not be identifiable to the ordinary Elf, but Clay knew them well; having spent time with them as a gull himself, transformed, not hidden with a glamour. Hannah always extended her wing feathers a fraction longer than a true gull and Ivan had a split tail feather that stuck up awkwardly; he thought it made him look jaunty.

Addressing Mara, Breeze asked, "Should we go on down to the beach?"

"Sure, do you have lessons you can teach me there?

"Of course, there are lessons to be learned anywhere in the world, and even more out of it," Breeze added mysteriously.

***

Tessa was disappointed that she was not accompanying Mara. She watched as Mara and Breeze walked to the gate leading to the trail down to the rocky shore. As they neared it, Mara hung back and Breeze went to open the gate confidently, when suddenly Breeze fell over the same way Mara had the day before.

Muttering under her breath, Tessa ran to offer assistance. Breeze was up again, of course, by the time Tessa arrived. Breeze was fuming. "Who does he think he is, not letting me out? So you are saying that only Clay has the key to let us out, or is Clay stuck here as well?"

Mara glanced at Tessa and then dismissed her from her mind; she had told her there was magic, she could learn of its truth or not as she chose to believe. "I don't know for sure. I did not ask him, I know that Morvayne trusts him and left him in charge of my training. Can you Travel?"

Breeze made a line of Light and looked at a blank wall within. "No! That rotten, scheming—I am going to beat him at his own game. That is what I am going to do! I will convince Clay that I am ready and willing to defend my Honor. I promised to serve the Light as we all do before we continue our training. Further, I will convince Morvayne that I want nothing more than to see all Humanity reduced to serving the Fair Ones." Calmly, she added, "This will be nearly as fun as living in the Land of Dreams. Intrigue has always been one of my fondest games. I hope you learn to trust me, Mara. I swear to serve you by all the Light and Power which I hold."

Tessa was openly surprised to see the elegant Breeze bow down to the earth before Mara. And equally surprised to see Mara take it in stride. In fact she regally acknowledged Breeze, commanded her to rise, and allowed Breeze to offer her a kiss which she then returned. They seemed at a loss about what to do next, so Tessa bobbed and offered the use of her phone.

"Mara, you wanted to use my phone to call your Grandfather; now would be a good time, Signorina."

She must truly be important for Breeze to bow to her; the situation is becoming more and more puzzling. The Master now has two women being held captive—evidently, by magic. She fought the urge to cross herself and failed. *Good magic,* she kept telling herself, *surely, there is good magic.*

"Yes, I would like to talk to a familiar voice, thank you, Tessa."

Mara was soon dialing the well memorized number adding the additional overseas numbers, of course.

One ring . . . two . . . "Hello, Ironwood Estates."

"Grandpa! I am so glad you are home!"

"Mara, how are you? You are still captive I presume?"

"Yes, I am. Does Clay keep you informed?"

"Yes, he has been sending reports every six hours, as do

Daisy and Jasmine. I understand Morvayne has Traveled to the bottom of the sea, but Clay was nevertheless unable to locate the longitude. Yet we are scouring the maps looking at the places along the latitude he was able to identify. It is a great help even if he does not think so. Clay is prone to despondency, so do what you can to encourage him, Mara. He is your best hope."

"I know he is, Grandpa. Does—does Aerrvin contact you too?" Mara asked plaintively.

"He has done so once, just to vent; he says there is nothing for him to do. He is quite fired up, that whippersnapper is. He surely loves you, Mara, and you were a lucky one to find him."

Mara loved hearing her Grandpa's voice; the familiarity was comforting. Mara realized she had not even called her mother to tell her she was engaged. She felt like doing it right away.

"Grandpa, I love you. I will call you again when I can." She soon hung up and turned to Tessa.

"Tessa, I need to call my mother. I will pay you back for the charges."

Mara sat down on the glider that Tessa kept near the open window. A gentle breeze fluttered the curtains.

"Mom?" Mara said, just realizing she did not know what time it was in Washington.

"Hello, Mara, it's late. Is something wrong?" Amanda asked.

"Sorry, I wasn't paying attention to the time. Were you asleep?" Mara asked apologetically.

"No, not yet, what did you want?"

"I just wanted to tell you that Aerrvin gave me a ring!" Getting teary Mara sobbed, "He wants to marry me, Mom!"

Amanda was surprised, but she could see it coming in the short time she had been there. "Mara that's wonderful. I hope those are tears of joy."

Mara had always been able to talk to her mother about anything (as long as it did not involve magic) so she went ahead, fabricating as needed. "I went to the beach with another guy, and he kissed me," she sobbed.

"I don't understand, Mara; why were you going out with someone else when Aerrvin had just proposed. I assume he proposed before this other guy kissed you?"

"Yes, he did, I don't know what to say. It's complicated, it was a teaching assignment. He was supposed to be teaching me some different ways to look at nature, and—I don't know. One minute we were diving in the ocean and the next, he was kissing me, but I left and he knows I don't want anything to do with him. The problem is Aerrvin is upset."

"Well, yeah! Why did you tell him? Little mistakes early on don't need to be mentioned. You said it was nothing." Amanda was confused, but wanted to help her baby.

"I didn't tell him, there were witnesses and he found out before I could talk to him. Now he won't make himself *available* to talk." Mara complained.

"Okay, Mara, take a deep breath. Welcome to the world of romance. Did you ever consider that you rushed into commitment too soon? I mean he is a catch and a half, with the looks and the money. But maybe, since you are just now allowing yourself to date, you should let yourself explore a variety of guys. I mean, if he is not even going to listen to what you have to say, maybe he is not the guy for you after all. You know?"

Mara kept control of her voice, but tears fell from her face causing dark splotches on the aqua fabric of her dress. "Yes but, I know two weeks is so very short, but it seems like I have known him for ages."

"Has he asked for the ring back?" Amanda asked.

"No, we are still engaged. He just won't talk to me." Mara pouted, starting to feel belligerent.

"Alright, honey, you will just need to be patient then. If he really loves you, he will come around. In the meantime, consider seeing others before you decide who to marry. I know I was hasty, and I loved your Dad more than is humanly possible, but sometimes I wished I would have gone to college and had a career first. I am sure you would have been my little girl regardless of the year you were born. Really, think it through, and hang in there. Love hurts. Isn't that what they say?" Amanda hated being so far away, but she did the best that she could.

Mara smiled at her Mom's quirky slogan. "Okay, Mom, thanks for letting me talk it over. I love you. Good night."

Breeze and Tessa tried to be unobtrusive, but they were in the room and had heard the entire conversation, at least from Mara's side. Seeing Mara hang up, they both moved in to console her.

"Long engagements are common among our people." Breeze said. "It is surprising that he would propose so quickly, but I must say, your Fairy Dust is the most potent I have ever experienced aside from Gwennara's. When he is in your presence, he probably cannot help himself. Maybe now that you are separated he has to rely on his true emotions. He will need to reason out if he really loves you, rather than the passion that your Dust engenders. I know that I will do anything for you simply because the Power you exude compels me to. You are even affecting Tessa."

Mara felt as if she were thinking in many directions at once, so she changed the conversation, "Then why doesn't my influence cause Morvayne to leave me alone. Can't I compel people away as much as draw them near?"

"Yes, but it will take training and usually that is a lesson taught after your Birth Day ceremony. But I guess desperate times call for desperate measures. You are certainly bright and I mean smart, as well as luminous. Compulsion spells are frowned upon, but everyone usually learns a few along the way."

Breeze walked Mara over to the sofa in Tessa's small living room. "I will teach you lessons that none of the men were probably ever going to teach you."

Mara saw Daisy in the window and motioned her to join them. The window did not have a screen, so Daisy scampered in and resumed her Elven form. Catching Tessa as she passed out, Daisy carried her to her bed and returned. "Sorry, I thought she might have been ready for that. I changed her memory. She will not recall a squirrel entering at all, and she will sleep for an hour. I would like to help with your education as well. Breeze, it is good to see you." Daisy hugged Breeze and sat down on the other side of Mara.

"Okay," Breeze said, "My mother taught me this trick when I was just about to leave for school. First, let me give you a few tips she told me as well. Fairies and Elves like to tease right?" Mara nodded. "Wonderful. We love to play a game called Gathering Dust have you heard of it?" Breeze asked.

"Not by that name, but Aerrvin has collected my Dust into pretty vials, and Jaera and Gareth accepted it gladly when he gave it to them. He said mine would be quite valuable and Fair Ones would clamber to have some, essentially. I concluded that it must be a game to try to get others angry or embarrassed enough to glow, so as to be able to collect the Dust." Mara looked back and forth between the two Elves for confirmation.

Daisy clapped daintily, "Yes, Mara you are always so perceptive. So anyway, I would like to hear Breeze tell her technique before I tell mine, as I am sure they are different. Breeze?"

Breeze paused momentarily before speaking. "Daisy, why are you here anyway? You seem to know Mara quite well and she knows you, but you were a part of Morvayne and Tigerlily's New World Party. Mara did you meet Daisy here?" Breeze meant the palazzo grounds.

Mara answered quicker than Daisy could. "Daisy is one of my sworn Attendants. Tigerlily bestowed six upon me at my birth. Clay is another."

Breeze raised her eyebrows at that. "Oh. Well that would explain his attachment to you. I thought he was totally besotted with you because you remind him of Tigerlily and Arianna all wrapped up in one package."

"I know I look like Tigerlily, as do you. But Arianna has golden hair. What makes me like Arianna?"

"Tigerlily always wore her dark hair smooth, and Arianna always accentuated her curly blonde hair, so your hair has some similarities. But we go right back where we started. Your Fairy Dust has a scent that is exactly like Arianna's and it drove Clay mad with desire. He could barely keep his hands off her when she glowed. Yet, she used this trick to control how much scent she allowed her glow to have. You will still lose control of your temper or embarrassment but you can always control the scent. Okay, it starts the same way as controlling your Light. Close your eyes and gather all of your Light."

"Wait," Mara said. "I have all of my light gathered and stored in separate pockets. Do you want me to release it all at once, or can I do it one pocket at a time."

"I do it all at once for convenience, but if you like you can do it piecemeal." Daisy interjected.

Breeze waffled her head and answered, "Do as you please. I was hoping to view your Power if you must know, but if you would rather not that is your choice."

Mara nodded and released her two front pockets and her hankie. "Okay, I am ready."

She waited in silence and peeked. Yes, two was overpowering especially this close. "Fine, keep your heads bowed, but please tell me what to do. I have it out so speak up."

Daisy had experienced her Light before, so she was not as stunned. She offered, "I take the yellow specks and separate them out. They contain the scent. Then I lock them up in a trunk and bury it under a rock. But wait! Before I do that, I take a spoonful and scatter some back in among my light, making sure to swirl it around evenly. You don't want to be completely without scent, that would be too odd."

"Okay I got it, as long as I separate it out and put it in a secure location I should not be attracting everyone within a mile of me, right?" Mara tucked away the two pockets of light and left the hankie poking out of her breast pocket. She would take care of the other two later. They were firmly secure anyway. If they opened up the Light would overcome the person regardless of the scent. At least that had been her experience so far. "Please, don't cower before me all day. Heads up."

Daisy gave Mara a hug from where she was sitting. Breeze was crying, "I did not really believe Gwennara could be dethroned. Are you sure she still lives?"

"Brand delivered her letter to my Grandfather Ironwood in person. I read it myself. She said that she had been taken captive and was being held under the sea with others. I have the Chair of Desire in my house; it is well protected, but Morvayne has been trying to get inside for the past thirty years. I think that is what Aerrvin said." Mara gave Breeze a pat on the knee. "When I sat in the chair, all of Gwennara's Power and Light flooded into me, literally suffusing me with Glory, I guess you could say. To say the least, it was amazing. I was raised as a Human and did not know what was happening. And that was only a week ago!"

Daisy stood up. "It must have been such a sight to see. Hannah was peering in and saw it; she said it was absolutely glorious. She has yet to share that vision with me. Well, I have rounds to make, take care, Mara." Daisy kissed her on the top of her head, causing Mara to think of something that had been niggling at the back of her mind.

"Wait, the first time Morvayne kissed me, I had to wash off his kiss because his kiss was binding me to him. You guys kiss me, what does that do to me? And one more before I forget; he kisses my Dragon skin now since I always cover up. Does his kiss still soak in or is he weakening my shed somehow?"

Daisy replied, "That one I do not know. You might need to ask Brand. He is the oldest person living who owns a Dragon shed. As for my kiss, it is a simple blessing, nothing to fear." With that Daisy resumed being a squirrel and left.

"Breeze, you have been awfully quiet. What's up?" Mara asked.

"I am thinking I have slept far too long. I do not know that I could have made a difference, but I can make one now. Come on, let's see to Tessa and then find Clay."

7

Whiling Away the Time

Aerrvin remembered that his house was supposed to have been completed by Saturday. So he Traveled to take a look. It was an empty shell, but all of the walls were beautifully primed and ready for paint, paper, fabric, whatever he should desire. The Brownies would be awake, but they were all in the forest model waiting for his directions. But Aerrvin wanted to be alone.

He knew he was not entirely alone, since Bronwyn had convinced him to come to his senses and return to some normalcy by allowing his companion to accompany him; discreetly, as always. The Dryads in their trees were mostly concerned with their own thoughts, not bothering with what was happening with the palace built up around them. Aerrvin completed the circuit, having looked at every room. He decided to begin with the entry hall.

The Brownies had installed the flooring. Taking his cue from the slate gray marble floors, he covered the walls in silver silk, striped with flat silver scroll-work applied along each seam. The silver scrolls were etched and cut to look like rose vines climbing the walls, creating a pleasing three dimensional effect.

Aerrvin viewed it from varying angles and decided to modify the look. It didn't 'feel' right. Therefore, he changed the silk panels nearest the door; they became texturally pleasing as he made those panels from rough raw silk—dyed to the same slate gray as the floors. Then each succeeding panel became lighter and more refined until one came to the end of the twenty foot entryway. At that point one would find oneself surrounded in the glorious light of the silk as it shone silvery smooth in the natural light coming in from the great windows facing the inner courtyard.

To complement, he caused the silver scroll-work nearest the front door to be tarnished and dull using the same degree of refinement; each succeeding rose scroll became more brightly polished. Then mirroring the theme, he removed the polish and smoothness from the marble nearest the door.

Standing at the entryway, he surveyed his work. "Well, Bronwyn, what do you think?"

"I must say, Your Highness, your taste and sense of aesthetic is impeccable. Your guests will feel as though they were leaving the dull and tarnished world behind as they enter and make their way in toward the beautiful glow you have created here at the end of this foyer. When the moon is full, it will truly feel magical," Bronwyn answered as truthfully as ever.

"Thank you, Bronwyn, you have grasped the concept precisely. Now, one final touch, and this space will be complete," Aerrvin said, adding a chandelier to the 20-foot ceiling.

Normally, in construction, people do all the painting first, but Fair Ones like to save it for last in order to get the precise color to match all the other design elements. The ceiling was a great arch, like a twenty-foot long tunnel from the door reaching to the end of the 10-foot wide entryway with hallways branching right and left at the end. Aerrvin tweaked the ceiling's color twice to get the precise shade of periwinkle touched with gray; then having applied the paint wet, he removed the stopper from a vial of Fairy Dust and induced the wind, or rather commanded Mirri and her sisters, to carry the sparkling mood enhancer up to become embedded in the paint, thus creating a faint luminosity.

Having used the bottle which contained both Aerrvin and Mara's Dust, he could not maintain his gloom. Smiling for the first time in hours—perhaps a day, which is a near lifetime for Aerrvin when depressed—the prince sighed. "Bronwyn, now it is complete. Call the other Brownies, I have assignments for them."

Once the Brownies were assembled, Aerrvin instructed them on how to finish the library, kitchen and courtyard.

"Remember, Jaera and Gareth will want to decorate their own wing so leave that space for them, and I will do the western wing as that is reserved for me and Mara. You may do the basement similar to what I have at the O'Shea Mansion. I am not sure when I will be back, but rest assured I will expect to see progress. Bronwyn, please pay the construction company in the morning and thank them for a job well done. We will leave in a moment."

Aerrvin went out the expansive French doors leading to the courtyard and minimized to his normal six inches.

Flying to an uppermost branch, he sat and enjoyed the night air, as well as the song of the Dryads. It was a song of peace and greenery, gentle breezes and family, beauty and love.

***

Sunday, Monday and Tuesday went in flurry of lessons and instructions. Mara felt as though she had learned a full year's worth of information. Wednesday dawned and Mara was greatly dissatisfied with Aerrvin's neglect. He had not even been on the beach flying about. Gareth came by briefly and said that Aerrvin had returned to Washington to attend to some business matters. He did not know when he would return.

Clay had told Ironwood that the latitude for Morvayne's window was 36 degrees with some minutes and seconds, but Mara didn't pay attention to the details. That could put him outside of Athens or below Washington D.C., even somewhere off the coast of California near Big Sur, or anywhere in the two oceans in between. Including the Yellow Sea or the Sea of Japan. It was a clue, but it was still thousands of miles to search.

"Maybe Grandpa has other clues." Mara sighed, as she padded her way to the shower. "Not that they have to be hidden in the Lost City of Atlantis, which surely is here in the Mediterranean. They could be in any Mermaid colony."

Clay met Mara and Breeze for breakfast as calm as ever. "I trust you slept well."

"Yes, I did. Clay? I just thought of something. I meant to ask yesterday, but then got busy learning and all. Can you leave the property? And can you remove the force field around me?"

Clay nodded his head gracefully while eying Mara appreciatively. "Yes, I can leave; no, you cannot. I am not able to release the capsule Morvayne placed on you, and it would crush you, were you to try leaving."

"Then what is the purpose of clearing the Brownie exit, if I cannot leave?"

"Once we convince Morvayne to remove the capsule, you would still be unable to leave the boundary by walking across the line—the same as Breeze. However, those wards only extend down a few feet. The Brownie tunnels are 100 feet deep, Breeze could leave now should she wish." Clay raised his glance to Breeze.

"You mean I can leave and no one told me?" Breeze exclaimed, startling Isadora as she brought fresh baked muffins to the table. "Hmph! It is nice to know, but I guess I will stay until Mara can leave as well."

She smiled at Mara and placed a muffin on her plate.

"Ah, my happy little family," Morvayne said as he exited the patio door. "It is so good to see you again. I am sorry, but duty calls and sometimes I am the only one who knows how to attend to such thinsg. Ah, well let us not talk business. Clay, how have Mara's lessons been going?"

"Morvayne, glad you could make it back so soon. You must have that magic touch." Clay smiled smoothly.

Seeing them together, Mara could see the family resemblance; both were lean, smooth and elegant. Morvayne still oozed smarm, if that was a word. It just made his beauty distasteful. Mara moderated her thoughts in order to control her features. *I am a leaf fluttering in the wind*, she thought.

Clay continued to answer Morvayne, "Mara is a quick study, and Breeze has been an immense help."

Breeze added, "It has been a pleasure, really. Morvayne, I should have left my Dream ages ago. I have not had any real challenges for such a long time. I quite enjoy trying to understand the poor girl. Sorry, Mara. I think Clay is taken with you and has given you a more glowing report than would be accurate."

Morvayne had already noted the nearness of Clay's chair to Mara's, as opposed to where Breeze sat. "Yes, well any progress is commendable. Mara, please show me a trifle of what you have learned." He flicked his fingers at her, excusing her from her seat so she could stand and demonstrate.

He took her vacated seat and ate her remaining breakfast.

I am a leaf. I am a leaf. Mara chanted within. Maintaining a calm exterior Mara produced her own meal consisting of a bowl of cereal and an orange juice. Nodding to Morvayne as he clapped condescendingly, she sat next to Breeze to eat her nutritiously superior meal.

"That was wonderful, Mara. I am going into the villa today, would you and Breeze care to accompany me?" Morvayne asked. "I will buy you anything you want."

Breeze clapped her hands and said, "Wonderful! I would love to. Mara say yes, it will be fun!" Breeze put her arm around Mara as though they had become the bestest of friends. Morvayne smiled appreciatively.

Mara simply nodded, allowing herself to blush lightly.

***

Before leaving, Morvayne called Clay into his office to discuss matters with him, "Well, Clay, have you taught her all of the background history she needs in order to take the Oath?"

Clay raised his brows arrogantly, and waited for the next question. "Did you teach her at night to prevent that pipsqueak Purple from contacting her?" Morvayne drew close in a near menacing stance.

"I never saw the Fairy as I taught, and when I left her I made sure she slept in the second level," Clay replied. "She has taken in all I have given, and is ready for Lessons of Conduct."

"You mean to tell me you taught her in her Dream? She has wards on her Dream! How did you gain her trust? I have tried to be so ingratiating to her, it sickens even me!"

Clay put a calming hand on Morvayne's shoulder. "You forget, Morvayne, I am your older brother. I will always be one step ahead of you. Never fear, I will not steal her from you. True she reminds me of Arianna, but she is *not* Arianna, nor could she *ever* replace her. You keep your promises and I will keep mine."

Nodding his head, Morvayne went to his desk and unstopped the wine bottle he had set there. Pouring a glass for himself he offered, "Care for a drop?"

"'Tis poison."

"I know it is, but it has curious properties which I have been studying. Did you know that if a Fair One drinks a glass a

89

day he gains the ability to, shall we say, see things differently? New thoughts and ideas blossom forth daily. I stopped writing them down, but look." Morvayne went to a shelf holding several leather-bound journals, taking one out he handed it to Clay.

"These are my findings from when I first started my investigation. Now, I nearly live on it as it sustains me and keeps me focused on the plan, which I have developed as a result of gaining this—new perspective."

"Fascinating." Clay said dryly. "I will peruse it in my spare time."

"Oh, you will have that. I have a favor to ask, and then you can do as you please. I have noticed quite a number of '*seagull*s and *insects*' flitting about, though I have not seen a particularly bothersome Purple. Be that as it may, would you mind cleaning it up a bit before we get back from town?"

Clay grinned with toothsome delight, "It would be my pleasure. One comment before you go; I think it would be okay to relax the restraints on Mara while on the property. She is easily swayed and trusts me, and Breeze too."

Still grinning, he opened Volume I of *Controlled Wine Experiments* by Morvayne the Scot.

Dismissed, Morvayne made no reply.

***

Going out front, Mara was disappointed in not seeing Aerrvin's Viper; of course it only held two people. Morvayne had a driver and the three sat in the back of a sleek black limo. Breeze managed to maneuver herself between Mara and Morvayne to Mara's delight and Morvayne's discontent. Though he hid it well. The drive was a short ten minutes and soon they were walking among shops selling the new day's offerings.

Mara did not enjoy the sights, not having anyone to share

her delight with, and having to cling to Morvayne put a severe damper on her joy. But Breeze chattered on about this and that, even convincing Mara to buy several new outfits. Amazingly, Morvayne permitted the purchase of a pair of Capri's, which was a small triumph. They stopped to enjoy small bowls of gelato, refreshing themselves for the heated walk back to the car.

The trip only lasted an hour and a half. Mara suddenly felt like she should have tried to enjoy it more. The thought of going back to the property felt so stifling. Once in the car she began to hyperventilate.

"Mara, what's wrong?" Breeze asked with concern. Instantly she had a cool cloth in her hand. "Here, put this on your neck. It will help to cool you down. Breathe evenly, I'm here okay? It's going to be all right."

Turning to Morvayne sitting beside her she said, "Can't you relax the restraints on her? I think she feels mental stress from lack of freedom."

***

Morvayne squinted at Breeze as he pursed his lips, then sucking air in between his teeth he replied, "I will relax the restraints if she shows improvement in her abilities. Mara would you like that?" He tried to sound soothing. "You must understand, all parents put these capsules on their young to prevent them from harming themselves. Your father was a colleague of mine, remember?" Morvayne sighed. "I meant it when I offered to assist you. Mara, having been awakened to your true nature has put you in need of training. I am not too proud to admit that I am not the best of teachers after all. Clay and Breeze will continue to assist me in my endeavor to see that you are properly prepared for what the future holds."

Morvayne paused to see if she responded positively to his efforts to soothe. Her breathing had slowed and she was resting her head on Breeze. Morvayne thought it a pity that Amanda refused to accept her own identity; the youngling really needed a mother right now. Breeze would have to do; she was a vast improvement over Kiera. In Morvayne's view Fairies were almost as bad as Brownies, the pesky things, *they are all right for fun and parties, but useless as an army.* He had tried so hard to get those Orange Fairies to be diligent in their task. *They have a belligerent nature and like to band together, but they are about as Bright as a fluorescent light bulb!* Morvayne forgot what he was thinking about, so he simply gazed at Mara. *She looks so like Tigerlily,* he thought fondly.

***

Clay went outside as soon as Morvayne left. He found Gareth sunning himself as a lizard. "Gareth?"

"Aye, 'tis me," Gareth replied. "Anything new?"

"Not really. Morvayne wants all the Fairies flitting about to be gone before he gets back from town. He expects me to scare you all away."

"I don't know you that well, Clay, what kind of things can you do to scare Fairies?" Gareth was seriously interested.

"Well, I have an attractant spell that collects all living creatures within a quarter mile, they come together in a great lump. Then I can separate out what or whomever I desire and bury the rest beneath the earth or wrap them up within a capsule and send them to the polar ice caps. I suppose, I am only limited by my ingenuity. Obviously, I cannot use my power to cause loss of life, but I can make it difficult for anyone to come near me when I do not desire it. It takes a year to weaken the capsule, and should I wish, I could come along every six months and restore it to its full strength. In essence, I could keep a band of enemies out of commission indefinitely. They would not die, but neither could they be free."

Gareth changed to his miniature self while remaining

hidden in the shade of the rock. Whistling to show he was impressed, he thought a moment and then said, "So that is what he has done, most likely, with the Queen and perhaps her daughter and great grandson?"

"Most likely." Clay liked the Blue Fairy, he was smart and would serve Aerrvin well as his Sworn Defender and leader of his army.

"Then why not capture Morvayne in this way?"

Clay raised a finger as if awarding a point. "Morvayne crafted counter wards against such actions centuries ago. Once he knew such capsules could be used on others he worked feverishly to create his protections against them. I recently read about it in his journal."

"So really, we just need to do a better job of tailing him and we might be able to locate where he has hidden them. We have nothing to do here anyway, so we will begin searching along the 36th parallel. Tell Mara we have not forgotten her." Gareth offered a delightfully precise bow and flitted away, careless of being seen at all. Soon all the Fairies winked out and were gone, leaving Jasmine, Hannah, Ivan and Elwood. Hannah and Elwood approached as Clay tossed hunks of bread.

Clay asked, "So, Elwood, what does the local population have to say?"

Elwood was more gray than white and he was slightly larger than the other seagulls. "Most do not take notice of Morvayne as he rarely comes here, but when he does, he usually has one or two parties where any who wish may attend. But really he prefers Elven kind to any who might live here, and he does not appear to know that an Ogre lives up the way, even though she has been there for centuries. Essentially they say he is a partier with very little substance."

"He seems to have fostered that image on purpose,

because he does not portray himself that way in the UK. Oh, he always has a pretty on his arm, but who wouldn't if they could? Hmm, something to think on. Thanks Elwood."

Clay turned his attention to Hannah. "Has Seamus returned to the tunnel yet?"

"No, but he should be ready soon. I helped him to Travel as you asked me to."

"Good, he should be done with his report in person to Ironwood and Brand as well as getting their input, so bring him back and have him enter the tunnels again. He need not march very far as we will want him to leave again in a few days. Tell Ivan and Jasmine to become neighbor cats or something, Morvayne wants the winged population dispersed. Though, I do not believe he saw through your transformations. It was just that all the flitting Fairies had become an annoyance."

Clay left them to their patrol; it was rather useless, but what else could they do? They had sworn to protect Mara at her birth as he had, and they were compelled to be as near as the wards would allow.

Clay wore a ware spell, alerting him to Mara's return. He Traveled his way back into the library with a ripple and a bend of Light. Mara was uneasy, bordering on controlled panic, so he casually exited the library once he heard the door shut.

Leaning in the doorway he asked, "The heat getting to her again? Perhaps a cooler clime would do her some good."

Morvayne snapped, "We are not going anywhere. Perhaps she should stay inside and we will go out at night if we feel a need. Honestly, it is not that hot; its only 85 degrees."

Breeze spoke up, "I think the capsule is draining her too quickly! Why don't you just release her from that? Mara will you show Morvayne that you are able to control your power? If you do, perhaps he will allow you that much freedom, at least. I do think it will make you feel better." Breeze looked from Mara to Morvayne and back.

Morvayne huffed a sigh, "Fine! Mara please show me your Power at full force and do a trick that is better than a bowl of cereal." He waved his hand in an intricate gesture and the capsule dispersed completely.

Mara felt lighter already. "Please, oh never mind." Mara was thirsty and reached into her refrigerator at home grabbing an orange cream Sobe. It was the last one. Jill was going to notice, so she wrote a note telling her she was still captive, but had been granted some freedom to test her powers. Smiling at that freedom, she sat down to rest, drawing a breeze towards her to cool her flushed skin. The three Elves all stood there gawking.

"Was that good enough or do you want something else?"

From the Elves point of view, they had not seen the location of the drink only that she had gotten one nor had they seen the note, Mara had done that in her mind and the note appeared in the refrigerator. The only other thing they saw was Mara glow lightly, and relax enough to sit and then draw the wind. Not all Fair Ones have that power so it was a revelation to see her do it.

"Breeze, did you teach her to command the winds?" Morvayne asked.

"No, she was taught meal and fabric creation, as well as holding Power and Light in reserve. She already knew flying and entering Dreams. As you told me, she had been learning to Travel, but we have not tried those here. With the capsule it would be too draining. We have taught no songs, or chants, or any such spells." Breeze went and sat down next to Mara, retrieving her own drink from a private stash she kept elsewhere.

"That's it exactly!" Clay said with uncharacteristic

animation. "Mara, you did not create that drink, you actually took it from somewhere. Am I right?"

Mara looked sheepish, "Yes, I was thirsty and knew that I still had this in my fridge. So I—I don't know I wanted it and got it." She shrugged. She realized that Clay was acting; he had, after all, taught her to reach for an object when visiting Meriel in her cave.

Clay smiled at Morvayne; Morvayne smiled briefly before becoming serious. "That was wonderful progress, Mara, but do not try it with a living being. It will harm them, and most likely kill them. I have not tried it myself as I have taken the Oath and cannot do it if I wanted to. But you have not taken the Oath and could kill countless numbers unknowingly. Which, as I have said before, is why children are kept in restraints until they learn control. I see you have control, but you still need knowledge because you are far more powerful than any ordinary twenty-year-old filled with magic."

Morvayne paused, considering how much to reveal. Then reaching into his breast pocket he pulled out a fluffy seedpod. "I have received the announcement that Gwennara has transferred her power to *you,* Mara, her only surviving heir. You are the future Queen of all the Realms." He bowed, observing Clay and Breeze bow at the news, but only briefly.

He had been expecting the news to arrive any day. Actually, he had gotten tired of waiting for it and caught a seedpod back in Washington while he was out.

"Mara, I feel it my duty to the Crystal Throne to keep you safe. As well as you, Breeze. If anything were to happen to Mara, Breeze, you would then be next in line for the throne. As you well know, all of Tigerlily's sisters are gone." He pursed his lips looking almost comical.

Breeze nodded. "I thank you for your concern. When did

this transfer occur?"

Morvayne faced Mara as he pulled up a chair. "I do not know, the announcement was brief." He handed the pod to Breeze so that she could receive it personally. "Mara, did you feel yourself receive this added power?"

Mara did not want to tell him her wondrous experience, it was too personal for scum to hear. Yet she knew he would have to hear something. "Yes." She tried to think up something fast.

"Well?" Morvayne asked.

Breeze handed the pod to Clay as he finally deigned to sit. He declined it saying, "No, thanks. I received the news already."

This earned a slit-eyed glance from Morvayne. He hated having a big brother fifty years ahead of him. *Why would he be lucky enough to have already received the news? It just isn't fair!*

Mara twitched as though about to say something and then took a drink, her bottle was nearly empty. "More like, maybe, you know? These past two weeks have been a turbulent awakening. How am I supposed to be able to pinpoint when I received more power? I mean, it seems to get stronger all the time. Am I making any sense?" She looked to Clay. She didn't know what to say, she was just rambling.

Mara noticed a ward go up around her, and noticed as Breeze and Clay become tense as well.

Morvayne held his hands in a placating gesture. "No worries, I just placed a seal on this room. Mara, I ask that you reveal your Light, all of it. I wish to know for certain, you understand, to verify that you have received all of Gwennara's Power and Light, My Lady." He bowed in breathless anticipation.

Mara felt like a child being brought out to play the piano for the adults. She stood as Clay and Breeze stood and then she opened the two front pockets and the hankie, the action caused her scented Dust to swirl about the room. Never, ever would she reveal the Light from her back pockets to Morvayne, at least not until she was free and could pass judgment on his crimes. Then he would see the full wrath of her Power and Light in Justice and Glory!

Morvayne did not keep his head bowed, he reveled in Mara's Glory as he thought of it as his own. He smiled as the rainbow sparks settled all over the room. He could influence armies with that Dust! With a sneer, he realized that Breeze and Clay had sunk lower as the Light shone longer and the Dust continued to gather. "That will do, Your Highness, I do believe. I will swear my heart and soul to you when you take the Crystal Throne."

Mara's compassion for Clay grew; she knew she must be torturing him with her scent. Looking at him, she was surprised to see he had a smile on his face as he collected a small vial of dust for safekeeping. Morvayne gathered the rest, not with wind as he did not have that ability. Not that one watching could see much of a difference. He used a gravity attractant much like a magnet; all the dust came rushing to his vial, but there was too much so he filled a second smaller one and allowed Breeze to have it.

"We shan't be greedy."

Mara looked about and saw that everyone was quite pleasantly smiling, herself included. "Well that was 'hungrifying'. Is it lunch time yet?"

Everyone laughed and Morvayne replied, "I should imagine it was. You won't be required to display this much for general tasks. Breeze, go check on Isadora. Let her know we will eat inside today."

Mara remembered she was supposed to be ignorant, so she asked about the vials of Dust. She sat down on the couch and

Clay joined her. Morvayne puffed himself up, pleased to have something about which she was willing to learn from him.

"Well, you see, this is called Fairy Dust. Fair Ones collect and trade it for goods and services. Each individual has unique qualities in the Dust they put out, thereby making one more valuable than another. Yours is particularly *Compelling*. Once you gain full control of your abilities you will be able compel nations to do your bidding—" Morvayne's eyes glazed over as he thought of the magnificent consequences of such power under his guidance.

Mara glanced over at Clay, her eyebrows raised in a question. Clay merely shrugged and wrapped his arm around her protectively as they sat side by side on the sofa. Mara was once again struck by how nice it felt to be in contact with Clay. *Perhaps he exudes some kind of Elven peace pheromones. Most likely,* she thought as she leaned into him. He smelled like fresh cut grass. She couldn't help but take a deep breath. Morvayne had finally started speaking again, but she had missed his first few sentences.

"…so it will be a remarkable era when we reach it."

Breeze returned, assessed the situation with coolness and then said formally, "Lunch will be served now in the dining room." Turning without waiting to see who followed she walked gracefully ahead; they too walked with casual grace, as though without a care in the world.

***

Tessa was glad to see Mara was not in a tizzy for once.

Morvayne's return had frightened Tessa as she was beginning to see him in the same light as Mara portrayed him. For now, everyone seemed quite mellow and appeared to be enjoying one another's company. It was odd how silent they were though, each seemed locked in their own thoughts.

Breeze invited Morvayne and the others to go swimming in the pool. Mara declined, not wanting to be near Morvayne in the water ever again. "No thanks, I would like to do some photography. May I retrieve my camera?"

Morvayne replied with expansiveness, "Please, feel free to enjoy the rest of the day as you please. I will take a dip, but then I must retire to my room as I have some contemplation to attend."

Mara grabbed her camera and went out into the wonderfully warm sunshine, inviting Clay and Tessa to join her. Tessa hesitated, "Are you sure the heat will not be too much?"

"I am," Mara replied. "The heat was just an excuse. It has not been too warm at all, I love it."

Mara looked to Clay, who had not risen yet from the table. "Are you going to have thirds?"

"No, you go on ahead. I want to get something, then I will join you in the garden," Clay answered as he smoothly rose and stacked the plates.

Tessa hustled over. "No, no, no! That is for me, sir, please go on. Mara, I will join you when I can." Tessa bowed slightly and proceeded to clear the table.

Mara decided to change out of the dress she had worn to town.

It was a bit sticky, and there was still a good amount of Fairy Dust stuck to it. She changed into the white Capri's she had bought, noticing, for the first time that she had gotten a tan from her day on the beach. She wanted a tank top, but had not seen one in town and her closet only held cotton or silk tops, dresses or skirts. Looking again in the drawers, hoping to see something new, she found among the swimwear a tankini top that would work. It was white with pink polka dots. Not her usual style, but who was going to see her anyway? The white really showed up her tan. She admired herself vainly in the mirror.

When Mara went out, she saw that Clay had beaten her. "I guess he didn't need to do much, whatever it was."

She started snapping as soon as she remembered her camera was in her hand. She reluctantly took a few of Morvayne splashing Breeze. *These will make great action shots for my portfolio.*

"What am I thinking?" she said to herself. "I am never going to have a studio, never have to prove my work to another to make a living. I should be pleased at having the world nearly handed to me on a magical platter. How come it feels so empty?"

Clay sat in the rose garden drawing in a sketchbook. He looked so melancholy, a solitary figure surrounded by a symbol of love. Mara felt the call to preserve the moment and snapped pictures from several angles. Like Aerrvin, he barely moved, only his hand and eyes appeared to have any life. *Beautiful. If I could photograph the Fair Ones I could be so successful*—there she was, at it again.

Dejected, she sat down next to Clay.

He had of course felt her roller-coaster of emotions since she came outside. "Mara, why so sad? You have always loved taking pictures; ever since your first camera at nine years old, you have been snapping pictures with joy and pleasure. I have always enjoyed being near you when you were practicing your art."

"You really have been with me since birth. It is kind of weird to meet people who know so much about me, and I barely know them. I do love taking pictures, it's just that, what's the point? I had plans of opening a studio and maybe receiving recognition for being a great photographer. You know? Maybe even having a fancy coffee table book of my photos, and being on display in art shows and museums. Now it seems there is no need. All the wealth of the world is at my fingertips. What else is there?" Mara sighed having talked herself lower.

"Is that what you really believe? That money is the only reason to do a thing?" Clay asked, glancing up from his sketch to look her in the eyes.

"No, of course not. Not when you say it like that. I have never really cared about money. I have been content with my life with Mom, even when she was single and living off of the survivor benefits she got. Then when she married Rick, we had more, but we were never the wealthiest in town or anything. I have had a pleasant life, aside from losing Daddy. Now it's all upside down and inside out! I don't know what I think about anything. I don't even know if I really love Aerrvin, or if it was just magic Fairy Dust making me think I did."

"Mara," Clay groaned, placing his sketch and pencil beside him. He turned and took her hand in the two of his. Looking deep into her eyes, he saw that she was indeed Mara, not Arianna nor even Tigerlily. "I love you. I would even love to be with you. But you are confused. You *do* love Aerrvin, I can feel it. Here let me show you. Stand up."

Facing each other. Clay said, "Dance with me." A sweet melody played for their ears only. He danced with such practiced grace and elegance; fluidity that only an Elf with his years could attain. It was pure heaven, and to Mara he smelled richly of the outdoors, mingled with the scent of the roses in full bloom.

For his part it was enjoyable, yet controlled. He was the teacher, she was the student. He had learned years and years gone by, to enjoy what life gives you at the moment it is given. Even though deep down he mourned a loss so deep, he could never be free from it. They danced through several songs until Mara found they were in the grove of trees near the cottages.

Morvayne had quit the pool and noted the pair, but left them to their dancing. He was determined to remain focused on his goal. If he could not have Mara yet, it was no matter. Clay could break her from her attachment to that puny Purple Fairy.

Later, he would teach her that she need not be attached to one single being for the rest of her life. Yes, Clay was a step ahead of him, but it would all work out in the end.

8
Lessons Accepted

Mara forgot what Clay was trying to teach her, or maybe she never knew. He was so sleek and well-muscled, they must have barely skimmed the ground as she never tripped once. She looked up at his perfect Elven face, pale and taut, his eyes slanted just a hair upward and his cheekbones reflected the light filtering through the branches above. He had released his shoulder-length hair, which was so smooth, a salon would love to have him model their products. She realized she had started to think about photography again and smiled.

Clay looked down at her, aware of her mirth. "I love it when you feel happy, Mara."

With precision and control, he cupped her face and kissed her on the lips. Once.

She thought she wanted more, but realized she did not. She stood there frozen in a stupor of thought. "What just happened?"

Clay dropped his eyes momentarily and then answered, "I just proved that you do not love me—more than Aerrvin."

He created a sofa and sat down; pulling Mara to him, he cradled her in his arms. "Mara, we enjoy being together because in part I cradled you as a baby; all of us did." He nodded toward the shore, "It is like we are your Nest Mates. We love you. We Fair Folk enjoy life to its fullest and wish the best for each other.

Attraction does not equal romantic love. Nor does love mean marriage is impending. I enjoy being near the rest of your Attendants; they are my Hold Mates, as Elves prefer to call them. We do not have Rings and Nests. I created it with Arianna, Tigerlily, Ivan, and Morthe—my dear Ogre friend. Hannah and Daisy too, but we were still studying and improving our skills so we were not always together. Then when Morvayne came along he was a natural member. Later I added Elwood and Jasmine in there too.

"For whatever reason, none of us have found someone willing to marry us or we them, though Daisy has received two proposals. Of course, Tigerlily, as you know, found love with both Jacques and Rupert. That was hurtful to both Morvayne and I. We each had hopes, separately, that she might desire to wed one of us. As you know, Morvayne desperately loved Tigerlily to the consumption of his soul. I do not think I can save him after all, and that pains me." Clay paused and squeezed his eyes shut.

Mara knew now that she loved Aerrvin more than anything, so she felt safe in softly brushing the hair back from Clay's face. She smiled at him as he opened his eyes. "I love you too, Clay. Thank you for opening my eyes."

Clay continued, as he needed to express his pain out loud, "I love Arianna, and I know she is not dead! We were close enough, once, that I have a strong connection to her. I will know when she is well and truly gone." Closing his eyes he took a deep cleansing breath, before slowly opening them to see Mara's shocked expression.

"Clay! Why haven't you searched for her? She should be Queen!" Mara sat up straight, still perched on his lap.

"Because—Mara, I swore to serve Tigerlily, and then you. I have not been free to search." It was a mild misdirection of truth, but he felt it was close enough to reality.

"And you have never told anyone?" Mara asked.

"My closest friends are sworn to your service as well," Clay replied, taking one more deep breath, and then releasing it in a loud sigh.

"So you are saying that the only way to search for her is for me to go searching for her, and you would have to follow. Right?" Mara asked thoughtfully.

Clay shook his head, "Mara, I could never ask you to do such a thing. Your safety is my highest priority."

Mara felt as though she had never loved someone as much as she loved Clay right then. Twisting around so she could hug him, she wrapped her arms around him and kissed him squarely on the mouth and then on each cheek, while thinking good thoughts and wishes for success. She didn't know how blessings were given, but it seemed as good a way as any.

"Then you shall have to keep me safe."

"Let it be as you wish, My Lady." Clay bowed his head ever so elegantly for one sitting with a maiden on his lap.

Mara turned toward the rock and said regally, "You may show yourself now, Aerrvin. I wish to speak with you."

***

Aerrvin had spent the last several days working on the palace. His western suite was fantastic and he just knew Mara was going to love it. It was a labor of love, his feelings for Mara increased as he worked out his anger and pride. By the time Tuesday evening settled on the palace, he felt ready to speak with her. He knew from Gareth that no real progress had been made. They were proceeding with the plan to get Morvayne to relax his controls and then sneak Mara out through the Brownie tunnels.

Aerrvin swept onto the beach as his second favorite sea

bird, once again a seagull.

He spied Mara immediately, she was in the garden taking photos of Clay. He could not detect her feelings from that distance, but he could read her body language, one minute excitedly snapping and the next dejected at something, until finally she slumped next to Clay. He hoped Clay could improve her mood. He hated seeing her so sad. It only served to make him feel helpless. Soon they were dancing. Aerrvin saw the direction Clay was moving, so he landed near the rock and switched to being a skink. By the time they were into the trees, Mara was feeling peace and then merriment. He could barely see her, but he saw Clay kiss her and she felt empty, a kind of shock. Then feelings of love for Aerrvin washed over her, in turn melting Aerrvin's heart completely.

Skinks don't hear words too well, so he improved his disguise to a squirrel and sat against the rock in the shadows. Pangs of jealousy wriggled through him as Clay pulled her onto his lap. He stamped his little foot, but refrained from chittering.

Clay taught Mara an important lesson, and it was in Aerrvin's best interest if she understood how things work in the magical world. Aerrvin echoed Clay's thought that it was dangerous to search for Arianna, but he agreed with Mara that is was the right thing to do, and not just for Clay. Aerrvin felt his respect grow for Clay with his smooth charm and wisdom. He realized that he could probably benefit from a few lessons himself. That was when Mara called him forth.

"Let it be as you wish, My Lady," he mocked, bowing as well as a squirrel can. "Thank you, Clay, for the wonderful lesson you taught; I have been inspired to reach for greater integrity and eloquence."

"May you have success in your quest," Clay nodded towards the prince. "Aerrvin, I would love to give you privacy, but Mara is not to be left unguarded. She can enter her Dream while I hold her and in this way you can have your privacy." The sofa became a recliner and Mara snuggled up beside Clay as he wrapped one arm protectively around her. To Morvayne it would appear that Mara had been smitten with strong feelings for Clay. Clay was sure he would not intrude even if they stayed past dinnertime.

Mara emptied her mind and sought the Void. This was becoming easier each day, almost as easy as counting. Soon she was in her Dream bedroom, with Aerrvin knocking at the window.

With joy, she ran and let him in and then remembered to set her ward against spying eyes. Mara thought it would be just like Morvayne to want to watch her making out with Clay, as he would assume they had fled to the Land of Dreams to enjoy freedoms they did not have here in the backyard. Pushing Morvayne far from her thoughts, she hugged Aerrvin and kissed him repeatedly until he gasped.

"I wish . . ."

She kissed him again and said, "Your wish is my command." She offered what she hoped looked like a mischievous grin.

Aerrvin read her mood and tried not to laugh at her smile. "I wish to be forgiven," he said as he sobered to the task at hand.

"No, Aerrvin, you are not to blame! I would be upset if I saw you drinking and having fun with some girl, especially if I knew you did not like her."

"Mara, listen to me. I am not mad at you for enjoying sensations. I saw, in shared Dreams, how much you drank. Everyone I know would enjoy any amount of touch after having consumed a glass of Honeysuckle Dew. It is ten times as strong as Rose Elixir. Add in the time between sips factor and it is amazing you had as much control as you did. It is extremely powerful magic. I know; I had a bottle once and didn't share but one glass."

He paused and then added, "I am livid with hatred for Morvayne though!" Aerrvin's voice rose with his emotions. "If I could have gotten close enough then, I would have killed him."

Mara interjected, "Why couldn't you get close? You've been near him before."

"He has a new piece of jewelry which prevents those intending harm to do as they desire," Aerrvin replied. "You do know that part of the Oath we take states that we are not to use the power to kill, right?

Mara nodded. "Yes, Clay and Breeze have been doing a great job of teaching me. I just hate being trapped here. It has been lonely without you. I even thought that maybe I did not really love you. Mom said that I should think about dating more, to make sure that you are what I want. When you wouldn't talk to me—I don't know. I thought maybe you were a shallow Fairy just high on my Dust or something, I don't know how you say it all flowery."

Aerrvin hugged her tight and tried to breathe in her scent; being a Dream there was barely a memory of it.

"We call it getting Dusted, being Dusted. I guess it is not very poetical anyway you say it. I suppose that is guy talk. To you I would say, 'I bask in your Glow and Glory in your Light.' Which is code for, 'I love getting Dusted, your scent is intoxicating!' And I must admit: I love it when it happens."

He flew her over to the dresser to sit on Growly. "I bet you didn't know that one night when you forgot to set your ward, I came in while you were sleeping and slept in Growly's place?" He kissed her under her ear, which just so happens to be a place where Fairy Dust collects. "You do need to set your wards better. Still, I would have warned you had Morvayne tried to enter. Lucky for you I was there."

Mara blushed and then blushed again realizing she had fallen for it again. "You! I'm on to your little Fairy games. I'll soon be one of the best at the sport and will have a trophy wall of all the Dust I will have collected."

She paused and thought awhile, allowing Aerrvin to stroke her hair. "So, sincerely, you were attracted to me before I started dropping sparkly Dust all over the place? You did not even know I was Faire at all, right? What did you like? And then, wait, I'm not done, what is so great about my scent anyway? I didn't feel like asking Clay."

"Mara, I could go on all night. I guess it's not really night—someone will be coming soon to offer you dinner. Let me see, your hair caught my attention first; my fingers itched to run through these silky soft spirals. The fact that you were attracted to me helped. Some prefer Gareth."

"Wait, I looked at both of you. How could you tell that I preferred you?" Mara asked.

"Ah, the moment of truth," Aerrvin said sheepishly. "I use a ware spell. It lets me know when someone close by is thinking of me, and you were definitely thinking of me."

Aerrvin's fingers slid down the smoothness of the silk ribbons on her nightgown. "Why do you choose this night gown as your default attire?"

Aerrvin was in tunic and leggings.

"Because it seemed to me that you liked it," Mara replied a bit shyly. Really, she did not know Aerrvin much better than she knew Clay or Robbie from her math class. She had gone to the movies with Robbie and a group of friends a few times.

"I am learning that we Fair Ones do a lot of things by instinct, no by—I know there is a word; it's a sense of emotion, an innate feeling that something is right or wrong. Right?"

Aerrvin pulled the ribbons free and kissed her neck before answering. "You are right, I do like this nightgown. We Fair Folk practice the art of living true to our core.

"Sometimes living so close to our emotions gets the best of us; hence my pride blinded me for a moment. But your absence proved to me how very much I need you in my life. I love you for your joy at seeing beauty and wanting to capture it on film. You have a talent and should not let it die. We Fair Ones can adapt to modern conveniences. You may have noticed by now that there is pleasure in living in the moments of everyday life.

"Yes, we could instantly be clean, and we could take nutrient capsules for sustenance. We can Travel and be anywhere. We can make, create, or sometimes take whatever we want. We may or may not wear clothes. But where is the joy? We revel in beauty, peace and joy. Indeed, we seek it in all that we do. That is our true essence and purpose." Aerrvin pulled Mara to him and, speaking mere inches from her face, he said, "Mara, you embody all three for me. Without you, I would lose beauty, peace and joy —forever."

Mara felt the truth of Aerrvin's declaration every bit as much as if she were wearing a ware spell. Truth seemed to enter her core and light her up from within. Freeing her Power and Light, she gloried in his presence as he released his essence in a shower of blue sparks mingled with purple, white, silver and gold. With a laugh of pure delight, Aerrvin swooped her up and out to dance in the rain and dark of night—trailing clouds of glory as they flew.

Alas, it did not last all night. Clay poked at her Dream, and she allowed him to enter. "Mara it is 6 o'clock. We should go in."

Mara shared with Aerrvin a final hug and a kiss. "I love you," they said in unison. Aerrvin went to Clay and hugged him too. "Thank you. Your gift is priceless." And then Aerrvin left.

Mara sighed and woke up. Clay stretched languorously, while Aerrvin returned to his seagull form and flew away, sending Mara feelings of goodness and light. "How does he do that?"

"Do what?" Clay asked as he stood up.

"Aerrvin can send me his emotions now, or I can feel them anyway." Mara said with wonder. "At least while he was within a hundred yards or so." She scrunched her nose in disappointment as his essence faded.

Her mentor replied, "You are bonding. The more time you spend together the more you will be able to feel each other's emotions. It is similar to a ware spell, but only works between mates. It is a sign that you are compatible and perhaps meant to be. Once you wed formally, your vows will allow you to feel the bond anywhere or anywhen each of you may go."

"Anywhen?" Mara asked as they walked back through the gardens.

Clay took her hand as they walked and smiled gently. "You have much yet to learn, youngling."

***

Tessa was bewildered with Mara's fickle behavior. She claimed to be engaged as a reason to reject Morvayne. Yet she became so readily attached to Clay. *Don't ask me*, she thought, *I'm just the maid!*

"Mara, Clay; I can bring you dinner now. Where would you like to eat?" Tessa inquired.

Mara would have liked to eat in the kitchen, but she remembered Isadora's jealousy. "The patio is fine."

The evening went by quietly. Mara was becoming bored though.

She did not watch much TV, but being forced into a situation where there was no TV or PC was beginning to tell. "So what do you do all day long anyway?" She asked as Breeze came outside.

"Do?" Breeze asked.

Mara replied with great drama, "Yes! What do Fair Ones do? I mean sleep is not necessary, but you do a lot of it. Probably because you are bored to tears! You must have something to occupy yourselves with."

Breeze and Clay shared a smile. Breeze sat down next to Mara. "I enjoy exercise, like swimming and walking. I hike in the mountains and explore caves. I collect anything light enough to float on a gentle breeze. My parents named me well," she smiled.

"Okay, those are nice, but what do you do with your mind? Besides we are trapped here." Mara hammered the table with her little fist, and looked from Breeze to Clay.

"We work on developing our social graces, like patience." Clay smiled lazily, looking at her through half-lidded eyes.

Mara blushed, prettily sending sparks blowing in the breeze. Then she groaned slumping in her chair. "I guess I am not phrasing my question correctly. While you are carrying out your mindless activities, like walking, what do you think about?"

Clay answered, "Close, but still not the right question. We think about whatever is on our mind. Perhaps the question you want is this: What is your purpose in living? When I have a moment to speculate, I find I ask myself this question: How can I find joy in this moment?"

Breeze interrupted, "He's right, when I climb a mountain I am enjoying the sights, the smells and the texture. My thoughts are focused on the entire experience. I don't have time to be bored. Here in the garden I can get lost watching a rose unfold and enjoy the shadows of the sun as it changes the shape and hue of the bloom, it is breathtaking really. Join me tomorrow morning, you will see."

Mara brightened. "Oh, I think I see! I have not been given the whole Wart being transformed into a hawk experience yet. You know, King Arthur being a fish and all when he was a boy?"

Clay burst out laughing. "I saw the movie from your window, but I could not hear it very well, it was raining. Nevertheless, yes we have classes like that at the Academy. When we were your age we were more easily bored. It was so long ago, I forget sometimes how it felt. I have learned to sit in contemplation for days on end. As surely you have read in *Enchanted Lives,* we can take a year or more to create a thing of beauty. We relish in each stroke or action. Taking your pictures brings you joy, but surely developing them and cropping them and all that you do to get them just right takes up all of your focus, and it is as easy as breathing and suddenly you find that it is midnight because you got lost in the moment."

Understanding dawned. "Oh! Yes, I have had moments like that. I get so caught up that I have no awareness of the outside world at all."

"That is the goal everyday of our lives; we banish boredom by living fully," Clay declared.

Breeze added, "Yes, but we Elves in particular get caught up in living so fully that we exclude those around us. Because we are so fully engaged with ourselves, we do not always interact as much as we should. This is why you will find Elves more often than not staring off into space, rather than having serious dialogs or romping through the forests. Fairies are far more fun if you desire excitement. I guess Gwennara, and you, Mara, have gotten it right choosing a Fairy for a husband." Breeze smiled wickedly. "Though if you want discussion, you can always find an Elf willing to debate theories. Even so, eventually every Elf will want to romp, especially on the High Holidays."

"I concur, Breeze, well said," Clay complimented.

The setting sun caught Mara's eye and she felt inspired to enjoy it fully, knowing that Aerrvin would be somewhere watching it as well. She went to the bench in the rose garden and took it all in it with more rapt attention than she had ever tried before.

The clouds gradually changed shape, both from the moving of the sun, as well as from the breeze that pushed the wispy streaks northward. The purples ranged from her favorite periwinkle to a deep plum and a dusky gray as the sun sank in a blazing array of brilliant pinks and oranges. Fleetingly, she felt Aerrvin as he flitted by. His joy was full.

9
Visiting Dignitaries

Mara woke early in order to enjoy the sunrise with Breeze.

She was shocked to see Morvayne already there in the garden, facing the rising sun. The first rays had just broken through. Breeze directed Mara to focus on a particularly well shaped bud, which was partially bloomed. Mara found that she had stood for three hours before Morvayne interrupted her admiration of the handiwork of He who creates all things.

"Mara, that was very commendable concentration. Breeze you are an excellent teacher. I have stood in this garden countless times for hours on end, enjoying the fragrant beauty and craftsmanship of nature's hand. But today we have a field trip, so you need to change and then we will breakfast in the car."

"How am I to dress?" Mara asked.

"You will find your clothes laid out. Do be quick. I want to be out the door in twenty minutes," Morvayne advised.

Morvayne found Clay in the library. "We will be leaving soon, you may come or not as it suits you."

"Where are we going this fine Thursday morning?" Clay asked amiably.

"You are in a fine mood today. I trust you enjoyed your little rendezvous with Her Royal Highness?" Morvayne asked.

Clay inclined his head briefly. Morvayne wagged a warning finger. "Remember, it is not permanent. She is mine, and you are just softening her up for me. I must admit you are quick. I have given myself one hundred years, so I have plenty of time to let you play your little games. She may despise me now, but one day all the world will praise me for what I have accomplished."

Morvayne began to retreat into his imagination, but Clay interrupted his thoughts.

"What, pray tell, is it that you wish to achieve which would engender the praise of the world?"

"Have you not been listening to me?" Morvayne spat. "Mara is the key to my plan for salvation. With her love for me, I shall be ruler of all the Realms. I will not sit back and allow the Human encroachment to continue. Have you not been awake! They are polluting the waterways and destroying the forests. We hide away in our caves and Holds while the Earth dies! What will become of us then? Have you even thought that far ahead? No, I doubt it. Only I have been involved in such forward thinking, while all the rest of the Fair Ones flit about partying and playing as though there were no change at all in all the world! Meanwhile, most of the Elves spend their lives, like Breeze, living entirely in the Land of Dreams. What will become of us if we all enter the Land of Dreams and the world dies? Will the Dream die because there is no one to Dream?"

Morvayne calmed his tone after seeing Clay raise his brows at the last supposition. "See? New thoughts brought about by my studies. Take that one to your next Hold meeting; I would love to get the Elves alert and thinking again."

Clay replied, "I see. I do recall you mentioning a similar plan before." He stood and stretched asking, "So where are we going today?"

"We are going on a whirlwind tour of my Holdings. I wish

to introduce Mara as the future Queen that she is, thus allowing them to see that I truly am in a position of power. Lately, they have begun to doubt my plans will work. I wish for them to be renewed in their support of me and my desires." Morvayne's eyes glazed over as he imagined the glory he would receive.

Clay revised his clothing, dressed in white leather leggings and a pale green tunic, he would blend easily in most springtime Holds. "Morvayne, do you mind if I bring my bow?"

"What?" Morvayne looked up and glanced at the bow in Clay's hand. It was such a natural part of his ensemble that Morvayne waved him off. "Oh that, of course. I need to look like I have Attendants. I have my Oranges, four of which will be accompanying us."

"Doesn't Mara need to look like *she* has Attendants?" Clay asked.

"Yes, that's what I meant. Mara and myself it is the same. Oh, but yes, you should be assigned as her Personal Attendant, as well as Breeze. No that will not work—she is too well known as the Queen's niece. I tried to have some of my pretty Fairies befriend Mara, but that went about as well as my teaching techniques did."

Morvayne thought outloud, "I really should have maintained better contact with our frieends." He had been so caught up in tracking the royal family, that he neglected his contact them.

Craftily, Clay offered, "I could contact Jasmine or Hannah. I have kept up on their whereabouts. They have easy manners which should not alarm Mara. I know where Daisy is too, but well, you know how she is." Clay grinned.

Morvayne smiled at the shared memories. "Yes, no we do not want Daisy, but if Jasmine is willing that would be lovely. I completely forgot about her as a Hold Mate, because as a matter of fact I *have* kept a friendship with her. She invites me to her events." He stood straighter accepting unspoken praise. "I wish to leave in five minutes. If she is willing, bring her here." Morvayne left to check on Mara's progress.

Having received permission from Morvayne allowed Clay to bring Jasmine in without harm. She was dressed in nearly sheer pink leggings, with a fluttery silver and white top. Her dark wispy hair had been pulled up in to a waterfall ponytail, ringed with flowers. The loose stands wafted gently in the draft from the ceiling fan.

***

Entering her room, Mara found a delicate gown made from spider web silk. She had not yet worn the soft silk, but had felt the things Aerrvin wore, and recognized it for what it was. The problem was, it was lacy and sheer and Morvayne had not provided an under dress or slip. She put it on and found it delightfully soft and beautiful, yet there was no way she was going out of her room dressed so indecently. She expanded her body armor to her wrists and ankles and decided that would do.

The sparkling swirls from the Dragon skin made the lace even lovelier. She admired herself in the mirror. "I wish Aerrvin could see me like this." With a start, she turned to find Morvayne entering as he knocked.

"Beautiful, Mara, the Dragon skin makes a charming touch. My friends will be envious." He smiled smugly. "But you need to do something with your hair, and we do not have time for Tessa to do it. Create something; I will tell you if it is acceptable."

Mara tried to keep her perturbed expression to herself, as she turned to stand before the mirror to consider a look worthy of the gown. She looked as though she should be wearing a crown, yet she knew that would be wrong, as she had not yet been crowned. Then again, she was a princess in a way, wasn't she?

"Morvayne? Is it appropriate to wear a crown, you know like a tiara? Aunt Lily had several, but I don't know which one is for what."

Morvayne smiled greedily. In an oily voice he replied, "Why, Mara, that is a wonderful suggestion. Please, any crown she owned would be fine."

Mara could not help but feel uneasy at having brought it up, yet since she had, she was trapped into having to retrieve one. Surely, Morvayne would not try to take it away from her. Mara knew he was getting restless, so she thought of the simple silver tiara with no jewels on it at all. It was delicate and oh, so finely wrought, actually twisting in on its own self as it spiraled up to a center point. Mara imagined her hair braided through it, firmly securing it to her head. It was more enchanting than she would have thought.

"That is perfect, Mara, and yes, please only release a portion of your light when I direct you. We do not need lower beings seeing you in all your Glory. Reserve that for special occasions." He held his arm out for her to take. "Come along then. I believe Clay is procuring another Attendant for you. You must present yourself properly before your future subjects."

Breeze came out of her room dressed very fairy-like. Mara had not been around Elves much, so she did not know what their ordinary attire was like. *They probably all prefer a medieval look or the barely there look*, Mara decided. *With the exception of Brownies who dress to match their surroundings, generally in the brown section of the color wheel, but still decidedly 'Robin Hood-esque.'*

She complimented Breeze on her blue and purple gauze. "Breeze, you look as though you were a cloud; ready to drift beyond the horizon!"

Breeze smiled in delight. "My intentions exactly. You

appear to be the sun and the moon all wrapped up in one. Perhaps a little less light, until we meet Morvayne's friends?"

Mara had forgotten. "Yes, of course, thank you for reminding me."

Mara stopped short at the bottom of the stairs, she had not expected to see a familiar face. Morvayne thought she had stopped in fear, so he offered a soothing pat.

"Mara this is an old friend of mine. Jasmine, so good to see you again." He left Mara to give Jasmine a kiss in greeting. "I thank you for being willing to help out on such short notice. I trust Clay has filled you in?" He looked to Clay and then back to Jasmine.

Receiving confirming nods, he continued, "Jasmine, it is my pleasure to introduce you to Mara Lilyana – ap Jamis, our future Queen." Morvayne was loathe to mention that last name, but it was her name so it must be given. "My Lady, this is Jasmine ap Weaver. I have requested her service for this trip. She will act as your personal lady in waiting, shall we say? Clay will be presented as our Personal Protector, and Breeze is, of course, family."

Mara offered a genuine smile to Breeze, she was so happy to have a female relative. She turned back to Jasmine and nodded in what she hoped was reserved grace. "Jasmine, thank you for attending me. I look forward to getting to know you."

"The pleasure is mine, My Lady." Jasmine offered a proper curtsy, executed with a graceful flourish.

Mara's ability to keep her thoughts in her head had improved. She thought, *Perhaps I should have stayed with ballet a little longer. No matter, aikido and fencing taught me balance and grace as well. I am getting hungry, though. Hopefully the food is not too hard to eat in the car.*

Morvayne ushered them out to a limo where they were shown to the furthest back seats which were arranged coach-like so the pair and threesome could face each other. Mara did not like feeling like she was Morvayne's prom date. But at least she got to look at Clay, Jasmine and Breeze. The driver looked familiar, but Mara could not place him. She noticed too, that four Orange Fairies were placed in the seats in front of them, along with weapons similar to Clay's. A divider separated them, so she could not hear what they had to say; they appeared tough, but jolly. Maybe boisterous would be a better description.

Once in the car, it immediately Traveled to a hot, dry highway headed south. Morvayne then produced breakfast. Wine, of course, as well as milk. The heart of the meal consisted of croissants, strawberry cream cheese spread, and additional strawberries with whipped cream.

Mara noted when the car turned off of the highway, eventually leading to a desolate country road in the near desert surroundings. They came to a stop at a gate where a sign read:

Eagle Ridge Sanctuary: Wildlife Refuge.

Other signs declared the land to be private property, and keep out signs were on either side of the gate. The driver had a pass, which the guard took inside his little building and then returned after a scant minute. Driving past the gatehouse, Mara discerned that the guard was wearing a Mask of Deception, or glamour, because his disguise flickered worse than Morthe's had. Yet, what she viewed in that brief flash was not an Ogre.

Trolls, she concluded, with a shiver.

They drove on for another three miles, down into a hidden ravine. At the bottom lay a moderate ranch structure, butted up against the canyon wall, as well as several barns and outbuildings. Mara ventured a question. "Is this Arizona or California, or what?"

Morvayne smiled indulgently, "You have read Ironwood's books I see. Yes, there are sanctuaries in many of the southern states. This one happens to be in Southern California, just outside of Ridgecrest. Trolls, like Ogres, require plenty of red meat. It was my idea to set up this cattle ranch as a sanctuary for them. They have taken well to beef and save most of the sheep, which they also raise, for the High Holidays. Yet, if the chance arises, they still have no problem with plucking a tasty Fair One for a snack. Especially Fairies as they taste particularly sweet to them. Have no fear, they see me as a mentor and listen to what I have to say."

Morvayne then snapped a bracelet around Mara's wrist, entrapping her, similar to the capsule he had been using. Mara panicked and started breathing unevenly. "Now, Mara, this is simply a precaution, calm down. This allows me to go wherever you go. Should you think to Travel, or should someone try to take you somewhere, by any means, I will be brought along as well. See? We are here. You must gain control of yourself."

Mara tried, but she feared he would keep it on her, ruining her plan for escape. She looked wildly to Clay and Jasmine.

Breeze took command first. "Morvayne you have panicked her. Let her know this is temporary. You will take it off once we return to the palazzo. Correct?"

Morvayne replied, "Yes, that is true, Mara. In fact, I can do better; I will remove it when you are in the car. None can Travel from within this vehicle, so I can assure you that you are indeed safe within these confines. Now, I must go and greet Olkin before he becomes incensed at the delay. Breeze, come with me. Clay, Jasmine, please calm her down. This is an important meeting, The Troll King is expecting an introduction to royalty and I would prefer, no slight meant, Breeze, he were to meet our future Queen." Morvayne departed, leaving Mara alone with her two Attendants. The four Orange Fairies trailed behind Morvayne, with Breeze on his arm.

"I'm sorry." Mara apologized. "I have been trying to keep a calm exterior, but I just hate being bottled up this way." She lifted her wrist. "Is all jewelry filled with magical properties?"

Jasmine scooted across the way to sit next to Mara. "I think you are handling yourself well, considering the situation. Were you to suddenly accept everything, he would be suspicious of you. Clay and I will do all in our power to keep you safe.

"Trolls are not as bad as they are made out to be. Yes, they are hideous and smell somewhat, but they do have some redeeming qualities from time to time." Jasmine smiled and gave Mara a gentle squeeze around the shoulders. "I like your armor; the pattern is so different from Hannah's." Jasmine pushed Mara's sleeve up to see it better. "May I?" Jasmine asked holding her hand out to touch it.

Mara smiled, she was not used to people admiring her skin. "I suppose. I asked the same of Hannah when I saw hers."

Jasmine caressed her arm a few times. "It feels pretty much the same as Hannah's. Clay have you felt it?" Jasmine asked, pulling him forward by the hand.

Clay smiled, "Impulsive as ever Jasmine. Yes, I have felt her armor, it is quite impressive." He briefly stroked her wrist with his thumb and then took her hand. "Come along, let us be done with this."

Exiting the car, Jasmine linked arms with Mara while Clay followed from behind. At the door, a cowboy in sunglasses waited to let them in. Only he wasn't a cowboy. Mara was not certain she wanted to meet Trolls. The pictures in Ironwood's books were very detailed, yet they were black and white sketches. She was not certain she would like seeing green-skinned beings. *Maybe I can get used to the wavering of their poorly wrought Masks.*

Once inside, it no longer resembled a ranch house. The main entryway was large, but the ceiling was low, as were the lights. Bright lights bother Trolls; they prefer to come out at dusk and Trolls prefer enclosed spaces. It was early evening, so they would be venturing out soon. A female Troll guided them deeper into the home, which eventually gave way to cavern walls as they passed through a large set of double doors. The female did not look too terrifying; she was a few inches taller than Clay who stood six foot four inches. Of course, Mara only stood five foot six, so the She Troll was essentially a foot taller. She had deep auburn hair pulled back into an intricate braid tied off with a leather thong. She was as wide as Morthe, and her flesh was bubbled here and there. One or two even oozed an offensive odor, causing Mara to wrinkle her nose which she stopped at a signal from Jasmine. If not for the sores, green skin and extra width, she was a pleasant looking woman. *Probably considered pretty,* Mara thought.

The tunnel widened, Mara could see Morvayne and Breeze, standing before a Troll on a throne. The She Troll stopped them at the entrance and waited to be called in.

The Troll nodded and Morvayne spoke in a moderate voice which carried well in the cavern. "Master Olkin, it is my sincerest pleasure to introduce Mara Lilyana ap Jamis, our future Queen of all the Realms."

Jasmine motioned for Mara to go on alone, while she and Clay took up a stance on either side of the door, having pushed the Orange Fairies down the wall with their stares.

Mara took a deep cleansing breath, chanting in her mind: *I am a leaf, I am a leaf.* She imagined a newly unfolded leaf, gently swaying in the wind. The gentle fluttering was so delightful, she realized with a start that she had arrived at the foot of the throne, and the hideous Troll had stood to greet her.

She had a lovely smile upon her face, so she simply nodded

and said, "Olkin, I have read of your exploits; you have a masterful mind and keen intelligence. It is an honor to greet you."

Olkin was as horrible as she had feared. He had five oozing sores that she could see, and his pale green skin was ashy, giving it the look of a lizard changing from green to brown.

He smiled, wetly sucking in his slobber before speaking, "My Lady, the honor is mine. Morvayne has kept me apprised of your progress. You appear to be just as powerful as his tales. Tell me, do you really intend to bring greater justice into the world, when you gain the Crystal Throne?"

"Why yes, I do. I could never seek to do otherwise," Mara answered truthfully.

Mara knew that Olkin thought of himself as truly superior to anyone else. Yet, she also knew he had a one-track mind, which was to gain followers, and to provide for all those he gained. Most likely he wanted to roam free and eat who, or what, whenever he chose. That had never been allowed by any previous Queen; nevertheless, it was his fondest desire. A Troll's idea of justice would be equally as different as Mara's would be compared to Morvayne's. Mara also knew that a Troll might try to trap one into promising something they did not wish to give. Hence, Mara was grateful that the first question had been easy to answer without deception.

Drool slipped down onto Olkin's cotton tunic as he prepared to ask his second question. Sucking the rest in, he asked, "Will you include Humans in your rule, meaning, do you intend to judge Humanity for what has transpired these past few centuries?"

"I am sorry, Olkin. I have not yet received any training regarding my roles and responsibilities as Queen. If it is part of my responsibility, then surely I will do it."

Mara saw Morvayne grin proudly, as though he had told

her what to say. Whether that was good or bad, she did not know. She glanced about, but was unable to turn completely around as it would have been rude, but it was only then that she realized the size of the room and that there were shelves of stone benches carved in two tiers of the cave's wall. All were filled to capacity; even cute toddlers were sitting raptly staring at Mara and the other Elves. Mara did not know it then, but to the Trolls, the Elves and Fairies all smelled delicious, and Mara in particular was highly enticing even without her Light and Dust.

"Very fair, My Lady. Very fair indeed. My final question then is this: Do you love Morvayne as he suggests?"

Morvayne started at the question. "That is not the question you agreed to ask, Olkin!" He whispered harshly.

"It is the question I desire to know the answer to. Be quiet, Morvayne."

Morvayne appeared to visibly steam, but he soon quelled all outward emotion and bowed lightly to Olkin. "They are your Questions, Master Olkin. Mara, proceed to tell him how you feel."

Mara was herself startled, both by the question and Morvayne's response. There was something in the exchange she would need to think about later, but right now she needed a good answer. If she said no the Troll would denounce Morvayne and refuse to help in whatever future plans he had. If she implied she liked him, Morvayne might relax further control; allowing her to learn more about his other captives. But could she lie?

I hate him. No, I need to repel those thoughts. They created emotions which perhaps the Trolls could smell or sense. She thought of Clay and his Hold Mates all tending her as a baby. She felt love as she thought of it. She loved them and they her. Clay still loved Morvayne and hoped to save him. Mara felt compassion as she thought of Clay's love for his brother. If her sisters had chosen to go astray, wouldn't she still love them? As Queen, wasn't she responsible for caring for all?

Olkin restated the question freeing Mara to answer as she now truly felt. "My Lady, do you love Morvayne?"

Mara became infused with a soft glow as she released a portion of her Light and replied, "Yes, I love Morvayne."

The room gasped, Mara could not tell who gasped louder.

Putting away her light she saw many still bowed from fear, or awe she could not tell. But she knew that they were becoming agitated as well.

Morvayne spoke to Master Olkin. "I fear we must depart now, but I will see to your requests as we discussed as time goes by. By your leave, Master?"

Olkin needed to eat soon, so he allowed the hasty retreat. "As you have said, Morvayne. My Lady, I pledge my honor to yours. I will swear my service to yours when you ascend the Crystal Throne in Justice and Glory. Be gone. I hunger."

He motioned and great sides of beef were brought forth for all assembled. The beef was raw. Mara and the rest left swiftly, but not before hearing juicy smacking noises. Clay and Jasmine each had hold of an elbow as they traversed the tunnel back to the ranch house.

Once in the car, Clay reprimanded Morvayne. "That was too close for comfort. Couldn't you have arranged to meet sooner?"

Morvayne acknowledged the timing was off. "Yes, precisely why I was in a hurry to leave. I should not have indulged Mara by allowing her to study the roses at dawn. Next time I will be more diligent in my planning."

Clay grunted. Breeze soothed him by rubbing his arm.

Breeze asked, "And how many more Holds do you have planned for today?"

Morvayne recovered all of his slickness. Taking Mara by the hand, he said, "Mara, I gave you the hardest task first, forgive me for not warning you. I was surprised myself at the final question, but I am well pleased with your answer." He looked into her face trying to read her expression. "I see you still fear me, but I felt your emotion; it was real. One day, Mara, we will remember and cherish this day with joy and celebration." He sat back to Dream about that glorious day, forgetting to answer Breeze, as well as his promise to remove the bracelet.

It hardly mattered though, because it was only thirty minutes between Holds. They visited three more. One was in Washington, filled with Orange and Yellow Fairies. Another was in Chile, up in the cold of the mountains. A small group of Elves lived there in the cave of a glorious golden-scaled Dragon. He slept, and would not wake, so Mara did not actually get to meet him. They stopped briefly in a meadow for lunch and then continued on to meet in some caverns of Egypt.

The group was once again small, not more than twelve, as far as she could see. But she was fascinated by meeting her first Elven baby. This group had three children; an infant girl not quite two, and the other two were the second set of twins she had met among the Fair Ones, although the other set were Fairies, not Elves. The twins were six years old and quite rambunctious. As with all the other groups visited, they felt dissatisfied with life and wanted to see change, preferably less Humans and more openness.

Mara held the baby, delighting in her silken, sweet smelling skin and hair. She remembered her sisters had felt much the same when they were young. This baby had black hair and large dark eyes that sparkled. She had a sparkly presence that tickled Mara's senses. "What is her name?" Mara asked the mother.

"Feather of Light, but we just call her Feather." The mother shared the same features as her daughter and Mara could not tell who the father might be. "One day, I hope she can be in the world and not have to hide who she is. I Dreamed for centuries, waking to find the world as it now is. I am ashamed that I neglected to do my part sooner. I tried to live among the Humans, but her father rejected us when he learned the truth. Now I have brought her into this world, and must never cease my efforts to return it to the joyful land it was before I slept."

She brushed her hand over the baby's curls, causing the little girl to squirm out of Mara's lap, reaching up to her mother.

Mara had no words of comfort. "All I can say is that I intend to pursue Honor, Justice and Virtue all the days of my life. She is delightful, and I am sure she will be a joy to you despite the world we live in."

"Justice is all I ask, My Lady."

It was well after noon in Italy now. Mara sat back in the car feeling exhausted. Morvayne looked over at her, slumped very unladylike in her exquisite gown. "Sorry, it has been a long day, I know. I do have one more stop I would like to make, but if you prefer we can save it for tomorrow."

"I don't care," she sighed in her whispery voice. "I guess it would be better to get it over with, but I think I will need some energy drink or something. A granola bar maybe?"

Clay grinned at her and said, "I am sure Morvayne can find something to satisfy you. Right, Morvayne?"

Morvayne retrieved a chocolate energy drink and a power bar. "This should hold you until dinner, in fact, where we are going they may invite us to stay the night. The Mermaid Colonies are always quite receptive to visitors, despite their exclusive nature."

"Mermaids?" Mara sat up, accepting the proffered treats.

Morvayne smiled as though at a dear granddaughter. "Yes, My Sweet Buttercup, I thought that would pique your interest.

"Surely, your father filled your pretty little head full of tales about Mermaids. This group is one we found together, perhaps one of them will tell you about her days spent with him. Any connection to your father must be better than none, yes? Think of it as a gift from me. We will need to change to more appropriate swim-wear. Your bracelet will not prevent you from exchanging your gown for a swimming suit," he finished, ignoring her saddened countenance. Looking up at Clay, Jasmine and Breeze, he exclaimed, "What?"

Clay said, "That was unnecessarily harsh. If I am to continue helping you in your Quest you will maintain a more dignified manner."

Chastened in front of three beautiful women, Morvayne sought a drink before replying, "Mara, I did not mean to bring up sad memories for you. You will enjoy the Mermaids, and I will maintain my distance. Stay close to your Attendants." He switched his Elven finery to blue-green swim trunks. "I would teach you how to design a breathing apparatus, but since you have your armor, as you like to call it, you can simply use your gills again." He looked to see if she would blush, and was gratified as a small cascade went falling to her lap.

Jasmine and Breeze fashioned cute swimming suits and Clay wore what appeared to be diving pants leaving his torso bare, though they could have been any ordinary leggings which the Fair Ones preferred. Mara designed her shed into the same diving suit she had made when she went surfing in Aerrvin's pool. *How many days ago was that?* She thought. She refrained from the board shorts, as they would cause drag. As long as Morvayne kept his word, and the others stayed near, she could stand to go into the water in his presence; she desperately wanted to meet Mermaids!

Traveling to locations underwater requires that those wishing to Travel together be underwater already. Diving off a short cliff was fun. Clay went first, followed by Mara. She had been cliff diving before and had no need of coaxing. Once in the water, Morvayne instructed everyone to follow him through the Window. The portal revealed a sparkling blue paradise.

Swimming into the water, Mara could feel a definite change in temperature. It was pleasantly warm and the white sand sparkled brightly. Before heading toward the obvious entrance, they swam about, enjoying the sea life living on and near the coral. Mara recalled a vacation a few years back that she had taken with her mom; they had gone down near Cancun. This looked similar, but she doubted that was the location. It was certainly warmer than off the coast of Washington, even warmer than California. She assumed Clay would recognize the location. He had Traveled the world five times over she was sure. After about an hour of being at one with the sea, Morvayne led them to the entrance of the Mermaid Colony.

A Merman barred the way, asking for the purpose and identification. Morvayne had a necklace given to him from the leader of this particular Colony, which gave him automatic entry.

They were led to a sea cave, lit by glowing balls of Light. Mara wondered how they were made, but chose to wait until later to ask.

The cave opened up as they were led down a spiraling ramp, as though they were entering a giant shell which was more spacious inside than it appeared. The colors were creamy white and pink, with green seaweed and kelp for foliage. Brightly colored tropical fish swam about. The Mermaids and men were every bit as beautiful as Elves. They came to a stop before a couple, husband and wife Mara presumed, sitting upon a Disney-like coral throne in the purest white; the spires jutted up at least twenty feet behind them.

They were announced by a young Mermaid, who had been informed of their status and names. It was odd hearing near clear voices under the water. Mara had learned earlier that Mermaids had magical abilities, not unlike other Fair Ones. They could not Travel, but they knew a few spells. If someone deigned to teach them, they would have been able to do more, but Fair Ones guard their knowledge closely from one another.

The Water Lord asked, speaking directly to Mara, if she and her retinue would stay for dinner. Mara had not tried to speak yet with her Dragon armor, she had gills and could take the water right in, so it was with great surprise and delight that she found her voice as melodic as a Dragon's, without the hissing sound.

"I thank you for your hospitality and would be honored to stay for dinner. Thank you."

They were given a tour of the watery world in which the Merpeople lived. Morvayne declined, having business to attend to with the Water Lord. The remaining four were led about by two young Mermaids; at least they appeared young. Mara eventually asked how old they were and they were not offended at all to tell her they were four hundred and ten and four hundred and twenty-three years old.

"Do you have a school here to teach Drylanders?" Mara asked, thinking of Aerrvin's experience under the sea.

"The younger of the two laughed and said, "No, not here, but we do have one that only takes a half day to get to from here…" She stopped at a gesture from the older Mermaid.

Evidently they had instructions to keep the location secret. Not in itself a clue, but a possible clue; these folks were supporters of Morvayne after all.

"Well, everything seems well-schooled and organized here." Mara said, not realizing she had told a pun, until everyone was grinning, including Clay. "Oh, do Mermaids travel in schools?" She blushed which was pretty even in the water. The Dragon skin gave it an oily quality as it held together before separating and going off with the current.

Dinner was an interesting affair among the Merpeople. They did have a dry kitchen where they could grill fish; they even had wood for an added, smoky flavor. Yet, they also had plenty of Asian style dishes with kelp or seaweed featured prominently. They appeared to have a penchant for sweets as well, having developed their ability to create desserts with a unique flair.

Jasmine asked about the Asian influence. "I assume the sushi rolls were introduced to Asia through Merfolk?"

Dain smiled, "Ah, yes we have been eating it forever in this style. Merpeople do wander up onto dry land from time to time. Not often, and we can only stay dry for a week. None of my relatives have been up into Asia. But I believe Lissa's family has." He paused looking expectantly at his wife.

"Yes," she answered stiffly. "My cousin and Great Aunt chose to live among the Humans in Japan, as it is now called. They have long since died."

"Then let us speak of happier times to come," Morvayne offered.

"Let's do!" Dain smiled again, looking to Mara he said, "I have yet to inquire about your upcoming reign over all the Realms. Gwennara was fair, yet she chose to remain blind to the woes which have befallen us with the encroachment of Mankind. I would support you more fully as my Queen, if I knew you would be in favor of influencing Humans to protect the waterways. What have you to say about your plans and goals?"

Mara had removed the dragon skin from her face for dinner as they ate at a table with an air pocket above their waists. Brushing a loose tendril of hair aside, she said, "I am sure you know I have only been awakened three weeks. My father was an

Ocean Scientist; therefore, I am very concerned about the health of our oceans, rivers and streams. Of course, I will use whatever influence I deem prudent. I will also trust my counselors and advisors to guide me, in my first years especially. I would hope to have your support, and look forward to gaining your trust."

"Well said. We shall see what the currents bring, won't we?" Dain acknowledged.

After dinner, Dain directed his Mermaids to perform a water dance for their entertainment. Mara found it enchanting and clapped in delight, though it was ineffective for producing sound. They left without having received a promise of support.

10
Deceptions

Morvayne produced a Window to swim through, and they were once again on the surface of the ocean. "I should like to see if you have enough energy to fly up to the cliff tops, Mara," Morvayne said, as he rose out of the ocean to stand above the water.

The other Elves also rose up, effectively drying themselves before shrinking down to fly. Mara willed herself up and found her desire granted. She reduced her size and flew, not needing to dry anything as she was essentially in her bare skin, leathery and rainbow patterned as it was.

Mara was tired, yet the Dragon skin's properties renewed her somewhat. She returned to her former attire and size and managed to sit in Clay's seat, surrounding herself with her two female companions.

"I do hope this was the last stop because I am drained and need to rest," she sighed as she lay her head on Jasmine's shoulder.

Jasmine felt sleek, strong and cuddly all at once, but the hop to the palazzo was immediate, so Mara was able to go straight to bed. Jasmine settled down on the couch in the front room.

Mara called before going to sleep, "Jasmine? Morvayne has

not removed the bracelet. I think it is draining me.”

“Oh, sorry, let me go and get him.”

Morvayne sat with Clay in the library. “Excuse me. Morvayne, Mara wants to see you.”

Morvayne’s eyes lit up. “She wants tucked in, does she? Clay, excuse me, I will be right back.” Morvayne swept up the stairs gracefully. Jasmine trailed at the same pace.

“Mara, you called for me?” Morvayne entered her bedchamber confidently, noting the lamp turned low and Mara dressed in one of the silky gowns he had designed for her. He thought her full armor ruined the look somewhat.

Mara held up her wrist. “It weakens me. Please, remove it.” Mara tried not to sound weak, but she was truly tired and her soft whispery voice encouraged one to think of her as weak. She saw Morvayne’s reaction and knew he liked making her plead; it sickened her, but she had no choice.

“So sorry, Buttercup, I became preoccupied. Will you forgive me?” He allowed his fingers to linger as he undid the clasp. Mara simply nodded, so he continued, “Thank you, I have enjoyed this day. Sleep well.”

Mara did not want to trouble Aerrvin in her weakness, so instead of running to her Dream she quietly sobbed to herself. *How could I love such a wicked, evil slime ball?* she thought. This only caused more tears. She was not as quiet as she had hoped, soon Jasmine entered and held her as Mara sobbed herself to sleep.

***

It was 2:00 p.m. in Seattle. Jaera had just finished English and was heading to math class. She had Mara’s cell phone on her so she answered it as Mara, “Hello.”

“Hi, Mara, it’s Mom. I hope you weren’t in class or

anything?"

"No, I am on my way to math class, then I will be done for the day. What's up?" Jaera asked.

"I am calling to let you know we will be coming up the day before your graduation because the girls will be out of school already. But you have not called about coming over for Ricky's graduation. It's this Saturday, remember, at 10:00 a.m.? So anyway, will you be coming out tonight or Friday afternoon?

"Oh, Mom, sorry! I forgot all about that! Tomorrow I have just one class in the morning and then I can come out. Is it okay if I bring Aerrvin?" Jaera asked, hoping she would be able to catch him.

"So you patched everything up with him I take it?" Amanda questioned.

"Yes, he gets a little emotional sometimes, but he is very forgiving. I love him and he loves me. We're great." Jaera did not know the situation, so she just made something up.

"That's wonderful! I do like him, but remember, if it ever feels like it's not right, you can always back out. Better to do it now than later," Amanda admonished.

"Yes, Mom. My class is about to start so I gotta go. I'll see you soon. Bye."

"Goodbye, dear," Amanda replied.

After class, Jaera went straight home by Traveling from the girls' bathroom. She went to lay down on Mara's bed so that she could visit Mara and Aerrvin. Aerrvin was right where she expected, with the kittens.

"Hey, Aerrvin, I miss you."

"Jaera!" Aerrvin jumped up and hugged her. "I miss you too. I could probably come home as there is not much to do here.

Mara has been gone all day today. Not just from the house, but all over the world it feels like."

"I am sure 'tis hard. I just spoke on the phone with Mara's mother reminding Mara to attend Ricky's graduation; 'tis this Saturday. She said you may come with. Please do, I don't want to go alone." Jaera clung to him as she begged.

Aerrvin smiled at Jaera's antics. "Very well, if I have to."

Jaera hopped up and down. "Goody! Now what is this about some argument between you two? Amanda told Mara that she should consider dumping you if you don't seem to be the right guy."

Jaera stood there, head cocked with her hands on her hips, tapping her tiny foot on the ground.

Aerrvin pulled her down to sit between Fluffball and Growly. "It's a lengthy story . . ." He proceeded to explain things from his point of view and included Mara's lessons learned from Clay. "So, yes, things are all better between us. But it still rankles deep down."

"Aerrvin, I am so sorry all of this happened. It is not your fault. Mara would have been awakened by Ironwood eventually, maybe only a week later. Morvayne has had his plan in place for years. We just happened to step into it. Most likely it is providential. Part of the pattern we were meant to play out. You know?" Jaera was cuddling Fluffball and scratching behind her ears.

"Yes, I suppose you are right. Who would have thought little Jaera would be giving me advice on romance?" He ruffled her hair engendering a wrestling match. Even the kittens joined in; since it was Aerrvin's Dream he made them a little more rowdy than they actually were at that age.

Finally trapping Jaera under Mama Cat, he said, "Let's go

find Mara; we will need directions to her house."

***

Mara was sleeping soundly when Aerrvin and Jaera arrived. She was dreaming of the time she went scuba diving with her father for the first time. They had driven down to California to visit her mother's parents. Mara was eight years old and already a proficient swimmer. Suddenly, instead of seeing the baby shark, which had excited her, she saw Aerrvin knocking as if on a glass wall. She pulled him and Jaera in and they swam to the surface.

"I guess we should go to a drier location." She imagined a warm beach with deck chairs. Sitting down she realized she was still eight years old, so she changed to her normal appearance wearing her favorite blue swimsuit. "I had a busy day. The last visit was to a Mermaid colony! I guess that was why I was dreaming about scuba diving. Jaera it is so good to see you! How am I doing in school?"

Jaera laughed and kissed Mara before sitting down cross-legged in the middle of her chair. "You are doing great! I can review everything for you; that way it will be as if you had learned it all first hand."

Mara exclaimed, "You can? That would be wonderful!" I mean, I hate math, but I really wanted to complete school. Can you do it now?"

"Sure," Jaera said. "Just sit back. Have you ever actually been all the way to the Void? Well, no I guess not. They don't teach that until you take the Oath."

Mara looking confused, so Jaera continued, "I guess you have not had any lessons on Dreams yet. Besides what little you have done on your outings with Aerrvin here." She grinned insinuatingly, causing Mara to blush. "Okay, well this will be a brief intro, because I have a lot of information to give and there is not much time before your dawn arrives."

140

Mara asked, "You mean my Dream is not really in the Land of Dreams?"

"No," Jaera replied. "It is stage one; where all can go, even some Humans learn to control events and create their own wacky wards to keep others out.

"Stage two is where you get your real REM sleep that your scientists talk about. Skilled Dream Walkers can enter there as easily as stage one, which is why we were able to get your attention. Stage three is in the Void, where we go to learn all the basics. Okay, so this is difficult to explain: The Land of Dreams is an alternate reality, as is stage three. To get to stage three you must have a guide take you there the first time, after that you can go there yourself."

Mara interrupted again in a panic. "But Morvayne said I could die if I Traveled out of the palazzo!"

Aerrvin took her hand. "Not by this method. Your body will remain as it does when you sleep. Your essence will Travel, nothing more. Just like when we helped your friend in the nursing home. Or some of our nightly adventures." He paused to wink before continuing, "Your body will remain in stasis; no harm can come to it while you are out of it. Elves and other Fair Ones have stayed in the Void for decades living alternate lives. This is why they can gain so much wisdom, stay so young looking, and still claim the ages they do. Fairies do not tend to stay for more than ten years at a time; we need more mortal living than Elves seem to require. Anyway, proceed, Jaera." He smiled in apology for interrupting the lesson.

"Okay, take my hand and watch how I make the Window." Jaera held her two middle fingers to her thumb and raised her pinkie high while flicking her wrist twice. She was also thinking of the desired location, which she instructed Mara about once they arrived.

The location was not anything Mara would have expected. They stood in the center of two intersecting hallways, each pointed to a cardinal direction as shown by the large N, S, E, W, letters inlaid in silver on the white marble floor. All was white on white, much like Aerrvin's room. *Who would have thought there were so many shades of white?* Mara marveled. Jaera walked down the eastern hallway. They passed several doors on either side.

Finally, she stopped and opened a door. "This one is empty," she sang.

Mara had seen no differences in the doors. "How could you tell?"

"The colors. You will learn to differentiate the shades over time. This one was duller white, meaning no one was using it."

"So it is like the Brightness of our Light? Mara asked.

Aerrvin hugged Mara to him, relishing her bare arms against his bare chest. Unfortunately, for him, it made her conscious of her attire. While it was appropriate for the beach it made her uncomfortable in this sterile location. She donned jeans and a tank top. Aerrvin turned his trunks to leggings, but otherwise remained bare. Forgetting to answer the question, Jaera conceded to Mara's sensibilities and returned to her normal leggings and filmy flowing top in shades of green.

"Now, are we ready to proceed?" she asked.

Without waiting for a response, she created a soft pile of feathers for them and plopped down gracefully, inviting her companions to join her.

"Now then, I am going to review the past week for you, so get comfortable. Once we are in the Dream, you will see everything from my point of view, as though we were the same person. Aerrvin will see it as well. If we had the room filled all would see it as I will project it. This is only one aspect of the

Void; these rooms are used for instruction, among other things. You will be taught more after you take the Oath. Ready?"

"Wait!" Mara said, "How long will this take? You are showing me a weeks' worth of living. What will they think when they come to get me?"

Jaera said, "It will take an hour or so,. W can squeeze a lot of living out of someone and condense it into minutes. No one will notice."

Suddenly Mara was living the past week as if in real time.

Only it was strange, most of the time it felt like her own life, but when speaking to Jill, Jaera always took on her own identity. Other than that she took notes and wrote an essay for English, on which she was sure to get an A. Jaera showed a flair for words; Mara hoped it was not too much better than what she would have written. She marveled and felt Jaera's joy at creating Jill's apartments. Mara thought her photography display was perfect and wished Jaera would have hung around to get more responses from her classmates. Jill moved out the day before.

When it was over Mara was crying. "Thank you. I miss Jill." Jaera and Aerrvin each huddled up to her like kittens in a nest. Mara was facing Jaera. "You have done wonderful living my life for me."

Mara smiled as Aerrvin kissed the nape of her neck. She pushed her shoulder into him; he nudged back, wetly kissing her again and then blowing a shiver down her spine.

"Aerrvin!" Mara squealed as she rolled over to stop him. She pinned him, but his strength was greater, of course, so Jaera piled on as well.

"Get him!" Jaera yelled. "He's ticklish on his neck."

"Aerrvin is ticklish?"

Mara suddenly forgot her melancholy and tried all the techniques Jaera suggested for tickling Aerrvin; as it turned out, Mara learned he was pretty much ticklish everywhere. Had the room not been soundproof, any walking passersby would have heard piteous howling as Mara and Jaera plied their torture. Signaling an end, Mara lay her head down on Aerrvin's chest.

Getting his breath back, Aerrvin said, "We actually had another reason for coming to see you. Your mother wants you over for your brother's graduation. She said I can come along too."

" Oh, I had forgotten that! Good thing she called. So, teach me how to send my memories to you. You might need a few to be able to talk about everyday stuff with my family."

"My turn," Aerrvin said shaking a finger at Jaera. "Alright, it really is just like everything else you have learned. The hard part was getting here. So close your eyes and imagine the night sky you see when looking at the Dreams of others. But because of where we are in the Void, instead of all the lights being other people and their Dreams, these ones are your memories. Look them over and you will recognize them, touch the one you want to share and it will be so."

Mara had not thought of some of the memories she saw before her for some time, so she reviewed them even though they were not needed for the task: Saying goodbye to Grandpa and Grandma before moving to Sequim, which turned out to be the last time she saw Grandma Jamis. The drive and first few days in their new home. She saw Sylvie out of the corner of her eye while unpacking boxes. Definitely hard and trying times. She skipped over hating her Mother for dating Rick, and instead viewed the marriage and that first week when her stepbrother, Ricky, moved in. She watched the day each of her sisters came home and a few happy memories they had as a family before she moved out. And then for good measure she included a drive home she had taken one summer. Then she thought of herself back in the white-walled room.

Jaera hugged Mara, saying, "Thank you for sharing yourself with me. I understand you better."

It was time to leave, so Aerrvin hugged her tightly and whispered into her ear, "I love you Mara Lilyana ap Jamis." He smiled as he looked into her eyes. Kissing the top of her head he said, "We have to go now, more lessons later."

11
Emotional Entanglements

Jasmine noticed when Mara went to the Third Level of Dreams.

Mara's body went inert, sending out cold energy and a field sprung up around her. Jasmine assumed Mara was with Clay or Aerrvin as she knew Mara warded her Dreams; Morvayne would not have access to her. Nevertheless, Jasmine went on alert and ensured that the rooms were secure. Then she went back and sat beside Mara, waiting for her to wake.

Mara woke at dawn, just as the light broke through her balcony window.

Jasmine sat beside her on the full sized bed. "Morning, Mara. I trust you are refreshed?" Jasmine asked gently.

Mara smiled gratefully at Jasmine as she recalled falling asleep in her arms. "Yes, I feel better now, thank you. I am starving though."

Mara rummaged through her dresser hoping to find something, and remembered she could pull items from her own drawers at home. She chose her trashiest t-shirt, one Aerrvin had missed because it was not in the closet, and a pair of cutoffs. She was feeling defiant. She showered quickly and fairly flew down the stairs on her way to wherever the food was being served. She bumped into Morvayne as he came around the corner of the hallway. "Oops! Excuse me. Sorry I—I am hungry. Where are we eating today?"

Morvayne looked her over from head to toe, with no change of expression. Then raising one beautiful eyebrow he said, "In the sunshine, of course."

With a smile she went to the patio to await service. Clay sat with Breeze looking out on the sea. Seeing her, they both smiled, but made no comment on her clothes. The absence of a comment was almost as puzzling as being told she was a fool Human who had no sense of style. Mara decided to ignore them too and see what happened. *I am a leaf,* she thought, chanting her new mantra.

Tessa arrived with hot water for tea and a choice of mint, lemon or chamomile. Mara chose the Chamomile, but pouted, "Don't you have rose and lavender?"

Tessa bobbed and said, "Pardon, My Lady, but we do not. I can look in the shops today."

"Oh, no don't! I didn't mean to be a bother." Mara hastened to ease Tessa's discomfort at not having what she wanted.

"What is this? You asked for something and she did not give it?" Morvayne's look made Tessa cower in shame.

Mara rushed to stand next to Tessa, "No, it was just a request for rose and lavender tea, she has none and that is quite all right. I can drink what she has brought."

Morvayne started to say something when Breeze intervened. "I have some in my stash. Let me go to my room and retrieve it."

"That will do nicely, Breeze, thank you. Tessa, you may continue with the breakfast service." Morvayne waved her on dismissively. "My apologies, Mara, I did not know you were fond of such specialized tisanes. I do not care for it myself." He prepared his own cup of mint tea as they waited in the calm of morning for their breakfast.

Breeze returned before Tessa. "Here you are, Mara. I left a packet in the kitchen so you can have some whenever. This is a blend I made myself; it also has a touch of chamomile I hope you don't mind; it is very light."

"No, that is the way it was made the last time I had it; I'm sure it will be just as lovely. Thank you. I did not mean to cause a fuss."

Clay chuckled, "Get used to it, My Lady. It will only grow greater as the year progresses."

"In that case, I should like to have my lessons on the beach today. Morvayne, can you provide me with safety to the beach, so that Clay can give me my lessons as I swim and sun?"

Morvayne almost glowed at such a simple request. "Of course I can, Mara. Since you are progressing so well, I will not attach my bracelet, as it taxes you so. No, that would never do for you, My Buttercup. I can create a bubble over the beach and a portion of the sea. Clay take note of the size and stay within the bounds, and all should be well. I will be Traveling and Breeze will accompany me. Jasmine can do as she pleases, with Clay's permission of course."

Jasmine arrived just as Tessa did. Breakfast was pleasant and filling. Mara ate two omelets and a scone, dripping with honey butter. Licking her fingers, she then wiped them on her shirt rather than the napkin which lay untouched; seeing the mild side eyes, she used it to wipe her mouth and then walked out to the rose garden to wait for Clay. She really was sticky and should have washed up, but she wanted to see what she could get away with.

Mara chose a rose to study and watched it shift as the sun

continued its climb.

Slowly becoming aware of her surroundings she noticed that Clay had been sitting there for quite some time.

"How does that work?" Mara asked as she turned to recognize Clay's presence.

"What?"

"How did I realize you had been sitting beside me for thirty minutes, yet I had been completely unaware of you, until I released the hold on my focus?"

Clay shifted on the seat, where he had remained immobile the entire time since he sat down. "You really like to do things out of order don't you?" His eyes twinkled. "Jasmine tells me you went to the Third Level within the Void." He paused waiting for her to accede the fact.

"Yes, how did she know? Oh, she was in bed with me. They said no one would know." Mara nearly whined.

"When you leave for the Third Level your body goes into stasis; it gives off a cold energy. Jasmine was awakened immediately. Do you mind telling me who 'they' were?" Clay asked, looking at the sunshine-faced daisy on her shirt, beaming its quirky smile.

"Later," Mara said as Morvayne started towards them.

"Mara, let me walk you to the beach." Morvayne proffered his arm and reluctantly she took it.

"I could drive the cart, but you have not been getting much exercise besides yesterday's swim, of course. It is such a mild day you should have no difficulties with the heat. So where are you in your studies, My Lady?"

"I don't remember. We did not do any lessons last night. Clay, where did we leave off?" Mara turned to look at him as he walked behind them.

"We were halfway through Lessons of Conduct, though I must say you did remarkably well yesterday. You could refine some of your spell techniques, but essentially your basic training is done."

"Morvayne, isn't there more things Clay can teach me? I grasp the topics so well when he teaches, and I would hate to see him go." She had no need to fake her fear of his impending departure.

"Mara, were you not paying attention? Clay is now your Personal Protector and Jasmine is your Personal Attendant. These jobs are not taken lightly; they will stay near you forever, unless you release them. Clay, you may need to review the Rights and Responsibilities again. Here we are, Mara, stay near the shade during the heat of the day or go beneath the sea."

Taking her hand he once again kissed it, his eyes crinkled in mirth as she sheathed it. Then waving his hand he created a barely seen bubble; Mara knew to stay away from the edges.

"Clay, you have the authority to release the bubble when you leave. It will shrink around Mara until you return to the property and then it will vanish. Until we meet again." He Traveled away directly from the spot.

Once he was gone Mara asked Clay, "Have you learned anything about him kissing my Dragon skin?"

"Sorry, I found nothing in my reading and I have not contacted Brand about that topic. Forgive me. I will see to it shortly. Let me examine this Traveling Shadow first."

It was the same signature and location as the Mermaid Colony, which Clay had noted while they were there. He had already alerted Brand and Ironwood. "I think his hidden location must be near that Colony but not in it. Presently, he has gone directly to the home of Water Lord Dain."

They went over the Rights and Responsibilities again, and then finished up the other lesson before going swimming. It was not as fun as hoped, because everything to be seen she had seen with Morvayne and it reminded her of that terrible moment just before she burst to the surface. Clay seemed to enjoy the swimming, so she stayed a while longer. Eventually he acknowledged her despondency and they went back to the beach.

"Mara, you are nearly as melancholy as I am! It has taken me years to develop this attitude, you are far too young for this. I take it you are still upset about enjoying your senses with Morvayne. True?"

"Yes," Mara replied quietly. She stretched out, face down, on the blanket to enjoy the warmth of the sun. It seemed to her that her Dragon skin rejoiced in the warmth. It certainly felt glorious to her. "Clay? You never answered my question about morals."

Clay lay on his stomach on another blanket, facing her nose to nose. "You know, Mara, you have far too many questions to be answered in such a short amount of time. Some of the things you want to know take years, hundreds sometimes, for Elves to be able come up with a satisfying answer. They publish them and you can find them in the libraries around the world. I am talking about Faire libraries here. This is another thing we do to occupy our time; we research others' thoughts and then we gather with like-minded souls and debate and add to or detract from the core belief. You asked, 'What are morals? Because, what is moral to one may not be moral to another.' In the context of your recent episode with Honeysuckle Dew, I would have to conclude you are completely innocent."

"But how can you say that? I enjoyed it—for a moment!"

"Yes, but you were given a drink you knew nothing about,

supposing it to be like the elixir Aerrvin gave you. Which in a way it is. It is as though a man secretly gave someone alcohol or pills and then took advantage of her. Do you condemn her or is she innocent?"

"She seems innocent. But what if she knew he was bad news, but she went with him anyway?"

"That would be a poor choice for a Human girl to make, but she would still be innocent. Mara, that is not your situation at all. You are a prisoner regardless of the freedoms he affords. It is immoral to keep any sentient being captive. Fish, and other pets do not count. As a captive, you are not responsible for pretending to go along with his plans. That is what we asked of you. I am more responsible for your misadventure than you are. And I am sorry I did not get invited in sooner."

Clay paused to look her in the eye; she saw his sorrow and closed her eyes a moment. He continued, "Yes, each person has their own set of morals, it is true, but the basic underlying belief for all superior thinking creatures is this: 'Cause no harm to others.' This is a hard principal to live up to when others want something and you must deny them their desire. This is not upheld strictly for emotional harm, but physical harm is frowned upon and death is seen as wrong by all, except for the Trolls and Kraken. Dragons have a unique belief system which you will have to study later. Even the Ogres weigh the consequences carefully before they sentence another to death."

Clay sat up and produced a thermos of apple juice; he poured Mara a cup before drinking his own.

"Okay, but what about war? The Elves and Fairies have been involved in as many wars as Humans have. We say we believe it is wrong, but we do it almost constantly anymore. How can a war be moral?" Mara sipped the cool liquid, enjoying its sweet tangy bite.

"Causing death is wrong, but if the death of those seeking to deny rights brings freedom for those being held captive, it can be worth the loss of those seeking to stifle them. Americans have always fought for freedom; they use similar logic do they not?"

Clay pulled a comb from the air and proceeded to groom himself. Mara had never seen a guy comb his hair after swimming before, though it was true most did not have hair below their shoulders. Putting it out of her mind she answered him, "Yes, that is true. So basically, I can infer that since I am living among Elves and Fairies, I should not take my Human upbringing too seriously, because the rules are more relaxed; therefore, running around dressed in a nearly see-through old cast off skin of a Dragon is not indecent in the least. As long as I 'cause no harm,' right?"

Clay smiled at her lengthy example. "Right. Aerrvin has no cares at all for who sees you dressed in skin-tight Dragon armor. He does, however, hold a jealous point of contention against Morvayne for sharing that sensual moment with you, mainly because he intended to introduce you to its pleasures himself. Morvayne caused pain to Aerrvin and you, and I may as well include myself." Clay paused to drink his juice before continuing. "By the same logic, I believe we will not lose our virtue should we need to go to war against Morvayne's band of followers. Remember, he intends to use your Power to influence Humans to get angry or greedy enough to cause more wars, thereby reducing the population of the most aggressive Humans in the gene pool.

"He has, of course always been a proponent of abortion and birth control. He joins causes all the time, and donates millions to them, all for the same evil plot to reduce the spreading terror of Mankind. And let me confess, I have supported this cause at times myself." Clay's hair was once again silky smooth and dry, shifting in the gentle breeze. He put the comb back and waited to hear Mara's response.

"Now see, to him that is moral and right; in his mind he is benevolent and a savior of some sort—saving the world for the Fair Ones," Mara complained.

Clay smiled toothily, "See? You are getting it exactly. There are always going to be differing views. It is up to us to make the choice that brings us closer to the Light in *our* opinion. We will be judged by the Supreme Being for staying close to the truth as we have received it. Sometimes that may be two opposite directions and both may be acceptable."

Mara moaned and held her head, balancing her elbows on her knees. Speaking toward the ground she said, "You are just speaking in circles now. Okay, new subject. Do we have time?"

"Maybe, how detailed is the question and how detailed should I answer?" Clay caused the sand to pile up beneath his blanket, allowing him to recline comfortably. He was facing the sea so Mara sat beside him, looking out at the waves.

Mara produced a fruit and cheese platter and ate a few bites before asking her question. "So, I went to the Third Level to learn what Jaera has learned at school, and then I shared a little about myself, because she has to go see my Mom today, due to the fact that tomorrow is Ricky's graduation. Sooo my question is: How could she condense time like that, and does it relate to your mention of anywhen?"

"Mara, I understand the need, but you were not supposed to go there until after you have taken the Oath. Do not return unless I or your Grandfather grant permission. I would appreciate it, do you understand?"

"Yes, I guess. Is there danger?"

"There are dangers. You could get lost without a guide and proper training. And yes, I will try to tell you how or why, but it is easier to understand if you are taught there. So here we go: Do you remember the string theory we discussed? Good, now last year you also worked with photons, remember the lesson about the comb?"

"Yeah, that was fascinating. We learned that the reason a comb can't make a sharp shadow is because the light has not made up its mind which side of the tooth it wants to travel through, so it takes both paths. Who knew light could make a choice—whoa! Are you saying that, wha–never mind explain it to me." Mara snuggled up beside him, enjoying the coolness of his body compared to the blanket. *How does he stay so cool?* she wondered. *Ah, ah, ah no more questions.*

***

Clay was in Heaven and Hell. Mara smelled heavenly and he was fighting his desire to caress her, causing severe anguish. *'Cause no pain,'* he thought. *She has no clue, and here I sit, salivating for a whiff of her scent. Obviously, Breeze taught her that horrible trick of hiding it. But I am so attuned to this particular fragrance that even the barest note is near satisfying. Anything is better than nothing.* Unable to resist, Clay leaned his face into her hair and inhaled deeply.

"Sorry, I can move away . . . " Mara started to say; Clay interrupted her retreat by clamping her to him with his arm.

"No, please stay," he begged. He caused an umbrella to appear over them and lifted the breeze momentarily, having noticed that Mara was too warm. Then he addressed her question.

"Einstein's hypothesis that quantization is a property of light itself is considered to be proven, and I can tell you that he is correct. You would need to take Earth Science as taught at our Academy to understand it all, Mara. But I can explain it this way: When you go to the Land of Dreams you are entering an alternate reality. Like the photon you can choose one of the many different paths through the obstacles of life. Both are true until you complete the 'thought experiment' as explained by Heisenberg. You do recall that when he actually made the decision for the photon it could then only take the one path?"

"Yes, and that still hardly makes sense." Mara replied, nibbling on a piece of cheese.

"It makes perfect sense when you recall that all things are free to act and be acted upon. We can live as many different realities as we can think of choices to make—when we go to the Land of Dreams within the Void. That is why it is so alluring. I could go and imagine Arianna never left me, because I never offended her; in essence I could go back in time and change the course of my life. Hence, we have anywhen."

"Then why haven't you done that? You obviously love her deeply." Mara felt compassion and guilt for stirring up his feelings.

"I have. I have spent a thousand years with her, while this body lay in stasis for one hundred years, in twenty-year increments, of course. But most still ended poorly. I eventually had to leave my Dreams, because I feel a responsibility to this life; I see it as my original existence. Now, please understand, those lives still play on, as does this one and any she might have lived. We have not proven it, but the theory is that all possibilities play on as we make minute changes daily. Our lives are split into myriads of shards like our Fairy Dust, all of them just as real to he or she who lives it. So when you go to the Land of Dreams you can look into the Void and see all your possible lives and choose any of them to experience. In this life I miss her. Among those I have viewed, some say lived, in three of them she died, twice in my arms and the third because of Morvayne." Clay's voice dropped to a whisper near her ear.

"How many different lives did you sample, if that is the right word?" Mara asked.

Clay stiffened momentarily and forced himself to relax. The conversation was getting touchy for him.

"I have lived ten different lives, Mara, three of them included you." There. He had intimated as much as he would, he would not tell her how her lives had gone. She needed to make her own choices without being influenced by him.

Mara scooted closer if that was possible and whispered breathily, "Did I live, or die horribly?"

"Yes," Clay replied, wrapping an arm around her as he recalled the memories.

They held onto each other for perhaps ten minutes, each lost in their own thoughts. Mara had never supposed life could be so complicated. *I lived and died already? I could have been attracted to Gareth!* She thought of several scenarios one after the other; she could have never gone to college, maybe even married her prom date. Her Dad could never have been taken away, her sisters would not be. She frowned at that. Although, her mother believed her girls were meant to be hers, so maybe her parents would have had more. *Do men believe they were meant to have certain children assigned to them? Clay was always a part of my life; am I meant to be his? No, that is too far off the track for me. I could never marry someone that old, one hundred and ninety is my limit.* She giggled, and sat up.

Clay felt relief as her spirit lifted; he smiled at her as she looked up at him.

Mara said, "You never quite answered how time was condensed, but I'm hot; one more quick swim and then we can return to the house." She ran to the sea while he took his time, still collecting his thoughts. Tucking away the memories, he recalled that he needed to ask Brand about the sheds being kissed.

Slipping into the Void he quickly located Brand and knocked politely on his window.

"Clay, please enter! What news?" Brand asked intensely.

"Not much, Morvayne returned to the Mermaid Colony a

few hours ago. But Mara has a question she wanted me to find the answer to."

"Proceed," Brand directed.

"Mara sheaths herself in the Dragon shed armor each time Morvayne kisses her, she has not removed the kisses as she thought that the shed would protect her, but now she is worried that he is doing something to the shed itself. Is it possible and what would it be?"

"Bright and bright she is," Brand commended. "Yes, she was right to clothe herself thus, and Morvayne can trace the shed wherever it goes if he creates a strong enough connection to it. She can start washing it with the lemon and mint or the vinegar and pepper, but it is probably too late to remove all of his connection. He would be able to locate the shed if he were within a thousand miles of it. I am sorry to say she will need to remove it when she makes her escape. Pity all the work she did to gain it."

"Pity too, she looks lovely in it." Clay responded.

Brand looked sharply at Clay, then feeling his pain, he grunted, "A real pity."

Clay sensed a need to return, so bidding farewell to Brand he awoke just as Mara called, having burst to the surface, "Are you coming or not?"

"I'm coming!"

12

Hometown Experience

Jaera and Aerrvin rode in the back of the sleek gray sedan, lost in their own thoughts. Aerrvin wished for his Viper; the trip would have been much faster *and* he would be driving!

True they could have Traveled, but really they had nothing to occupy their time with anyway; they would just be sitting around waiting until it was time to arrive. Aerrvin relived the past three weeks again, firmly entrenching within his soul every little detail.

Jaera thought about Gareth He had been gone a week and she missed him terribly. With both Aerrvin and Gareth gone, she had felt utterly alone. She barely slept because of the emptiness of the Nest. While still located with Mama Cat and her kittens, without her longtime Nest Mates it just wasn't the same. She had stayed a few nights in Mara's house before Jill moved. So she had been totally alone in the Nest only twice. Aerrvin was now deeply asleep, but he cozied up as she leaned into him. She was ready to accept a proposal from Gareth, but he did not seem to be as interested. *True he has a battle to plan. But he should still find time to meet me in my Dreams!* Her angry attitude caused Aerrvin to stir, so she toned her mood down to a simmer. Eventually she fell asleep.

As they entered the small town, Bronwyn woke them up to give them time to prepare. Jaera needed to transform her looks with her Mask of Deception, and Aerrvin needed to get used to sitting next to one who resembled his true love.

Arriving at the home of Amanda and Rick, Jaera and Aerrvin climbed out and retrieved their luggage. They waved as the Brownie then drove away to procure a hotel room. "Might as well walk right in. I'm home, I guess." Jaera smiled a little too broadly for Mara's staid nature.

"Tone down the chipper attitude; she's a stoic remember?" Aerrvin reeled her in, slowing down her clipped pace.

"Thank you, Aerrvin." Jaera looked him in the eyes as they went up the porch stairs. Suddenly the door opened, Sarah and Becky screamed happy welcomes, jumping all over the two of them. "How come you didn't bring Gareth too?" Sarah asked.

"What, and not Jaera?" she could hardly refrain from asking.

Aerrvin interrupted to prevent a row. "They had other things to do, but we will get together again soon. I promise."

Both girls clapped and shouted hoorays. All the noise brought Amanda to the front room.

"Yay! You made it." She hugged each of them and sat down on the sofa indicating they should sit as well. "I hope you like barbecue; that's where I was, out back getting dinner set up. Rick should be home soon. He loves to cook out there, so I let him! Any chance I get; saves me from having to do it all."

Jaera and Aerrvin sat back on the plush couch, each with a girl on their laps. Jaera spoke up, "Mom, Aerrvin does not eat red meat. Do you have anything besides ribs for the grill?"

"Oh, that's right. I think you did mention that once. Sorry, Aerrvin. I can run down to the store and pick up some fresh fish." Amanda blushed at her forgetfulness.

"Oh, that's alright, I can just go catch something off the

pier. If you have a pole I can borrow?"

Amanda smiled at the thought of this pretty boy catching a fish. Yet, he claimed to have come from out here on the peninsula, so why not?

"Sure, follow me." Amanda led him to the double garage where they kept all their outdoor gear. "Pick what you like, but don't stay out too long, we will eat in two hours or so."

Aerrvin smiled in thanks and chose a suitable pole and lure.

Amanda's place was situated in a quiet cove. They shared a pier with five other neighbors. Aerrvin thrilled to be near the ocean, no matter he had just been swimming yesterday in the Mediterranean. It continually sent waves of peace and joy through his soul. He harbored the belief that surely some ancient ancestor of his was a Water Sprite. Humming Mara's Lullaby, as he had come to call it, he walked gracefully to the pier. Soon joined by Sarah and Becky. They tended towards chattiness, but he continued humming so they sat down beside him and listened instead. Looking at each other and then at him alternately until he turned and asked, "So, how many fish did you catch this month?"

Free to speak, they regaled him with their stories of all three fish they had caught on the weekend.

Aerrvin was hungry, so he called three good-sized kelp greenlings in by waggling his fingers in the water. It took half an hour to catch the ones he wanted, so he just sat on the dock another twenty minutes just enjoying the girls' happy chatter along with the salty breeze.

Inside, Amanda helped carry Mara's suitcase upstairs, Jaera grabbed Aerrvin's. "Do you have a place for Aerrvin or should he stay at the hotel?"

Amanda turned indignantly, "The hotel? No, he can stay

here. Unless he is too good to stay with us; this *is* a humble home compared to his mansion."

"No, he's not too good, he will sleep wherever, even a tent if you have one." Jaera smiled remembering the time they actually tried camping—Human style.

Amanda gave her an odd look and continued up the stairs. "I thought he could sleep in your room and you can sleep with Becky. Good enough?"

"Sure, Mom, that will be fine." Jaera carried the suitcase to Mara's room and set it on the end of the bed. She walked about the room touching the things Mara had touched on her last visit.

"Talk about déjà vu. It seems like you did that the last time you were here." Amanda took the photo in Mara's hand. 'This was a fun trip. Do you remember seeing that octopus? It was so huge!" She smiled at her daughter., waiting for her to say, "Massively." But she didn't.

Jaera sat up against the headboard and said, "Yeah that was a lot of fun. We should do it again sometime."

"Right, like I will have enough money for that. Rick and I are going to Australia this fall with the girls. A few weeks after we get Ricky settled in at school, I can't remember the dates. If your rich boy wants to pay your way, you can join us."

Jaera made a face at the slight to Aerrvin. "Are you mad at Aerrvin? Because, we are fine."

Amanda sighed, "No, I'm not mad. He seems to be a little cool to you still. Have you discussed slowing down, to maybe date other people first just to make sure?"

"We know deep down that we are meant for each other. If I could get him to commit faster, it would not be fast enough!" Jaera realized she was speaking about Gareth. "Sorry for the outburst. I seem to be quite moody lately."

Amanda looked as though she had seen a ghost. Shaking her head as though to clear her mind she said, "Perhaps you should rest before dinner. I have to go over some bills anyway, it's payday and time to 'pay the piper' as they say."

She smiled and took the suitcase off of the bed. "Go ahead and nap here. I will wake you when Rick and Ricky come home."

***

Amanda brushed her daughter's hair away and kissed her on her forehead. *Something does not feel right*, she thought. Something niggled at the edge of her thoughts, but she could not bring it forth. She went to her computer to begin paying the bills.

She completed most by the time Ricky came home, with Rochelle hanging on to his left side like an additional appendage. Amanda stopped what she was doing, after checking off the bills she had completed.

"Hey Ricky, Rochelle. Mara is here already. Aerrvin is out on the pier with the girls, fishing. I don't know if he will catch anything, but he doesn't eat red meat. If he is unsuccessful, could you run down to the store to get some clams or fresh fish?"

"Yeah, it's doubtful he will catch anything the way the neighbors have been in and out all week on their boats. You should have given him the keys to the boat so he could really have a chance."

"Well he seemed confident, and I don't know what experience he has on a boat. It would be my luck that he would get lost and then Mara would hate me for losing her boyfriend."

That sounded too close to losing Brentwood, so she turned away to compose her face. *Why would I even think such thoughts, let alone speak them?*

The girls clattered in from the back door. "Look what

163

Aerrvin caught!" they cried with excitement.

Amanda introduced Aerrvin and Ricky to each other along with Rochelle.

Aerrvin had already cleaned his catch, so it was just six beautiful fillets in a tub that they kept by the cleaning station. He placed them in the kitchen sink to rinse.

Ricky whistled. "Those are beauts. You caught them right off the pier?"

Aerrvin nodded.

"We usually have to go a mile out to catch greenlings. I wonder what brought them in?"

Rochelle said, "I wonder if there are any more?"

"I don't know, we could try to find out. Mom, how long until dinner?"

"Dad should be home any time now, so probably twenty minutes or so. We're having shish kabobs, so they shouldn't take too long to cook."

Ricky left to see if he could top Aerrvin's successful catch.

This left Aerrvin alone with Amanda, as the girls chased after Rochelle.

"Well, that leaves a quiet moment to talk," Amanda said, leading the way out back to sit in the shade of the covered deck. "So how's things, Aerrvin? Mara said she hurt your feelings. Are you really recovered?"

Aerrvin admired Amanda's directness, but was more surprised that Mara had discussed so openly her situation with her Mother. He did not know what she had said so he remained guarded. "Of course I am hurt, but I do not blame her. It could have happened to anyone."

Aerrvin tried to exude calm, but on Amanda, it seemed to heighten her anxiety, so he scaled down his Light. Aerrvin was now certain that Amanda could perceive Light just as well as ever; he tamped his down tightly and presented a calm demeanor instead.

Amanda had looked away as he began to shine. *This is not happening,* she told herself while watching the girls hop around Rochelle. *Aura's around people do not signify magic,* she told herself. She'd read about the ability online. *It's just a manifestation of greater spirituality.'*

"Aerrvin, I have always had the ability to see auras or a glow around certain people; you were just glowing a soft blue mixed with purple. Have you been told about that before?"

Aerrvin smiled, "Yes, I have. Not everyone can see it; thanks for noticing."

Feeling more confident Amanda said, "You don't think I'm a kook?"

"No, how could I think of my future Mother-in-Law as a kook?" Aerrvin asked, while trying to guess where she wanted the conversation to go.

"I don't know, most people don't want to think about spirituality or mystic things. I am sure Mara has told you about my distaste for make believe magic. Even so, I have had an increase in my sensory perceptions lately, so I have been reading up on chakras, aura's, and the like. Rick says it's all nonsense, and he would rather I let him tell the girls fairy tales." She shook her head, wondering why she was opening up to Aerrvin like that.

Aerrvin nodded. "Well, I have taken a look at the current philosophy. I think they have something to them. Obviously I glow. However, the conclusions they draw inferring certain qualities to the various colors are seriously wrong. In my opinion anyway." He shrugged and grinned to soften his criticism.

"Yes, well . . . Oh, Rick is home, just a minute," Amanda said rising from her chair.

Amanda greeted Rick and went up to wake Mara.

"Mara, honey, are you ready to wake up?"

Jaera had merely gone to her simple Dream, so she woke easily when the door opened. Stretching out gracefully she got up. "Yes, I feel better. How did Aerrvin do?"

"Oh, he caught three nice fish. Come on down and visit. Ricky brought his new girlfriend over too."

They chatted and enjoyed their dinner as the sun lowered in the sky. That far north the sun always took forever to completely set, so it was still light when Amanda invited everyone to come inside to watch home videos.

"Oh, this should be great!" Jaera said, poking Aerrvin in the ribs. "Just what every future mate wants to see and every poor child hopes never gets shown."

Amanda thought the word choice was off, but the sentiment was right. *Maybe Mara is trying to show herself superior to regular folks, by using fancy language. She's more graceful somehow. She's as lovely as ever—I've got it!* Amanda thought, *Her aura is green, Mara was never green! Mara radiates like a rainbow. I don't care what Aerrvin thinks; I'm going to look up what green means. Maybe she's sick.*

Amanda stopped her daydreaming as she realized everyone had stopped talking as they waited for her to put the video in the player. "Sorry, thinking and walking at the same time, you know me!"

They watched videos of Mara as a baby; the girls had seen them before, and Rick held no resentment for the love that Amanda and Mara felt for Brentwood. Eventually they moved on to vacations with the new family, the additions of the girls, Mara's prom and graduation, ending with Ricky's prom which included

Rochelle as his date. Jaera was touched by the closeness of the family and felt bad that Mara had to miss out. She wiped her face on Aerrvin's shirt. He drew a breeze their way and gave her a hug.

"Well, hate to eat and run, but Rochelle's grandparents should have arrived by now, so I gotta go meet the family." Ricky hugged Rochelle and she punched him playfully in the stomach, gaining smiles from everyone. "Nice meeting you, Aerrvin, maybe we can go out on the boat sometime," Ricky said, opening the door.

"Yes, that would be fun," Aerrvin replied with a nod.

It was 10:00 and the girls were still wound up from having company, but Amanda insisted they go to bed.

Jaera said, "I will tell you a story if you are ready in ten minutes!"

Amanda thanked Mara and sat back and watched her daughter. She seemed more confidant and not self-conscious at all sitting on the couch playing with Aerrvin's hair. He barely seemed to notice, and appeared lost in his own thoughts, not even looking at the game Rick chose on the TV. *He's the same Aerrvin I met two weeks ago, just contemplative. But Mara is all wrong, as though she's been taken over by an alien.*

Amanda snorted, breaking Aerrvin out of his reverie. He noticed she was thinking about him and that she was also upset. *Not good, he thought. This is going to get messy, I can tell.*

Speaking to Jaera he said, "Come on, let's go tell those sisters of yours a story or two. Good night, Amanda, Rick. I will be retiring soon myself; thank you for dinner. It was delicious."

Probably not much of a compliment, he thought, with a smile as he walked up the stairs with Jaera. He had eaten a fish and a half by himself and a little bit of the fruit salad, and one soda; he did not allow Jaera to have one, so she had to have water as they had no juice. The soda had not really improved his mood much. He was still quite depressed, and the fact that Amanda could perceive it only deepened his distress.

The girls were not in their rooms yet, so Jaera began singing a counting song, having told them that when she got to fifty she would tickle them if they did not get into their beds before she finished, and that if she got to one hundred they would get no story. They hustled as Amanda came up to lay out their pajamas.

Right at fifty they ran screaming into their room as Jaera came up behind them to tickle them.

They tried to hide behind Aerrvin as he sat at the foot of the bed. Yet, Jaera was a master tickler so she caught them anyway, being careful to not torture them, as she often did to Aerrvin or Gareth.

Once in bed, Jaera said, "And where will I sleep? Mom said I was sleeping with Becky, but you two are in the big bed. I don't think I want to sleep on that top bunk. It looks too high."

The girls pleaded to let them all sleep together. "We don't take much room. You can sleep in the middle and I won't kick I promise," Sarah said holding her hand up like a scout.

Jaera turned to Amanda, "They don't pee in their sleep do they?"

They all burst out laughing. Yet Amanda was reserved as she said, "Not anymore. If you don't mind the crowd, you can do as you please. Goodnight girls; and don't keep Mara up. She had a long day today—she went to school before driving over here." Amanda kissed each girl, seeing their little tiny auras in the dark better than she could in the light. In fact, the room seemed to glow much more than usual with four distinct auras as well as her own, which she could only see in her mind's eye.

From what she had read, it was supposed to be easier to see aura's in a light room with the person standing in front of a light colored backdrop. *I'm probably going crazy.* She hugged Mara and accepted a kiss.

Amanda went downstairs as Mara began telling a story about a little girl who went for a walk in the woods. She sat down next to Rick. Waiting for a commercial, she pondered what to say.

Finally, a break came. He turned to her. "Can you bring me a drink?" She got up and brought him a soda. He looked at it, rolled his eyes and got up and retrieved a beer. "What's up? You look like you lost a puppy."

"I, uh, Mara—did she seem strange to you?" Amanda fumbled.

"No, she seemed happier than normal. Shouldn't she? I mean did you see that ring on her finger? She's got it made in the shade. You should be happy. Your little girl is all grown up, about to graduate, and get married, and have little grandbabies for you to fuss over," he laughed as he sat down next to her.

"No, it's like she's not herself. You know how I said I can sometimes see auras?" He rolled his eyes again and looked at the TV.

"I know you think it's nonsense, especially since I am so anti-pretend and pro-science. But I think it fits in with science, our bodies are sparked with electrons or something. We are made up of water, light and a little bit of matter. That's science, not pretend." Amanda knew she would get nowhere with the conversation, especially as the game came back on. "Are you going to watch the whole game?"

"Yeah, it's got two hours or so. I'll wait up for Ricky to get home. Going to bed?"

"In a while, I want to do some reading first."

Amanda had a study right next to her bedroom, so she went in and 'fired up' her computer. Looking up one site after another, she was struck as she read:

Everything is made of energy & vibrations. That's why everything has an Aura. An Aura is an energy field that reflects the subtle life energies within the body. It's a personal electromagnetic energy field around each being, shaped like an eggshell. It is a reflection of the body's spirit . . . As everything that is in our reality is created from electromagnetic energy, everything has an aura—plants, animals, etc.

"That's what I thought! It is not really *so* mystical, it's scientific. Not everyone has the eyes to see it."

She pondered on that for a while and then came back to Mara. When Mara was born, she had shone so brightly. Brentwood said it was her Elven heritage. She recalled that she thought he was on to something back then. She had been searching for answers as a teenager. Brentwood showed up so bright and hot. She recalled telling all her friends about the super cute guy she met at Sea World.

Amanda smiled at the memories, *That's what I get for watching old movies. Where was I going anyway?* She let her mind wander and then remembered, *Oh, Brent gradually got me thinking that magic was real and that he had an Elf for a father. And that I was most likely a Fair Folk of some kind too, saying he could see a faint spark of light in me. I would have believed anything he said; I was young and he gave me hope of leaving home.*

Amanda sighed as she continued to meditate. *Yet, Mara kept her glow. I got so used to it, I felt other children looked dull by comparison. Brentwood started scaring me with talk of wicked Elves wanting to kidnap Mara. That's when I began to shut down. I hate to remember it now. Why am I doing this? The fights with Brent—* Amanda started crying sitting there at her computer.

She thought, *I am so alone. I have no one to talk to. Rick scoffs at me the same way I began to scoff at Brent. Mara eventually did begin to lose her light, until one day she had no aura at all. When did that happen?'*

Sobbing, she acknowledged that it was when she married Rick and moved to Sequim. If she got very close to kiss Mara good night, she sometimes sensed a flicker of pearlescent glitter. Becky and Sarah each glowed a constant small flame, no glitter to them. Even Morris, that smarmy co-worker of Brentwood's had an aura; it was cloudy, yet he sparkled sometimes. She remembered ignoring it as she swept up the office where they worked.

I'm getting a headache. I'd better go to bed. Drying her face, she made her way to the bathroom and washed up. As soon as her head hit the pillow, she fell asleep.

Her dreams were her normal vivid scenes. She had learned years before ever meeting Brent how to direct events within her dreams. He claimed to have been in her dreams, but she denied those events from having happened as well. So here she was dreaming that Brent was coming home from work and Mara was a teenager. Brent brought home a new assistant, Aerrvin.

"Aerrvin, what are you doing in my dream?" Amanda demanded.

"This is a dream?" His face offered wide-eyed mischievousness.

"Yes, it's MY dream. Why are you here?"

"I was concerned about you. You seemed upset since you saw my Power emanating from me. I let it flair to try to calm you, but it only upset you more. I want to apologize."

"Well you can't be responsible for what your aura does, can you?"

"As a matter of fact, I can tamp it down tight, or leak it out until I am blindingly Bright." Aerrvin demonstrated. "But I do not go about my regular day this Bright. It would be rude." He tamped it down to a soft glow.

Amanda realized he was just barely luminescent all the time; she had been so struck by his boyish charms that she had failed to observe the glow until he had turned it up on the deck.

"This is just a dream. You can't really answer my questions anyway, but it sure has been nice to talk to you."

Amanda waited for him to fade away, but he just sat there. Mara entered the dreamscape, glowing softly as she did before Brent went away. "Mom, Dad wants to know what's for dinner. Can I help? Who is the hot guy?"

Aerrvin went up to her and introduced himself as her future husband.

Amanda was incensed, "Now hold on, this is my dream. You can't just come in here and take over like this. Get out, now." He kissed Mara and then vanished.

Crying, Amanda went into the kitchen. "Brent, can you help me understand this?"

"No, Amanda I can't. You need to ask Mara or Ironwood. Aunt Lily might be able to help. She has always helped me." Amanda watched as he faded away.

"Wait! Don't leave me," she cried.

"I will always love you, Amanda. You will always be my little Water Sprite," he hugged her and disappeared, leaving her standing alone at the kitchen counter in her dream.

Amanda fled to a deeper dream.

13
Awakened Perceptions

Amanda woke up to the aroma of bacon and eggs. Saturday morning, Graduation Day! She jumped out of bed and nearly went downstairs, before remembering she had a guest in the house. She showered and primped and went down looking as fresh as a stepped on daisy.

Rick looked up as he finished flipping the last pancake of a stack of four. "You didn't sleep too well with all that tossing and turning, so I let you sleep in. These are yours," he handed her the plate.

Amanda saw that everyone was at the table eating, so she went and sat down too. "Morning, everyone! Mara, did you sleep well with two little munchkins on either side?"

"Sure did, better than I have all week." She tweaked Becky's nose.

"And you, Aerrvin?" Amanda asked, not sure she wanted to look directly at him or not.

"I dreamed all night long!" He smirked with the exact same grin as he had in her dream, without the widened eyes. "Must have been getting to sleep in Mara's bed."

That caused the girls to say, "Oooh! Kissy, kissy."

Amanda watched Mara make kissy faces at him across the

table.

Aerrvin leaned back casually and accepted the air kisses on one cheek and then the other, causing the girls to start attacking him with kiss after kiss, blowing them at him as fast as they could. He feigned being under attack and hid his face with his empty plate.

Amanda could tell things were going to get out of hand in short order as Becky started to leave her chair.

"Uh, uh, missy. Get back in your chair and finish eating. You need a bath before we leave for graduation, so finish up." She smiled at Aerrvin as he exhaled an exaggerated sigh.

"Thanks, Amanda. One of your daughters is enough for me!" He looked at Mara and smiled an almost sorry looking smile, but he recovered his cool exterior and said, "How do we dress for this occasion?"

"Well it is a small school, but we still like to dress up for important events; nice slacks and a button shirt would do well, right, Rick?"

"Yep, I even bought a new tie," he replied.

Amanda brought herself to look at Mara, definitely green. "Mara, are you sure you are feeling well? You look a little off."

"Well you know, it's probably the stress of finals and everything. Jill moved out. Did I tell you?" Jaera asked.

"No, I did not hear about that! So she got her place up and running already?"

"No, just the apartment, but she's making payments, so you know, she couldn't afford to stay with me anymore. I miss her already." She frowned. emanating true sadness. "But that means, Ricky, you don't have to sleep in the basement after all." She grinned an impossibly wide grin, and after a look from Aerrvin, she moderated it to a more Mara-like smile. "Should be fun, Raccoon Boy." Jaera remembered a favorite nickname she had learned from Mara's memories.

Ricky made a sour face, but smiled anyway. "Sure will Motor Mouth."

It sounded like old times to Amanda; she had the urge to shush them, but saw they were just teasing so she let it be. *It must be Mara,* she thought, *well, of course it's Mara, what's wrong with you?* She hustled the girls up for baths and apologized to Aerrvin for not having another bathroom. Turned out there was time enough for everyone. Ricky left early to go over the program one last time, leaving his bathroom free.

The graduation was much like any other, long and boring except for when they talked about Ricky and his friends. Afterwards they had all the relatives over for a buffet in the backyard.

Rick's ex came with her husband, daughter, and parents. Rick's parents and two brothers came as well. Talk was about college and football. Small groups discussed Mara and her fiancé. Mara should have been shyer, but she was laughing and enjoying the attention. *Maybe having a boyfriend does that to a girl. She was certainly in a good mood when we went to the memorial commemoration.* Try as she might, Amanda could not get the feeling of wrongness to go away.

The afternoon wore down to evening, most guests had left. Rick sat in the living room watching a game with his brothers, his parents had gone home. Mara and Aerrvin helped with clean up.

"Well, Mom, I'd like to stay longer, but I need to finish up some stuff before school on Monday so I'm leaving tonight. You won't be too upset will you?"

"No, I understand; wouldn't want you to get bad grades at the end. I didn't see how you got here. Did you ride the bus?"

"No, Bronwyn drove us. My car got stolen," Aerrvin admitted.

Rick overheard that, "What! No way? You had it insured I hope." Aerrvin nodded, Rick turned to describe the car to his brothers.

Amanda felt a weird tingling sensation but pushed it aside as she said, "I'm sorry to hear that Aerrvin. Were you nearby when it happened? Do you know who took it?"

"I'm sorry I brought it up; yes I saw who took it, but we can't get it back just yet. He's bad news. Some Birth Day present." Looking out the window he said, "I think our ride is here."

Aerrvin had already brought their luggage down. He hugged the girls and then kissed Amanda on the cheek.

"Take care, Amanda," he said knowingly. It was too intimate; she almost cried as she hugged Mara-who-wasn't-Mara. "I will," she answered belatedly. She took her daughter's face in her hands and said, "Mara, I love you."

Jaera teared up and replied for Mara, "Love you too." Then hugging Amanda one last time and calling, "Bye," before kissing each girl on the head, she left.

"Bye," Rick called as the door shut.

From the window, Amanda watched Aerrvin put his arm around her daughter as he walked her to the car. Bronwyn had taken the luggage. Her appearance wavered, making her look like she had short red curls, before going back to the long, dark fluff Amanda knew and loved.

Amanda knew she was losing it. She didn't want to see a psychiatrist in her own town though; it would be bad publicity for the electronics store. It was such a small town, everyone would talk. Rick wouldn't want talk.

Amanda had the phone number for Mara's pastor, so she called him.

After the pleasantries were over she asked him, "Pastor, was Mara in church last Sunday?"

"Yes, she rarely misses except when she visits you. Is something wrong?" Pastor Mike answered.

"I don't know yet. She was just here for her brother's graduation, and she didn't seem to be all—I don't know. Something was not right about her. Has she been in to talk to you?"

"Yes, she has, but that is between her and me. You know that I have a clinical practice as well as a ministry. All I can say is she was concerned about both areas. If you think I need to contact her, I can. When do you think she will be back?"

"Oh, it will be late. You can talk to her tomorrow. Why is it that she no longer teaches her class? I forgot to ask her about that," Amanda asked, as she tried to get the courage to tell him she was the one with problems.

"Sorry, can't discuss that either. I think it would be good for you to have an honest heart to heart with her. You could both benefit from honest communication."

"Yes, you are right, thanks for letting me bother you." Amanda couldn't bring herself to discuss her problem on the phone.

"No problem, Amanda. Call anytime," the Pastor said, ending the call.

"Maybe I should just keep busy," Amanda said out loud. She put the girls to bed and went back to finish the bills. She paid most everything online, so she checked in to view her phone bill and was shocked to see a call from Italy. Immediately she thought of Ricky; he had called friends overseas before, but this call was to the house. It lasted forty minutes; Ricky was barely capable of a ten-minute phone call with Rochelle.

"What day was that?" She looked on her calendar and back at the screen. It was late, the only call she had—a chill went down her spine. "How on earth did she get to Italy! Why didn't she say she was there? I'm calling this number."

"Buon giorno," said a female voice.

"Hello, this Amanda, Mara's mother? Is Mara there?"

"Oh, Amanda! Mara's mother. Yes and no. She is out taking a walk. I can take a message, yes?"

Amanda did not know what to say. "What do you mean she is taking a walk? She just left my house an hour ago!"

"No, Mara is taking a walk. My name is Tessa, I am just a servant to Master Maurice. Mara said for me to tell her friends, Jill and Jaera, that she was taken to Italy by Morvayne. I think that is Maurice, and she said for them to talk to each other.

'She called you herself. I think she did not want you to know, but she said her friends will rescue her so calling the police would be bad. Miss Amanda, I think I might be in trouble for telling you, but Mara is very moody; some days she is happy and other days she is sad. I feel so helpless. Are you still there?"

Amanda was barely audible, "Yes, I'm still here. Tell me: What does she look like? Maybe it is not my daughter."

"But it is. She called you remember? She is fair with long almost black curls and blue eyes. Her skin, it sparkles sometimes, and she is engaged to a man she calls Aerrvin. But she walks about holding hands like a lover with Clay, a man here who is her teacher. He is brother to Maurice."

"How long has she been there?" Amanda asked looking at her calendar. Aerrvin's birthday was marked the 23rd of May.

Tessa answered, "Saturday, May twenty-three."

Amanda's heart sank further, if that was possible. Maurice sounded like Morris. He appeared to leer at Mara quite a bit at the restaurant. *I should have never let him near her.*

"What does this Maurice look like?" Tessa described him to a slimy T. "I think I am going crazy, Tessa. Do not tell Mara I called. I may call again; please take care of her for me, if you can. Tessa this may sound funny, but—are you magic?"

"Me? No!" She spoke rapidly in Italian. "Sorry, no, but Mara she says she has magic skin. I have seen it too, it is like the rainbow! I think there must be good magic, yes? She is too good to be evil. I do worry for her. I will help her if I can. I have to go now."

"Thank you, Tessa, for telling me. It was the right thing to do."

Amanda was fired up. "No, I am not crazy! I knew it. That was not my daughter."

That meant that Brentwood had been right. *Morris killed Brentwood, and I danced with him?* Amanda felt sick. *No! No! No! I have to do something.*

She went down to talk to Rick. The game was almost over. No point in interrupting. He would not be able to pay attention and she would not say what she had to say in front of his brothers anyway. She went up to her room and began to pack her bags.

"What's going on?" Rick said, walking into the room. He walked over to her; she collapsed into his arms.

"Mara has been kidnapped!" she wailed. "I need to go find out what I can do to help."

"Hold up. What the heck are you talking about! She just

left two hours ago. I didn't hear the phone ring."

"You won't believe me, but that wasn't Mara, that was someone in disguise." She proceeded to tell him about the call from Italy, and the one she just made. Amanda told him what Tessa said about the situation.

"Okay, I see you really did get a call from Italy, but this still makes no sense. Why would Aerrvin have someone pretend to be Mara? Did he kidnap her? Why would anyone want her anyway? To blackmail Ironwood? He's the only one with money. Have you called him yet?"

Amanda had hoped he might be understanding, but telling him the whole truth was hard. "The world isn't what it seems. Brentwood told me years ago that an evil person had plans to kidnap our baby girl. I had already lost my son; I could not bear to lose another child. I refused to believe him and stopped listening to his stories about magic and mythology. As you know, I have told you before, he really believed that fairy tales were true. I forbade him from telling them the same way I have asked you to refrain. I never told you the reason though." Amanda cried as Rick held onto her. He walked her over to the bed and sat down, pulling her down as well.

"So are you going to tell me that you believe this evil guy was some troll, or something?"

"No, he's an Elf," she cried.

"Aw, well that makes perfect sense. Amanda, come on! You don't believe this bull!"

"But I do! That's the problem, Rick. I am a magical being myself. Brentwood and Mara are Elves and our two daughters are Water Sprites just like me. I tried to pretend it wasn't true when Brent told me that Mara was in danger. When he disappeared, I went even deeper into denial, until I was barely able to see truth at all. I mean, I can see more than aura's. I could see Mara's

Brownie, you know, Sylvie? That she always talked about, even though I insisted she did not exist. I thought that if Mara did not know who she was she would be safe. I even began to forget and really believe I was an ordinary Human."

Rick sat there dumbfounded. "No, Amanda, you must be mistaken. Mara was just here and Becky and Sarah are two beautiful little girls. Maybe you need to see a counselor or something. I can't let you leave in this state."

"Let me go!" Amanda hissed as Rick clamped down on her wrist. "Mara is in danger!"

"Tell me; what you can do to help? Do you know where in Italy? Who says you would not be taken as well, then where would we be? Think things through, Amanda! You can't go running out in the night." He let go as she relaxed.

"Then help me think what I should do, Rick. This is real!" Amanda cried at him.

"Call Ironwood. Call Jill or this Jaera. You said the Italian lady said they knew about the situation. Give me a number I'll call." He called Ironwood since they did not have Jaera's number.

"Hello, may I speak to Ironwood?" Rick paused as he listened. "He's not home. All right, can you have him call Amanda when he gets in? It is urgent, about Mara. Anytime, please have him call. Yes. Thank you."

Rick looked at Amanda; she sat slumped on the bed. "Honey, I think you should go to sleep and we will discuss things in the morning. He brought her a couple of sleeping pills, which she used often to get a good nights' sleep. His hope was to keep her in the house while he slept.

***

Ironwood was in Greece, swimming toward the Mermaid Colony located off the shores of its southwestern cliffs and beaches near Alika. Johann, Gareth and ten of his battalion were with him, as well as two of Lorelei's cousins. Gareth had been to this school before for his Sea Studies. It was the same one Aerrvin had attended; as such, it was very highly recommended. Once inside, Ironwood requested a visit with the School's Headmaster.

"Mistress," the Mermaid greeting them corrected.

"Very well, Headmistress, if you please," Ironwood amended.

They were taken to a waiting room where two students sat; one was quite agitated and the other looked depressed. There were three doors, so Ironwood hoped the other two were not waiting to see the Headmistress. A door opened and the depressed student was summoned. A second door opened and the Mermaid looked at the crowd and then shut the door. They waited an hour, before finally being summoned into the third room, which had received no students. Ironwood maintained his calm even though he was anxious and thought poorly of the reception received.

The room was small, so only Ironwood, Gareth and Johann went in. The Headmistress was a very lovely Mermaid. Yet at the moment, she was quite stern.

"I am very busy, as I have just received some troubling news. Are you here in relation to this allegation?" She held up a missive for Ironwood to read.

He grimaced and responded, "Indeed, I am." He went on to detail his heritage and subsequent search for missing relations.

He handed the letter to Gareth and Johann. In essence, it said that no one within the school grounds were permitted to leave until further notice, and that a guard had been set to ensure compliance. The allegation was that The Headmistress was responsible for the kidnapping of Gwennara.

"I can vouchsafe most assuredly that I am involved in no way in the capture, nor keeping of Gwennara, nor any other persons Elf, Fairy or otherwise. I am hoping that since this is your Quest, you will use your band of defenders to help prove my innocence," the Mermaid declared.

"I will, but I find myself feeling near hopeless. Morvayne is behind all of this and he has captured every last member of my direct family who manifests Power and Light, not counting Brand the Bright." Ironwood explained Mara's capture and location in Italy. "Morvayne does not know the location of the Crystal Throne, but he will not cause our Queen's demise until he gains that knowledge. Without the Throne, Mara cannot complete her coronation, properly."

"So what can we do while we are quarantined?" she asked.

"Well, first I do not know your name," Ironwood said courteously. "Nor have I introduced my companions." He motioned to those in the room as well as those outside.

"Sorry, Ironwood. My students call me Mistress Lumina, but you may call me Mina. And I know Gareth already, one of my finer students in years past." She smiled at her own memories. "That leaves your Fairy here." Swimming over to greet Gareth with a kiss, she then turned to Johann as Ironwood introduced him as his assistant. "Secondly?"

"Secondly, I seek permission to inspect all possible locations for prisoners." Ironwood said.

"That might be tricky. I don't want the students to be aware of the enforced lockdown. They are not permitted out without a teacher already, so the teacher's will simply change their lessons. I will use stall tactics on students who wish to quit. How long do you think this will last? Will it come to an actual battle?"

"We are hoping to have my granddaughter freed before Midsummer. That would be three weeks. I believe we will indeed have to fight to be freed from this prison, as it has now become. I do not know why he has laid this blame on you. But surely the Queen must be nearby. Honestly, Morvayne is losing his wits, and I would be hard pressed to be able to follow his logic. If she has been hidden in a storeroom, and we find her before he leads his soldiers in to incriminate you, we may find we have the upper hand. Shall we proceed?"

Mina agree, it was as good a plan as any, so calling ten discrete assistants, she divided them into eleven teams to disperse and begin the search. She kept Gareth to herself.

"Tell me, Gareth, is the danger as ominous as Ironwood suggests?" Mina asked, playing with his hair as she directed water currents to twirl around them. He shrugged, unable to answer before she asked another question. "And Aerrvin, how is he? You look so much alike I can never see you without thinking of him."

Gareth laughed, "Yes, we look so much alike that you could stand to keep neither of us and broke our poor hearts as you sent us on our way."

"It was for your own good. Truly, it takes a rare individual to commit to living with a Mermaid. Well, what is Aerrvin up to?" Mina said, as she led them down a rarely used water tunnel.

Gareth filled her in on the last one hundred plus years, ending with his engagement to Mara the Future Queen and center of all the commotion in the Faire Realms.

"Goodness! He should thank me for rejecting him! When you talk to him, tell him I sorrow for this trial he faces. He will ever be a fond memory for me."

They went through several rooms, both wet and dry, finding nothing. Truth be told, Gwennara could have been shrunk down to a thumb-sized being and placed in stasis for all anyone knew. Finding her would be just as easy as finding a pearl dropped from a sailing vessel upon the sea.

***

Rick woke with a start. Amanda was not in the bed. "Amanda?" With relief, he saw her bags on the floor. She came in from the other room, her 'study' as she called it. "Oh, I thought you had snuck out on me."

Amanda came over and kissed him. "No, I slept soundly and feel refreshed." She looked at the hope in his face and dashed it. "No, I have not given up my foolish notions. There must be something I can do, and I would rather do it in person. I am going to Mara's house to see what I can learn. Jill and Jaera have information, as does Aerrvin. I could feel his tension the whole time he was here."

"Do you promise to stay in Washington State? I'll have none of this boarding a plane and going off to Italy business." Rick said, as he got dressed for breakfast.

"I promise I will not buy any plane tickets, nor board any planes." Amanda promised holding her arm up in a symbolic pledge.

"The girls still have four days of school. What are your plans?" Rick asked.

"Your niece, Heidi, can stay in Mara's room. I'll pay her to make dinner too. She will love it," Amanda replied, sounding sane as ever.

"I want to talk to that Tessa lady. What time is it in Italy right now?" grunted Rick, as he sat to pull on a pair of socks.

"I think they are nine hours ahead so—maybe four or five. She is probably working. But we can try."

Amanda went to her study to retrieve the number; she had it on a small note pad already. Dialing it, she handed the phone to Rick.

"Hello, is this Tessa? Yeah, this is Amanda's husband, she said she talked to you yesterday? You did; well what is all this about Mara being in Italy? Yes—"

Amanda wished she had put it on speaker phone. "What is she saying?" She whispered. Rick held up his hand. "Yeah, who is this? Clay? I don't know a Clay. Amanda do you?" Amanda grabbed the phone from Rick.

"Clay, is it really you?"

"It is. How did you get this number?" Clay sounded as smooth as ever. Amanda recalled his sleek wiry form as he held baby Mara in his arms. She always calmed at his touch.

"Mara called me; it's on my phone bill," Amanda answered. "Why do you have Mara in Italy? Tessa said Morris is your brother. How come you never said anything about that? Why didn't you come to the memorial?" Amanda wanted to rail further, but she choked on her tears.

Clay used the same calm, soothing tone she remembered. "Amanda, peace. Please, take a breath. I promised to watch over Mara; do you recall?" He paused, but she barely verbalized a response. "I *am* Morris' brother, his true name is Morvayne. He stole Mara last Saturday. My brother does not know that I am here to watch over her, he believes I am here to help him overthrow Humanity. Amanda, we went away because you sent us. We could not even come into your presence had we wanted to, Brentwood forbade it and made it law."

"Then how come you can be with her now?" Amanda asked, puzzled at what he said.

"Brentwood only forbid us from you, not Mara. We have been with her every single day of her life. As soon as she leaves her residence, we follow discreetly, guarding and protecting as the need may arise. Daisy and Jasmine are here with me, and out on the shore, Ivan, Hannah and Elwood wait for an opportunity to do more than look as they fly by."

Rick had been listening on the other phone. He broke in by asking, "Then how come she got captured in the first place? And if you really have Mara, why don't you just leave with her?"

"Rick, it is complicated and leaving is not that easy. The perimeter is guarded and the barriers are impassable. We are preparing a tunnel escape, but it will take a few more days before we can attempt it. There will be loss of life and it will be difficult for us to proceed. We are seeking alternatives, but so far none have presented themselves."

"Look, why don't you just call the policia or whatever they call them? Sheesh! Man! You have a phone!"

Amanda broke in, "If they call the police, Morvayne will just take Mara elsewhere. Then we would not know where to look. Clay, I want to help, she's *my* daughter! Maybe it's my fault, because I didn't protect her from the right things. I thought Brentwood was wrong." Amanda sobbed as she whispered, "Please, forgive me. Can someone come and get me?"

Clay paused, then he said, "I am not sure we can come in your presence; Brentwood made the command and he has not rescinded it."

"But his command would be voided with his death!" Amanda argued. "Surely you can do it now, if I desire it. Can't you?"

Clay's voice lowered. "Amanda . . . "

"No, don't say it!" Amanda hung up her phone leaving Rick on the other line with Clay.

Rick ventured the question, "Are you saying Brentwood lives? Where the heck is he then? I can't believe he would abandon his family like that; to hear Amanda tell it he's the greatest thing since sliced bread!"

"My brother staged his accident and has him held prisoner somewhere; his uncle was eaten by the denizens of the deep. Sorry, you did not need that information. Amanda must need your attention, I need to get back to Mara. Tell Amanda I will consider options for her help, and we have missed her."

Rick hung up and returned to his bedroom. Amanda lay curled up in a ball on the floor. Scooping her up, Rick held her until she stopped shaking. Unfortunately, Becky peeked in and ran away. Rick was helpless and felt like crying himself.

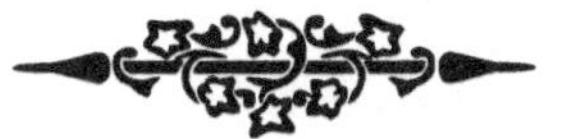

14
Sunday, Sunday

Sunday afternoon, Mara felt bad about missing church.

Pastor Mike wouldn't even notice, because Jaera would attend for her. She had hoped that Jaera would take her to a white room in the Void to share Ricky's graduation with her, but Jaera and Aerrvin were busy with something. Besides, Mara barely had an hour to try to contact them, because Morvayne returned and wanted to talk about his grand plans for her. *As if I heard it enough I would accept it.*

Mara sat in the orchard attempting a sketch; her subject was the magnificent olive tree. Her picture looked like a tree, just not the tree in front of her. Clay approached and looked over her shoulder. Making no comment, he sat down and started splitting a blade of grass apart. "So what did Tessa want?" Mara asked thankful for the lack of a critique.

Clay sat and slowly tore another blade apart. Mara looked up. "Clay, what? Tell me," she waited and added, "Please?"

He sighed, "It was your mother. You neglected to recall that she would check her bills to see where the call came from, besides, had she looked she probably has caller ID and would have seen it sooner."

Mara was stunned; she had been careless. "Is she in danger, are my sisters okay? I just wanted to hear her voice!"

Clay continued to sit, so Mara had to reason things out herself. "So she knows I'm not there. Did something happen to Jaera and Aerrvin? Who did she think Jaera was? No, not the right question. She believes again?"

Clay nodded. "I had to tell her."

Mara looked stricken, "No, you told her about Daddy? Oh, Clay, why?" She held her head in her hands. "Tell me everything."

Clay recounted the entire conversation, while Mara sat trying to absorb her mother's pain. "I don't know if she is strong enough to handle this much heartache at once," Mara finally said.

"She might surprise you," Clay replied, picking up her drawing; he sketched a miniature copy of the tree next to hers with precision.

***

Morvayne sat in his study daydreaming. *Everything is set in place; all I need is for the Water Sprites to tell me they are ready. Soon they will deliver the message to the Mermaid Academy. They will discover the bodies in stasis and will charge the poor little Mermaids with complicity, working with the Trolls to steal the Crystal Throne away from the Elves. He smiled as he pictured the pretty Mermaid claiming her innocence. Poor pretty Mina, she does not even suspect me.* He thought about playing it all out again in his Dream, but instead postponed it to have dinner with his beloved guests.

***

Dinner included Morvayne's preferred assortment of guests; he missed his usual frivolity. Tonight he wanted to celebrate his upcoming coup. Mara looked adorable dressed as an 1880s courtier. She appeared to have had lessons dancing the minuet, as she performed it flawlessly.

Getting his turn on the floor with her Morvayne said, "Mara, my dear, I do believe you are growing up; your grace is beginning to show." He offered his perfect smile and ignored her stiffened jaw. "It would surely be a pity for you to miss your graduation, after all the years you put in. Would you like to attend?" Morvayne asked as though offering a prize for good behavior.

"Of course, I would," Mara said guardedly, suppressing hope.

"Very well then, we shall move to my place on Vashon Island tomorrow and visit campus bright and early." Morvayne smiled as the dance neared its end. "You are troubled still. What is it, my pet?"

"What is the point of moving when we could Travel from here just as easily?" Mara said, as she tried to moderate her emotions to appear casual.

"No point, really, I just like to change locations often. Besides, I get bored with not having enough to do. Getting caught up in the big city life energizes me. Surely you love Seattle too?" Morvayne replied.

"I do. I could not wait to grow up and leave Sequim. But this warm beach life has grown on me. Thank you for showing me another side to life." Mara hoped she was not going overboard, but she had nothing to fear; Morvayne had been aptly named.

The music ended and Clay cut in for the next dance, a classic waltz. "Mara, I have hardly seen you all night, may I?" He looked at both Mara and Morvayne.

Morvayne relinquished his hold and kissed her hand seconds after she sheathed it. "Tomorrow, then."

Clay fluidly guided Mara about the floor, easily gliding between the other light-footed Fair Ones in attendance. Morvayne's kiss reminded Clay that he had not yet told Mara what he had learned about kissing the Dragon skin that Mara wore. Apologizing, he told her the bad news.

"No wonder it gives him so much joy," Mara said glumly. "I love this shed; it is from Meriel's daughter. It's just not fair!" She pounded Clays chest, wishing it was Aerrvin's. "Did you know he was moving us to Vashon?" Mara asked abruptly changing subjects.

"He told me just before dinner," Clay conceded.

"Now what will we do?" Mara whispered, drawing Clay's head closer to hear above the mini orchestra.

Breathing deeply before answering, he said, "We will play the game as it is set before us."

Clay had indeed lived three lifetimes with Mara in the Land of Dreams. But it had been years since he had even thought about those lives. He had a vague memory of dancing with Mara as he was now when he was introduced to her on her naming day. *No such celebration exists in this existence*, he mused.

For the most part, lives from the Land of Dreams fade over time, just like true dreams. Only now that he was at the crucial juncture, where different choices were to be made, did he begin to recall with pain and joy those precious lives, once again. In all three, she was so malleable in his hands; whatsoever it was he desired, she trusted and complied. Her death was his fault he now recalled. Steeling himself, he shied away from that memory. *We can learn from our alternate paths. What has Morvayne learned though, that is the question?*

Mara did not want to stay up any longer than was required, so Clay and Jasmine escorted her to her rooms shortly after 10 o'clock. "Thank you. I am going to see if I can find Aerrvin or Jaera. I'll see you in the morning." Mara hugged them and shut her bedroom door.

Jasmine sat on the couch pulling Clay with her. "Clay, I have begun to recall some past lives that I have lived with Mara. Are you experiencing the same?"

Clay inclined his head once. Then he looked up with pain in his eyes, Jasmine was a true friend in every life he had ever experienced. Seeing his sorrow, she took him into her arms to offer comfort, not knowing if his memories were the same, yet she knew hers were not all pleasant, nor anything near what Mara now desired. Aerrvin was in none of the old memories.

"Clay what are you going to do?" Jasmine asked after some time. Clay had stretched out with his head resting on Jasmines lap while she soothed his head, twining intricate weaves in his hair.

Clay sighed and tried to take a cleansing breath, which got cut short by an errant thought constricting his chest. "I know now where Gwennara is being kept. But the battle might be harsh." Clay did not wish to mention more, so Jasmine had to force it out into the open.

" . . . and, Arianna? Clay what will you do? I need to know; my visits to the Void do not end so well and it appears yours do not either."

"In one life path, my desire for Arianna led to Mara's capture and imprisonment by Morvayne, eventually leading to the death and slaughter of millions. I taught Mara to trust me and told her that the world did indeed need to be brought into submission." Clay paused to gain control. "I told her she could trust Morvayne and listen to his advice; she listened and lived a long and cruel life. Morvayne gave me Arianna, but I had to keep her hidden from the world. It was a sick life. Her joy was never full, so she eventually Faded, leaving me bereft and utterly alone. I offered to battle against a Troll army and died."

Jasmine wiped a tear from her cheek. "Oh, Clay, I am so sorry. I did not live that one. But I did live one where you nevertheless traded Mara for Arianna. Mara chose death, saving Humanity from her vast power.

"Arianna eventually found the Crystal Throne, but it took centuries, because both Gwennara and Brand had died in the Great Battle, as it came to be known. The battle was so great, that Morvayne's desire was partially met anyway. Humans recognized our existence once again, and many, many died. We did not need to hide, but neither did we become worshiped as heroes or gods. The Humans continued with their destruction of the planet and increased their numbers further—if that can be comprehended. I lived exceedingly long. Long enough to see them send out spacecraft with colonists seeking a new frontier. Sometimes, I think we should never have visited the Land of Dreams."

"It is harsh," Clay agreed. "Morvayne is preparing to offer Arianna to me; tomorrow we go to his home on Vashon Island, which is where he made the offer in the otherwhen. Jasmine, I have not made up my mind, even now with those memories returning. Maybe I can change the outcome . . . " He paused considering what to tell.

"In one of my lives, I captured Mara's heart before Morvayne could. We married and lived a long and joyful life. We even had three children, all of them very Bright." He smiled at the returning memory. "Right now I could sway Mara to leave Aerrvin; over time she would see it was the right thing to do. She loved me so deeply!" Clay looked up into Jasmine's eyes seeking judgment, but found only compassion.

With a soft down-turned smile she said, "Clay, did you never live a Dream where I became your wife?"

Generally, speaking about adventures in the Land of Dreams is taboo. This sharing of past/concurrent lives was a very intimate thing to be doing. Jasmine's hazel eyes changed in a blink to shining merrily, as she brought her head down to kiss him.

"Maybe I will have to locate one or two." He smiled, shutting his eyes to concentrate on the feel of her fingertips pulling on his hair.

Morvayne walked in, not knocking, of course. "A pleasant evening I presume?" Sitting down in the recliner, he waited for a response.

Clay remained as he was, allowing Jasmine to caress his brow. Sighing, he replied, "Nothing of consequence to report, if that is the intent of your question. Mara has retired and we while away the time. Her education is sufficient; the rest needs to wait until after her Oath Taking Ceremony." He opened his eyes to glance at Morvayne. "Your guests have left?"

"Not all. Breeze is spending the evening in the garden with a few lingering guests and Kiera cuddles nicely, as Fairies are wont to do." Morvayne smiled casually. "I will just check in on Mara and be on my way."

***

Mara had changed quickly, taking down her hair and then giving up when she could not comb through it all. Tessa had used a good amount of hairspray. Plopping into her bed as she thought about Aerrvin, she marveled at how quickly she could now transfer herself into her Dream. Aerrvin waited at her window.

"Come in, where have you been?" Mara asked briskly.

"I have been at Ironwood Estates; bad news, Gareth and Ironwood and their company have been trapped in a lock-down of the Mermaid Academy off the coast of Greece. It appears that the school will be charged with the kidnapping of Gwennara. They do not think that their presence inside the school is known by the enemy. They were inside already when the quarantine order was issued." Aerrvin stood straight and confidant, but Mara doubted he felt that tough. She hugged him in order to be hugged in return.

"Did they send any instructions on what we should do?"

"No, it appears we have arrived at a spot where we have to fly facing the wind." Aerrvin said

"What's that supposed to mean?" Mara questioned, wrinkling one eye as though thinking was very hard.

Aerrvin laughed, "Sorry, you are too cute. It means instead of letting the breeze take us where it will, we will fight against it. It will be tough, but it is necessary. Yet we are still subject to the wind and must go to where it is strongest in order to turn it away."

"Oh. Well, I tried to visit Jaera's Dream. Where is she?" Mara asked.

"She is visiting your mother's Dream. Your mother has suddenly awakened herself and is very angry and hurt and afraid. I think she was able to detect that Jaera was not you." Aerrvin chucked her under her chin. Also, she could see my glow, so I had to keep it tight. Your sisters glow softly and she can surely see that. I think realizing that you were in Italy sent her over the edge."

"Maybe I should go and see her now. I didn't do it before because, well, she was anti-magic talk. But since she has had to face reality so harshly—oh, did anyone tell you that my mother learned about my fathers existence?" Mara asked.

"No. I did not have time to talk much since I needed to pull the battalions together to prepare for this entanglement. I have been trying to decide how many we will need to leave for your tunnel escape."

Mara's voice keened, "Oh, Aerrvin! Morvayne is taking me to Vashon tomorrow. I don't know how long it will be. I tried to tell him how fond I have grown to the beach, but he says he likes change." Aerrvin held Mara as she sobbed, stunned that his plans were being ruined further.

"Why?" he questioned the universe. Aerrvin sighed. "Very well, let's go visit your mother."

Mara stopped him as he was about to step out to the Void, "Wait it must be afternoon there, isn't she awake?"

"No, Rick is keeping her on her sleeping pills while he decides what to do with her," Aerrvin replied.

Entering her mother's Dream was weird, like going back in time. It was the house Mara had been born and raised in, until her father's tragic 'accident'. Amanda was sitting at the kitchen table talking to Jaera as they ate apple pie.

"Mara! What are you doing here?" Amanda asked with a smile. Without waiting for a reply she said, "Mara, this is my friend Jae, Jae this is my daughter Mara. She has been off to college and should be in class right now." She turned a disapproving glance at Mara and then noticed Aerrvin. "And Aerrvin you should be at work. Brentwood needs his assistants helping him, not moping around his daughter."

Aerrvin grinned mischievously and replied cockily, "But she's so cute!"

Mara no longer felt weird, she was alarmed. She started to open her mouth and Aerrvin pulled on her hand while Jaera shook her head slightly. Mara slumped into a chair. "I don't feel good; could I have some chocolate milk?"

Amanda fussed over Mara as she always had, talking about nothing important. *Dang it! She's my own Mom!* Mara thought. *I can ask her whatever I want.*

"Mom, what is Dad working on?"

Amanda looked Mara over and then said, "I can't talk about it in front of our guests, dear; maybe later."

Jaera ate her pie quickly and stood to go. "So good to meet you Mara. Amanda, I will be back, okay?"

"Sure, come on over anytime," Amanda sang out as Jaera left.

"Come on over and sit down, Aerrvin, you know what Brentwood is up to as well as I do." Amanda motioned for him to take Jaera's abandoned seat. "Mara, what I am about to tell you is sensitive information. Your father wanted you to know, but I wanted you to have a normal upbringing like mine." Amanda paused, looking at her teacup.

"What, Mom? I won't be shocked. You can tell me; we talk about everything, remember?"

"This is harder than I thought, but I think it is the right thing to do. Mara, do you remember the book Dad used to read to you as a little girl?"

Mara nodded, smiling to encourage her mother. "Yes, it should still be sitting on the shelf in his study. Do you want me to go get it?"

"Yes, that would be a wonderful idea." She turned to Aerrvin as Mara left the room. "Am I doing the right thing?"

Aerrvin reached over and patted her hand. "I think you are." Mara returned and casually opened the book to the picture of Tigerlily and her sisters. "Here it is. I have loved this picture ever since I was a little girl."

"Yes, well, do you notice anything peculiar about the princesses now that you are grown?"

"Yes, Mom, now that you mention it. She pointed to the stunning Tigerlily with her smooth black hair. She looks just like me, or rather, I look just like her. Doesn't Dad have an ancestor with this same name?" Mara pointed to the name beneath the drawing.

"My goodness, Mara, you are taking this so well," Amanda said with relief.

"Taking what so well?" Mara pushed.

"This Tigerlily is your Aunt Lily now, and these are not silly tales, but a family history." Amanda squeezed her eyes shut. "I never thought I would tell you such a thing, and I don't know why I want you to know now. But I feel it is important. Are you shocked or frightened, Mara?" Amanda's hand began to shake.

"No, Mom. It sounds right." Mara stood and pulled her mother into an embrace. "It sounds like truth. Thank you for telling me." Mara felt like weeping, but she didn't know if it was for happiness, sorrow, or fear.

Amanda recovered with a quick cleansing breath. "Now, Aerrvin and Dougie have been working with your Dad on his search for Mermaids willing to talk about the Lost City of Atlantis."

"I thought that Morvayne, I mean Morris, was Dad's coworker on this project, wasn't he?

"Yes, well he is, but I don't like him,. Let's not discuss this any further." Amanda rubbed her forehead.

"Sorry, Mom, that's okay. Do you want to take a nap? I can fix dinner."

"Yes, that would be nice. The girls should be home from school soon. Maybe a quick nap before they get here, that would do me some good."

Mara blinked in surprise, as Amanda left to lie down on her bed. Mara walked about the house looking at photos. There were the familiar ones from her childhood, but the ones of Rick and the girls going fishing and such now included Brentwood, her father instead. "No, this is still not right, how do we get her to move to Sequim?"

"We don't, at least not today. She revealed a large portion of truth to you, let her get used to that. Maybe in a day or two you can try introducing Morris again. She is going to have to go through that horrible day of loss once more, but for now let her rest." Aerrvin took Mara by the hand and Traveled to the Fourth Level with her.

"Clay said it was unsafe for me to be here," Mara said, unsure of what the dangers were, she looked about warily.

"It is unsafe for you to come here alone, but I am experienced and can keep you safe. Come, I wanted to share my weekend with you. Jaera should be along soon." Aerrvin guided Mara through the Eastern hallway as he searched for an empty room.

Just after they shut the door, Jaera caught up with them and knocked to be let in. They experienced Aerrvin's version first, including his visit to Ironwood Estates. Then they experienced Jaera's version. Mara was amazed that Jaera got away with telling the girls a fairytale; surely her mother knew that story by heart, she had sat in often as a tiny girl when her father had told her that story.

"I guess Becky and Sarah *are* glowing Brighter, at least seen through your eyes. I did not really notice anything about them when they were at my house before," Mara said.

"No, but you would notice it now yourself. Your eyes are opened completely and since they came into contact with all of our Fairy Dust, it activated their—hormonal response system, I guess I could say, for lack of a better description. In other words, they are now capable of Glowing. Water Sprites do not sparkle like Fairies and Elves, but they still respond to the pheromones in the Dust. Just because your Mother is very weak does not mean her offspring will be. Her true mother was very careless in sending her away to live among Humans. In reality, they cannot hurt anything unless they receive training; they will simply Glow, but will not be able to cause strong 'magical' things to occur.

They will be noticed, though, by all of us in the real world. But they would most likely be left alone." Jaera taught.

"Why do you say *most likely*?" Mara asked, panic rising at the new threat.

"No one has need to bother non-believers, but since they are related to you that makes them a potential hostage to make you agree to do whatever it is Morvayne or his minions want from you."

Someone pinged at the door.

"What is it?" Mara asked in alarm by Aerrvin's reaction.

"It could be Morvayne, he can't enter. But he may have found your body in stasis." Aerrvin said.

***

Morvayne found Mara in stasis. "Clay get in here! What is she doing? Did you teach her to go to the Land of Dreams?"

Clay was truly distraught, "No! Oh, Mara what have you done? No, Morvayne I did not teach her anything about the Land of Dreams, except to tell her that it was dangerous and that she was not to go there without a teacher."

"So you are not so perfect after all," Morvayne sneered at Clay. "She obviously found a teacher willing to take her, probably that puny prince!" He spat in rage.

"Morvayne, she is curious," Clay said, regaining his calm demeanor. "Tell her about something and she wants to try it. This can work to our advantage. Calm yourself. I am sure she will return at dawn. Just think of the things she can be influenced to do in her innocence, believing that it is for the good of all her Realms. She really does intend to reign in justice; it all depends on how she interprets justice." Clay smiled slyly, hoping to shift

Morvayne's attention to his Dreams, rather than the reality before him.

"I will go and find her and will make sure she returns safely. Go relax; you have company. I have much to gain, as you well know. Trust me, I will continue as Mara's protector until she sends me away. She is safe, I can tell. I have a connection as you surely are aware." Clay eased Morvayne out of the room.

Morvayne responded, "Yes, well you probably know that I have gained a slight connection as well, to her shed. As long as she believes that it keeps her safe, I will be able to locate her anywhere at all. Very well, Clay, you have rarely been wrong. I can afford to wait for her to return. But she will need to be blocked from doing this again, or I shall have to find her another protector, one who will not make a simple mistake with one so valuable."

"You are right. I will ensure that she is not left alone to visit the Void like this again." Clay went and sat on the end of the bed.

Jasmine sat beside Mara. "Good night, Morvayne; we will attend to her. Never fear, all will be as you wish come dawn."

Morvayne left, slamming the door as he did so. Jasmine wondered, "Why would she do this? Aerrvin took her there, yes?"

Clay smiled ironically, "Now that is a nonsensical question, if Aerrvin wanted to take you there, wouldn't you go?"

Jasmine smiled and agreed, "Yes, I suppose I would. You did tell her not to go again, right?

Clay worked his jaw. "Yes, she is becoming quite willful. Not the same sweet little girl we knew and loved. It is the Royal blood asserting itself. Morvayne is going to have his hands full if he gets his way." Jasmine looked seriously at Clay. "Is he?"

Clay understood and shrugged. Then he lay down next to

Jasmine as she scooted Mara over to make room for three. Clay entered the Void. He found the room they were in. They were surely alerted by Morvayne pinging their door and now he and Jasmine had done it again by moving her body.

Mara had three options. She could stay in the room for twenty years; at that point the door would open and the occupants would be required to leave. Mara could open the door and hope no enemy awaited outside; or if Aerrvin chose to take her, she could take the leap to the true Land of Eternal Spring and live countless adventures. But there was a fourth option completely unthinkable, which was why Clay did not count it as an option. Mara and whoever was with her could choose which one path they wanted to be judged by; and by so doing they would cease to exist in this life and would go and live that single life. Just like the photons, Clay recalled trying to teach Mara about, once the path choice was thought, the photon no longer took both paths. *Mara!* Clay thought helplessly.

Mara felt like she could feel Clay seeking her. "I think we should open the door. I am not ready to go to the Land of Eternal Spring, or to look at alternate lives yet. It sounds like it should be interesting living my life over in different ways, although some of them might be far too tragic. Maybe I won't sample too frequently,' she rambled. "Anyways, we might as well go. I do want to go to my graduation, at least, before I die my horrible death. Are you coming?" Mara had her hand on the door handle as she looked back at Aerrvin.

"Wait, let me go through first." Aerrvin said, echoed by Jaera.

"Wait, one more thing." Aerrvin bulked up to seven feet tall and had huge muscles like a comic book character. He asked Mara to shrink down and told her to sit in Jaera's satchel, which she had slung across her chest. Taking his sword out, he nodded and Jaera opened the door.

Clay stood there looking relieved and then puzzled. "Where is she?"

"All's clear, you can come out, Mara. 'Tis only Clay," Jaera called softly.

As soon as she was full-sized, Clay seized her by the shoulders and chastened her. "Morvayne came in and found your body! I told you to never come here again."

"You implied, and I responded evasively," Mara corrected. "But you are right, it was foolish. Do not blame them. They were sharing with me my brother's graduation. I wanted to experience it."

Clay glared at them. "I will blame them; they know better. Unfortunately, now Mara has to have tighter controls placed upon her. She will not be able to return to her Dream. Mara you will have to come to mine. Morvayne expects me to keep you safe and free from distraction until his plans are achieved. We will have to play along until another opportunity makes itself plain.

"Aerrvin, please tell Seamus he can return to Sylvie for a while, unless of course you have need of him. Sylvie is a nervous wreck by now I am sure."

Mara hugged Jaera and then kissed Aerrvin and clung to him, he smelled so fresh and clean. "Can you mail me a package of your Dust?" She smiled.

"I can shower the yard with it," he replied smiling at the request.

They walked to the intersection and each made their own line of Light back to wakefulness. Mara woke to find her two friends lying beside her. "A little tight isn't it?"

Clay sat up and said, "It was tight alright. Don't make decisions like that on your own again. Consult one of us first. Have you even visited Hannah, Daisy or any of the other's in their Dreams?"

"Not mine," Jasmine pouted.

Mara looked down and replied, "Fine, I will visit my Protector's Dreams and I will consult one of you before making any major decision. As long as it does not include clothes!"

15
Vashon

Morvayne entered just as the sun broke forth its first golden ray. "Good, all is in order. Mara you gave me quite a scare. I see you look somewhat chastened. I shall overlook your disobedience this once. But surely, you are now aware of the dangers? Yes?"

Mara nodded meekly. Morvayne instructed that they would be leaving in one hour. Precisely one hour later, they left in Aerrvin's car. All the Fairies were in the trunk and Mara's two attendants along with Breeze were minimized as well. They hovered near Mara's shoulders, causing her to think about what it would be like to have them always hovering near her like that or sitting on her shoulder like Seamus sat on Aerrvin's.

"I don't like the hovering," she said at last. "Please, sit on my knees or something."

In a blink they were at Morvayne's Washington property. So it really hadn't mattered. Morvayne released the Fairies and gave them quiet instructions, then he came around to the passengers' side, allowing Mara to get out.

"Smells like Washington!" Morvayne said, breathing deeply. Clay and the other two Elves resumed their normal forms.

Morvayne acted as though Mara truly were a guest being invited to stay as he went about showing her the house. A wall-sized salt water aquarium took up one side of the living room. It was stunning with pure white sand and sparkling stones littering the aquarium floor. The beautifully back-lit water theater showcased the tropical fish in bright blues, yellows, and oranges as they darted here and there.

"Lovely," Mara commented truthfully.

Her bedroom was done up very much like the other house, with lots of white and purple. Though it was more richly hued with four different shades of purple, starting with a medium plum carpet and getting darker from there with the drapes and bed spread complementing each other. The bed had dark flowers on a paler purple, the curtains were just the opposite. Mara peeked into the closet and was pleased to see ordinary clothes.

The room belonged to a suite which had a sitting room in front of it, as well as another bedroom sharing the same sitting area, much like the rooms in the O'Shea Mansion. Breeze was given the other room.

"I apologize for the inconvenience you will experience in sharing a bathroom, but I am sure you will work things out between yourselves. Remain here while I show Clay and Jasmine their rooms."

Morvayne shut the door softly. As he left they strained to hear if he was locking them in, but it appeared he had not. They dared not go check.

"Well," said Breeze airily, "Might as well make ourselves at home." She glided to the overstuffed white sofa and sat down, holding the bright red pillow in her hands. Mara joined her, bored already.

"Mara, when you find yourself in quiet moments, it is a good time to practice the exploration of minutiae."

"Thank you, Breeze. I will try." Mara picked up the hot

pink pillow and explored its silky smoothness, as well as the cool feel it imparted and then reveled as it warmed up beneath her hand. She felt it with her face, her lips, her bare arms and was about to feel it with her feet when Clay returned, inviting them to come downstairs.

"How long were we sitting there?" Mara asked, just as she realized it was two hours and twelve minutes.

"Two hours." Clay replied. "Morvayne can be quite detailed when he wants to speak about his goals and plans."

Morvayne waited in his library. One wall of the aquarium was visible from that room as well. Mara sat so that she could watch the fish.

"Mara, I have something I need you to see," Morvayne said.

Inviting Mara forward, he opened a large box. Within it sat a six-inch Fairy. He stirred as the lid came off.

Mara was incensed. "What is the meaning of this? Why is George trapped in a box? What did he ever do to you?"

Morvayne replaced the lid. "I wanted to see if you knew him; he has been trailing us every time we left the property, and I did not know if he meant to cause you harm."

"Well, of course, he means no harm. Let him out now!" Mara demanded.

"What will you do for me?" Morvayne asked.

"Why should I have to do anything for you? What have you done for me that I could not have gotten elsewhere? Forget it. George lived a good life. All he wanted was to return to his mother and pursue a Dream. Why don't you just let him out, so he can ask me whatever it is he wants to ask? Obviously, he has something he wanted to say, or he would not have been trailing me." Mara was angry and completely unaware of having lost control of her two pockets of Light.

Those in the room were humbled, but still looked at her through their lowered lashes. Morvayne's smile grew. "Mara, I simply I wanted to see your reaction that is all. It was a mere test. Come along then, release him yourself."

Mara lifted the lid, simultaneously pocketing her light. "George, oh, George! I am so sorry. Please, come here. What did you want?"

"Mara, I wanted to thank you. But then this feller had some of his Orange flunkies bind me up and they put me in this box. Not any way to treat an old man, I say."

"No, it's not." Mara said emphatically. Glaring at Morvayne and Clay too, since he smiled as well.

"George, maximize yourself. I want to see you better." George complied and Mara was pleased to see he was looking much healthier, even younger, perhaps a vigorous sixty years old.

"Oh, George!" Mara hugged him. "You look wonderful. Have you returned to see your family yet?"

"Yes, I saw them briefly, but I wanted to thank you. So I returned and found that your house was warded, and then you went to Italy and you were warded on your person when you were not in the warded palazzo. Mara, what's up with all the wards?"

Mara nodded towards Morvayne. George addressed him. "May I inquire, sir, why you like locking Fair Ones up so much?"

Morvayne feigned innocence, "I do not enjoy it one bit, Mara is my utmost concern. I am doing my best to keep her safe. Why else would I capture a Fairy trailing her? You do know she is the Future Queen, correct?"

"Yes, I did learn of that. My lady, I feel honored to have

known you as a simple Human. I look forward to your Reign of Justice and Virtue." George bowed as regally as any Mara had ever seen, delighting her completely.

Mara turned to Morvayne. "Will you please let George go? He has nothing to do with anything."

"Mara, if I do, you must agree to do something for me in return." Morvayne would not budge.

"What?" Mara asked in exasperation.

"As you know, I loved Tigerlily more than anything. She had a ring which I gave her, perhaps you saw it? It was large and almost gaudy. Ah, I see recognition on your face. Fetch me your ring and I shall free George."

"Oh, George," Mara said. "I am so sorry. I cannot retrieve that ring."

George shrugged.

Morvayne spluttered, finally saying, "You would not get me a ring that was mine in order to save your friend? What kind of a woman are you? Have you no compassion?"

Mara spilled tears both of anger and sorrow. "I cannot retrieve that ring, it has been given to another."

"You gave my ring to that snotty little Purple? How—" Morvayne started, but stopped as Clay put a calming hand on him.

"Morvayne, she speaks the truth."

Morvayne stated quietly, but distinctly, "Who has my ring?"

"I gave it as a gift to the Dragon who gave me this shed." Mara replied.

"Impossible, Ironwood gave you that shed! Tell me the

truth! You would not even know how to find a Dragon's lair. Unless you had help. Did you?"

"Yes, of course, I had help. I met an Elf named Hannah; she had armor and I wanted one too. She probably didn't think I could get one, but she brought me to Meriel's cave. And I was very charming and here we are; Meriel has the ring and I have the shed," Mara concluded, now grateful Meriel had the ring.

She still did not know what it could do, but obviously it was powerful.

"Clay, you said you kept in contact with Hannah, go find out if this is true."

"I can feel her truth Morvayne, she is not lying." Clay replied.

"Then just go get her! I want to ask her myself!" Morvayne yelled, losing his composure. Mara had not seen his Fairy Dust before; it was sparkly, but had an unpleasant after scent.

Breeze tried to soothe him, "Morvayne, come sit by me while we wait." She stroked his hand and moved to his neck easing his tense muscles as he sat hunched forward on the couch.

"I don't understand why you would have chosen that ring to give away. Surely, Tigerlily has boxes of jewels fit for a Dragon?"

Mara feigned regret, "I am sorry, Morvayne. You know Mother did not allow me to hear anything about magic. Lily told me nothing. I thought it was something a Dragon would like; I did not think I needed it, so I gave it away; it's as simple as that."

Morvayne shook his head. "Mara, Mara, you are such an innocent youngling. You should not be let out on your own for one hundred years or more. That ring has magical properties which enables the wearer to—"

Clay stepped into the room with Hannah. Dressed in her traditional garb of armor, and her thistle-like skirt. Carrying her bow and quiver full of arrows, Hannah greeted the room briskly. "Hey, it's been so long. How's everyone doing?" She offered a hug to Jasmine and Breeze and ended with Morvayne. "Clay said you had a question for me? I see this Mara girl, is here, so it must have something to do with her armor?"

Morvayne returned her hug and then answered her. "Yes, it has been a long time. What interest do you have in Mara, and where did you meet her?"

"I met up with her on her college campus a few days back. I have been taking classes just for something to do. One never knows whom one might meet. Mara was pretty persuasive. I see she has her Light under control now, but when I met her, she was flashing and blinding Fair Ones left and right. Not to mention drawing ever increasing numbers of suitors. I took pity, as well as being influenced, and wanted to see what she could do. I can attest, she is one powerful maiden, and Meriel rather likes her."

"I see. So, Mara, you are telling the truth. Forgive my doubting nature. Hannah, did you know she was going to give Meriel the Ring of Truth? Why did you not stop her?" Morvayne asked still frustrated at the loss.

"Morvayne, surely you know I would not go before Meriel so soon without a summons. My armor is not that old. No, I did not accompany Mara, and she did not discuss gifts with me. Like I said, I was interested in learning how persuasive she could be."

"Yes, it could be a fun game sending younglings into a Dragon's lair," Morvayne conceded. "Yet you should be aware who it is you are sending. Do you know who Mara is?"

Hannah smiled and shrugged dismissively. "I do now, and she was successful. What is the problem?"

Morvayne raised his voice. "The problem is that I want my

ring back!" Then hoarsely he asked, "How can I get it now?"

"I love puzzles as you well know. I can sit and think of a solution if you would like, or I can visit the Land of Dreams and search. What would you like Morvayne? I feel I owe you something," Hannah replied sweetly.

"Very well do one or both, just try to be quick. I really wanted it today as I have some important decisions to make, and it would have been helpful. My house is too crowded, so return to your own Hold or wherever you hale from. Knock at the door when you have some insights or suggestions." Morvayne sighed as he struggled to recapture his suave exterior, "It is a pleasure to see you again, Hannah, and I welcome your friendship. It was a sorry break up, and now I would like to bring all my friends together again in these perilous times. We should have dinner sometime."

Morvayne waited for Hannah to depart and then gave Mara the box containing George. "You may keep him in your room, but he may not leave the premises. He can pursue his Dreams from the box as well as the woods; no harm done."

Mara received the box and took George to her room immediately. "George, I am truly sorry you got captured. But you may create your own environment here in this corner." Mara placed the box in the corner beyond the sofa in the front room. George instantly transformed the space beneath the end table into a miniature forest floor with a few ferns and he filled the box with feathers, having sunk it into the floor so that the feathers were level with the carpet.

With a tiny, "whoopee!" George jumped into the pile and cozied up with a soft scrap of fabric. "Thanks, Mara! Tap on my door if you need me."

***

Morvayne assured himself that Mara was situated in her

rooms with Breeze, and then invited Clay into his study. "Clay, I have reached a point where I must reveal my soul to you. As you are well aware I need the Throne of Desire, my Ring of Truth and to be wed to She who sits upon the Crystal Throne in order to achieve my ultimate goal of cleansing the earth."

Morvayne revealed nothing new to Clay, sitting casually in the fine leather chair he responded, "Yes, this is known."

"If Mara were to meet with misfortune the Throne would fall to Breeze," Morvayne said, looking to Clay for a response. Clay merely nodded waiting. "Unless another preeminent heir were found."

Clay asked calmly, "And who would this heir be?"

Morvayne opened a window showing Clay a still form, a form in stasis.

"Truly? This is my Arianna? Where is she? Why have you kept this from me?" Clay allowed his emotions to run free. Morvayne's presentation did not make sense though. "Wait, you want Arianna to assume the Throne? You never loved her. You cannot marry her!"

Morvayne smiled oily, gaining the response he desired. *Yes, Clay still pines for Arianna.* "Clay, you misunderstand. I truly do desire Mara. She is more powerful than Tigerlily ever was, and looks nearly the same. No one could ever replace my Tigerlily, and I know you feel the same about Arianna. I do wish you to break down Mara's resistance against consorting with Elves, rather than fawning over that silly Purple Fairy. But I feared your feelings for her might get too involved, unless you knew of Arianna's existence. When Mara becomes mine, Arianna can be yours. She is still as stubborn as ever and refuses to say more than a few words to me. I want her to tell me where the Crystal Throne is hidden.

"Therefore, I will grant you access to Arianna for one

hour. That is if you swear to do all in your power to convince Mara to turn away from Aerrvin, and accept my way of thinking." Morvayne finished his little speech and observed Clay with raised brows.

***

"I would do anything to be with Arianna. I must warn you, she may continue to reject me as she has all this time. What else do I get for helping you?" Clay had thought through this scenario many times and still had not prepared a reasonable response. While looking at the gateway through which he could view his true love, he tried to perceive the location. Surely Morvayne knew he could always see the latitude, he did not seem concerned with Clay knowing it. Clay felt he almost had the elevation as well, longitude was still a mystery. *There I have it! She is not below sea level, curiously. So she is not with her mother.*

***

Morvayne paused before answering, he had not thought more would have been necessary. He observed Clay: He seemed totally besotted with Arianna, yet he was cautious. *Why did he always have to be so mysterious?!*

"I can make you czar of any realm you choose. Obviously, you would answer to Mara—and me. Once we rid the earth from the scourge of unbelieving mankind it might even be a pleasure to rule over Humans."

"Very well," Clay replied.

"No! You must swear." Morvayne insisted.

His eyes narrowed as he tried to comprehend why Clay would want to weasel out of such a prosperous deal. *Surely he does not mean to have both maidens?* Morvayne himself had planned to have as many as he could convince. *Breeze and Mara are assured, but Arianna will have nothing to do with me. Removing Daffodil had been an education though it remained a mystery as to where she went. Getting rid of Tigerlily's daughter had been sporting and necessary; she simply was not strong enough to produce the desired posterity.* He smiled lightly at the memory. Leaving the others had played out well; Mara was exactly what he had been waiting for.

Perhaps Clay will soften Mara up enough to get invited into her home. Yes, I am willing to wait for that. I shall lighten my control. As long as Clay swears. Clay sat leaning forward as he drank in the vision of Arianna with his eyes.

Morvayne shut the window with a snap, no sound really just a suddenness which Clay was not expecting.

Clay looked at Morvayne and then smiled, "Sorry, I got lost in thought. Yes, I swear to do all in my power to convince Mara that marrying a Fairy is not in her best interest, and I will convince her that mankind's eyes need to be opened to the Truth. Please, tell me: Where is Arianna?"

"Not so quick! I did not say I would reveal her location. You may have one hour with her; I will bring her body to your room. It is up to you to locate her Dreamself in the Void. Her normal Dream is locked tight. Which you may have noticed had you ever searched for her these past few centuries."

With a shrug, Clay went directly to his bedroom. Obviously, there was a catch of some sort. Proving Clay's suspicions correct, Morvayne wove a bubble of confinement sealing Clay and Arianna into the room.

"You understand," Morvayne said, not really asking. "I need your help as much as you need Arianna. I cannot trust her. She will try to escape and surely, you would be tempted to follow. I do trust you, of course, you have never failed me," Morvayne stated, but it seemed a question.

Clay replied as he lightly stroked Arianna's cool form, "No, I have never failed my family."

Morvayne looked at Clay coolly and then departed, shutting the door on Clay. Clay was aware that he had played that poorly, yet he could not waste time worrying.

One hour, one precious hour was all he had. With her body in his arms he reclined against a pile of pillows on his bed; he felt confident that she would invite him in. He slipped into the Void as easily as slipping into a body of water. He knew Arianna's preferred hallway and went directly to her door. He knocked: A coded knock that only she and he had shared.

He waited. He recalled waiting outside that door for a month without a response. She knocked back timidly, but correctly. He responded with the proper sequence and she opened the door.

Rushing in he did not wait to hear what her full-lipped mouth tried to say. Taking her in his arms, he kissed her, and then wept. They stood that way for an hour until he managed to gain composure and found that she too had shed tears.

"Morvayne has given me one hour to spend with you as he tries to blackmail me into trading the future Queen of all the Realms for you."

In a sweet, controlled voice the Princess began, "Tries? Do you mean to say you are not going to do it? He has kept me trapped in a djinni bottle most days. But now he has a new form of enforced stasis. And you cannot rescue me?" Arianna asked with animation, yet without anger.

Clay created a pile of pillows and tumbled down with her, she allowed him to nuzzle her neck. Breathing deeply to take in her scent, he replied. "I have sworn to protect Mara Lilyana ap Jamis all the days of her life, not once but twice. I have sworn to seek you until the ends of the earth do crumble and fall. I love you more than words can say. But how could you respect me if I were to fail in keeping my promises?"

Clay wanted to fall to weeping once more, but could not bear to close his eyes again. Arianna was a vision he never thought to see again in reality, or even in the Land of Dreams, having sworn off visiting those paths years ago. He had lived one perfect life with her, and feared all the rest would end as miserably as the ones he had previously visited. He could not bear repeating the torment of losing her over and over again. She returned his gaze as he soaked in every detail, her dilated eyes indicating her compassion and love.

"I knew you would be honorable one day," she breathed. "This is the one I have waited for all my life."

"This one? You mean this Dream?" Clay asked in shock.

"Yes, I barely visited this Dream once, long ago when I was Dream hopping, barely staying a day here and a day there. In so many you were much like Morvayne; it scared me away from you.

"But this one, I visited this future moment way back before you even crossed the ocean for the New World. I left the Dream before giving or hearing my answer. But I remember the emotions. I loved you for your integrity and hoped to find you here someday."

Arianna let a tear slip and cuddled close, allowing Clay to inhale deeply as she shared her Light with him. She transformed the Dreamscape to a shadowed springtime glen. Clay joined his Light with hers; chasing all shadows from their hidden arbor beneath the close growing foliage on the edge of the open meadow. Clay's meadow. All too soon, a ping sounded at the door. The Dream vanished and they were once again inside the small white room.

"Arianna, show me your favorite Dream," Clay asked with pleading in his eyes. He needed a pleasant Dream to keep him sane once they were parted.

Arianna smiled knowingly. "I did have a good Dream involving you, here let me show you."

Above them the dark velvety expanse of the Void appeared and Arianna pointed out a glowing star-like spark representing the alternate life she had experienced.

Clay noted it and promised to visit it. Then he showed her his favorite Dream, which was different. It was good to know that there were two of life paths with happy outcomes. He knew statistically there were never ending numbers of every scenario, he just had not found them and he preferred real life over Dreams anyway.

The ping sounded again and Clay feared being ripped from Arianna, so he quickly kissed her, leaving her with a promise, "Til the ends of the earth do crumble and fall."

He opened the door and found Morvayne standing in the hallway, craning his neck to catch a glimpse of Arianna. However, she was behind the door and slammed it shut as soon as Clay was out of the way.

"I see she still has her temper," Morvayne said dryly. "Yet, you appear to have enjoyed yourself."

"Aye, that I did." Clay answered truthfully.

Never did he expect to find joy simply in the knowledge that she admired him for his integrity. It would sustain him until this crisis was solved, even if it took the next one hundred years.

Clay smiled a toothy grin at Morvayne. "Thanks Mo, I owe you." He sighed one last cleansing breath, wishing he could breathe in her essence always. Nevertheless, now he was free to do what had to be done.

16
Graduation Day

Mara thrummed with excitement; it was Friday and she was graduating in front of her friends and family. True she was wearing Morvayne's tracing bracelet, but other than that she was free. She had called Jill and Dougie. Having left a message with Rick, Mara did not know if he would share it with her mother or not. He said he would bring her down to talk to Ironwood and Pastor Mike, since she had indicated she was willing to talk to someone, but he did not say when. Mara visited her mother often in her Dreams. Some progress was being made; at least she was less jittery when Mara brought up magic and her father's research. Football, television, living next to the ocean in Sequim were not safe to mention at all.

Even better, Morvayne said he would not be in attendance; he trusted Clay and Jasmine as well as his bracelet. Mara could see her group of friends right up front. They used their winning ways to get seats near Mara's assigned seat. Aerrvin and Jaera came into the hall where she waited to enter the stadium.

"Mara, it's really you!" Aerrvin said into her ear, as he breathed in her sweet scent, and then nibbled at her neck.

How she ever doubted his love and perfection she could never say. His hair hung loose except for the one braid tied up for Seamus to hang on to at need. At the moment, he was in Aerrvin's carpenter jeans side pocket. Which was good. Mara did not want him so close when she snuggled so tightly.

Eventually, she had to let go so she could greet Jaera. "Thanks for everything, guys. You are the best. Where is Gareth?"

Jaera looked down as Aerrvin said, "He's with Ironwood, remember?"

***

Amanda had slept so much she was sick of it. She refused the pills when Rick brought them to her on Wednesday, and had not had any since. He stayed home with her most of the day, and left Ricky with instructions to call if she started to leave the house when he needed to go out. She had of course been instructed not to go anywhere. So she baked cookies with the girls, and watched movies with them. Eventually they ran off to play, so she tidied up the house. It had become quite messy.

Dusting the shelves the next day triggered her willingness to accept psychiatric help. While dusting some of the photos she thought, *That's not Brentwood.* Suddenly a whole storm of memories flooded her, as she recalled dream after dream from the past few days.

Dream Jaera was a big help she realized, but Dream Mara was bigger, if pushier. Amanda went to her old photo albums which held pictures of Mara as an infant and toddler.

"Yes, there is Clay. Just as he looks in my dreams, he *is* real." Amanda could hardly wait for Rick to get home. She even remembered the ceremony where each of Mara's Attendants promised to protect her for life, or until released by Mara. She had found it emotionally touching back then. She now recalled hugging each one, they all became dear friends over the next three years. Then fear struck and she sent them all away. Now she knew; they had never been very far away at all.

Amanda met Rick at the door; clean and dressed with dinner ready as she did any other day before she had 'taken ill' as he called it. They dined and chatted with the kids. Once the kitchen was cleaned and all was in order, Rick thought he would get to watch the game, but Amanda excitedly pulled him to her office.

"Rick, I have some more evidence that I am not crazy!" She smiled at him, not too wild-eyed, yet certainly animated. She showed him the pictures of all of Mara's Attendants. Then she showed him the drawings in *Enchanted Lives*.

"See, these are old family friends. I cannot Dream hop because my Light is dim, but Clay, Mara, Aerrvin, and Jaera have all been visiting me while I was conked out on those pills!" Amanda saw sorrow in Rick's eyes. She calmed her enthusiasm, grateful she was not crazy, yet recognizing Rick's need to accept truth slower, after all it took her eighteen years to re-accept it.

"Look, Rick, I am ready to go and talk to Pastor Mike. Remember I told you he was a psychologist or some such? Also I would like to talk to Ironwood; I think he will be of some help to me now."

Rick swallowed and then nodded. "Okay, we can drive down tonight and you can see him tomorrow. Mara called, and asked if we were going to be attending the graduation."

Amanda looked up sharply, "She did? Was it really Mara? Why didn't you tell me? What did she say?"

Rick reluctantly told her Mara's exact words. He hated feeding into the fantasy, but Amanda did seem to be feeling better and was not planning on running away as soon as his back was turned. And he preferred the idea of her seeking help away from the community. No sense in getting negative publicity.

On Friday morning Amanda walked into Pastor Mike's office. "Amanda, welcome. Yes, please take a seat. You said you had some worries you needed to discuss? Let me remind you; I cannot discuss Mara's visits. So, begin where you will."

She explained her abandonment and adoption. How she never quite felt like she fit in, but yet she became popular—all the boys trailed her about wherever she went. She was a star on the swim team, but she felt like something was missing. So she sought religion. Her parents were Christian, but in the most generic sense, they never set foot in a church building except for weddings or funerals. She told about how intriguing Brentwood was, and his explanations for the mystical things she experienced. Pastor Mike stopped her there.

"What kind of mystical things did you experience? You may not know, but that is part of my specialty; in training and studies. I am always searching for unique stories to write down. Do you mind if I make notes?" he asked.

Amanda smiled in relief. "You mean you might actually believe my experiences?"

Pastor Mike assured her he had a very open mind, and requested that she continue. Amanda told of seeing fluttering out of the corner of her eyes in the late evening or early morning hours, and how she later learned they were Brownies, having met several after marrying Brentwood.

He merely nodded as he wrote, so she told about seeing sparkles falling away from certain people, when she was in high school in particular; it happened quite a bit at parties. And now her ability to see auras had just returned, or rather strengthened.

"Okay, what triggered that, do you suppose?" Pastor Mike asked.

Explaining her uneasiness with Mara at her house last weekend, Amanda admitted that it had never really truly gone away. She realized that her visitor was not Mara when she accepted that Mara had been kidnapped. Amanda told everything she knew about Tessa and the phone calls. Pastor Mike became visibly shaken as though he truly believed her. Amanda didn't know how to feel about that yet, but she continued by telling about her depression and fear, her dreams and ending with her looking through the photo album and Enchanted Lives.

"Yes, Mara showed me the similarities of her own looks and Tigerlily's," he mused. Then he reddened. "Oh, excuse me, I should never have mentioned that."

Amanda smiled; truly happy to know that the Pastor had helped ease Mara into accepting who she was. "So then tell me this: Do you believe Fair Ones have eternal souls?"

Pastor Mike issued a deep belly laughed. Clapping his hands in delight. "Oh, you are Mara's mother, that I can tell you." He wiped moisture from his eye. "As a matter of fact I do, even more so since having talked with all members of Mara's family, I mean Ironwood. He has always been a favorite professor of mine. I read everything he publishes, and some he does not. And I love, love, love when I am free to hear one of his lectures.

"Yes, Amanda, I believe in good magic and salvation for all God's creatures, including beasts, fowls and otherwise."

Amanda wept; another similarity. Pastor Mike pushed the tissues toward her.

"No, Amanda, you are not crazy, and I am worried about Mara. Did you say she would be at her graduation?"

Amanda wiped the tears away. She smiled and replied, "Yes, Morvayne is trying to lull her into believing that he trusts her and cares about her welfare. He very well may. *He* is the one who is crazy. He—he was responsible for the disappearance of Brentwood, as well as other members of Mara's ancestry." Amanda hiccuped. Squeezing her eyes shut she composed herself. "Thank you, Pastor, you have been a great help. Would you be willing to talk with Rick as well, from time to time?"

The Pastor smiled, "Of course, Amanda, you surely need family support in this difficult time. I find it difficult myself, now that I have turned this corner and added a chapter of belief in something greater than humanity. It strengthens my Christian faith though, and that is of utmost importance to me. Light and Truth is as real as Darkness and Counterfeit teachings. I will never deny truth when it is staring me right in the face."

Amanda flinched, at first thinking he was condemning her, yet looking at him she saw he was merely stating a fact that he had learned to accept this truth.

"Yes, never again will I deny what I have known to be true. I have a daughter to protect and save, somehow." Amanda sat up straight in her chair, once again the poised confidant woman the Pastor had met a few weeks earlier.

***

After the graduation, Jill invited everyone to her catering shop for a get together. Amanda made sure she was in the car with Mara. Seeing Clay and Jasmine across the street was almost surreal. Amanda held Mara's hand tightly as she fought to control her emotions. Rick was pretty impressed that Clay was even there, and that he looked exactly as young as he did in the picture of him cradling the infant Mara in his arms. Though Amanda had barely changed either. He just thought he was lucky to have snagged such a catch. As it turned out Rick and Jill were the only Humans at the party. He was feeling pretty dazed as he sat there, surrounded by beautiful people on every side.

At one of the tables in the far corner, Jill sat down next to Rick. Stroking the leather tabletop she asked, "Pretty overwhelming, huh?"

Rick looked at her, "So you believe it all: but you also believe you are human, right?"

Jill smiled sadly, "I know it is hard to take it all in so fast.

But the evidence is before us. Jaera decorated my rooms upstairs in two days, and she was being slow on purpose. Gareth designed this room and had his Brownie friends build it, including Dougie," she smiled an awkward smile, "in less than three days. You *know* this would take weeks or more to accomplish. Look at it!"

Rick looked around. It was truly beautiful; people would shop there just because it was so cool. Then they would fall in love with Jill's cooking.

"They say Brentwood still lives," he said quietly.

Jill realized, finally, the reason for his reluctance in admitting what was plainly before his eyes; there were real live six-inch Fairies dangling from the light fixtures!

"Oh, Rick, he does, but Amanda won't leave you; she loves you! I have seen it in her eyes. You may not have had time to talk about it, but you need to. Right now, she is concerned with freeing Mara, as she should be. Things will work out, I can feel it," she smiled hopefully at him.

Rick nodded and took a drink of his beer. He noted that he was the only one drinking. Probably wise since they believed Mara needed to be rescued. Rick thought, *How could so many people all be delusional?* Ironwood was not in attendance, which was odd; he had said he would not miss her graduation for the world. Amanda appeared to be getting fired up, so Rick stood to walk closer to hear what she was saying.

"I mean, anything at all?" Amanda demanded.

Aerrvin took Mara by the arm, and replied quickly, "Sorry, Amanda, not yet."

At that moment Morvayne strolled in followed by two up-sized Orange Fairies. "Mara, so glad you could have a few friends join you in celebration of your accomplishments. Amanda so good to see you again. I trust Mara has told you she took me up on my offer to assist her in her trials, as she navigates through the next stage of her life?"

"Wait up a minute, mister! She's got a father already. Who do you think you are?" Rick asked, getting in Morvayne's personal space.

Raising his eyebrows at the audacity, Morvayne replied, "Yes, she does," he smirked. "Perhaps something more personal would fit the description better. Mara?" Morvayne held his arm out for her to take. "It is time we get going. I have much yet to get done. Where is Ironwood by the way?"

Mara reluctantly left Aerrvin as she walked towards Morvayne at the same time as Breeze; gratefully she took the hand Breeze offered instead.

Amanda answered, "Ironwood, is not here and why do you care? Mara, you don't have to do this."

Rick added, "Mara just come here, stay with us! We have not visited long enough yet. Aerrvin, say something!"

***

Morvayne had had enough; *let them handle the aftermath as they will.* Creating a window with a ripple and a bend of Light he walked out of the room, taking Mara and Breeze with him. Clay and Jasmine followed from the street, as did the other four Attendants.

***

Amanda screamed plaintively. "No! Mara?" Aerrvin stood to comfort her first as Rick was too stunned to move.

"Amanda, Rick, we cannot keep her with us yet, because he has a tracking device on her by way of the bracelet. Without Clay being in her presence the bracelet would shrink in on her, paralyzing her. We have to free her from the device, and immobilize Morvayne before she can be completely free."

Rick finally gained some sense of reality and said angrily, as he pointed at those still in the room, "Why didn't you just zap him with some kind of magic of your own? Couldn't you just kill him?"

Aerrvin guided Amanda over to a table and sat down, inviting Rick to sit opposite of him. "It would be great if it were that simple. But here is the whole situation—.Are you ready for this?" Aerrvin paused looking first at Amanda and then Rick. Rick turned to Amanda for her response first.

Amanda's heart was racing; she was furious and wanted revenge, whatever it took.

"Yes. I would like to hear the whole truth." She looked at Rick realizing he must be in shock; he obviously believed she was delusional, before. *What sane human being would think otherwise?* "Rick?"

Rick was lost in thought. He had seen what he had seen. *No denying it. Mara was gone. Brentwood lives? Mara is gone; I love her as any father would. Why are they just sitting here?* Snapping out of his thoughts, he heard Amanda say his name.

"Heck yeah! Why are you so calm? If I had—"

Jaera laid a hand on Rick's shoulder, calming him.

Aerrvin continued, "Rick, I know it seems impossible to believe all of this, but let me tell you how things stand, in order or as much order as I can give it. Okay?"

Receiving a nod, Aerrvin told about Morvayne's passion for Tigerlily, his part in the loss of some of her descendants, and then the loss of the other princesses and finally the abduction of the Queen. "This made it necessary to give the Power and Authority to the next heir of the Crystal Throne."

Rick did not get it, but Amanda did. "You mean to tell me that Mara has become the Queen—of all the Realms? She does seem brighter . . . " she ended with a mumble.

Aerrvin started to speak, but Rick interrupted. "Mara is the Queen of the fairies? Oh boy, this gets richer and richer!" he barked.

Aerrvin held up his hand. "Yes and no, Mara is the Future Queen of all the magical Realms. She is an Elf, so she supersedes other classes. The Fairies have their own Queen, who in turn gives her allegiance to The Elven Queen. The Fairy Queen is my own mother." Aerrvin could not help but glow somewhat, while he again held up his hand to forestall another outburst from Rick.

"Yes, it does get richer. I came to New World to establish my own Kingdom; therefore, while my title is currently Prince Rosewin of the Rose Crown, soon I shall be crowned as Fairy King of the New World. I have not come up with a more lyrical title so it will have to do. I intended to be crowned with Mara on our wedding day. Depending on how things play out, I may have to be crowned without her."

Rick exploded again, "See? That is exactly what I am talking about, you are so laid back about this. I still haven't heard why you haven't just killed him with some magic potion, or dropping a boulder on his head. Just tell me about that!"

"Okay," Aerrvin replied calmly. "I do not mean that I am giving up on Mara. We Fair Ones are very long-lived. Morvayne and Clay are over eight hundred and fifty years old. I myself am very young, having just turned one hundred and ninety. When we turn twenty-one, we take part in a ceremony whereupon we are granted greater Power and Light as we promise certain things. One of them is to not use our Power to kill or cause harm. If we want to kill Morvayne, we would have to use our own strength, by sword, arrow or spear. I suppose modern weaponry would kill as well, we have not taken a liking to those advances, so it is doubtful we would ever use them. The Trolls or Ogres on the other hand may decide that they do like them. That is something to think on." Aerrvin looked for Gareth, before remembering he was not there.

"You mean all the bad stuff is real too?" Rick groaned as he took Amanda's hand. Looking at her she seemed determined to hear everything Aerrvin had to say. "All right, so you can't just kill him. But isn't he causing Mara harm by holding her prisoner?"

Aerrvin sighed, "Evidently emotional or mental harm is not included in the Oath to the same extent. If Mara gets too depressed, Morvayne will feel a constricting on his person, a kind of inability to breathe. Therefore, he won't be able to cause her too much harm, because he will become uncomfortable. If we try to use our Power to cause physical harm or death, we become paralyzed until we no longer desire to use our Power in a manner in which we have promised not to do. So that is part of the problem. What we are trying to do, is cause Morvayne to trust Mara, thereby allowing her greater freedom. He plans to take one hundred years to pull her over to his way of thinking. That is the main reason we are not running about in a panic. Lest you think we never do, let me assure you; when she was first abducted we were a flurry of action and found her fairly quickly in Italy. We had a plan in place within days. Unfortunately, he moved her into his place on Vashon Island, so now we have only the trust-Mara-plan as well as Clay's plan to bring in more of Mara's Attendants."

One of Lorelei's cousin's stood behind Aerrvin; she said, "Clay is Morvayne's older brother." She paused, allowing that to register. "Clay has kept his allegiance to Tigerlily and her posterity a secret from Morvayne. It has been quite a feat too, since Morvayne has been lurking about these last two hundred years. Nevertheless, it is true. Morvayne believes that Clay is willing to teach, or train, Mara into believing the same things that Morvayne believes. Which is, once she accepts Morvayne's line of thinking, she will be willing to marry him, allowing him to be co-ruler with her, at least those are his plans."

"Why does he need Mara?" Rick interjected.

Dougie placed a hand on Aerrvin's shoulder, letting him know he wanted to answer. "Morvayne blames mankind for his loss of Tigerlily when she chose Humanity to gain Salvation. He desires to reduce the population of Humans to less than half of what it is now, perhaps one third. He needs Mara as Queen so that he will have access to the Crystal Throne as well as the Chair of Desire. With her on his side, when he sits in the Chair of Desire his wishes can be granted, overriding the Oath we take."

"So, you are telling me, you have a mad elf on the loose who intends to destroy the world as we know it? You can't kill him with your powers, but I can? Right? I could go up to him and blow his head off, right?"

Aerrvin continued, "Right, you could if you managed to get close enough. He wears an article of jewelry, which has a ware spell; it allows him to know when others are thinking about him. He cannot read your mind, but he would be able to feel your emotions, and know you meant to cause harm. It also stops those with magical powers, making them unable to do anything negative when they are close, such as suddenly stabbing him. The other problem, is that he has the Queen Gwennara and her daughter Arianna held hostage, along with Brentwood. And we have just learned that Ironwood and Gareth are trapped as well. We need to untangle some of the knots before we eliminate Morvayne. Some of his spells might not disappear with his unbeing, and his leaving this world might cause other spells to be activated. Haste is really not the best first response."

Amanda asked, "So what *can* we do?"

Aerrvin replied. "I have one more bit of bad news. Rick you need to take this seriously. Mara had a friend, George, he lived in her retirement center. It turns out he was a Fairy and had been living as a Human these last sixty years. He wanted to return and was lost. I helped him return along with Mara. He has been trailing Mara in order to thank her. Then Morvayne's guards captured him. He put George in a box and presented him to Mara to see how she would respond."

Amanda was horrified. "What kind of response did he want?"

"Well," Aerrvin continued, "he was trying to blackmail her, by saying he would free George if she would give him a certain ring which he had given to Tigerlily. As chance would have it, Mara did not have it, as she had already given it away. But Mara would have refused to part with the ring anyway even with George's continued entrapment. Mainly because she knows he has lived a good long life, and all he wants now is to Dream, so she could have stayed strong and not given in to Morvayne. But if he had one of your little girls . . . "

Amanda fainted. Rick felt nauseous, *what kind of nightmare is this?* Amanda came to quickly, with the help of some lovely Elf whom Rick had not met.

"Take me to them now!" Amanda commanded.

Aerrvin drew a line of Light in the air, creating a window into Amanda's back yard. Rick followed after Amanda, amazed at what he was doing. The girls were three doors down, they walked as swiftly as they could without looking ridiculous. Knocking on the door, they were relieved to see the girls happily playing cards with Tina and Joey. Thanking the neighbors, they left and quickly went back home.

"Now what?" Rick asked. "What about Ricky?"

Aerrvin said, "Ricky is not in danger. Morvayne cannot take him hostage. We are sworn to leave Humans alone as much as possible. The girls have too much of a glow for Morvayne to leave alone; even though they do not understand, he would not care."

"I don't believe it. He's crazy! If he can break one rule he can break others. Where can we go that would be safe anyway?" Rick was getting heated, but tried to keep calm in front of the girls, who were totally confused.

"Ricky is crazy?" Sarah asked.

Amanda answered, "No, not Ricky, a bad man. He has kidnapped Mara and we need to go hide to stay safe. Aerrvin thinks that the man does not want Ricky. But I want all of us together."

Rick nodded. "I'll call him." Amanda went up to pack the girls some clothes. Ricky arrived ten minutes later.

"What's the rush? Dad you look like you've seen a ghost, and why are you here anyway? You were not due back for another day."

Becky filled him in before Rick could finish sighing. Amanda came down with a suitcase.

"Good, you are here. Go put some things in a bag and hurry!"

Ricky hurried.

"So, Aerrvin, where is it safe to go?" Amanda asked.

"Mara's house is completely warded against Morvayne, as is Ironwood Estates. The girls would probably feel more comfortable in familiar surroundings; besides Ironwood is not home to invite you in, and I could not presume to take you there."

Rick spoke up, "We left our car . . . "

"I can go retrieve it and you can drive it back . . ." Aerrvin started.

"No, take us to safety now! We will explain later—I can't do it." Amanda shook her head at Rick, unable to explain her inability to deal with the thought of losing another loved one.

Ricky came down and Aerrvin created a window into Mara's backyard. "I can't enter someone's home without an invitation," he explained as he motioned for Rick to go first. The children were stunned to silence, although the girls smiled in wonder.

Ricky started looking as terrified as his dad.

Once in the backyard, the girls started asking questions one after another. Amanda shushed them, "Wait until we are inside, I will explain everything." She went to the front and used her key to enter the house. As she walked toward the back door, Sylvie went skittering into the kitchen. "Wait, Sylvie! I believe! I need you. Please, wait." Sylvie stopped.

"Amanda it has been years that I have waited to be recognized. Have you come to keep your daughters safe?" Sylvie asked.

"Yes, let me let them in, don't go too far away. I want to talk with you later. Thank you, Sylvie." Amanda said hurriedly, as she unlocked the back door.

The family came in and trooped into the living room. "So I guess you have a great explanation for this. Was that a worm hole or what?" Ricky said exuberantly.

Aerrvin spoke to Amanda and Rick. "I can erase their memories, they will sleep and wake up remembering having greeted you on Sunday and then driving here. You will still have to tell them why you have decided to live here though."

"What?" Ricky said. "We are all going to live here? If there is some bad guy snatching people out of thin air, what stops him from getting us here? No, I want to remember this. It was creepy, but cool! I don't want anyone messing with my head and my memories. Thanks, but no thanks."

Rick and Amanda agreed.

Amanda told her life story one more time, again showing the pictures in *Enchanted Lives* as well as the pictures on the wall in the study. For the first time, she recognized Morvayne as the guy standing next to Tigerlily. She pointed him out and told the girls to never talk to a man who looked like that.

Sarah said in awe. "So I am a Water Sprite? What can I do, can I learn magic? Aerrvin can you teach me?"

Aerrvin looked at Amanda and Rick, they looked at each other.

Rick finally shrugged and Amanda said, "Something small."

Aerrvin said, "You are very young, most do not begin using their power until they are ten or so, except for getting things they want like hugs, kisses, and dessert. Close your eyes; do you see that glowing light?"

"Yes," they said in unison.

Sarah said, "It's always there. What is it for?"

"It is your Power and Light, it can protect you and keep you safe. Keep your eyes shut and walk to me."

Aerrvin caused a chair to land silently in front of them, they walked around it confidently without opening their eyes, as well as a few other randomly placed obstacles. When they reached the window where he was standing, they were amazed along with the rest of the family.

"Wow! How did I do that?" Becky asked.

"It is just one of those things; do you ever turn the lights on at night to get a drink?" Aerrvin asked.

"No, I can always find my way," Sarah said proudly. "You mean that is my power? I have super night vision? But I walked with my eyes shut. What about that?"

"You have both; you can see where you need to be in places where there is limited vision because as a Water Sprite you might go swimming in some pretty murky water. You have this Power to keep you safe while doing that. Even I can't walk about with my eyes shut, at least not as well as you."

"One more! Please, what else can I do?" Sarah begged. "Well, since you are a Water Sprite, you can learn to stay under the water for days at a time, even months if you really wanted to, like say you want to visit the Mermaids, you could do that."

Amanda teared up at that. Mermaids were Brentwood's passion. *Why didn't he just marry one of them in the first place?* She thought angrily, and then quickly repented. Without him, she would not have produced Mara. *Mara the future Queen of all the Realms!*

"But you have to wait until you are older for that." Aerrvin laughed softly as they squealed and jumped up and down.

"Mama, did you hear?" Sarah asked.

"Yes, honey, I heard." Amanda smiled sadly. This reality stunk.

Sarah returned to Aerrvin. "Is that why this house is safe?" She asked as she pointed to all the low glowing wards on the windows he was standing in front of. "And are you going to rescue Mara?"

Aerrvin pointed out all of the wards around the house explaining who made them and what they did. Rick and Ricky followed, even though they could not see a thing. Amanda saw them as she always had, they still seemed like simple reflections of light if she thought of them that way. However, there was no denying the snowflake on the mantel. She stopped and stroked it now. Sarah and Becky stood next to her.

"Mara was looking at that when she said Santa was real," Sarah recalled. She looked first at her mother and then at Aerrvin.

Aerrvin nodded. "Yes, I have asked about this mantel. It was created by Ironwood, but then he managed to get Santa to bless it with his kiss. No one can enter that chimney except Santa, not even his helpers! He is a very busy and important Elf, but if there were a true emergency, he would send help. I don't think we can call upon him yet."

"Not even for the future Queen? Does he rise above her in importance?" Amanda asked incredulously, both at herself and the questions.

Aerrvin smiled ruefully. "They are near equals, he loves her as much as he loved Tigerlily and the Queen, but he would have the same restraints that hold us back."

"Okay, how did Tigerlily leave her house without fear of abduction? I mean we want to stay here, but not forever. We want to be able to go to the store at least, if not the zoo and museums."

Aerrvin flinched at mention of the zoo. "I would stay away from the zoo. Morvayne has a large following there, with a Fairy Ring made up of mostly Orange and Yellow Fairies. It is not safe right now. Rick and Ricky can continue normally, I can place a simple safety spell on an article of clothing like their shoes or a watch. It will warn them when they are nearing a dangerous situation, so they can change course. It can't really stop anyone from hurting them, but it can give them time to respond."

Ricky raised his hand. "I'll take it!"

Aerrvin continued pointing at the stairs. "Mara has all of

Tigerlily's jewelry. I haven't had time to tell her of their properties, but a combination of them would keep you safe enough to go shopping and the like."

Going up to Mara's room, they all went silent. The house suddenly seemed empty without Mara there. Aerrvin went into her room with a familiarity that slightly disturbed Amanda. He went right to her closet and removed the jewelry box that Mara had been given after Lily's death. Seeing all the jewelry brought tears to Amanda's eyes as she recalled Lily wearing multiple jewels wherever she went.

"She wore this one at all times," Amanda said as she picked up an emerald ring.

"Yes," Aerrvin said with a nod for emphasis. "That is the one I was going to suggest. She has a spell on this one — specifically forbidding Morvayne from being within a city block of the wearer. That is what made it so hard for him to spy on her. This necklace is endowed with charms, which prevents anyone from remembering bad thoughts they might have had about the wearer, they need to be within eyesight, or comfortable hearing distance. It engenders a kind of love, but not obedience; you cannot force someone to do anything against their will."

Then he took out two sapphire encrusted hairpins each in the shape of a dragonfly. "These would be perfect for little Sprites. They repel evil doers from touching them. If an evil being is on the same sidewalk, they will flee as though in horror. It actually squeezes their lungs, preventing them from gaining oxygen until they get far enough away. If you are in a sufficiently crowded space they will not even be able to get near enough to identify who wears the ward."

Amanda looked up in sorrow, meeting sorrow in Aerrvin's eyes as well. "If you knew, why did you not tell Mara to wear all of these?"

Aerrvin scrubbed at his forehead in frustration. "I had just met her! I did not know she had an enemy at first and then she was captured before I knew it. I thought she was safe when she was with me. Bronwyn is right, I am vain and conceited. I trusted in my own strength when I should have realized Tigerlily had these jewels for a reason, and had given them to Mara for the same one." He dropped his head as he realized the full impact of his arrogance. His blond hair fell like water over his face.

Amanda recognized her own neglect, and reached out to Aerrvin giving him a brief hug and to brush his hair back behind his ear. "No, Aerrvin you are not to blame, I am more at fault than you. If I had allowed Lily and Ironwood to train her as they wished, she would have been prepared. Instead I insisted she wait until she turned twenty-one…" Amanda paused and stared at Rick. "Oh, that's it!"

Rick asked, "What?"

"I have to go to the bank! Brentwood left important information for Mara. I read some of it at his disappearance and did not want to accept it, but it was his wish for her, so I could not keep it from her. However, I had it sealed until her 21st birthday. I can release it though; we need to go and get it now!" Amanda already had the ring, but she took up the necklace and held it up to Rick expectantly. He complied by fastening it around her neck. "Why couldn't Mara have chosen this one to wear instead of the purple one?"

"Ah, that was partially my fault, Amanda." Aerrvin replied sheepishly. "I wanted to see it on her, not realizing that she had had a previous experience with it." He explained the story of her having put it on without permission and the resultant consequences. "It does, however, have redeeming qualities besides spite. The wearer is induced to question things more fully, and to think things through before making decisions. Something a Queen needs in order to rule with justice. I simply wanted to ensure that she accepted my proposal thoughtfully." He laughed. "She still can't take it off; she has another day or so at least."

Amanda shook her head with pity for all of the errors, and then asked, "Okay, Aerrvin, can you take me right to the bank?"

"No, Traveling requires that I have been there before. I can take you back to Jill's place and you can get your car. Who else is going?"

They were stumped. Ricky decided to stay at home with the girls. But Rick was torn; he was not sure if he trusted that the house was safe. He also did not want Amanda going to town without him.

Amanda left the room suddenly, returning with Sylvie in her Human sized form. "Girls, guys, this is Sylvie; she is Mara's dearest friend and is a Brownie. Her family lives beneath the house and will protect all who live here."

"How did she get so big?" Sarah asked, followed by Becky saying, "Yeah, I thought they were tiny like Fairies."

Aerrvin nodded, encouraging Amanda to change her in front of them. Sylvie returned to her former size momentarily and then back again. She bowed to Aerrvin and said, "I am well and truly shamed at having to reveal myself this way. But I will do anything for Mara. Are you sure this was necessary?"

The little girls ran to her and hugged her as Aerrvin nodded. "Aye, this family needs to see and believe for their own safety, as well as Mara's." Turning to Amanda he said, "Would you mind if I left Seamus here as well?"

Amanda looked at the glimmering shape sitting on his shoulder. "Is that who that is?" She shook her head wearily. "No, the more the merrier, I guess."

Seamus became visible as he climbed down off of Aerrvin's shoulder; upon reaching the floor, Aerrvin maximized his form. Rick and Ricky both sat staring from the couch.

"I don't think I can tell my friends about this even if I wanted to!" Ricky exclaimed.

Rick replied, "You don't want to." He paused to look about the room. "Alright, I will go with you, Amanda, as long as you trust these guys."

17
And So It Begins

Morvayne was curious about Ironwood's absence. Ignoring Mara's hurt expression he pressed, "Where was your Grandfather? Surely, he would not have missed such an auspicious occasion. Is he so fearful that he cannot leave his house now?" Morvayne had indeed tried to gain access to the estate, but the wards were equal to Tigerlily's, or his own.

Mara stuttered; she did not want to tell what she knew, but Morvayne was going to keep pressing. "I have been w-with you. How am I to know where he is? I sent an invitation to him and hoped to have seen him. Maybe he was in the crowd at the stadium, but I did not see him."

"Ah, but you have been receiving visitors in your Dreams, and still you deny me access. How can I trust *you* when you trust me so little?"

Morvayne was losing it. He was actually shaking. Clay handed a glass of wine to Morvayne. He downed it in one swallow.

"Morvayne, I think Mara should be seen to her rooms," Clay said, smoothly guiding Jasmine and Mara toward the suite reserved for them. "Let us retire to the study; you have much on your mind."

In the study, Morvayne opened a bottle of wine and poured himself a larger serving, drinking it more slowly this time.

"You are right. I do have much on my mind. I sent some of my followers on a lead I had, to find Gwennara. She was being held by the head schoolmistress of a Mermaid Academy. But when my guards went in to search, she was not there."

"Who was not there? The mistress or Gwennara?"

"Both!" Morvayne spat. "I don't understand where they could have gone! I had placed a bubble over the school to prevent Traveling. They should have been there still." He pounded the table. "It has to be Ironwood and Brand. The Fairy managed to get away from me, but I have not seen his presence anywhere; though my patrols report that he was at Aerrvin's birthday celebration."

Clay observed Morvayne closely. He was slipping, unaware that he just revealed his part in Gwennara's capture. Clay had been watering down the wine with a synthetic non-alcoholic replacement. The flavor was the same, but Clay wanted to see the results of taking an Elf off of the addictive drink.

It was as fascinating as Morvayne's earlier books detailing the increased consumption. When Morvayne first began, he was truly able to think up masterful plans and spells. That was how he developed the spells he taught to the Fairies, helping them learn how to craft counter spells. Truly a masterful accomplishment. But as the decades wore on, Morvayne's writings became more convoluted. Sometimes just rambling commentary, mostly about his desire to hurt Tigerlily as much as she had hurt him. To hurt her by destroying those whom she loved.

Especially Ironwood, Brentwood and Mara. Ironwood proved to be too elusive, always on the go and far more powerful than one would expect considering he had never fully converted by taking the Oath. One of Morvayne's books was completely devoid of words, except for the occasional threat written beside the countless drawings: scenes of war and torture, drawings of bombs and weaponry. Morvayne had been a muse for those who had developed weapons of mass destruction. Clay literally threw up after viewing that book. Still he had mixed feelings; he could not tell whether taking alcohol away would help at all.

Morvayne sat staring off into space, lost in his own thoughts, unaware that he was being observed as a scientific experiment. The diluted alcohol eventually worked to restore his equilibrium. Sighing, Morvayne stood and said, "I must go and see the school myself. I need to see if anything was missed. Would you care to join me?"

Clay felt it might be a trap, but he did want to see the location. Stretching languidly, he replied. "A swim would be nice, let me tell Jasmine first."

Morvayne agreed and waited for Clay's return. The window opened to a beach off the shores of Greece, Clay recognized the location immediately. "Ah, Greece, a favored land."

Once in the water, Morvayne again opened a window, taking them right to the gates of the Academy. Water Sprites guarded the opening with a few of the Mermen from the colony they had visited earlier. They offered Morvayne another brief overview of the events as they had played out. The Water Sprites arrived with permission to search the school. When they requested to see Lumina, she was not to be found, nor were her guests who had arrived moments before the quarantine. The description of the guests left no doubt.

"Ironwood! How did he manage to get here first?" Being in the water hampered Morvayne's ability to storm away loudly, so instead he requested to see Lumina's rooms and office. The office was closer and he doubted it would reveal much. Mina was quite spare in her décor, so there was very little to look at. What he was looking for no one could guess. He caused all the furniture to fall apart to inspect the insides.

Nothing.

Next they searched Mina's apartment, in the same minute detail. Holding up a basket with a lid attached he said, "Gwennara was inside this basket. She still sleeps, I checked this morning, neither will she rouse until I release her. But how did they remove her body?"

Clay ventured a question. "How can you hold her against her will?"

Morvayne looked proud as he replied, "I assume you mean by what means, not by what moral authority?"

Clay smiled crookedly. "Exactly. I wish to know how it is done. It appears you have bested me at something, little brother!"

Morvayne replied vainly, knowing it was inevitable. "My research took thousands of years in the Land of Dreams; if a Dream appeared to hold little research, I fled in search of one which did.

"Occasionally I found a Dream I wished to experience and stayed with it. Mara was truly a wondrous wife, for a while. She betrayed me in the end. I mean to make it work this time, even if it means destroying all else. My research included."

Clay had hoped for a clear answer, so he pushed it once more. "Is it similar to the bubble you placed over the beach the other day?"

Morvayne returned Clay's open-eyed questioning face with a mocking stare. "Wouldn't you like to know? Yes, it has some of the same properties. But, surely you understand the need for keeping this to myself. My goals reach beyond you and me. I will restore the world to its proper balance! Future generations will adore me as their savior. At that point, my knowledge can be shared with a select few. When you prove faithful, I shall share my knowledge with you. You, who have taught me so much."

That was a clue that would take pondering. Clay stored it

away and continued to tear apart bits of this and that. Eventually Morvayne agreed there was nothing to learn and returned them to the beach. "You may stay and swim as you like. I have other business to attend to. I will see you tomorrow at noon."

Clay kissed his brother on each cheek, not knowing if it would be his last chance. "I love you, Morvayne," he said honestly.

Morvayne was touched, even through his crazed thoughts. He hugged him back and said, "You have been true to me all these years; yes, you will rule in glory with me." Smiling, he changed into archaic stockings and a jerkin, then he created a window to a desert in California and stepped onto the porch of the Troll compound.

Clay dove down into the water and swam mindlessly as his brain concentrated on a deeper level, puzzling out what Morvayne had revealed. The bubble was like an enlarged capsule or restraint that parents use on their younglings to protect them from their own Power. Somehow, Morvayne found a way to strengthen the power of the capsule, making it act like a stasis chamber. *He said it could only be released at his command.*

Meaning there were still two paths of light leading to it. If he could convince Morvayne to allow him access to Arianna, perhaps he could study the capsule around her. He had not looked at her body in stasis that closely, as he had assumed it was in a normal stasis condition. As well as being anxious to speak with her and more. Clay swam to the surface and walked out of the water; he needed to find Brand.

Entering the Void, he searched for the Fairy's Dream but found that Brand was deeper, so he went to the Void in search, but he had no clue about which door he should knock upon. Realizing the futility, he returned to the real world to seek Ironwood.

Daylight still ruled in Washington as he knocked on the front door of Ironwood Estates. Clay was relieved to find that Ironwood was indeed home. Greeting Lumina and Gareth, Clay asked how they had escaped.

Gareth replied, "Brand the Bright has many magic tricks up his sleeve, which he says will stay secret. All I can say is that we found Gwennara in Mina's own apartments. She was a tiny statue, part of an entire diorama given to Mina by one Master Maurice a scholar of oceanography. Yes, there were others in the diorama, but no, not she whom you desire. Sorry. Nor Brentwood." Gareth hung his head in near defeat.

"But Brand did not go with you to the Academy. How did you escape?" Clay insisted on an answer.

Ironwood entered the room and responded, "Brand taught me, as an heir, one of his secret skills which enabled him to counteract the magic which Morvayne used to entrap the Queen, as well as her Attendants. This was a skill Brand had just developed, and had not yet shared it with Gwennara. The attack has left him full of regret. Anyhow, we were able to leave right in plain sight of everyone. We scattered ourselves to such a degree, that we were able to filter right through the barrier just like water, air or fine particulates. Each of us carried one of the bodies in stasis and they filtered right along with our clothes, it was truly amazing, Clay!" Ironwood exulted.

"So, can Mara learn this technique?" Clay asked.

Ironwood nodded, "Yes, as long as she can master a Mask of Deception, and then learn to Transform, then yes, she can do this."

Ironwood then dissolved right before Clay, becoming a fine mist, almost finer than Fairy Dust. The mist floated to a far corner and then coalesced into the not so old gentleman once again.

"Fair Ones may have used this trick before in ages past, but with peace for so many centuries it became lost. Brand happened upon an old text, which mentioned Traveling on the Mists of Time. While this is not that, it lead Brand to experiment and this was the result. He named it Vaporization. It may well take Mara time to learn, but she can do it."

Clay smiled. "I am sure she can as well. I have a theory on how Morvayne has put his captives in stasis. Is Gwennara or another of her fellow detainees present?"

Ironwood nodded. "Brand is spending time with his wife. He can feel her essence and mood; he thinks she can feel his as well. Curiously, he cannot find her within the Void. But come to my study, the rest are on my desk."

Clay was amazed to see that they had been shrunk down to three inches, rather than the normal six for Fairies. Though only two of them were Fairies. One was a Mermaid, another an Ogre, two were Elves and the last one was a Dryad. Picking up the Dryad, he studied it and then explained what he had learned from Morvayne. Lorelei was in the study and became fascinated with the theory of unraveling the spell by following the paths of light.

"Here let me try." She reached for the Dryad and held it close so as to study it.

As she worked Clay confessed, "Morvayne brought Arianna to me, but she was full-sized. Can we enlarge them while in this state?"

Lorelei replied, "Let me take this Dryad to my lab. We will study how to make the binding and then perhaps we will see how to release the capsule. Thank you for your insight, Clay." She smiled as she hurried out the door.

Ironwood smiled wearily. "If anyone can solve it, she can."

"Very well, as long as it is being worked on. I should return to Mara. Tell Brand I rejoice in his joy and sorrow for his loss. Arianna strives for freedom in the same state as Gwennara and seeks for honor always. We will be victorious if it takes one thousand years." Clay bowed to Ironwood and left.

***

Mara sat propped up with pillows on her bed, wondering what she could do to help herself. She reviewed her experiences in a Dream state, yet she had not gone to her Dream, nor had she entered the Void or anything like it.

"This is new!" she marveled. She even allowed herself to recall her times spent with Morvayne on the beach and elsewhere as she searched for clues. "That's one. Morvayne said it was a pity Dad could not see the Lost City of Atlantis, for which he had found the final clue. He can't see it, but he's there!" She reviewed her memories further, "Two, he wants my necklace. No one has told me what it does, beside be spiteful. Hmmm, one more I'm sure."

Breeze walked by, "Did you say something?" She backed up, entering the bedroom.

"Oh, I was just talking to myself. I am collecting clues, trying to see a pattern to the puzzle." Mara repeated what she remembered so far. "… and he wants Tigerlily's tiaras and crowns. Probably all of her jewelry. Oh I know! Why does he want the Ring of Truth, besides sentimental reasons, what does it do?"

Breeze settled on the pillows beside Mara. "Your necklace guides you into asking the right questions and helps you solve mysteries. A good enough reason for not wanting you to wear it. He would want it to help him see the best way to destroy Humanity. It also helps you dispense justice by way of asking the right questions. Tigerlily received it when her older sister became 'no more.' The Ring of Truth is almost self-explanatory. The

249

wearer can discern when another is lying, a fine tool for a monarch to have. It also has a prophecy attached to it which is the real reason Morvayne wants it, and he must never get it…” Breeze paused as Clay appeared in the room, stepping in from a bend of light.

“Sorry for being so direct. I thought you would want to know right away. I need to share something; let us retire to my Dream!” His eyes shone with hope. Jasmine joined them from the couch so all four met in the Dream.

Clay’s Dream was a lovely meadow with the sun shining down and a soft breeze blowing through the grass. Joyfully, he related his news and they hugged one another at the revelation. Breeze and Mara’s two attendants began practicing the vaporization technique and had it mastered in minutes.

“How can you master something so quickly when it is something no one has tried for ages?” Mara wondered, while she practiced keeping her Mask of Deception from wavering. She was once again the blonde with the spiky hair. Why she kept trying that girl she didn’t know.

“It is really quite easy once one has the Mask of Deception in hand. Just like Ironwood said,” Clay replied after he returned to his normal sleek self. “Here, Mara.” Clay put a mirror in front of her and told her to try looking like Breeze. “It will be easier if you don’t try someone from an old memory. It should be a strong vision in your head, not a wish only of what you want.”

Mara looked at Breeze from all angles and closed her eyes, easily seeing her as though Dreaming. “This is like my waking dream state,” she said in wonder. Then opening her eyes she saw Breeze in the mirror without wavering, she twirled and moved just as gracefully as Breeze ever did. Laughing she turned to see what the others thought.

They smiled, but Breeze and Clay walked closer, inspecting

from very close. Clay sniffed and then nodded. Breeze grinned and then shook her head.

"What?" Mara exclaimed. "Didn't I do it right? I'm not wavering or anything, try to scare me or tickle me I bet it will stay, it feels very secure, somehow."

"Oh it will stay alright." Clay grinned at her. "But you skipped right over the Mask of Deception and Transformed yourself into Breeze, right down to her smell. I would have to say you failed if you were in my class."

"Oh, pooh!" Breeze inserted, "Your professors would not fail you, Mara, they would know that they had not given you the correct instruction. You have been jumping around all over the Land of Dreams where you should not be going this young. Somehow, you skipped over the first level in the Void, the place you go to find other people's Dream stars. While there, you should have picked up your mask. Instead you went right into a Dreamscape and Transformed. So close your eyes and return to your own self."

Mara did, returning dressed in her default nightgown with the ribbon properly tied. "Sorry!" she quickly changed, as she blushed, spilling Fairy Dust all over the place. "Maybe not the best choice of clothing, it's just, never mind…" She continued to blush as the others shook their heads grinning.

"Never you mind, Mara, you look just as lovely in cut offs and smiley faced flowers," Breeze said in a sisterly fashion. "Now in order to select a mask, you need to enter the Dreamer's Void and nowhere else; it works best if you do it from the same location every time, that way it becomes second nature and can be accomplished almost instantly. So look up and visualize what you want. A mask will appear. Reach for it and it will fall upon you. Open your eyes."

Mara looked and saw Jasmine's face greeting her in the

mirror.

Clay came near and smelled her scent with a sigh. "Yes, that is you Mara."

He proceeded to tickle her, causing her to lose it, but she held on for a minute first. He complemented her, "Very well done. You will need to continue practicing daily until you can keep it without thinking about it. In addition, we will do it in real life. You can be Breeze and Breeze will be you. Sound fair?" He asked, wrapping his arm around her waist; all that scent she cast about was intoxicating.

"Hey, wait a minute! How come you have scent, I mean *real* scent not just a memory of it, in your Dream? Aerrvin and I don't." Mara asked, suddenly turning on Clay.

Clay smiled warmly. "It comes with getting older." He dared not reveal that his Dream was really a part of The Land of Eternal Spring. He had studied time and space to such a degree that he had learned how to transform his Dream. It was permanently attached to The Land, or True Living, however one wanted to see it.

He could experience reality as much in this place as anywhere else in the Land of Eternal Spring or in his waking state on Earth. This was dangerous, because if he died here he would die there, unlike being in normal stasis within one of the white rooms where one could die repeatedly and live to do it all again.

Clay frowned as he realized their bodies were in reality in The Land of Eternal Spring. Morvayne's binding capsules did not prevent visiting The Land. But if Morvayne came looking for them, that might be bad, even though they were not fully free to exit into the world through different portal.

"Perhaps we should practice in Jasmine's Dream next time." Clay collected all of Mara's Dust and deposited it in an exquisite hand blown vial, capping it with a silver stopper. He placed it somewhere so quickly that Mara could not see. Well almost, she saw a cavern wall with three other vials in a niche. But it was an after image, so she wasn't certain that she really saw it at all.

They awoke and Breeze went back to her crocheting in the recliner, Jasmine remained on the couch, and Mara wondered what she should be doing now. Dusk turned to evening, but she was not tired, having just napped while she visited Clay's Dream. Clay seemed content to just lie there on her bed.

"Clay? I have determined that my father is in the Lost City of Atlantis. Do you think it is possible, or rather probable?" Mara asked as he continued to rest there, unmoving.

Taking a deep breath, which he seemed to do a lot of lately, he opened his eyes and turned to his side to look at her.

"Ah, Mara, you make things so hard!" He sat up and placed extra pillows behind him. "No, not your questions, just your presence. Yes, I do think that your father is in the Lost City as well as Arianna. Nevertheless, the Mermaids are so closed mouth on the subject that it may take another ten years of research just to get a few clues. The same as it took your father. You were in a conversation with Breeze when I came in; what was it about?"

Mara told him all her thoughts about the puzzle before them, and then remembered another clue, "Oh, what is the prophecy anyway? Is that why you requested the ring be returned at the right time, or at need, or whatever it was you said?"

"Yes, the ring needs to be on the hand of she who sits upon the Crystal Throne, when the Day of Reckoning is brought to pass. Whether that is the final Judgment Day or something else, we do not know. Most speculate it is a day reserved for a time before that final day. A day as defined by a great writer and philosopher Plateaus, who said:

'…it is a time of punishment or retribution, a time

253

when he who destroyed will be made to answer for his crimes and mistakes.'

I think Morvayne wants to be the one wearing the ring, so that he will be the one judging. I think he interprets Humanities' actions as the crime. They have expanded their mistakes by increasing their numbers and pushing nature away. Many of those in the magical realms are mixed in their assessment. Which is why Morvayne has gotten away with all that he has done so far."

Clay looked at Mara, proudly noting that she no longer quivered or cried at the thought of Morvayne and her incarceration. She was thoughtful and seeking answers. *She is putty in my hands; I could sway her whithersoever I would. Or could I?* She was gaining wisdom and Power at an alarming rate, faster than any student he had ever taught before. True, he rarely took on teaching positions, and it had been 160 years since the last assignment had been accepted; nevertheless, she was amazingly bright and Bright.

"Oh, I just remembered the other thing that I wanted to try." Mara caused her armor to become a pair of gloves and then two bracelets. She removed a bracelet and asked Clay to wear it. He put it on and then caused it to become body armor.

"Mara this is wonderful! You just thought of this? Why didn't Hannah ever think of this? Never mind, we Fair Ones are too vain to want to give up having something others do not have. She would not have been unique among us had she shared. I wonder?" Clay caused his to become ten bracelets then took all but one off and tried again but it only split into two more. "Mara we can have forty suits of Armor from this one shed! I wonder how potent Morvayne's tracing kiss is when it is diluted like this?" Then he frowned. "Too, I wonder how protective it is." He covered his arm and then took a knife and sliced at his arm softly and then with more force suddenly he winced. "I guess it is too thin."

The sight of blood shocked Mara. "Clay what have you done? Let me help!"

Clay waved her off. He swept his hand over it, and it healed. "It was very superficial, we have simple weaves to repair such scratches."

He continued testing with Jasmine's help until he determined that the optimum number of times it could be split and still be protective was six. At eight no one could slice a knife through, yet Jasmine was able to stab a spear through his side, but no matter how hard she tried at six it was just as strong as it was when whole.

"Then my shed can make two more. Jasmine and Breeze would you care to accept this gift?"

Jasmine took hers readily; she had coveted Hannah's all through the years. "I know Morvayne can trace it, but surely the strength is weakened *and* he will not be a problem forever. Besides, we can confuse him by going in opposite directions."

Breeze accepted the other one. "Good thinking, but also, Mara, I think you should divide one a few more times and allow Morvayne to kiss it and then when we leave we can attach it to a fish and he will go chasing after it." She laughed at the thought.

Clay nodded. "Yes, that should work. Just do not divide it too much; you still need its protection. No one is going to try to stab you or anything, but still . . . safe is better than sorry. Yes?"

Mara smiled, happy to have recalled her desired test. "Yes! Do you mind if I visit Mom's Dream? I want to be sure she is not overly worried about me." Clay agreed and left her in Jasmine's care.

Morvayne returned through a portal as Clay walked toward his own suite. "Any progress, Morvayne?" Clay wondered what part the Trolls were to play in all of this scheming.

"No, not really, join me for a while." Morvayne motioned toward his sitting room. Clay followed and chose to stretch out on the couch. "You shouldn't be that tired, Clay, you barely swam for a few hours," Morvayne chided.

"You forget I am tasked with watching over Mara's Dreaming as well. It becomes tedious being with such a youngling. It is Jasmine's turn tonight. I shall be refreshed tomorrow; have no fear. I just want a little time alone. You know how I can get." He sighed thinking of the vials of Dust in his grotto.

Which Dream to sample? Not bothering to keep his face as still as granite, he smiled at his choices. He knew Morvayne could feel his emotions anyway.

"You don't appear to be desiring alone time to me, big brother," Morvayne said dryly.

Clay waved his hand delicately in the air. "Be that as it may, what did you wish to discuss?"

"Nothing, really, I am just disgusted that my plans fell through. Amanda has moved her entire family into Mara's house. For the summer, or what, I do not know. That blasted Amanda was wearing Tigerlily's jewels, which prevented me from getting close. I hate it when I cannot get what I want! The Orange Fairies are beginning to fight with the Yellows and it seems that everything is slipping away."

"I can see why you would be feeling low, Morvayne, but we have Mara. That is the important thing."

Morvayne interrupted, "No, you don't understand! The Chair of Desire is inside Mara's house. If Amanda has come to her senses and accepts who she is, then I will have a harder time getting that chair out of there."

"Oh, no I did not realize that the chair was there. Do you

also know where the Crystal Throne is? That would be beneficial if we could get them both in one location." Clay sat up feigning enthusiasm.

"No, but I still have ways to get that information."

"Really, do you think Arianna knows? I never got around to asking her. It was our first meeting in centuries, you know." Clay grinned unabashedly.

"That might be one way, but I also thought that causing enough disasters around the world might convince Ironwood to be more forthcoming with what he knows." Morvayne chuckled. "Well, I will think on it. You appear to have a Dream in mind, so I will wait to send you to Arianna's Dream. Perhaps tomorrow. Sweet Dreams, Clay," Morvayne crooned as he ushered Clay out toward the hallway.

18
Past Loves

Amanda asked Rick to drive directly to the bank to retrieve the contents of the safety deposit box. Leaving the policies, bonds, and photos, she took the letters and a journal. Placing them in her giant purse, she fretted that they could be snatched from her at any moment. Once in the car she asked Aerrvin if he could just pop her into the garage.

"I can look and see if it is empty. Yes, it is, but I need to be driving to take us there."

Trading seats was not a problem. Rick and Amanda were in a hurry and moving through a portal was far faster than driving all those blocks in the late afternoon rush hour traffic, traffic which lasts nearly all day long!

Once in the house, Amanda sat at the desk in the study, scanning the journal for clues to Brentwood's location, noting each clue onto a single page. Between the final pages she found the letter Brentwood had written to her. She set it aside, knowing she could not read it in front of Rick for fear of crying. She felt conflicted over the idea that her first husband still lived, but she did not have the brain space to work through those emotions while dealing with the current crisis. After looking through the journal, Amanda finally made herself open the letter for Mara; she smiled as she read the nickname Brentwood had used often when referring to their daughter.

My Dearest Marvel,

This letter was written when you were nine years old. I want you to know that I love you more than anything. If I am not giving this letter to you personally I am sorry. It is for your 21st Birthday and I so wanted to be there for you. You know that Mother has asked me not to tell you about your true heritage...

Amanda skipped down past the history lesson.

...Now you know why I am so busy, my work is important to me because I believe that there are great treasures which can benefit all mankind, the stress is on kind— the Faire included. We are meant to be counted among all the earth's sentient beings. Counted as equals I mean. I took the Oath at twenty-one and encourage you to make the same choice.

Talk to Aunt Lily and Grandpa Ironwood. They will be a great strength to you. I trust your Attendants with your life. If you have not met them yet, ask Grandpa to introduce you. And please stay away from Morris, your Mother knows who he is. Grandpa Ironwood and Aunt Lily will tell you more details too. He is no longer my assistant, though he pretends to be. I have learned that he intends to steal information from me. This is the important final clue which I have learned: The City of Atlantis can only be reached by entering the Land of Dreams. It does not have a physical location, in this time frame anyway. The other clues are in my journal. Perhaps, if I am missing, you will find me there.

Sweet pea, I send you all my love, and hugs, and kisses, forever and ever, Daddy

Amanda cried anyway. She let the others read it with it's nearly perfect penmanship. Something she always noticed. She had accused him once of messing up some of the words on purpose and his only reply was to wink at her. After Aerrvin read the letter, he asked to see what she had written in her notes.

"Is it true? You know how to get to this, Land of Dreams?" Rick asked.

Amanda shook her head, "No, I am not strong enough. Aerrvin, can you? Can Mara?"

Aerrvin nodded as he pushed a lock of hair behind his ear. "Yes, I visit often. Mara has not taken the Oath, so she is not supposed to go. Ironwood had never taken the Oath until just recently, but I am sure he has been there anyway. You know how he is, he will do anything for knowledge." Aerrvin failed to admit that he had taken Mara there as well.

Amanda shook her head, "It appears to run in the family." She looked about, "Well, I guess you should hurry and let Ironwood know about this—Your Highness. I am sorry to have bossed you around today." She bowed her head, not knowing how much reverence to give a Fairy Prince.

"Your direction was right for the circumstance, and Aerrvin is fine, Amanda. Save the royal bowing for formal situations." Sylvie came in and bowed, asking if anyone would like to eat since a light dinner was ready.

Aerrvin grinned at Amanda first, knowing that allowing the Brownie to bow looked questionable. He then replied, "No, I have duties to attend. Thank you, Sylvie. Seamus, time to go."

Sylvie bowed again and left. Seamus came in and waited to be shrunk down, then he climbed up to sit on Aerrvin's shoulder, holding on to the braid behind Aerrvin's ear.

"By the way, Amanda, you are not as weak as you think.

Brownies can only change size by command. You caused Sylvie to be Human-sized, and only you can reduce her. Please remember to do so before you retire for the night, she would feel so bad if she were not able to perform her duties. Right, Seamus?"

"Aye, you said it true." Seamus beamed.

A good Brownie always admires another who takes their duties seriously. My Seamus was smitten as well and good as any Fairy Prince in the room.~ Bronwyn

***

Morvayne decided it was time to try visiting Mara again in her Dream; then he remembered that she had been told she had to visit her Attendant's Dreams instead. "That must mean she is with Jasmine," he mused before slipping into the Void.

Jasmine had her Dream warded so he knocked angrily, but it was useless. He stormed over to the women's suite. Breeze was still up, busily crocheting what appeared to be a shawl, a very fine and delicate one made of spider silk. The sight reminded him of his mother, instantly taking him out of his senses momentarily.

"Breeze, how are you?"

Breeze could see his anger, but acted as though she did not. "Fine, thank you. Would you like some company? I can work on this later." She set it aside and rose to greet him warmly. "You look as though you could use a good massage; you shouldn't allow yourself to get so worked up." She reached behind him after hugging him and kneaded his tense neck muscles. "Really, Morvayne, you should take better care of yourself. Where would we be without you?"

"That does feel good," he admitted. "I wanted to visit Mara in a Dream, but Jasmine has her Dream locked up tighter than a Level Four door. Ah, well it wasn't anything urgent. A swim and a soak in the hot tub would do me wonders I am sure.

261

Join me, Breeze, and I shall soon be pleasant company, and yes, please, a massage would be wonderful." He smiled at her, genuinely grateful for the offer.

In the morning, everyone woke up feeling refreshed and at peace. Morvayne had a butler in Vashon, rather than a cook and maid. The butler was a master chef and created beautiful culinary delights for every meal. He was also a Yellow Fairy, very intelligent, but easily offended.

Mara had learned that lesson on her first night there. She had scoffed at a delicate candy sculpture that he had placed atop a spinach and strawberry salad. It had not looked practical, but it turned out that once it was broken it added the perfect crunch and sweetness to the salad. No amount of complements appeased him. Today he graciously served each guest and then swiftly placed Mara's, without a nod acknowledging her thanks.

This was becoming tedious to her. Suddenly her anger flared and she bound him tight with air and caused his head to bow.

Morvayne had just noticed the slights of his butler, for the first time. Seeing Mara's sudden surge of anger startled him. "Mara, let him go. What did he do to you? Hans tell me?"

Mara was still seething as she released him. He remained bowed before Mara's Light and Power.

"Master forgive me; she did not like a creation of mine and I have been rude. My lady, forgive me."

Mara was both troubled and pleased. She had never been one to lash out so suddenly; this was appalling. Yet, she felt it was just. He had been rude and she was the future Queen! *How dare he treat me so poorly?* Yet, she was pleased because, even though she had lost control, she had nevertheless kept her two back pockets of Light firmly in place with never a thought of releasing them. It was as though they did not even exist.

She smiled now. "I forgive you, Hans, don't let it happen again."

Morvayne and the rest of those at the table simply stared at Mara in contemplation. She could not read their expressions as she looked at each before taking a bite of her fruit compote.

Then Morvayne caused Hans to go to his knees. "Hans, shall I make an example of you? Do you not recall that she is my future bride and your future Queen?"

Hans quivered as Morvayne caused some unseen pain to bear down upon him. "No, Master, I mean, yes Master—I—I forgot in my anger, but I will remember my Queen always in her Glory. My lady, my life is yours."

Mara stood to gain Morvayne's attention, she had yet to put away her Light. "Morvayne, stop it! He has apologized and I have forgiven."

Morvayne was troubled at her confidence and command, but with that much Power and Light he could do nothing but obey. "As you wish, *My* lady," he smiled ingratiatingly. He thought desperately, *Please let me gain control of her before she gains control of me! Why me? Why can't any of my plans go my way? It is simply not fair!*

Mara was not sure what had happened, but it appeared that a shift of power had occurred just then. Clay's eyes sparkled briefly, before he tamped his ebullience down to his usual calm demeanor. Hans brought in the rest of the meal, serving Mara first with the greatest amount of grace and deference.

Breeze chatted away with Jasmine as though nothing of significance had occurred at all.

Morvayne chose to present a calmness he did not feel, "I will be gone all day after all. I had thought to stay and learn what you have been taught, but it appears I have no need. You are ready to take the Oath, Mara, and I have a few surprises I wish to prepare for your Birth Day. Mara, My little Buttercup, you can put away your Light; it truly is too much."

Mara blushed, sending more Dust to join with that which she had sent shooting in every direction in her anger, only now it cascaded gently to the floor as it fell from the silk dressing gown which she had worn to breakfast.

"Sorry, I forgot."

She truly had, but she thought it was funny anyway. So now, she smiled and hungrily ate all of her breakfast, requesting seconds. *Another whole day without Morvayne, hurray!*

Once he was gone, Mara told Clay and Breeze about her visit with Jasmine to see her Mother.

"So she has all the clues and will be staying in my house until this matter is settled completely. Also, Clay, who should we give the extra sheds to?"

Clay had stretched his lengthy form on the couch and lazily watched the fish in the giant tank as they swam languidly from one corner to the next. He was in a complete state of relaxation having overdosed on Mara's Dust. At least that is how Mara saw it. Inside, Clay was a mass of emotions at war, yet the best way to get Mara close to him was to maintain complete calm—so he did. Mara sat on the floor in front of the couch facing the tank. Clay reached out and gently pulled her hair through his fingers.

In answer to Mara's query Clay said, "I think we should not give the other ones to your Attendants because we need to stay with you. We should to give them to Water Sprites. They can scatter in several directions and Morvayne will be completely confused. I will need to stay with him while you make your escape. He will still believe that I approve his plans and support him in his efforts. I am not asking to be released from your service, just for a temporary reprieve, so that I can do what needs to be done here."

Mara turned and knelt in front of his face, tangling her hair in his fingers briefly. "Ow! Clay, I don't want to be away from you. I trust you; you make me feel calm. Who will keep me as safe as well as you?"

"Mara, you have not gotten to know Ivan or Elwood very well; they are very skilled and equally devoted to you. You trust Hannah and Daisy, do you not?"

Mara screwed up her face as she thought and then replied, "Yes, I guess so. I mean, yes, I know they are trustworthy and skilled. Hannah feels like she should be my best friend forever. But you . . . "

Inexplicably Mara began to cry. Thinking that she had stopped doing that days ago, it only made her cry more.

Clay had been dying to hold her, but he had not meant to make her cry. Sitting up, he took her on his lap. "Hush, Mara, Shh… I will return soon. Daisy mastered the Art of Vaporization and was able to leave Morvayne's property. It works! Today you will continue practicing your Mask of Deception techniques. When we judge you have it under control, you can then Transform into fish and whatnot. Like Wort. Remember?" He brushed her cheek with his own.

"How do you do that? I was so upset and now I'm not."

"It is my gift. We all have unique gifts and talents. Mine is to calm others. That is another reason Morvayne accepts my presence; he is calmed when I am near. He lessens in his heated passion of hate. I do not think he notices the effect, at least he has not mentioned it lately. Mentally he still believes what he does, but emotionally his fervor is dampened."

Mara abruptly changed the topic. "Do Elves grow beards?" She stroked his perfectly smooth face, causing Clay to take a sharp inward breath, followed by a slow sigh.

He grinned, "Mara you are so incredibly delightful. I am experiencing déjà vu. This was a part of a life I sampled, but there was no Aerrvin at all. You became my wife, and it was a wonderful joyous life." He allowed his eyes to linger on her face for a moment.

Now Clay was crying. Mara was shocked; no Aerrvin? She thought to move, but as always Clay kept her where he wanted her.

"Mara, I need Arianna if I am to stay in your presence. It just hurts too much. I love you just as much as I loved Tigerlily, and nearly as much as Arianna. Meeting with her reminded me how very much I need her. I will go to the Land of Dreams and find a way to bring back both Arianna and Brentwood, but I need your permission or command, either will do." Clay sobbed once more accepting Mara's comforting hug.

Once again she kissed him on either cheek. While thinking good thoughts of success Mara blessed Clay, as she tasted the salt of his tears. "I will grant you your request, but you must share this Dream with me. It is not fair that you should shoulder this burden alone."

"Mara, I have behaved badly. We generally do not share details of our Dreams with one another, at least not the ones from our alternate life paths We are not supposed to influence each other by what we have experienced."

"But it's not right! Is it?" She paused thinking. "I guess it is. If Aerrvin came to me with a Dream that showed us living happily ever after in order to convince me to marry him, it would not make it true for this life. Nor would any of the Dreams you have lived. You said I died horribly, was that from this experience?"

Clay smiled again. "Oh, Mara how do you get me into these messes? I am supposed to be suave and coolly mysterious!

You have turned me into a crying fool telling you of my secret lives! This is wrong, I tell you," he paused to take in her pearlescent visage, "but I will tell you." He added the last part softly, producing a cool cloth to wipe her face and then his.

"I told you before that you were in three of the Dreams I have lived. In one, you married Morvayne, you ruled the world with severe justice based on his ideology. You lived a long and cruel life. Morvayne gave Arianna to me, but it did not bring me joy. Another one was not much better; you became my bride, but Morvayne still sought to have control. Poor choices on my part caused your death. Your betrayed eyes haunt me." He stopped to squeeze his eyes shut for a moment.

"However, Mara, this moment here is the one which brought me happiness and a long and joyful life with you, well not this exact moment, the part where you asked about beards . . . that was a turning point. Had I chosen to answer exactly as I had in the otherwhen perhaps we could have had the same results. But I doubt it. As I said, there was no Aerrvin in that scenario.

"Eventually, we had three beautiful children who went on to have many lovely grandchildren for generations. The world was at peace and life was wonderful for all. That was a very rare Dream indeed. Most end in violence and death. That kind of perfection is hard to find, you might never find it on your own. Very well, Mara, I will share that Dream with you, as it is ours. But, not until I return."

Mara nodded graciously, "Thank you, that is fair."

Her mind was so full of questions that she blurted out a new set of problems. "Where will I go? I can't go to my house; it's too crowded. Ironwood Estates might work, but Morvayne would wait for me come outside sometime. Don't I need to go somewhere that he does not know about? At least until we can imprison him somehow? What kind of punishment should he get anyway? I mean what kind of punishments have been given in the past for similar kidnapping and the like?"

Clay hugged her and laughingly replied, "Too many questions at once! Aerrvin has prepared a place where you can hide, he has placed wards as strong as or stronger than those at either Ironwood's or Tigerlily's homes. Do not look so surprised; we have been planning your escape together. And I am not the one to judge what kind of punishment Morvayne should get. You are.

"However, I can tell you what they did to Jules when he stole the Crystal Throne and tried to rule in the Queen of the First Garden's place. She had been away in the Land of Dreams; never had anyone ever made a move against the Queen and her Throne, so it had not been guarded while she slept for five years. This is what she did; she caused him to be placed within a capsule similar to the ones Morvayne uses. Then she allowed twelve persons who had been wronged by his brief rule to sit in the Chair of Desire. Seven chose to have personal desires granted, but five chose various forms of vengeance against him. So severe were those consequences that he Fled to the Land of Eternal Spring with a promise to never return. As far as anyone knows, he has not. Sentencing Morvayne to make a final life path choice and live it would not be too harsh. It would be compassionate and just."

Mara tried to climb out of Clay's lap gracefully, but instead kneed his thigh painfully and plopped down beside him.

"Sorry! I'm just a kid 'member? How do you gain grace anyway, never mind. That comes with age I'm sure. I will practice my lessons, but first tell me, seriously, I want to know. Do Elves grow beards?" she tried to sound commanding, but Clay was so dumbstruck that she had returned to the question that she rolled over laughing.

"Please, just tell me!" she giggled.

"Yes, Mara. Have you never seen a picture of Santa Claus?" Clay grew a significant beard right before her eyes to demonstrate. He looked like Merlin suddenly and then he returned to no stubble at all.

"Amazing! How do you do it?" Mara asked.

"No, that was your last question. You have more pressing lessons than hygiene sciences."

Mara happily went to try her Mask of Deception lessons with Jasmine. Just knowing that she would never have to shave again was news enough for now.

Clay went to find Aerrvin. He found the prince with Jaera and Gareth, sitting in Ironwood's vast library along with Lumina.

Lumina was in the process of asking, "I would like to know when you think it would be appropriate for me to return?"

Lumina had been standing when Clay arrived, brought in by one of the Brownie staffers. As he entered, she deftly slipped in between Aerrvin and Gareth on the couch where they sat.

Jaera exuded fierce jealousy, but being the first to see Clay enter from behind the others she joyfully ran to him and pronounced, "Clay should have an answer for you."

Clay allowed Jaera to guide him to the soft leather chair placed adjacent the couch. Soothing Jaera's jumbled nerves as she sat in his lap, he said, "Indeed, I have great news! Perhaps you should get Ironwood and Brand so I shan't have to repeat myself."

Gareth started to rise by removing Mina's hand from his thigh, when a Brownie poked her head in.

"I have sent for them, sir, they should arrive shortly."

Mina observed Clay holding the now becalmed Jaera. "You have a way about you, Clay; she has been spitting fire all morning!

You would think she were a Yellow!"

Aerrvin and Gareth grinned, but only Gareth responded, "I like her just the way she is!" Jaera blushed for the first time in ages.

Aerrvin collected her Dust quickly and passed the bottle to Gareth after shaking a small amount on his wrist. "Still as sweet as ever," he declared, after taking a whiff.

Ironwood and Brand arrived along with Lorelei and a few of Ironwoods assistants. "Clay! You have good news I hope?"

Clay stood to greet Ironwood and bowed to Brand, reminding the others to stand and bow as well. Ironwood caused more chairs to appear. Gareth wisely chose a chair and pulled Jaera away from Clay, arranging her on his own lap as he savored her scent. She had a vast collection of Dust and rarely wore her own, Gareth had nearly forgotten how sweet she truly was.

Mina frowned briefly at the slight, but then turned her attention to Aerrvin caressing his hair once before taking his hand in hers and turning her attention to Clay. "You can return me to my Academy?"

"I have a plan, so I would say, yes."

19
Battle Plans

Aerrvin quickly shared his shed with Gareth and Jaera, even as Ironwood divided his amongst his assistants and Attendants, while Mina looked on jealously. With a sniff, she sucked it up. If this would help secure her home, she would accept it.

Lorelei had news as well. "Thank you for letting us know about Daisy. It is good to know the technique can be learned so quickly and works so well against Morvayne's wards. I have been able to enlarge the Dryad with no apparent harm; we can see the light trails more easily. We have undone most of the weave, but if you would care to take a look? Perhaps you can see what the next step should be."

Clay stood immediately; this was his true desire, to understand the weave and how to remove it. Standing in the lab with Lorelei, he was impressed with her studies. She was obviously an eminent scientist. "Lorelei! Why have I not seen your publications?"

She bowed her head and said, "Because I have not published anything. Well, that is not true I did publish *How to Weave Clouds* under the false name Rain ap Surrey. It was many centuries back."

"Rain? I love that book; it is for younglings true, but it was delightful nevertheless. Your talent should be shared, not all of course, but surely you have countless discoveries and insights to share."

"Yes, Ironwood has said much the same thing. Come, here is the Dryad."

Clay saw that it had indeed been unraveled and the ribbons of light hung loosely in a pile to the side.

"Can you not simply cut the excess, now that it is unraveled?"

"Perhaps, but I would not want to risk it. The difficulty is here." Lorelei colored the light section she meant with a soft pink glow.

Clay moved closer to see more precisely. "Lorelei, can you color each ribbon a different color? We should be able to see the tangle better that way."

She complied as she said, "How obvious! I should have thought of that myself."

Clay observed how she altered the light to get the two colors, one pink the other yellow, simple and amazing in itself.

The knot was convoluted, but now that it was in two different colors, they quickly solved the difficult part, undoing it within the hour. As soon as the light fell away and then disappeared with its unmaking, the Dryad became aware. He hummed a plaintive cry.

Joyfully they called the others and went to release Gwennara.

***

Aerrvin and his two companions left after honoring Gwennara in her return. It had been sobering to view her without her Power and Glory, but her regal bearing remained and Brand cared not that she was no longer Queen. They rejoiced in each other and wept when Clay said he would depart soon to quest for and retrieve Arianna and Brentwood.

***

Entering the Water Sprite resort in Italy, Aerrvin greeted the Blue Sprite with a kiss. He turned to his companions and said, "Kiana, this is Jaera and, of course, you know Gareth. We have a mission for any of your people who might want to assist. Can we meet your Grotto Leader?"

Kiana assured him that Queen Aegle was in residence and would surely meet with him.

"I never knew that Queen Aegle ruled from here, did you?" Aerrvin asked his companions.

Gareth and Jaera each shook their heads in wonder. Aegle was truly ancient and revered among Water Sprites; indeed all water creatures honored her.

Kiana returned saucily and invited the group to enter a tunnel, which opened up to a particularly large cavern with natural light spilling in to shine directly upon the dais upon which the daughter of Zeus sat. All three Fairies bowed deeply before rising when called.

"My children rise. What is it you wish from me?"

Aerrvin stood, flanked by his two companions. "Mother of the Graces, it is with great awe that we request your help in the depths of the sea."

He told her of the attack on the Academy as well as the search for Arianna and Brentwood in The Lost City of Atlantis. He told her of Clay's plan to disorient Morvayne, as well as how he planned to secure the school for Lumina.

"Yes, I have just received news and details of that attack. You say Lumina is with you? May I meet with her?"

Gareth bowed and winked out, returning shortly with Lumina. She bowed deeply and went forward without waiting. Aegle rose from her chair and met Lumina half way as they embraced. "My dear child, I thought you lost to me." Aegle returned to her throne and caused a bench to appear for her guests to sit before her.

"I wish to meet this Brand one day and thank him for his newfound talent. Truly wondrous this Vaporizing. I knew of it by another name, but never practiced it. I suppose I did meet with his Queen Gwennara when she first took the Crystal Throne many ages gone by."

She sighed gracefully, her beauty surpassed any words the poets had written in their efforts to describe her.

"Lumina is a favored great-great-great granddaughter of mine." She smiled once more at her. "Of course, I wish to help her return. I shall give Clay a proper tour of the City of Atlantis, not lost to me at all. We can secure the schools today. I want to assure that all of the colonies and Academies are secured and evil doers routed out. I fear I may have stayed in Atlantis far too long, I do have duties to perform. Do you have the sheds you wish to share?"

Aerrvin blushed in his youth before such beauty and wisdom, Brightness and Power. It was humiliating to not have Clay with him to hand over the tainted sheds. "No Mother, Clay has them. I shall fetch him."

Clay had already left Ironwood Estates when Aerrvin returned. "Did he say where he was going? A cell phone surely would be useful."

Ironwood grinned. "Yes, Humans do have some mighty amazing inventions; we should not be written off so completely. Ivan and Elwood each have a phone; let me try them."

He called.

"No, he has not contacted them yet, they will call you when he does. I took the liberty of telling them your cell number."

Aerrvin found Clay himself when he decided to check in on Amanda who was still living in Mara's house. Opening the door to let him in, Amanda greeted him warmly. "Aerrvin, please come in. Clay is telling me about your new discoveries and plans. I want to help, but Clay doesn't think there is anything I can do."

"How is it that he can now be in your presence?" Aerrvin asked perplexed.

"I sat in the Chair of Desire, and he popped into the room! Who knew it had such power?"

Aerrvin saw a twinkle in Clay's eye, but had urgent news so he pushed on.

"Amanda, Clay. I have been to visit the Water Sprite Colony on the beach near Morvayne's Palazzo. By surprise, I learned that Queen Aegle has a residence there *and* she requests your presence."

Clay acknowledged surprise by lifting one brow before soothing his face once more. "I would be honored."

"Who is she?" Amanda asked. "I mean obviously she is Queen of the Water Sprites, but you appear to be in awe of her."

Using his teaching voice, Clay replied, "Aegle is the daughter of Zeus and is over Thirty-five hundred years old. She is the Mother of the Graces, those Charites known as they who influence Humans and others in beauty, mirth and good cheer. Her husband is Helios also known as Apollo. She lives in the Land of Eternal Spring and is rarely seen anymore."

"These deities exist?! I don't know what a Charite is but— how can my daughter be a Queen of all the Realms compared to a daughter of Zeus?" Amanda nearly shouted as she tried to comprehend her ever-changing reality.

"The Charites are Muses. The title of god is fairly new, but the position stems from the Fair Ones who lived in the First Garden. The Greek and Roman gods are not actual gods; they are simply Fair Ones who had more fame and power. Apollo does not drive a chariot to pull the sun. Those are truly myths. Really, Amanda, you need to get an appropriate education. Ask Ironwood for some good books to start with, you can learn as you teach your daughters." With a sweep of his graceful hand he changed his attire to a simple white toga. "She does prefer the era of her fame."

Amanda admired his calves as she collected her thoughts, "So muses influencing others is real, but ancient gods are not. Yes, I need to get educated. I know nothing. It is a good thing I was planning on homeschooling. Aerrvin wait!" She called as he made a Window to the Colony. "Can I come? After all, she is my Queen." She looked pleadingly from Aerrvin to Clay.

"Very well, how should you like to present yourself?" Clay smiled as Aerrvin closed the Window.

Amanda looked at her shorts and blouse. "I have no idea. Do Water Sprites always go about nude with perhaps a strand of sea weed? That is all they have on in Ironwood's books. I won't meet a queen in the nude, I will tell you that!"

"You could wear a toga or you could wear something like this." Clay caused her clothes to become a gauzy top, which barely came to her thighs which were clothed in lacy leggings. "Generally, Sprites do prefer to swim with nothing on as it creates less drag." Just then Rick walked by the study. Pursing his lips, he eventually whistled.

With his eyes raised in a question, he asked, "A costume party?"

"No, I don't have time to explain, but I am going with Clay

and Aerrvin to meet my Queen. I mean the Queen of the Water Sprites."

Clay added, "Not just the Water Sprites; all of the water world, especially Mermaids. Neptune has retired and the throne passed to her. He no longer lives in this world either. He retired completely into the Land of Eternal Spring. He probably lives in Atlantis—I would suspect."

"Oh, well if that is all." Rick quipped. Amanda smacked him on the shoulder. "Isn't there some kind of protection you can place on her? I mean, Morvayne uses that capsule thing; I don't want Amanda trapped, just protected."

Aerrvin responded, "She still has the ring and necklace. But I can give her one additional device. Mara gave it to me for a birthday present." Suddenly two bracelets appeared on his arm; removing one he handed it to Amanda. This is from a baby Dragon. It is the skin it sheds as it grows."

She put it on, feeling its softness even though it appeared stiff. Aerrvin nodded as she caressed it in wonder. "It will respond to your desire." Aerrvin demonstrated by causing his bracelet to become gloves. Then full armor, he removed his tunic for emphasis.

"I just wish it to cover me?" Amanda asked, as suddenly she was covered head to toe, causing Rick further shock.

"Yes, but only imagine it covering your body. Like a body suit. Yes that's it." Aerrvin smiled as her arms and legs glowed with the oily glittery shapes that shifted on her person. "Now watch." He tossed his sword to Clay who caught it and swiftly sliced at Aerrvin's ribs.

Amanda screamed, causing the three children to come running down the stairs. Aerrvin calmed them all as he explained the qualities of the shed, including using it as a diving suit with gills ready-made. He demonstrated his gills and webbed hands as he covered himself completely, allowing the kids to feel its softness. Ricky wanted one, as did the girls.

Rick stroked Amanda's arm. "It *is* incredibly soft. Okay, dear, you may go with my blessing. But do not stay away long or we will worry. Aerrvin, Clay—keep her safe," he charged sternly.

Stepping through the window they entered the lobby of the spa, since it would be rude to appear directly before the Queen. Once again, he called Kiana and asked her to escort them into Queen Aegle's presence.

Amanda noted that most of the Water Sprites were indeed almost all nude and they were every color of the rainbow, but mostly watery blues and greens. Fairies made up most of the guests and they were mostly clothed if topless or dressed in gauzy, lacy, or sheer fabrics.

"I see I need to develop a new wardrobe," Amanda murmured to Aerrvin.

"It will be fun!" Aerrvin replied with a wicked grin.

"Could my children have been born in colors like these?" Amanda asked with a wave all about her, but particularly to the deep blue legs of Kiana in front of them.

Aerrvin smiled. "No, they learn to change their skin colors with a simple formulae, or wish, really. I have told Mara, but she may not have had time to tell you. Magic is not magic when you understand it. It is mostly math and science. You will love it, Amanda, hardly any mysteries at all."

" 'Hardly' he says," she snorted right as they reached the opening to the great cavern.

Kiana introduced them and, following Clay's lead, Amanda bowed deeply before the most beautiful creature she had ever seen. *No wonder they were called gods,* she thought. She dared not look up; the Queen's Power affected her strongly.

"Please arise and seat yourself. Aerrvin, I assume this is Clay." She nodded in return to Clay's smooth nod, smiling at his beauty and grace. "Who is this *Amanda* you have brought." She did not look at her, but at Aerrvin.

"Mother, she is the one whose daughter I seek to free. Also her husband is Brentwood, whom Clay seeks to recover, along with Arianna."

Kindly, Aegle nodded to Amanda, "Ah, the mother of our future Queen! Welcome Amanda. Rest in comfort. I knew not what kind of girl this Mara was. Her great-great grandfather is Brand the Bright, a Fairy of great renowned. Gwennara too is well thought of and greatly respected. I sorrowed upon hearing of her entrapment in one of my Academies. Now I see that my own heritage is to be represented in the new Queen of all the Realms. Truly, she will unite the world in justice and truth, I can feel it. What is your heritage, child?" Aegle asked.

Amanda looked down. "I was abandoned, Mother, I know nothing."

Aegle commanded, "Come here. Right up on the dais. Come on." Her fingers beckoned.

Amanda hesitated, she felt so lowly compared to such grace and beauty. Nearing her, though, she felt love, and ventured to meet her eye to eye. Aegle took her hand.

"Yes, as I thought. You are weak, but not as weak as you have been led to believe. Someone has placed a dampening binder on you. I suppose they thought since you were to be raised Human, they did not wish you to harm yourself. Nevertheless, you are grown now. I will remove it. This tells me that whoever left you, cared about you enough to want you safe." Amanda blinked back tears as any adopted child would.

"Now. Do you feel a release?"

Amanda tried to feel a change and closing her eyes was surprised to see her soft glow was brighter. Beaming, she replied, "Yes, Mother, thank you!" She felt compelled to bow, but was too close, so she lowered her head gratefully.

The Queen reached out and caressed her face. "Please, sit with Lumina." She pointed towards the bench with a low back on it, where a beautiful woman sat. She was not an Elf, so Amanda wondered who and what she was.

Turning her attention to Clay, Aegle said, "I assume you have the sheds you wish my warriors to wear?"

"I do," Clay replied, reaching into his satchel which had not been there moments before. "We wish to wait a few days; Mara is not ready to Vaporize yet. She learns quickly; if she can keep her mind on her task, she should be able to accomplish it within three days. That is barring any unforeseen moves by Morvayne. He is becoming increasingly agitated, but Mara is becoming increasingly commanding in her bearing. She may become strong enough to command her release without any casualties at all."

The Queen thought for a while and then said, "Fascinating. Lumina can you bear to stay with me these three days before you return to your beloved students?"

Lumina nodded and smiled, "Of course, Mother, it will be my pleasure."

"Clay, I understand you wish to seek these relatives of our future Queen within our most glorious fortress. For what purpose do you desire this thing?" Aegle inquired.

Clay stood. "Your Highness, I am Mara's sworn Protector. But above that, I love her with all my being. I cannot stand by when she knows there is a small chance that her father can be returned to her. It causes her pain, which causes me pain."

Amanda felt her heart clench at the thought of meeting Brentwood. She loved him desperately, but had a new life with Rick. *How could I leave him?* She could not. *Surely, Brentwood would understand.*

Aegle asked Clay, "What is your true motivation?"

Clay stood a little stiffer. "Those are true and pure motives. But you perceive rightly, Arianna is my true love, and I cannot survive this life much longer without her."

Aegle smiled lovingly. "There. Was that so hard to admit?" Clay looked abashed, but he nodded anyway. "Yes, Mother. Truly hard."

With a near roll of her eyes Queen Aegle said, "Very well, you are dismissed. Return to me, Clay, in three days and we will begin this reclaiming of the seas." Clay turned to collect his companions. The Queen added, "Have you a plan for detaining Morvayne?"

"We have considered a binding, but we do not know one of sufficient strength, he has been studying the art with the best that he can find. As we know, he visits Atlantis frequently in order to secure his captives and rouse them from time to time. Or tries to anyway." He grimaced recalling Arianna's entrapment. If you know who has been teaching him or can send someone to find out, it surely would be a boon."

The Queen shrugged and stood for a moment, before stepping down to bid farewell to each of her guests with a hug.

Lumina came forward as well and gave Aerrvin and Gareth familiar hugs and kisses. "I wish you well, dear cousins." Before Jaera could get fired up, she hugged her as well and said, "He is ready for you now. I wish you the best."

Jaera shyly went to Gareth and held his hand. Amanda was lost, but accepted everything as it came.

Leaving the spa to stand on the beach Clay said, "While we are here we might as well take a swim. Do you want to give it a try Amanda?"

They were all still six inches or so. Seeing the world from this size was too odd for Amanda, so she requested that they maximize to their Human form.

"Sorry, I know this is my true size, but it is going to take time. I don't know, but that I will always prefer this Human size to that Fairy size. Sorry!" Amanda said, pleading forgiveness from Aerrvin and his Nest Mates.

Aerrvin and the others all changed their armor into complete lizard skin. It was the first time for most, so Jaera called forth a full-length mirror.

"This is awesome!" She laughed as she added spikes down her back and webbing beneath her arms, going all the way down her side just stopping at her hips.

Aerrvin had his hair in the crest that Mara preferred. Gareth made his a double-rowed crest, and Clay sleeked his away completely, allowing one to marvel at his perfect bone structure while his face writhed with the flowing rainbow swirls.

Amanda had yet to complete her armor, standing in front of the mirror she disrobed and viewed her lizard-self in one swift stroke.

She smiled. "Yes, no, that is definitely not attractive. Since I am a Water Sprite, do I have to be a lizard? I mean I have never tried to stay under the water longer than three minutes, but that was because I was told it was not possible. I can can't I?"

Clay assured her that she could certainly give it a try and if she felt anxious she could simply extend her armor. "Besides Aegle released some of your hidden power. You glow Brighter even now. Let's try it." Taking her hand, they ran into the water.

Amanda was amazed. Her vision was perfect and she had no need to use any man made breathing device. Joyfully they swam about enjoying the nearby reef and all it held. She was equally surprised to hear her companions speaking in a musical voice enhanced by their dragon sheds. She laughed and found that she too had a sweet watery voice. She could have swum for hours and hours, but she had promised not to worry Rick, so she eventually swam to the surface to enjoy the luxurious Italian heat.

Clay created a blanket and they all gratefully stretched out to sun. Gareth transformed his clothes to swimming trunks, as he liked to tan. Not counting Amanda, the rest were fair and felt just fine in their second skin.

"Ooh, Gareth, you don't know what you are missing." Jaera crooned, "The heat feels like liquid honey is being poured down and soaking into my being."

Amanda noted that it did indeed feel different from ordinary sunbathing. "Do dragons really like to sit in the sun? Or is that just in stories."

Clay replied, "Dragons are just giant lizards, they really do enjoy soaking up the rays and if this is how it feels to them, it isn't any wonder at all." He sighed and closed his eyes.

It felt great, but Amanda was vain and wanted a tan just as much as Gareth did. "Gareth can you teach me how to create clothes for myself? I would like a swimsuit so that I can get a little bit of a tan as well."

"I don't know if I have the skill for teaching, and I am not sure you have enough power. You are Brighter sure but —"

"Nonsense!" Jaera interrupted, smacking him on the head. "Amanda just imagine the clothes you want. Shut your eyes. See yourself with them, I mean see them on you." She laughed. "You wouldn't want to just be holding them."

Amanda's lizard skin became a maillot. But no actual fabric materialized. "Well at least I had not imagined the skin into a bracelet and then the suit!"

"Sorry, Amanda. Maybe with practice. Would you like me to create you a swimsuit?" Jaera asked.

"No, I guess this lizard skin is quite comfy really." Amanda replied turning over to tan her legs from the back. "I do want to learn how those Sprites change their tint though. That should be fun!"

After an hour Clay said it was time to go. "I need to return to Mara. Amanda I think you already have the ability to change tints."

He brought the mirror and showed her. She was perfectly tanned as though she had spent a week on the beach. "I have always tanned easily in a day or two, but this is crazy!" she exclaimed.

"I think it is because it was your fondest desire to have a tan, you must truly desire something, not casually think it. Perhaps you did not *want* a swimsuit?" Clay smiled broadly as Amanda smacked him on the arm.

"I was thinking of a great tan while I was soaking up all this heat. Let me try one more thing." She imagined her nails done in a lovely coral, something she had been meaning to get done.

Looking down she crowed, "Look at that, I did it!" She then imagined the toga back in place and beamed as it appeared just as Clay had fashioned it. "Oh, I could kiss Aegle for this gift. Brentwood would be so proud–" she stopped shocked at what she had just said. "I–sorry. I don't know why that popped out. I have no intention of leaving Rick for Brent. Don't say anything please!"

Aerrvin held her hand, "Amanda, Brentwood *would* be proud. He will not hold Rick against you, he will be happy for you. I can promise you that. If he is like any other Fair One he will understand what you went through. For all you know he has had to find comfort elsewhere as well."

That only made her wrinkle her brow, but Aerrvin had been wanting to prepare her for that possibility for a few days now. "Amanda, listen to me, this is important. We Fair Ones can easily live over one thousand years and as you have just witnessed with careful skill we can live much, much longer. These few years will be but a short moment in your life. Rick will age and die, there is not much help for that.

"You can choose to die when he does; generally we Fade away in grief. Nevertheless, your daughters have the ability for this extended life as well. Do you really want to leave them before they are fully mature? I am still young at my age. Clay is getting old." Aerrvin smirked and ducked as Clay's fist swung towards his head. "Amanda, what I am trying to say is that you can return to Brentwood soon. Soon for us anyway, fifty years is kind of short. Think on it. For now, enjoy what you have. Surely you know that our greatest desire is to enjoy the moments of every day to the fullest."

Amanda nodded as she continued to take it all in. Aerrvin made a Window for Amanda to step through and closed it without following.

"I have elsewhere to be," he said and stepped away from his companions, as did Clay.

Jaera smiled impishly up at Gareth. "I guess that leaves you and me! Where should we go?"

20
Skills Perfected

Clay entered Mara's sitting room. Breeze sat next to Jasmine crocheting. She stopped as he came in. "Good news?"

"Yes, fairly good. Is Mara still in the fish tank or in her room?"

Morvayne entered the room, coming out of Mara's room. Smiling his weasel-like smile he wrapped his arm around Clay. "Ah, my dear brother, what good news have you to tell?"

"Hannah has made a few breakthroughs on your puzzle." Clay lied easily. He wondered why Morvayne was back already. It was barely past dinner.

"Let me check on Mara first." Evading Morvayne, he went to her room, but she was not there. He could feel that she was close, but she was not to be seen. "Where is she? Jasmine, where is Mara?" Clay exuded calm, but his heart was straining to race away. He kept it steady by shear will, as he did not want Morvayne listening to his heartbeat. Understanding broke through, but he did not like being made the fool. So instead, he left the room and asked Morvayne to talk with him privately in the study.

Once seated in the study, Clay said."Morvayne, I just wanted to tell you that I am ready to destroy the freeways in California. An earthquake should be going off in a few hours."

He smiled conspiratorially, awaiting Morvayne, who was not Morvayne, to respond. Morvayne smiled and melted away, becoming Breeze.

"Very clever; you must admit we had you fooled. Come, see if you can tell who is who."

Returning arm in arm with Breeze, Clay went in to find two versions of Hans standing near the credenza.

"Mara, I am so proud of you, and your teachers have done a remarkable job as well. Walk towards me so that I can observe you. They both walked forward and turned and swaggered as Hans was wont to do.

One of them watched him more closely, so he chose that one. "Surely, this is Mara?"

They both immediately returned to their own form. "How could you tell?" Mara whined.

"You can't keep your eyes off of me," he replied suggestively, causing her sparks to fall lightly.

He informed them about all that he had done and learned. "So now you get to start on the next technique. Sure to be stimulating. Have you eaten already?"

"No, we were waiting for you," Mara responded.

***

Aerrvin returned home to visit his parents in Ireland. Filling them in on recent events, he taught them the Vaporization technique, charging them to keep it secret for royalty and guards only. "That is what Brand hopes anyway. It will become known eventually, but a few decades are better than days. Right?"

Nodding, Laurel asked about his retreat. "Where is this hideaway you intend to take Mara to?"

"Well, that is why I am here, Mother. I have built a beautiful palace on the coast of Washington. But it is for a wedding present. It would be completely safe and secure as I have placed wards on top of wards throughout the entire structure. My difficulty is this: Should I marry her soon, before her Birth Day? That is, should she manage her escape. Or should I take her there to keep her safe, and then not have a grand gift to give when we actually do marry? Or . . . can you keep her safe here, until we are ready to wed?" He looked forlornly at his mother, awaiting her wisdom.

Laurel looked at her pitiful son and then turned to Jasper. "Dear, what do you think?"

He smiled and waited to hear what he thought.

Laurel went on, "I think she would enjoy a temporary stay with us. Not more than a year though, Aerrvin, really. Too many Royal females in one location will become difficult at best."

"Yes," echoed Jasper. "I would love to get to know your intended better before you are wed. Besides, she will need some training before she can rule with diplomacy. Laurel and Harmony would enjoy offering their knowledge and advisors to help train her. Yes, that is the least we could do for our Future Queen."

Aerrvin performed back flips for his parents to show his gratitude; it seemed as though it had been ages since he had let his Purple personality shine. "Thank you Mother, Father. I knew I could depend on you! You always know what to do. May I use my rooms tonight?"

"Of course, dear, they are yours, you are always welcome here. Where are Jaera and Gareth anyway?"

"Dancing, I hope!" Aerrvin allowed his eyes to sparkle.

The pair had been holding off because of him. They wanted him to marry as much as Harmony and his parents did. "I do believe Gareth has finally gotten the courage to devote himself to Jaera; at least they seem to radiate joy in each other's presence more brightly than ever before." Bidding his parents good day, he chuckled as he left to find his rooms.

***

Morvayne negotiated with the Trolls for hours. They insisted that they get one Fairy for dessert for every Human they remove. Obviously the numbers would not support very much of that. There were far too many Humans compared to Fairies. Eventually he reasoned with the leader who finally understood that they could have the deal for one week or they could have a small colony of Fairies incarcerated and they could save them for the king, to enjoy at his pleasure.

"Besides," Morvayne reasoned, "once they get a taste for Humans they may be satisfied with one a day for as long as a year. Perhaps more," he smiled conspiratorially at the green-skinned Master Olkin.

"Very well, Elf. However, if things do not go as you say, then we will seek revenge against you. Elves can be tasty too." He slurped a particularly ropy string of slobber in for emphasis.

"Tomorrow then," Morvayne confirmed.

Drawing a line of Light, he left. It wasn't much, this killing spree; he had let bands of five or six loose before. This time he had one hundred Trolls willing to hunt, but he was spreading them out throughout the world. His plan was to use the Fairies to Travel, since Trolls lacked that ability. Were the Troll compound to be discovered before Morvayne had true power to rule the world, then Humans would probably come in and bomb the site. No, Morvayne rethought that, with a snigger. *They would incarcerate them, because the Human softies would say that any sentient being required a fair hearing. It would take them years to come up with laws to deal with it.* But Morvayne could free them at will. Maybe he would simply destroy an entire village or small town in a day. *That might be fun.* He grinned at the thought.

How could Humans be the favored species anyway? It never made sense to Morvayne; *Elves are far more superior and beautiful; more graceful and talented than Humans could ever hope to be.* For that reason, Morvayne had always thought of the Supreme Being as unfair and unjust. *Perhaps He Himself is not in his right mind.* Yes, Morvayne felt that he had the right of it and he would prove it.

The forty Water Sprites that Morvayne had gathered to his way of thinking agreed to set off a tsunami to hit the shores of China and neighboring Asian nations. It was set to go off in a few hours. The wars in Africa were proceeding well. Morvayne loved stirring up trouble there, it was so easy to get those nations and tribal leaders all stirred up. Morvayne had plans in the works to provide killing frosts to most of the crops of the southern states.

One disaster after another and the Humans will be looking for someone to save them from destruction. But the killing will have to continue for at least another decade before the numbers would be low enough for me.

Yes, I have time. Mara is sweet, yet I know what she is capable of, having experienced her wrath in the otherwhen. One last check in with my followers in Egypt and then I will go home.

His 'family' was just finishing dessert when he arrived. "Oh, that does look good. Hans a dessert only please. My day went well. What did you accomplish today?"

Everyone looked at him briefly, amazed at his chattiness.

Clay offered an answer first. "I have learned that Mara's family has moved into her house permanently. I think it would be nice to take a visit tomorrow."

Morvayne considered and agreed. Mara was shocked. First, that Clay would mention it, and then second that Morvayne would agree. Breeze then requested a trip to the museum as long as Jasmine went with her. This too Morvayne agreed to congenially, he was in a good mood. Why?

After seeing Mara tucked into her bed, Clay and Morvayne retired once more to Morvayne's sitting room. "You are definitely in a good mood. If I make my request, will you grant me my desire as well?"

Clay grinned winningly at Morvayne. "I am pretty sure I can become quite friendly with Amanda, she appears to like my boyish charm. A week or two and she will be inviting me in whether Mara is with me or no," he bragged.

"Yes, I am sure you are correct." Morvayne sniffed. "What is it you desire?"

Clay smiled wickedly. "Arianna, obviously; remember, I forgot to ask her about the Crystal Throne. I will not forget this time as I have recently seen her and will not have so much making up to do. By the way, where have you searched already? If she tells me one of those, I will know she is not telling me true and then I can redirect her."

"Clever Clay, always thinking ahead. I have searched the Royal Palaces of Ireland, Scotland and Greece as well as their small home in Australia. They have a few caves, but I have never learned the locations of those caves. We speak as though I have already agreed to allow this. Hold on! Don't get all pouty on me. I will releae her to the Void, but you must allow me to enter for five minutes. With you, of course."

This meant revealing her preferred door in the Void as well as their secret knock. Clay weighed the alternative of not seeing her. "Very well, I do not see her being very forthcoming with you there, but it is a possibility."

Morvayne excused himself to his room and then returned with her body. *Had he kept it here the whole time?* Clay wondered.

"No, Clay, I see what you are thinking. I just did not wish you to puzzle out her location, she is a precious commodity to me."

"Please, can't I keep her all night in my room?" Clay begged, hating his brother for degrading him so.

Morvayne made no reply.

They went to Clay's room. Holding Arianna between them on the bed, they slipped into the Void. Clay went directly to her door and rapped his patterned rhythm. She answered with her own tap swiftly and he concluded the rap by adding an extra tap, hoping she understood. She opened it warily, rather than joyfully.

"So you had a coded knock. That would have been helpful, once upon a time, anyway. Proceed."

Clay swiftly glanced at Morvayne and then sat in the grass on the edge of the small stream that appeared. Addressing his true love he said, "Arianna, Mara is about to have her Birth Day and she needs to be crowned upon the Crystal Throne. Could you tell me its usual locations Or where it might be right now? Do you know?"

"I do. It is always kept wherever Mother wants it."

"Now look here . . ." Morvayne started, but cut off at Clay's flick of the wrist.

"Morvayne is anxious to have a place where he can search. Do you know the location of any of your Mother's favorite caverns?" Clay asked calmly.

Arianna understood and perhaps Morvayne knew she would evade, but Clay was doing what he had said he would.

Arianna replied, "One we always visited when I was a youngling was in India; let me show you its location as there are several residences there." She changed the setting of the room and suddenly they stood before a cliff, lined with carved porches and entryways. "Ours was the uppermost one, obviously." In an instant the view changed; they sat on the porch looking down toward a river. "I do not know if they have been there recently, but we loved it as a young family seeking adventure."

Morvayne cruelly made an elephant appear out of the brush, trumpeting as it came charging towards the river.

Clay tensed, but chuckled dryly, "Very funny. May we have our privacy now?"

"Very well, Clay, you did as you said you would. As a kindness I have released the bindings holding Arianna in stasis. You have four hours. Arianna, I look forward to you joining the family. It shall be glorious!" He casually walked to the door then looking back, he smirked, and closed the door.

Not very long after, they were lying upon a pile of pillows in Arianna's Scottish palace bedroom. Clay kissed her eagerly, but briefly. Forcing himself to stop, he quickly told her all the good news, especially about the release of her mother.

"Even better, we can untie your bonds as well. Here is my problem. We thought your body was with Brentwood in Atlantis, but right now, it is with me. Morvayne retrieved it too quickly for it to have been in Atlantis. I don't think he has learned time travel. Though, I suppose he could merely reach through a portal, *if* direct portals are allowed. Still, I need to locate where he is keeping you. Alternatively, we could free you now. The twist is that Mara will not try escaping until the day after tomorrow, we hope."

Arianna caressed his face and looked up at him with her clear blue eyes; Clay inhaled deeply in response.

"Clay, stick with your plan. Let's escape for a while." Standing up, the princess went and opened the door of the now white-walled room, carefully making sure that no one was spying.

"But first, let's see if I can visit my body; it seems like I need to stretch. I get these feelings when Morvayne releases the binding."

Clay stopped her. "Let me check to make sure he is out of my room." Waking he looked about and realized that there was, once again, a bubble of power surrounding the room. Clay added his own field, which would prevent Morvayne from entering and returned to collect Arianna. "Please, join me in my real life."

She laughed at his word choice and awoke from the Dream. Clay had her curled up body lying protectively within his own, as he had wrapped himself around her moments before entering the Void.

"Oh, yes, my muscles ache." Arianna stretched and then sighed as Clay expertly massage her stiff neck and shoulder muscles. He spent ages loosening each group of muscles until she said she felt good enough to dance. Slowly they danced to a swaying rhythm, which he hummed softly in her ear.

"Did you visit my Dream?" he asked. Breathing deeply to collect as much Dust as possible, knowing his chance was short in real time. He kissed her jawline before she answered with a smile.

"Yes, Clay, I did. I think it was better than the one I found. Though I had to speed through parts. I should like to view it again more slowly. Did you have time to view mine?"

"No, there is too much happening right now. This is the first break I have had and I would rather spend it with you than a Dream. Although, it is 2:00 a.m. If we returned now we could have a four-week mini-vacation. What do you say, join me in Glennferry?"

She smiled up at him, enjoying the firmness of his muscles beneath her hand. "I would love to. Will Merlin be there?"

***

Amanda always stayed up late, so Rick said nothing when she sat in the study and researched information online. Noting the time, she ensured everyone was tucked in and checked in on Rick before returning to the study. *Now, to read the letter from Brentwood.* Amanda had read it just the one time, but her emotions were too raw to deal with it, as well as being in denial. She was not sure she could handle it now either, but she thought there might be a clue. Brentwood had typed it, but had included a hand written p.s. at the bottom. She read that first.

P.S. Live your life fully my precious one. Make every moment count. You never know what life will bring you, but I promise to love you forever. XXOO

Amanda allowed herself a good cry. *Isn't that what Aerrvin had said? We need to experience our emotions completely. Somehow, Brentwood knew he might not return from his adventures.* Amanda allowed her temper to flare at his negligent behavior. *How could he have behaved so recklessly, knowing he had a young daughter to raise?* She knew she was being ridiculous, but it made it easier to read the main letter.

June, 5, 1997

Amanda,

I love you and apologize for leaving you this way. If there has been no body recovered, I believe I have been kidnapped. I know you will not want to believe this, but please do not throw away this letter! Save it until you are ready. Please ensure that my journal and other personal effects in my strong box are kept for Mara.

I wish to to bestow them upon her at her 21st birthday.

I have included a letter for her as well. Please, Amanda, I am begging you: DO NOT throw it away! Dougie is Sylvie's cousin, they will have important information about Mara's safety, as well as Ironwood and Aunt Lily (who is Tigerlily, as you well know.) First of all do not move out of our house! It will protect you and keep you safe.

Please call Hannah and Clay back into your life; they love you and Mara, as do the others. I know we have been over and over this. I can NOT stress enough the importance of Mara's safety! I know it is your greatest concern as well, which is why we argue. Please, let's not argue anymore.

I need you, Amanda. You two are everything to me, and Mara is everything to the Magical Realm. I promise you—this is not make believe. I have found the path to The Lost City of Atlantis. I will be taking a trip shortly and do not know how long I will be gone, I am hoping only a week. Morris is actually an Elf named Morvayne, as I have told you before. He intends to kidnap Mara. Aunt Lily and Ironwood will know how best to protect her, yet they will respect your wishes.

I have recently solved a riddle given me by a Dragon named Meriel, she gave me twenty years to return to her with the answer. I have known the answer for a year now, but have not had an opportunity to return. Meriel has promised to extend protection on you and Mara when I solve it. She also agreed to listen to a proxy if I cannot reach her. Send a friend like Elwood or even Ironwood—you will be protected. Here is the riddle:

> *Tell me now and tell me true*
>
> *This thing I wish to know from you*
>
> *Is something great and wise and true.*
>
> *Greater than he who sits on high.*

More evil than he who tells the lie.

The rich of the world have need of it

The poor and the destitute abound with it

Eat it now and for some time

Within a month your soul will fly.

'Tis something great and wise and true.

This thing I wish to know from you

Tell me now and tell me true

I am ashamed to say that the answer was painfully simple. I am planning to go see Meriel next weekend before I leave on my week long trip. But should something happen to me the answer is this; Nothing. Nothing is greater than God, or more evil than Satan. The rich need nothing, and the poor have too much of nothing. Eat nothing and you will die. I believe Meriel actually loves granting wishes and always gives simple riddles. Remember that; and she may become a lifelong friend. Until we meet again, my dearest Water Baby . . . Brent

Amanda did not know how to rid herself of the guilt she felt.

She had argued with Brentwood repeatedly and especially on the day of the accident. She had said some mean and hurtful things that day. She could still see the pain in his eyes as he left.

She had promised herself when she met Rick to never be that harsh again. True, she felt no need; they lived a peaceful ordinary life, until recent events changed everything. And yet, Aerrvin brought up the possibility of a future reunion with Brentwood. She had only dreamed of such a possibility and now it was a probable truth. *Would Brent really love still love and accept me?*

She read the postscript again.

Brentwood never lied. That would have to do. She needed a hug, but did not want to cry on Rick's shoulder; he was worried enough about Brentwood's return.

She called out softly, "Sylvie?"

She knew the other Brownies were trying to clean, they probably wished she would go to bed. One of them went and got Sylvie, who came in a minute later.

"Amanda? Did you need something?" Amanda maximized her and fell into her arms. She meant just to get a hug, but she started sobbing all over again. Sylvie patiently soothed her. Once Amanda was calmed, she noticed that Sylvie had shed her own tears.

"I love Mara very much. I miss her. But you are worried over many things, aye?" Sylvie asked.

Amanda nodded and handed the letter to Sylvie. When she had read it, she hugged Amanda again and replied, "I remember his last days at home. You were afraid, Amanda; he knew that and truly loves you. Dougie knows where Meriel's cave is, as does Seamus, though he cannot make a Traveling Window; a weakenss some of us have. Dougie is just across the street. Should I send for him?"

Amanda brightened at the thought of doing something helpful. "Would you?"

"Of course! I need Mara back with me soon; her absence causes true physical pain. How Dougie manages to enjoy life all these years is a marvel. Seamus is my anchor now. Without him, I would simply sit in my hollow and weep. Your little girls bring me joy as well; thank you for sharing them with me."

One last hug and she was gone. In less than a minute she was back with Dougie, who was pleasant as always.

"Thank you for trusting me, Amanda. I would be honored to meet with Meriel."

"I want to come too!" Amanda announced.

"As so do I!" Sylvie added.

Dougie looked at one determined face, and then the other. "You are not telling me the answer to the riddle are you?"

"No," they each answered.

"Very well, tell Velvet where we are going and then we will go." Velvet was in the hallway polishing the floors. Sylvie quickly related their Quest and returned with a shiny object in her hand.

"A gift," she replied as they looked askance.

"Do Dragons always need gifts?" Amanda queried.

"They like them, but Brentwood has already given her his gifts; she will remember."

"Then let's go!"

They appeared on the cliffs above the sea. The transition was a bit jarring as it had been night when they left and they stepped into the full sunshine of late afternoon.

"We will have to dive down and swim beneath the sea to enter the cavern properly. Dragons get testy if you simply come in from the sky to land in their private courtyard," Dougie instructed.

Sylvie was a bit nervous as she rarely went swimming, yet she had had opportunity enough when they lived in Sequim. They dove in together. Amanda was thrilled with the dive. She had never used her wings before, having only gained access the day before. The dive was like a slow motion free-fall as her wings took her as slowly as her fear requested; it came so naturally that she was tempted to swoop up into the air and dive down again.

The surface of the lagoon was a treat as well; the water was so calm and clear. Breaking free of the relative silence, a bugling greeting surprised her. The young Dragons were playing in the water as Meriel watched from her ledge.

A young green Dragon swam near suddenly and dove under the water only to rise with Amanda on his neck. "Welcome sister," he greeted as he swam to the small sandy beach.

Amanda was amazed at the sweetness of the young Dragon's voice as well as the attachment she felt for him. Holding onto the green Dragon's neck ridges to keep from falling, she recognized the delicate shimmer of his skin. "I share your skin?" Amanda asked in wonder.

"Yes, how did you get it?"

Amanda started to answer when Meriel interrupted. "No speaking, until I grant permission. Who comes to disturb my solitude?"

Dougie stood before Meriel and chanted:

Dragons High and Dragons Low

Give to me what I should know

Give me lessons by your Light

Grant to me your knowledge Bright

Give me lessons by your Light

Give to me what I should know

Dragons High and Dragons Low

"Meriel, I come in the place of Brentwood as his proxy. My name is Dougie and I have come to solve the riddle. Or rather, my companions have the answer and wish to receive the promised protection."

"Yes, I remember you and Brentwood. I expected him to answer my riddle sooner than this. Wait, before you reply I wish to know how this one happens to wear a shed of my dear Grimson? Tell me your name and how you gained this treasure."

"My name is Amanda Jamis Powers. Brentwood was my first husband and father of my daughter, Mara. She has not had time to tell me how she gained this skin, but she gave it to Aerrvin who gave a portion to me as a protection against the evil which threatens my family." Amanda was amazed at her bravery; she was now standing beside a baby Dragon while speaking to its very large mother.

"Mara is precious. You must be very proud of her. Please tell her she may visit me anytime. As you can see, Grimson loves any who shares his skin."

Amanda started to speak, but Meriel snorted and then said, "Wait! I need to know who this final Brownie is. Three Brownies in one month, amazing. Have all Brownies begun to adventure?"

Sylvie bowed deeply. "My Lady Dragon, I am Sylvie and I belong to Mara. We seek to gain protection and help."

"Yes, that was the purpose of solving the riddle. Mara did tell me that her father had disappeared in a boating accident. Which explains his not returning to solve the riddle, but if you had the riddle why did you not come sooner? Was it truly so hard to solve?"

Amanda replied, "No, I kept the riddle locked up in a box. I was lost in my Humanity and did not believe in magical things. Mara has been captured, causing me to return to my true self. I reread the letter and knew that this was something I could do to help keep her safe, and to request protection for my other two young daughters."

Meriel keened loudly, startling the three guests. "Why did you not tell me she was in danger? She is my Future Queen and I adore her! She is sister/friend to my dear Gwendyll. Tell me where she is!"

Amanda bowed in apology. "Sorry to upset you, we share the same fears. Morvayne has her within his warded home on Vashon Island. That is part of Washington State."

"Yes, yes I know. I have maps. Please, come inside."

She turned and swiftly slithered into the deeper portion of the cavern, returning before they arrived in her receiving room. Unscrolling a map, she requested a precise location. Amanda did not know and smiled gratefully when Dougie pointed it out.

"I see. Do you know the answer to the riddle? I must keep my standards."

"Yes," Amanda repeated the riddle and then replied confidently, "the answer is nothing."

"Very well, I will extend the protection to your young ones as well. I cannot leave yet, as my children are far too young." She caused two bracelets to appear before Amanda. "The stones in these bracelets render any ward useless against the wearer. So if Mara is trapped behind a barrier of magic, you can walk right in and not be stopped. The one who created the ward will not feel it break, nor will he be alerted. I can keep you and your family safe in any body of water. Simply call out and help will arrive through my network of friends."

Dougie looked up sharply, "Does this include helping Brentwood?" Hope shone brightly in his eyes.

"Yes, I suppose it does. Do you know where he is?"

"Yes, he is held captive in Atlantis," Dougie replied.

"Atlantis? Yes, he did mention he was planning a trip there didn't he? That complicates things. I assume this Morvayne has trapped him there somehow, correct?"

"Yes, and Clay of Glennferry has confirmed that Arianna is a captive as well."

"Another family member, Brentwood certainly hit the jackpot with this request. I cannot leave my children for another sixty years; at that point I can go there and free him myself. I will see if I can convince another to go in my place, but my friends are busy with their own interests. I cannot promise anything sooner than sixty years. I am sorry, Dougie, I can feel your pain." She felt Amanda's mixture of pain and relief, but did not comment on it.

"As for Arianna, I gather you do not know her location?" She received a nod. "I do have a favor owed me by one Zara, an Ogress. She is skilled at sniffing out those in stasis, the usual form of incarceration. Here is her location."

A window opened showing a cave situated on some high cliffs next to the sea. She included the coordinates for Dougie and he acknowledged that he had them firmly planted in his mind. "You will need a sample of Arianna's Dust to give to Zara."

"Thank you, My Lady Dragon. Your gifts are truly wondrous." Dougie bowed.

Meriel again turned her attention to Sylvie. "Sylvie, I see you have a gift as well as a ring upon your finger, a ring which once was mine; please explain."

Sylvie bowed, as she is ever wont to do. "My Lady Dragon, the ring was a gift from Seamus, he proposed to me and gave me this ring. I thank you for granting his desire. It is perfect and I love it. I have brought you a button which I have treasured for several decades. I love it, but wish for you to have it in gratitude for all that you have done and will do for Mara, my Mistress, whom I will serve forever."

Sylvie handed the button to Meriel. It was a Sea Dragon carved in silver; it curled around the outer edge and inside lay a clutch of eggs with one hatchling peeking out.

Meriel inspected it closely and purred in a loud, warm way. "Sylvie, it is precious, thank you. You may Travel from here, as I am sure you are anxious to remove Mara. Say goodbye, children."

Amanda had forgotten them, as they had been so quiet. She patted each one as they came near to say good-bye. Then Dougie opened a Window and they returned to the study in Mara's house.

21
Escape

"Should we get her now?" Amanda asked as she faced Dougie.

"No, Amanda. I know you want to be involved, but you have lived your life as a housewife. Gareth, Hannah, or Elwood on the other hand, are trained combatants, spies, and Protectors. Clay is the leader of Mara's Attendants and Hannah is second, so we can try contacting her to get her opinion."

Amanda sighed, "You are right, Dougie. Thanks for reminding me. No sense in walking in on Morvayne and getting myself killed by some trickery."

They called Elwood, who contacted Hannah. She arrived swiftly and accepted the two bracelets which Meriel had given them. She let them know that she would confer with Clay. He had a plan set in motion and she did not want to mess it up. "These may be necessary, so they are quite helpful. We will return them as soon as possible. Remember, you are safe here, so rest easy."

Dougie went home and Sylvie resumed her work. Amanda now knew why she never slept very long at night. She didn't need to. Or she could sleep forever. *How funny!'* she thought. She decided to watch a little TV before going to bed for a few hours. A tsunami had just crashed upon the shores off of Asia. It was bigger than the one that struck India a few years back. Amanda felt pity for the poor victims. Okinawa, the southern shores of

Japan. Taipei, and countless small islands suffered loss; many completely wiped clean. All of the channels were showing coverage. It was too overwhelming, Amanda turned it off. Collecting a sleeping pill, she went to bed.

***

Morvayne spent the night flying over the carnage as an Albatross, calling out from time to time in joy to his faithful Orange Fairy who acted as his bodyguard. "Henri, look how pristine! You can have that one for a new Fairy Ring!"

"I am honored, My Lord," Henri replied.

Morvayne viewed each island carefully and then went to witness the destruction of the larger populations. He regretted that he had not thought of doing such a deed sooner. Eventually he had seen enough and he returned home.

He had Arianna to put back, and he wanted to see what the news would have to say about the death and mayhem of the Trolls, sent mostly to South America, but a few had been granted opportunities in some of the southern United States.

Little did the Yellow Fairies know that they were to be dessert once they had completed the task of opening Traveling Windows to the desired locations. Morvayne really had little respect for the Yellows; they were too full of themselves and fought too much with the Oranges; they certainly lacked the fierceness in battle that the Orange Fairies displayed. *Yes, it will work out well.* He already had twenty Yellow Fairies in a holding pen on the ranch. Of course, they thought they were in a glorified scientific lab and connecting library. *Ha! They are so full of themselves, it serves them right.*

***

Clay bid Arianna farewell and returned to his room. He studied the protective barrier after removing his own. It was

306

similar, but held nastier consequences. Too bad all that intelligence went to such wicked pursuits. Clay realized Morvayne would be returning soon, so he curled up protectively around Arianna and took a quick nap. Hannah was there in his Dream.

"It's about time! Where have you been!" She hovered in his personal space. Then she broke into a smile. "So you have been getting Dusted have you? I can't tell the difference between Mara and Arianna." She held up her hands questioningly.

Clay smiled contentedly, "Arianna. We went to a figmentary Scotland; it was absolutely delightful."

Hannah nodded, "That is wonderful! I have news for you." She related Amanda's Quest and told him about the bracelets which were now in her possession. "The next time you get a moment with Mara they should work to take the bonds off of her immediately. Moreover, should your trip to Atlantis be unfruitful, Meriel said she would be free to go as soon as her young are grown."

She paused a moment as she inhaled the fragrant air of his favorite meadow. "We still do not have a definitive plan for entrapping Morvayne. Have you thought of anything yet?"

"No, but that is wonderful news indeed. I will collect the bracelets soon. Also, we have been given permission to visit Amanda in Mara's house. Of course, Morvayne wants me to study the wards and see what can be done about them. He may even tell me the counter spells that he taught the Fairies. That would be fantastic knowledge to gain."

Morvayne knocked at his Dream. "Ah, there he is now."

Clay invited him in. Morvayne acknowledged Hannah with upraised eyebrows. "Arianna kicked you out?"

Clay grinned boyishly, "No, I just wanted to ask Hannah about her progress on the task you set her on." They turned to her expectantly.

"Well it appears to me that short of sending someone in to dispose of, not one, but four Dragons, the best solution is to wait until her young are grown. She will leave her cave for days at a time in her joyous freedom. True the cave will have wards, but I understand you are developing quite an arsenal of counter spells. Is it true you gained your wisdom from drinking wine?" Hannah had moved closer to Morvayne, as though he was, oh, so attractive.

Morvayne was fooled, as the vain Elf he was, he believed all others inferior to him. "Yes, it is true that was the key to my initial success. Of course, I am now immune to its effects. My own intelligence guides me now. How old are Meriel's young?"

Clay answered. "They are about forty, which gives you sixty years to find or collect the Throne and Chair of Desire. All well within your self-imposed one hundred year time-frame." Clay leaned back on a fallen log, and picked at a twig, snapping it neatly into one-inch sections.

Morvayne turned to Hannah. "Thank you, Hannah, you have been a great help. Would you care to join us for dinner tonight? I feel like it will be a joyous day. Well worth celebrating."

"I would love to. May I bring an old friend?" Hannah asked.

"Yes, of course, male I hope. We have three females in addition to you and we shall have dancing."

"In that case, can I bring both Elwood and Ivan? They are my Hold Mates still, and it would be hard to choose whom to invite. Besides, Ivan still likes Jasmine." Hannah had hold of Morvayne's arm, as she begged prettily in her Dragon armor. At Morvayne's nod, she hugged him and kissed him soundly, before stepping out of the Dream.

Clay and Morvayne looked at one another in wonder momentarily, before Clay said, "Still the perky little fluff ball she always was. I have missed her."

"Yes, she does have an energy about her that no one else can duplicate. I have surely missed all of my former friends. It will be grand to be gathered all together again. We can let Mara and Breeze replace those not with us." Looking at Clay's momentary drop in countenance. Morvayne amended, "Arianna will join us once we have the Crystal Throne. For tonight let loose and enjoy life for a change; you have ever been far too somber. Let us wake."

Waking up, Clay breathed in Arianna's scent one last time as he nuzzled her neck and kissed her cheek.

"Really, Clay, I have never understood your inability to keep your hands off of her. Yes, she is lovely and she smells nice— but, so do plenty of other Fair Ones." Morvayne bent near and inhaled, "Yes, she smells like Mara. You seem to be able to control yourself with the youngling. What have you to say?"

"I love her," he answered simply, as he drank in Arianna's visage.

Morvayne felt a stab of pain and jealousy. "Yes, well see where love got me. As I recall Arianna rebuffed you as well. Do not get me wrong; I am glad she is giving you a second chance, if she is. All I am saying is, don't trust her. She will probably try to escape given the chance. If you want to keep her near so that you can enjoy her scent, you will probably do well to learn some of my binding spells."

Clay never expected to be offered, but he readily accepted. "Please do. I am not too proud to learn from my little brother."

"Of course, all in good time." Morvayne said jovially. "Right now I need to return Arianna." Picking her up, he took her to his rooms. Clay wanted to lie down and review his last four weeks with Arianna in their shared Dream, but Mara awaited. So, with a sigh, he showered and then dressed in simple jeans and a white button up shirt, left casually un-tucked. He enjoyed combing his hair and carefully pulled it back into a queue; tying it securely with a leather string.

Soon.

***

After breakfast, Clay and Mara were driven to her house by Hans. Mara felt oddly nervous; being free to go home. Clay felt her jitters and took her hand to soothe her.

"What is it?"

She shook her head, "I don't know. I think it has to do with being trapped for so long and then suddenly being free. I still feel like I am being watched. You know? I feel spooked."

Arriving home Mara choked up. Amanda came out as soon as the car stopped. "Mara! Honey, please come inside." She took her hand and nearly ran with her into the house. Once inside, she hugged her fiercely. "You look wonderful. Come on in, sit. Sorry we have taken over your home —"

"Mom, calm down! It's okay. I want you safe. This is perfect." Mara looked around, it was the same, if a bit messy, two little girls and two "vacationing" guys tend to leave a little dishevelment. "How have you arranged the bedrooms? We can change the furnishings to make it more efficient." Mara started to go take a look.

"No, we don't want to be a bother, Mara. Ricky is on the fold out couch and the girls are sharing Jill's old bed." Amanda said, as motherly as ever.

Mara smiled. "Nonsense, Mom! This is Ricky's house now. He should not have to sleep on a couch and have little girls running through his room."

Clay trailed behind, interested in observing Mara's skills. Mara went on back to Jill's old bedroom. It was classy and hip, but still too feminine for Ricky. Mara caused the walls to become a calm ocean grey-green, she even gave them a wide rough texture simulating waves.

Amanda gasped. "I had no idea! Your father never did anything like this."

"It is probably Aerrvin's fault. He taught me how to manipulate texture and such a few weeks ago. What do you think Mom, lighter curtains or darker?"

"Lighter, he gets moody enough without feeling like he is in a cave," Amanda replied.

Becky saw what was happening and ran out back to get Ricky. He came in and directed Mara in arranging the rest of the room. Clay even volunteered to travel with Ricky to pick up the rest of his stuff. With all of his electronics situated, he was truly moved in and ready to find a job.

Testing out the bed, Ricky remarked, "Now this is the way to move in, no rental trailer or long drive."

Just then Rick came in to see what was going on. "Hey, Dad, you should get a personal assistant who can teleport you back to the house every day. You could check in on the business and be home for dinner, presto change-o!"

Rick shook his head and then grinned. "This is all insanity! But, I would like to check the shipment that is due in today. I mean, Jim is a great manager and all, but I still like to check in every now and then. Maybe going back to the house every couple of days would be good. We wouldn't want the place getting musty. Who knows what is growing in the fridge?"

Amanda became concerned about her house at the mention of it. "I think we still have dirty dishes in the sink! Yes, it does need to be looked after. Clay I don't want to be a bother. Do you know a less busy individual who could help us out?"

"You probably have willing Brownies in your house there, I can go and see. They have not done any cleaning since you left. An empty home causes Brownies to feel bad, so they prefer to sleep. Or work on their own homes. I will be back shortly; since I am going, would you like to go along, Rick?"

He did. Looking over the house he assured himself that all was well. They had forgotten about the mail, so he brought it all in and sorted through it. Mostly junk, five bills. Yes, they definitely needed a plan. Clay appeared to have found a few Brownies as Rick heard them talking when he came down the stairs. They were still six inches and scurried to the shadows as he entered the room.

"It's okay guys, I believe in you. In fact I need you. Whatever Clay told you is true."

A male Brownie emerged from behind the magazine rack. "We miss your daughters and hope that they are safe. I can ensure that your home stays neat and if you would like, I am willing to be made Human sized, so that I can become your personal assistant. I will bring in the mail and pay the bills, whatever you would like."

Rick was stunned, he had never had a personal assistant, but it sounded pretty sweet. "I would love that, dude. What's your name?" Rick noticed Clay cringe, but did not know why.

The Brownie puffed out his chest and said proudly, "My name is Dude."

Clay now spoke, "You just christened him by calling him Dude. Having revealed himself to you in this manner and having been renamed he is now totally and completely at your service and fully your responsibility. Should you abandon him for no reason, you will cause him pain and mental anguish. You are his person and his desire is to please you. You, of course, cannot maximize his size. It would be wisest to have Amanda do it rather than me since the one who shifts his size is the only one who can return him to his original form. I will not always be available." Clay turned to Dude. "Do you have a wife, Dude?"

"No, My Lord. I am only ninety years old. This will be my first assignment!" Dude said, still beaming.

"Very well, Rick, go on and check your shipment. I will take Dude to meet your family and then when you are ready, he will assist you in returning home. You do have the ability to Travel, correct?"

"Yes, it is a natural ability in my family," Dude replied.

"One other thing, remember to set out milk and cookies. There is nothing better than that before a night of cleaning and repairing, right Dude?" asked Clay.

Dude beamed and gave Clay a thumbs up before following him through the Portal into Mara's back yard. They knocked and were soon inside with Dude learning everyone's names. Of course Dude knew the family already, but Aerrvin had arrived with Jaera and Gareth. After meeting them, he met Seamus and Sylvie.

Amanda proudly used her newfound talent to increase Dude's size and then sat with him at the computer to teach him about their finances.

Mara sat on Aerrvin's lap, finally free to express herself as she wished. She reveled in his scent and tried to think of ways to cause him to blush, so that she could collect his Dust to take with her. Clay maintained a cool distance, looking like his normal public self. Now that she knew him better, she recognized that he was mildly jealous. So she tried not to be overly flirtatious with Aerrvin and invited her friends to go back upstairs to help her finish the girl's bedroom.

"Clay how long can we stay? I forgot to ask and don't want to be too surprised when we have to leave." Mara called back down the stairs.

"Two hours, finish the rooms and then you need to practice Vaporization."

Clay went over to the Chair of Desire. It had a pull of its own. He wondered how much power it had when no one sat upon the Crystal Throne. Sitting down, he felt a gentle infusion of energy. The world seemed brighter and the clarity seemed crisper. As an Elf, he obviously had sharp vision, but while sitting there it seemed as though he had been in need of glasses. He enjoyed picking out the detail of the velvet pillows on the couch and then turned his attention to his own shirtsleeve. Noticing Mara, he realized that thirty-six minutes had fled as he enjoyed the chair.

"Truly a treasure, Mara. Have you sat in it since you got here?"

"No, I have not. I did not know if I should."

Clay stood reluctantly and motioned for Mara to sit.

She sat and instantly gasped, as the small restraint that Morvayne had placed on her, as well as the bracelet, which he snapped onto her wrist, each broke. The restraint simply vanished and the bracelet fell to the floor.

"I am completely free!" Joy lit her face. She stood and allowed Amanda to hug her before sitting back down. "Mom, I am still going back to the house."

"What! Are you mad? Aerrvin? Clay? Why would you want to?" Amanda was aghast.

"Morvayne has Arianna. If he thinks Clay helped me, he will keep Clay from seeing her. It's not fair."

"I didn't know Clay had a relationship with Arianna. Clay, you want Mara to return and put herself in Morvayne's hands so that you can—what? I don't know what Arianna means to you. You are sworn to protect Mara! Clay?"

Clay looked pained. "I *am* sworn to protect Mara." He swallowed noisily and took a cleansing breath.

"Mara, I believe that since you are free, it is best if you stay here, or no, rather, let Aerrvin take you to the place he has prepared. You will not be able to stay here."

"No, if I stay away Morvayne will double his attacks on this house. He will eventually find a way to weaken the wards. Clay, I love you too much to let you lose her."

Mara had tears in her eyes as she blew Aerrvin a kiss and then Vaporized. A fine shadow of sparkly mist wafted away and through the wall. They all sat there a moment, stunned by the abruptness of her departure.

"I guess she has mastered the Art of Vaporization," Clay said stiffly. "She will be able to leave without a problem, but Morvayne must not see, oh never mind, he surely knows already that the bindings have broken. I have to go!"

Clay stepped into Mara's bedroom at Morvayne's house. He had time to reach Mara's side just as Morvayne appeared.

"What is going on?" Morvayne demanded.

Before Clay could speak Mara explained, "I sat in the Chair of Desire and my bracelet fell off. I knew you would be worried, so I returned."

Morvayne was nearly as perplexed as Jasmine. He turned to Clay. "Is this correct? Tell me everything as it happened."

Clay complied and then added. "We left in such a hurry, it would be polite to return and give a proper farewell."

Morvayne considered briefly and then replied, "You may return and calm them. Let them know that she can return on Friday. I need to study the effects of placing additional wards on Mara. This is curious. Mara come with me." Mara brushed Clay's arm in thanks as she followed Morvayne out of her suite.

As soon as they were downstairs Jasmine pounced, "What happened, truly?"

"As stated, she sat and the bonds were dissolved. Then she Vaporized out of the house. She is a free Maiden now, and is here by her own free-will," Clay replied, barely containing his conflicting emotions of pride, wonder and fear. "Morvayne will find he has a very determined opponent. I will go talk to Amanda now. Go spy on them to learn what you can."

Jasmine found Morvayne and Mara in the study. Jasmine had transformed into a ladybug and sat underneath an ivy leaf near the entry. Morvayne tried several binding techniques and all of them fell away.

"Fascinating. Why are you still here? You can obviously leave now," Morvayne inquired.

"I care for everyone here and did not want you to mistake my freedom as a move against you," Mara replied honestly.

"Yes, well that was the hoped for response, but I had thought it would take years to achieve. You are a puzzle, Buttercup. I assume you feel a connection to Clay. If he were to be sent away on assignment would you still stay?"

Morvayne could not understand her motivation at all and hoped to learn what she was thinking. He felt her panic even as she stifled it and maintained a cool façade. He smiled slightly.

"I would prefer he stayed near me. He *is* my sworn Protector. I have come to depend on him. Where would he be sent anyway, and why should he listen to you over me?" she challenged.

"Oh, you are becoming feisty aren't you?" He continued to smile, enjoying the challenge even as it still made no sense to him. "Very well, I have no command over him it is true. You shall be Queen and we shall serve and obey. But the Crystal Throne needs found. Do you suppose you could talk to your grandfather about its whereabouts?"

Perhaps this could work out very well, he thought.

"I could give it a try. May I call now? Oh, but he would never speak about such secrets over the phone." She playfully patted his hand.

Jasmine would have shaken her head in dismay, had she had a neck. Mara had always been so shy and retiring as a Human. Her Elven nature was truly asserting itself.

"I could probably ask him Saturday; he has planned a birthday party for me on his property. Everyone I have met so far is going to be there."

Morvayne wanted to scream, *she is not even asking!* Yet he maintained his cool. "Mara dear, I had so wanted to participate in your Oath Taking Ceremony. I am not permitted on Ironwood Estates."

She just looked at him coolly, as she ran her fingers over his silken sleeve. The front door opened and they heard Hans and Clay enter.

"Very well, Mara, you are a free maiden; please think of me during your Birth Day Oath Taking Ceremony. I shall be thinking of you." He stood and taking her sheathed hand, kissed it not once, but twice. "We will have guests for dinner tonight, please choose something Faire." He retired his rooms upstairs;

The only television in the house was in his bedroom. Even watching the foreign channels, as they discussed the bizarre snatching of loved ones that had occurred, did not bring him the sought after joy he had hoped for. *Mara will bear watching; perhaps she and Clay have fallen for each other and Arianna is no longer a motivator for Clay. No, I saw Clay with Arianna. He was truly smitten; he must have convinced Mara that he cared for her though. She never mentions that puny Purple and none of the Oranges have reported him flitting about anymore, for at least the past week.* That thought did manage to lighten his mood. *Perhaps we can get her to find an interest in Ivan; he has a flair for art. Perhaps he would like to discuss photography with her* — Morvayne wandered off into his Dream, imagining Mara falling for this Elf and that, until finally she found that she did indeed enjoy Morvayne's superior style and wit.

***

Mara spoke to Clay and Jasmine briefly, before calling her grandfather. Clay assured her that everyone was calmed and nearly confident in her choice. Aerrvin especially understood and supported her decision. Jasmine related her opinions on Mara's verbal sparring with Morvayne. This time she was able to shake her head as she laughed.

"Clay you should have seen her, she is almost as commanding as–" She blushed as she realized she was speaking about royalty.

Turning to her charge she nodded lightly, "Sorry, I was going to say you remind me of Tigerlily. Mara, it truly was a treat." Jasmine collected her own Dust and handed it to Mara with a slight bow. "Forgive my impertinence."

Mara accepted the gift and then hugged Jasmine. "Nothing to forgive. Tigerlily was my mentor; to achieve her sweet demeanor and wisdom would be a treasure to me."

Clay mocked, "Mara, she meant you were coy and commanding. Two very exquisite skills of Tigerlily's, which were the envy of all who met her!" He hugged Mara tightly as she blushed her own scent-filled Dust all over herself. No one bothered to collect it, "Let Hans have it," Clay laughed.

***

Mara confirmed her Birth Day party with Ironwood. He had already spoken to Aerrvin by the time she'd called, so he was reserved in his joy at hearing from her. "This is wonderful, Mara. I look forward to your special day. 6:00 p.m. Saturday then?"

"Yes, that sounds wonderful. I will call Jill too. Love you, bye."

Mara was thrilled. She did not know what to do about Morvayne, but he did not seem to be taking it too poorly. Clay still did not know how to overpower him. Mara decided to mull it over it for the afternoon; perhaps she could think up the right questions. Clay had said that her necklace was designed to help her do just that. She decided to go out back; it was a lovely day seventy-eight degrees and calm. Not hot like it was in Italy, but nevertheless warm for her. She wanted to work on her tan.

Positioning the lounge chair toward the sun, she sat down with a sigh. Free to do as she pleased! She had never enjoyed so much freedom in her life. Not even leaving home, to live in Seattle at eighteen, had felt as wonderful as this.

"So this is what it's like to be a Queen. Hmmm, I guess I can handle it."

She smiled and then sat up as she heard someone approach. It was Hans. He bowed. "My Lady, I wish to know what you would prefer for our dessert tonight."

Mara lifted her hands in a questioning flutter. He brought forth three fanciful creations. "Please, if you would taste them and tell me your desire, it would bring joy to my soul."

"Very well, Hans, but why do you care? I mean, you know that all of your food creations are masterful." She took a taste of the flan; the caramel was perfectly golden and the custard firm, yet smooth.

"My Lady, surely you know that my greatest desire is to please you," Hans replied with a bow, yet he kept his eyes on hers.

Mara suddenly felt far too exposed in her bathing suit. "Hans, you know I am promised to another, right?"

He did not know about Aerrvin, as Morvayne had never mentioned him to the 'help'.

"I know that Morvayne woos you, yet I see he does not have your full attention and desire returned." He smiled handsomely, his eyes filled with hope. "Besides, My Lady, I simply desire to bask in your Glory, to please you with my culinary prowess will suffice if you so desire. The flan? Does it please?"

She took a second taste, since she had not had lunch. "It is perfect, as I would expect. But flan is not a favorite of mine." She smiled at his dropped countenance.

She had never had so many suitors in all her young adult life. *Lucky for me that I found my soul mate. I would be so confused with all of the attention — what am I thinking? I had been confused, and it had taken he who had contributed to the confusion to bring me to my senses.* She knew she was getting lost in her thoughts, as Hans shifted his foot, she realized she had sat there for three full minutes contemplating Aerrvin, and flirting, and being a Fair One.

"Sorry, I am still getting used to being awakened. Let me sample the chocolate one."

Hans brought it forth with a flourish. "I did not know that you were new to this. I know your heritage, but that is all. You behave as regal and faire as any Elf maiden I have ever met." He poured a raspberry syrup over the chocolate trifle and then placed a small dollop of whipped cream to one side.

Mara knew she would love this one. With a smile she

savored the bite, allowing herself to enjoy it completely. With her new senses, that meant it took a full two minutes before she took a second bite, to confirm that she had truly enjoyed it; the second time she made sure to get a bit of the cream. Coming out of her chocolate ecstasy, she realized that Clay had joined them, and Hans was abashedly bowing before her Sworn Protector.

"Clay? Is there a problem?" Mara inquired.

Clay turned to her, jealousy plainly expressed in his taut stance. "He was standing over you as you lay there sunning. I thought it inappropriate to your station."

Mara became aware then of how it would have looked. Yes, truly not how she should be seen by anyone other than her husband.

"It is partially my fault, Clay, leave him be. He is asking for my opinion concerning the dessert for tonight. I got lost in the savoring of the chocolate trifle. Probably my vote goes there." She tossed Hans a smile as he glanced up. "Stand up, Hans. Clay come and taste these with me." Both obeyed, as though they were little boys.

Clay sat on the next lounge chair as Mara fed him a bite of the flan, followed by the trifle. He chose not to give his opinion until the final dessert was sampled. Hans presented the final dessert as though it were a cherished object.

"My latest creation, please tell me your opinion." Mara did not know what it was so Hans told her. "It is a Mascarpone Panna Cotta served with fresh pears, plums and apricot puree. It is similar to a cheese cake, but lighter."

Mara could not help herself; she had to savor its flavor deeply, but she held on to Clay's hand to maintain contact with the world. It was delightful, but she would still prefer chocolate. *Probably the Humanity in my genes,* she thought. She gave Clay a bite and waited for his verdict before she gave hers.

"Well? Clay, tell us your opinions. We are all waiting with bated breath."

Clay smiled with his eyes, but otherwise kept his face severe. "I favor the third one, but would not turn any of them away if offered."

Mara clapped and turned to Hans. "Make both the Trifle and the Panna Cotta. I am sure none will go to waste. Hans you should meet my dear friend, Jill; she is a chef just starting her career. She has fed me these past four years and it has been wonderful; she treated me like a queen. I miss her."

Hans bowed and said, "Yes, My Lady, I can make them both, thank you for the honor. Your friend, she is Human?"

Mara replied, "Yes, as Human as they come. But she knows my true nature and accepts me as I am. She would love to meet you. In fact, I can introduce you tomorrow! I keep forgetting that I am free to go wherever I wish."

Mara grinned at Clay, gaining an approving nod in return.

"Sorry, but I do not understand. We have always been free," Hans responded, confusion plain on his face.

"Hans, I thought you were aware of Morvayne's plans? Do you really not know? Clay, is he lying?"

Clay responded casually, "Mara, slow down. You need to take time to sense the feelings and emotions around you. You won't need to always be asking that way. What do you feel?"

Mara stopped and allowed the energies of Clay and Hans to wash over her. Clay was once again calm and in control, if a little – dared she think, jovial? Hans was clearly confused and wondering, but very much wanting to please. *I guess I will have to get used to that one,* she thought.

"Okay. Hans is curious and really wants to know, right?"

They both nodded. Mara answered, "Morvayne kidnapped me; surely you heard the news about Gwennara right?"

Hans replied, "Yes, of course, Morvayne told me about it. I rarely go out, as I gather my ingredients from a private store."

"Well, he must have forgotten to tell you that he was the one responsible for the abduction! Anyway, I have managed to free myself from his bonds, and am here by choice," Mara told Hans pertly.

"My Lady, I am pleased to have you here, truly, but why are you staying if he is responsible for kidnapping you as you say?" Hans was still confused, but he appeared to believe her.

"I have my reasons," she answered mysteriously and gave him a saucy smile.

Once Hans was gone, Clay chuckled and leaned back to enjoy the sun. *Tigerlily would be proud,* he thought as he reminisced over bittersweet memories of one of his lost loves.

22
The Bonds of Friendship

Dinner had been delightful. Morvayne's mood was light and he even maintained his distance from Mara as he flirted with Breeze and Hannah. He seemed to want her to speak with Ivan, so Mara spent most of the evening dancing with him.

Ivan was tall and as broad as Clay, but was more solidly built somehow. Mara concluded that his muscles were more defined, though he was not bulky. The thought of a bulky Elf made her laugh. She felt nearly as comfortable with him as she did with Clay. She mused at the meaning of it, concluding that it was still due to just having been like their infant Hold Mate.

Her mother seemed to be getting her wish that Mara experience going out with a variety of guys before settling down.

"A very unusual engagement," Mara murmured.

"How's that?" Ivan asked.

"Oh, sorry, just talking to myself again. It has been an amazing six weeks, like an entire lifetime has been lived. I am a completely different individual than the one I was. My old friends would barely recognize me, I think. At least, that is the way it feels," Mara replied, just before Ivan spun her away and back.

She looked up into his impossibly green eyes, like moss flecked with gold. Like Morvayne, Ivan kept his hair cut short, above his ears, with the bangs long and smooth. They fell into his eyes from time to time, causing him to blink his long auburn lashes. With a practiced sharp twist of his head his bangs moved to the side. The deep red caught the low lighting and reflected back a light of its own.

"Trust your feelings, Mara. Once you learn to read emotions and feelings, both in others and yourself, you will rarely make a wrong choice," Ivan counseled.

Looking at him, Mara felt the urge to have her camera in her hands again. Her eyes gleamed at the thought and he could feel her joy rising. He smiled at her, wondering what was causing her elation.

She stopped dancing and said, "Wait." Reaching through a Window of Light she retrieved her camera. "May I?"

Ivan was as vain as any Fair One could be and posed encouragingly for Mara the rest of the night. Mara eventually took pictures of everyone as they all, seemingly, became picturesque. As she ran out of her second roll of film she sighed with contentment, murmuring, "I can't wait to develop these."

Morvayne overheard and encouraged her to take Ivan with her. "Surely you are not tired. My party has come to a close. Ivan, I am sure, would be fascinated with seeing your pictures. Jasmine and Clay would be happy to attend you as well, if you want. Hannah will stay and keep me company a while longer, won't you Sweetling?"

Hannah nodded demurely. "I have no pressing needs. I can wait for Ivan here as well as there." She waved a delicate hand at the air.

Mara was impressed at her ability to appear so feminine and vulnerable. As second in command, Hannah usually presented as powerful and blunt.

Mara thought about going to her lab at home, but it seemed rude to step into the basement while the family slept.

"I guess it really isn't my home anymore. I gave it to Ricky, not legally, but in essence."

As she pondered Ivan said, "I have a photo lab we can use."

"You do?" She hugged him joyfully for providing a solution to her dilemma. She could have gone to the school lab, but that felt wrong too, since she was no longer a student. Gareth had a lab, but for some reason she wanted to keep her distance from Aerrvin tonight; she did not try to determine why.

***

Morvayne resumed dancing; he was partnered with Breeze currently. He smiled at Mara's familiarity with Ivan. "She is getting quite flirty," he commented.

Breeze nodded, "Yes, her royal bloodline cannot be dismissed. She does remind me of my dear cousins." She paused and then added, "You should encourage her to invite me to attend her Oath Taking; perhaps I will be able to search the grounds for the Crystal Throne."

Morvayne was intrigued with the thought. "Yes, that might work, but do you know how to transport it? It does not move as easily as a car you know."

Breeze frowned, momentarily marring her beauty. "No, that is a royal secret not entrusted to me. Do you have any thoughts on how to move it?"

"As a matter of fact, I lived a Dream with Tigerlily in which she entrusted me with the incantation," Morvayne replied smugly.

Breeze was truly surprised. "Really? Morvayne why have

you not chosen to stay there? Why would you want to spend time in this existence when you have found that which you seek?"

Morvayne was touched by her concern, he hugged her to him and then replied, "It was a perfect Dream, but unlike you, I prefer this reality to those found in the Land of Dreams. I care about those here who need me to restore the world to its proper order."

Breeze smiled in wonder. "Morvayne, who would have known you had so much concern for the rest of us? You are deep and complicated, a true phenomenon," she smiled at him with adoration in her eyes.

Morvayne bowed at the compliment. He danced in silence a full five minutes as he contemplated his next move. "Very well, Breeze, I will send Clay and Jasmine along with you to Mara's Oath Taking Ceremony. She will invite whomever else she will, please encourage her in getting to know Ivan and Elwood. The more friends she acquires the better."

He smiled at his future position of prominence in Mara's life; none could possibly compare to him. Mara would surely see it one day. "I will reveal the spell for moving the throne, but you must join me in Dream to learn it; I cannot risk spying eyes and ears even in my own home, you understand?"

Breeze rejoiced inwardly, but quelled it skillfully. Morvayne was a master mood reader. "I am honored, Morvayne! Truly I understand the necessity; one never knows whom to trust, ever."

***

Hans always enjoyed creating culinary delights. When Morvayne hired him to be his chef and butler, he went eagerly. To serve an Elf was an honor, especially a Lord. But over the last one hundred years, Hans had come to see Morvayne for what he was. The first fifty years had been as hoped, what with parties and serving his master in his everyday affairs, but slowly Morvayne began bringing more unusual guests to his home. They would discuss the destruction of the world caused by Humans. At first it was something Hans supported and agreed with. Humans were causing undo stress to the ecosystem. But lately, Morvayne's friends would arrive and discuss why the total destruction of Humans would be an effective solution. It became alarming to Hans, but he did not know to whom he should turn. He had told a few of his Yellow companions and some of his former Nest Mates and they had said they would look into it, but they had never gotten back to him.

He knew that Morvayne trusted him, yet the Elf had no respect for Fairies at all. Hans found it strange, considering the fact that Morvayne used the Orange and Yellow Fairies for his guards. Not to mention Hans himself. Overhearing the plot to steal the Crystal Throne was the final straw for Hans. As soon as he had the house in order, he retired to his room, and then Traveled to Ireland to request a viewing with the Queen of the Rose Crown.

It took an hour, and he was beginning to worry, as he had breakfast to serve in a few hours. But he determined that he could 'create' it rather than make it from scratch if necessary. He had never requested a viewing before and was gratified that the heir to the Crown, Princess Harmony was also on the dais.

Queen Laurel looked down at him with sympathy for his timid nature. "You have requested an audience with us?"

Hans bowed as low as he had ever bowed before. He did it flawlessly though and looked the Queen in the eyes, having a penchant for direct eye contact. "Your Highness, I have urgent news I wish to relay." The Queen merely nodded encouragement, so he continued by telling her who his employer was and the state of Mara's situation.

"You mean to tell me she is no longer captive?" The Queen became animated as she looked to Princess Harmony and her Consort, King Jasper.

"That is correct," Hans bowed slightly.

"That is wonderful news, Hans, thank you! Does Aerrvin know?" Queen Laurel asked.

"I do not know, excuse me, but I did not know that you had known about Mara. She says she has only been awakened these past six weeks and she has been held captive these past three. What does Prince Aerrvin have to do with this?" He cowered at his boldness, but as a Yellow he liked to know everything.

Princess Harmony sneered beautifully, and said, "Hans you have allowed yourself to be insulated from reality in your service to Morvayne. Did you not hear about Queen Gwennara's capture or Aerrvin's Birth Day announcement? You live so close, surely you could have attended the party. Well?"

Hans bowed before her Light, as he reveled in being blasted by her fabled wrath. Yellows did not really cringe so much at one another's tempers, rather they played at goading one another.

"My dearest Princess, I must admit you are correct. Morvayne tells me the news, as I rarely ever leave his property. He informed me of the capture of Gwennara, but I did not receive an invitation to Aerrvin's party. Morvayne has Orange Fairies guarding the perimeter of the property; they would have intercepted any seedpod being sent to me." He stopped to think, as he realized that would account for his never hearing from his friends as well. "I thank you for your insight, I have much to consider. Still, I wish to know what would I have learned at Prince Aerrvin's party?"

The Queen laid her hand on Princess Harmony's arm. "Aerrvin proposed to Mara and she accepted. Mara is to be my daughter-in-law," she smiled at King Jasper.

Hans was truly shocked, he had not even suspected that she cared for Fairies; *well she did save George*, he recalled. Sadly, he had no chance at all in wooing her, he knew it for certain now.

"That is glorious news, Your Highness. I did not know."

He knew the date of Prince Aerrvin's birth as all Fairies did, calculating he realized that Mara had been abducted the day of Aerrvin's 190th Birth Day celebration. "I do not know what the prince knows, but I am not finished with my report. Morvayne has told Breeze that he will reveal the secret of transferring the Crystal Throne to a different location. Further she will be permitted to attend Mara's Oath Taking Ceremony with the promise of searching for the throne while on Ironwood's property. Somehow, my master intends to convince Mara to marry him so that he can rule the world. Pardon me for saying this, but she is quite besotted with her protector, Clay, who happens to be Morvayne's brother. I do not know what his involvement is, but Mara trusts Breeze, Jasmine, and Clay almost equally."

Jasper smiled jovially, "Clay and Jasmine are her sworn Attendants; she should be able to trust them with her life."

"Yes, Your Highness, I had heard that they were sworn to protect her, but I thought that perhaps they had sworn in such a way as to still be able to accomplish Morvayne's designs," Hans replied worriedly.

"Very wise you are Hans, but they were given to Mara at her birth by Princess Tigerlily herself. Along with four others: Hannah, Ivan, Daisy and Elwood. They have kept their continued relationship with Tigerlily, as well as this new assignment, secret from Morvayne all these years. Have you seen them?" Jasper asked.

"Oh, that is a relief; yes all of them except Daisy. I have not met her," Hans replied brightly, thankful that all was not as bad as he had feared.

Suddenly three Yellow Fairies appeared before the court unannounced. "What is the meaning of this?" Jasper bellowed, standing with sword in hand.

"Pardon, Your Highness. We have urgent news; the Trolls have eaten over half of my battalion," said the Brighter of the three glowing Yellow Fairies. They were very nearly spitting fire in their deep agitation.

The room erupted in gasps. Harmony looked as though she would faint, but then suddenly she shone Brighter than anything Hans had witnessed in a Fairy before, having never met royalty until meeting Mara.

"What provoked such an attack?" she demanded.

The leader once again spoke, bowing before her brilliance. "Princess, Morvayne has made a deal with the Orange and Yellow Fairies of our Ring in Seattle. I see you know this; he arranged for the Yellow Fairies to create Windows for the Trolls to attack small villages in South America and a few small towns in the southern portions of the United States. Upon completion the Trolls were given permission to snack on my Yellow companions! That was my Battalion, or half of them! The other half are still on the Troll compound, in a library and science lab. They have no idea they are in a holding tank—waiting to be fed to the King of the Trolls!"

Princess Harmony was furious. All the Fairies bowed before her fury. The King and Queen merely lowered their eyes. Harmony shouted, "How dare you make deals with Morvayne and Trolls! You deserve the same treatment! I would eat you myself if I thought I could stomach it. You lowly creature. What did he promise you that you thought it fair to murder innocents?"

"He–he promised knowledge, Your Highness. He has great stores of knowledge, which he has gained through his research.

We were tricked into believing he meant no harm to us."

Queen Laurel asked quietly, yet distinctly, "And yet, you thought it right to cause the death of Humans. Your crime is too great to ponder. How did you escape?"

The Yellow leader turned to his companion on his right. "Spinner here is evidently a double spy; he works for Prince Aerrvin and arrived as soon as he heard what was about to happen."

Laurel commanded, "Spinner, you may rise and stand before us. Tell us your story."

Spinner stood. Nodding once, he began, "Aerrvin met me a few years back. When Morvayne invited him to help spy on Mara, I made sure that Aerrvin knew who I was. He trusted me and tasked me with telling him all that I could concerning Morvayne's plans. I am sorry to say that I learned of the murders too late to stop them. But Morvayne has a deal to continue to provide Fairies for more death and destruction. I believe that he has added Fairies to his list of those he could do without. No doubt due to Aerrvin's involvement with Mara, his intended."

Another window of light appeared and Aerrvin, Gareth, Jaera and one more Yellow Fairy appeared. (*Yes, Seamus and several other Brownies were there, we don't count for much in these tales of Royalty*)

Aerrvin nodded swiftly and said, "Good! I see you have heard. I won't have to explain then. Morvayne has also caused the Tsunami off of Asia. A delegation needs to be sent to inform the sea folk in other waters; it is possible that they can calm the waves and free the shores from the backlash. Mother, Harmony, what do you propose to do?"

They made sure that each party knew what the last had shared.

"Place this Yellow and his companion into custody; he has

no need of further knowledge from us," declared Queen Laurel.

Guards came and took them away.

"Hans, we have sensitive matters to discuss. We thank you for your information. If Aerrvin has no further questions you may go." Hans turned to face the Prince, he so hoped to stay, but he knew his station.

"Hans, I thank you for your concern and commitment. I should like to meet with you soon, but today is far too chaotic. Inform Mara of my love, should you get the chance." Aerrvin produced a hankie, which he wiped his glistening brow with and handed it to the butler.

"I shall be honored, Your Highness."

He bowed to the Queen, and asked, "By your leave?"

She nodded and Hans Traveled back to his room. He felt drained and lay down upon his bed. Never had he had so much excitement! *Thrilling really,* he thought, as he reviewed the whole evening. He played a part in saving his future Queen. He placed Aerrvin's hankie in a private cubby only he had access to and slept for a few hours. He dreamt of being the hero who saves the future Queen of all the Realms and of the rewards he receives because of it.

***

Mara was shocked by Ivan's photo lab; it was not what she expected at all. The walls were sterile; white on white, just like the hallway on the Fourth Level.

"Where are we?" she asked in wonder.

Ivan smiled as his green eyes surveyed the surroundings. Then Mara noticed two of the walls rising, revealing a great window looking out on the vast expanse of space.

"Space? I'm in outer space? How on Earth, no, not on

333

Earth. How did you manage this?"

Ivan hugged her and said, "The world is very old.

Civilizations have learned to leave the Earth twice before. My Parents left this spaceship to me. They inherited it from my Great Grandfather."

"But, why do we not have any records or proof in archaeology?" Mara asked as she stood by the window looking down upon the Earth.

"We don't have time for a full history lesson. Come let's prepare the film and I will give you a brief overview."

Clay and Jasmine had obviously been there before, they excused themselves to visit the lounge. Ivan told Mara that there were some traces of proof among Egyptian, Mayan and other South American cultures, but scientists could not accept it.

However, the main reason for no traces were due to two things. One—The great flood destroyed all civilization upon the face of the Earth. Only those who had gone up into space or had built a refuge beneath the sea remained after the waters receded. (*Not counting those who fled to The Land of Eternal Spring, I am sure Ivan does not mind my clarification here*) Two—Noah's children retained a vast amount of knowledge and with help from a few Elves, some of his select descendants moved far from the general populations and built up another advanced society. It lasted only a few hundred years and fell into the sea when the continents broke apart.

At that point in his history lesson, Ivan laughed. "Don't look so shocked, Mara, it only took this current society 400 years to get as advanced as they are. Were Elves to present what we know, your Human society could be highly advanced within fifty years."

"No, it's not that. I believe you. I still get shocked to learn that those Bible stories are true. I believed, really I did, but to have it affirmed and shown as fact is astounding. Thank you, Ivan, for being a part of my life!"

Ivan nodded graciously and said, "Thank Tigerlily, she chose me." Then seeing she was about to cry he hugged her and got her busy developing her pictures.

Ivan watched awhile and then helped out a bit. Once all the prints were hanging on the wall to dry, he stood back to admire them. "Mara, you are truly talented."

He walked closer to inspect one of himself. Morvayne had a large patio where they had been dancing; the lights were low but sparkly, and Ivan was standing with the deep evening sky behind him. A few small lights drew interest above his left shoulder, on the right side of the photo. Ivan was facing the camera at a quarter angle, looking away from the lights. The flash from her camera highlighted his cheekbones beautifully, while he appeared to look joyfully at the shadowy couples dancing in the background.

"I love this one of me especially. Would you like to make these into a book?" He turned his pleasant face to hers, as he grew a mischievous smile.

"Yes, I would love to have a book someday. But —" Mara started.

Ivan laid a finger on her lips. "Wait, let me show you." He took down all of the photos, then leaving the darkroom he placed them face down on a scanner that pulled them in one at a time. Then on a large screen on the wall nearby they could view page by page the order he had put them in. Surprisingly, he had put them in chronological order seemingly by accident, but Mara was beginning to see that it was no accident. He was just fast.

"Would you like to change the layout?" Ivan asked as he sat down at the computerized control desk.

Mara took a second seat, amazed to see her pictures becoming a book. "Yes, I think some need to be cropped differently." Ivan taught her the various controls and soon she was editing her book.

She noted that he was content with watching her. "Ivan?"

"Yes, Mara?"

"Have you ever Dreamed of a life with me in it?" Mara asked innocently.

Ivan blushed and spluttered a moment. Completely caught off guard, he took a few seconds to regain control. Mara stopped editing to turn towards him in apology.

Ivan gathered his soft white Dust and handed a lovely pale green vial to her. "Forgive me, Mara. You are young I know. It is taboo to speak of our time in The Land of Dreams."

"Oh, Ivan I did not mean to embarrass you, please, um, I'm so sorry!"

He still held the vial out to her. "Your Highness, you have no need to beg forgiveness. If you wish to know I can tell you." He lowered his eyes as though in shame.

Mara felt terrible, she had wanted to collect Dust, it was true, but she had not wanted it from true shame or hurt. She accepted the Dust, as she inferred it would be rude to refuse it.

"No, Ivan, it is not necessary. Clay did tell me it was not talked about. I just forgot and was making small talk. I'm *so* sorry." Her eyes started to water, so she hugged him to hide her face. He hugged her firmly and then released her.

"We shall move on from here," Ivan said resolutely. He pushed a button and soon a complete book emerged from a slot to the right of the desk.

Mara picked it up in wonder. It had a deep green, high

gloss cover with a picture of Morvayne standing casually as he observed his party guests. Inside, the photos told the story of good friends at ease with one another. She could feel Ivan's mood as she turned the pages. She looked up to see him in tears.

"Ivan, what is it?"

Ivan looked at her with a bittersweet smile, then taking her hands he said, "Mara you have a beautiful talent and ability to capture the essence of a being in your pictures. This book reminds me of past times spent with Morvayne, happier times. We used to have such glorious parties so long ago. They had slipped from my mind until now. Thank you, this is a treasure."

Mara felt shocked; she had just been taking pictures of beautiful people. Ivan was definitely touched though. "I hope you are not just humoring me." She smiled to lighten his mood.

"I am not. May I kiss you?" Ivan asked. Seeing her surprise he hastily added, "I forget your innocence; we Fair Ones show gratitude by blessing one another with a kiss. Normally we do not ask, but you are my future Queen, which makes it improper to be spontaneous. I know that Morvayne does not ask."

He saw she was still confused, so he took her and kissed her forehead. "That is all I wanted, Mara, why do you fluster me so?" He smiled crookedly, while his eyes speculated.

"I don't know, Ivan. I feel like you should be a lifelong friend, but I don't know you at all. It's my youth I'm sure. Don't let me rattle you. I'm just a kid. And you have permission to kiss me with a blessing whenever the mood strikes you," she beamed at him, hoping to allay his discomfort.

He hugged her and gave her head a second kiss. "Ah, Mara, I love you," he said with a chuckle. "Let me set this to make copies for the others. Now, let's go show what we have made."

He led her down a silver corridor that opened up into what appeared to be a large recreation room. There were clusters of seating arrangements, some with tables for games, some were electronic tables, which did who-knows-what. Clay and Jasmine were seated at a hooded device, like a video game from the 90s with the seats built in. Seeing Mara's approach they exited. Of course they could see the two blessings upon her head, but they made no comment. They greeted them with tight smiles nevertheless, due to news they just witnessed on the viewing screen.

Clay spoke first, "I see Ivan convinced you to make a book. He loves that gadget." Clay smiled in casual friendship as he softly punched Ivan in the shoulder.

"Yes, he did! It is marvelous. I would love to have one at home," Mara said, then thinking, *Where will I live?*

She put that aside as she handed her book to Clay. Clay accepted it and drew Jasmine with him to sit in one of the lounge areas. Their reaction was much like Ivan's as they shed silent tears through their smiles, turning the book page by page. Jasmine or Clay would occasionally ooh over a picture, or laugh at another. Once they had looked it over, Jasmine stood and held her arms out to Mara in a beckoning stance.

Mara now understood, so she went and allowed Jasmine to place a blessing atop her head and on each cheek. "Mara, this is priceless. Thank you. You made me a copy, yes, Ivan?"

Ivan was nearly weeping again himself; he cleared his throat and merely nodded.

Clay sat looking at the cover of his brother.

Tears continued to fall as he contemplated the past and the very near future. Filled with compassion, Mara removed the book and sat in Clay's lap to give him a hug. Ivan had not been aware of how close they had become, but kept his reaction to a slight twitch of his eyebrows, which no one of consequence saw.

Clay buried his head in her curls as he allowed himself to be racked with sobs. Ivan and Jasmine joined him on either side, each resting a head on his shoulders. Jasmine smoothed Clay's hair. Mara did not pay any attention to how long they sat that way. Finally he eased away from her, or rather shifted so she knew to sit up. Jasmine produced a cool cloth to cleanse the salt and Dust from his face; Mara realized it was a ritual cleansing particular to her newfound friends.

He sighed as she washed his troubled face.

"Thank you, Jasmine, Ivan, Mara." He took his characteristic cleansing breath once more. "Mara, you have no idea how precious this is to me. It will serve as a memorial. The time has come to remove Morvayne before he causes more harm."

Ivan looked to the device they had vacated. "What did you learn?"

23
Evil Reports

"Come and see," Clay said, standing as easily as if he had no grown woman in his lap. Mara was placed gently on her feet and went quietly to see what this "device," which was now obviously not a video game, had to show.

She and Ivan sat in the two seats. Clay pushed a few buttons and a satellite picture began to slowly zoom in on the Pacific Ocean. They watched in silent horror as scene after scene showed waves cleansing entire islands free of its inhabitants.

"What are we seeing? Is this the future, something Morvayne plans?" Mara asked, not daring to think it real.

Ivan replied as Clay hesitated, "No, see the date is displayed here. This happened yesterday. Clay, are you saying he caused this?"

Clay pushed a few more buttons, which showed Morvayne on many repeated dates visiting the Water Sprites, and the final video showed the Water Sprites causing the huge waves to grow until they reached catastrophic proportions. Jasmine then reached in and caused the device to show the Mermaids at work in real time, counteracting the waves to dissipate further damage. Mara was amazed that they had surveillance under the ocean, but kept those questions for another time.

"If he has asked this kind of damage from the Water

Sprites, what has he asked of the Trolls and other groups he took me to meet?"

Jasmine responded, "You do not want to see. The Trolls have received help to Travel in order to raid villages and small towns in South America as well as Nevada, Tennessee and Kentucky. In addition, we have a report that the Yellow Fairies serving Morvayne have been sacrificed as treats for the Trolls. Over twenty-five have been—" Jasmine could not bring herself to say it.

"Eaten?" Mara felt surreal as if she was discussing a fantasy video game. "Morvayne has allowed Fairies to be eaten? Does Aerrvin know, and the Queen?"

Clay gathered himself together at hearing Mara's questions. He replied, "Yes, Aerrvin is with Queen Laurel and Princess Harmony. The Princess is especially livid, as all those taken are Yellow Fairies like herself. There are still twenty-eight or so being held captive. They are working to rescue them, as well as preparing to hold a trial against the head Fairy who convinced them to follow Morvayne. Those rescued will also be tried for treason."

Mara thought awhile and stated softly, "He was so happy at his party, and it was because of his progress at cleansing the world. He has lost all sense of right and wrong. Clay, what can be done? You said he has spells protecting him, right?"

Clay nodded, "He does. I do not know if I can hide my emotions enough to be near him. Once we return we may have to declare our opposition. Events will play out as they will. I had hoped to learn of Arianna's location. But I think she is lost." He gasped, choking back another sob.

"No!" Mara said sharply. "I will return with Ivan. I will tell Morvayne that you two are taking a little trip together and that I gave you permission. I will tell him that I have added Ivan as a protector as I felt it unfair to make you stay near me always. Think of some way to get past his wards."

Clay held up his hand to slow her down. "We have the bracelets from Meriel, retrieved by your Mother on behalf of your Father. They can bypass Morvayne's spells and wards. I do not know if they work on his personal protection."

"Ivan, what are you thinking?" Mara asked as she turned to face him.

Ivan looked thoughtful and replied seriously, "If those do not work on him personally? Really, I think the only thing you can do is to become Queen and command him with all of your Power and Light. That gives him three more days of death and destruction, but perhaps we can send forces to stop those other groups you visited. Clay, have you given me the coordinates for those Holds?"

"Yes, I have already logged them into your system."

"Wait a minute, three days? That is my birthday. You mean I am to be crowned as well?" Mara asked with a higher pitched voice than normal.

Jasmine responded, "It would be best, the sooner the better. Morvayne's Power will be diminished in your presence. He thinks that he can turn your thinking to his, in truth, he *has* done it in other life paths. He is obsessed with having that outcome in this existence. But he has never known about this location and the intelligence we are able to gather. This ship will come in handily. Ivan?" Jasmine looked at him pointedly and he shrugged his shoulders and invited Mara to follow him to an adjacent room.

"This is a stasis room," Ivan said, as the lights came on.

Mara saw that three of the walls held chambers, like bunk beds, but they had rounded doors that slid down and sealed shut.

"Humans, or any creature, can be placed within one of these and can remain in stasis for two hundred years without damage. This allows for space travel to other locations. Of course, once a Fair One has been to those distant locations they can Travel back and forth directly."

"What else can you do with them?" Mara asked.

Clay smiled grimly at her perceptiveness. "We can trap Morvayne in one and send him to a location far away, somewhere we have been so that when he arrives in two hundred years we can Travel there before his capsule opens and then issue his real punishment and prevent his return to this planet."

"Why didn't you use them before?" Mara asked perplexed.

"First of all, we had no proof for the small things we suspected of him, and secondly he had not done such evil things before," Clay answered.

Ivan added, "Besides, we still need The Queen of all the Realms to bind him. Gwennara wanted more proof before she would act, and by the time she had proof she was well and truly caught. You are our only weapon now. Which is a secondary reason for his wanting you as his wife. He says he will love you, but we see he is not capable of that pure emotion any longer. After his bitterness at losing Tigerlily, he turned to his studies, the alcohol surely ate away his conscience. He no longer has a feeling for right and wrong. Revenge is his driving force." Ivan shook his head in pity.

"So, if I had not learned the Vaporization technique, or Mom had not gotten the bracelets, I would still be his captive and we would not have a way to crown me Queen," Mara thought out loud.

Clay interjected, "You should be getting back soon. Perhaps a quick tour of the rest of the station, Ivan?"

"I would love to," Ivan responded.

Taking Mara by the elbow, he showed her the secondary control room, as well as the living quarters, which could hold up to two hundred. He then ended the tour with the shuttle port.

"This is amazing, almost like movies come to life. Can I ride in one?" Mara asked pleadingly.

Ivan smiled congenially. "Of course, Your Highness. Just not today."

Mara walked back with Ivan silently until they were nearly back to the control room, then she stopped and asked, "Doesn't it get lonely living in such a large space alone?"

"I have not lived here for fifty years, when last I did it was with a few companions. Daisy stayed here for twenty and my friends visit from time to time. Only the most trustworthy know that I have it, so the number has remained small as far as Elves go. However, I have a dear Ogre friend who is here always; he prefers the engine room, so we have not seen him. Furthermore, there are about forty Brownies here; surely you have noticed them skittering about?" Ivan asked kindly, his green eyes crinkling merrily at the corners.

Mara pouted momentarily. "Yes, I guess I did. I have been so used to ignoring them that I barely notice them. Is that rude?"

Ivan chuffed a soft whisper of air. "No, Mara, Royals rarely notice Brownies and the Brownies prefer it that way. Unless of course they are your personal servants and then they dance in delight at your every whim. You do know that Sylvie is in physical pain because of this separation, yes?"

"I have just learned that, yes. Dougie must be suffering horribly too. How can he be so cheerful?" Mara wondered.

"He has faith and hope. Come, we need to say good-bye and return." Ivan guided her back through the entryway into the main control room. They each hugged and then Ivan indicated that Mara open a window for their return.

Mara stepped into her bedroom in Morvayne's house, followed by Ivan. She had thought it the safest place to enter, but as it turned out Morvayne was sitting on the couch with Breeze.

"Ah, there you are. I had begun to wonder how many would be here for dinner. Where are Clay and Jasmine?" Morvayne said as he walked toward them.

Mara gave her prepared excuses and Morvayne appeared to accept it. "Very well, what have you got there?" He asked as he saw the books tucked under her arm.

"These are the photos I took. Ivan has a dream lab. I love it! I brought each of you your own copy."

Mara handed Breeze hers first and then gave Morvayne his. Ivan had two more for Hannah and Elwood. Morvayne sat down on the couch to gaze at the beauty she had captured. He was of course enraptured by his own person being featured on the cover. Mara marveled at her ability to squelch her abhorrence of his vile acts, while she felt compassion and pity for his lost soul. She loved him still.

Morvayne felt love emanating from both Mara and Ivan, true it was mixed with a soft dose of pity, but of course they would pity him. Looking at the pictures reminded him of all that he had been missing. All that had been lost.

"Mara, these are beautiful! You have captured the essence of my dearest Hold Mates with such clarity and perfection it makes me want to weep." Indeed a single tear escaped his left eye. "The only thing missing is you. We shall have to have another party and allow everyone to take a few pictures. I would love to have a beautiful book to remind me of our early years together."

Morvayne eyed her hungrily, reminding her that he was

smarmy.

The thought caused her to laugh instead of cringe though. Morvayne was completely confused at the shifting emotions she emanated. Mara could sense his emotions more clearly now as well. She decided to hang on to Ivan to see what it did to Morvayne. Ivan smoothly wrapped his arm around her and kissed her on top of her head. She beamed back at him as she felt Morvayne explode with jealousy and glee. Morvayne really wanted her, but he truly did want her to forget about Aerrvin by crushing on several Elves. *Just like Clay had said,* she thought to herself.

"I would like to take a nap, Morvayne, what time shall I be wanted for dinner?"

"Be ready at six. We will be going out on the town for a change. Something black and made for dancing will do. Ivan, welcome to my Hold."

***

Morvayne was glad to leave for a few hours. Mara's shifting emotions hurt his head. He marveled that her love for him was growing. He truly thought it would take more than fifty years to get her to enjoy his company, let alone love him.

Retired to his rooms, Morvayne looked through the book again. He wept more freely in privacy

"Tigerlily, why did you leave me?" he whispered. He chose a Dream he had visited before, one much like the previous night with all of his dearest friends dancing the night away. They were so free and fun loving then. Morvayne gave up his thoughts of current events and allowed himself to be taken by the Dream.

***

Aerrvin was frustrated at not being able to participate in the raid against the Troll's. "It just doesn't seem fair, Bronwyn!"

he exclaimed. "I mean, yes I know it is proper for me to rule from a safe vantage point. You know?"

Bronwyn responded with a comforting tone. "Yes, Your Highness. It is frustrating not being in the thick of it. But I am glad you understand that we need our King to remain safe to rule another day. Surely you do not wish to cause Mara undue sorrow."

"No! Of course not. I am worried for Gareth and Jaera. I would be lost without their companionship. I think I will just hover above as a hawk, do you want to come?" Aerrvin asked.

"No, My Prince. Take Seamus. He needs more flying practice. Mind, stay far from any trouble, arrows and otherwise," he admonished.

Aerrvin transformed into a hawk, as did Seamus. Then they Traveled to Southern California, just above the Troll compound.

Gareth had convinced one of Mara's chroniclers to leave her momentarily, so that his battalion could Travel inside the compound. She always maintained a discreet ladybug appearance and had convinced the Fairy battalion to miniaturize their size as well. They also wore cloaking devices, allowing them to be invisible and nearly scent-free. The Trolls have keen olfactory senses so the smaller the better.

Aerrvin watched closely, but saw no Window admitting his loyal subjects. He felt them, however, when they arrived. His ware spell allowed him to feel thir confidence and pride to be serving their future King.

Mara's chronicler was named Ivy. Gareth called her over to ask her which way she thought the lab would be. "Well, we went that way to the throne room. The kitchens are beyond that. So either they set up the lab right next to the kitchen for convenience or they really do have a nice laboratory and library already, in which case it would be down the northern or southern corridors," Ivy replied to Gareth's question politely.

It was a toss up. Eventually he sent two units north and south to scout the tunnels. They each returned within ten minutes having found nothing.

Gareth directed, "I guess closer to the dining hall was what we should have expected. I want this unit to stay put and the other three will follow my unit."

He led his unit toward the large cavern where Mara had met with the hideous green-faced Troll King. The room was occupied, but as they entered, they separated in various directions above the Trolls, thus dissipating any scent they might impart. Gareth saw that a few Trolls seemed to get a brief whiff as they looked about the room hungrily, slobbering on themselves. They went to the kitchens for food instead of looking for insects above their heads. Gareth noticed a door behind the Troll King's large throne. He assumed it led to the King's private quarters. "It might also have a library. Ivy, stay here and tell the other units where I have gone. Gorin's unit can scope the kitchen. Have him return as soon as he is done, by my orders."

Gareth found that there was indeed a room set up for the Yellow Fairies. It was not guarded, as the Trolls had all the main exits watched and the ward Morvayne had placed over the room kept them from Traveling away. Gareth realized that it was the only section with a ward.

"I should have thought of that first!" Shaking his head he Vaporized into the lab and was soon reassembled.

"I know you! You were at the Zoo a few weeks back. How did you enter?" a Yellow Fairy exclaimed.

Another cautioned silence. "Morvayne tricked us. Do you side with him?"

Gareth nodded a greeting at the group and said, "I have come to rescue you. Surely you now know the fate of your comrades?" He paused to hear their grumbled assent. "I come in the name of Queen Laurel ap Rose; she wishes to meet with you immediately."

"My name is Llewin. I am the current commander in charge. How do we leave?"

"Good question, Llewin. I will bring you out of here, but I need your promise to submit to the Queen and her will concerning your crimes. Evidently you believed Morvayne had more to offer you. Do you wish to discuss this first? You have one minute before I teach the technique."

With almost one voice, they said "No!"

Llewin spoke for the group. "We have seen the error of our ways. We will submit to our Queen and accept her punishment as just."

"All in favor raise your hand." Gareth observed the crowd, all but one raised his hand.

"You there, do you wish to remain here?" Gareth asked incredulously.

"No, I wish to be free from all restraints," the dissenter replied.

Gareth shook his head in wonder. "And you are Yellow! One would think you would all be smarter than you have been. Surely, you know that The Law keeps us free. Without rules, we would have chaos. Llewin, he is your responsibility. Will he come or stay?"

"If Gibb stays they will question him before they eat him. Better to bind him now and take him with us."

The mention of binding caused a stir. Most moved away

from Gibb. Two powerful Yellows focused their attention on Gibb, even as Gibb began a defensive spell. Gareth had a faster approach having received added power bestowed upon him as Aerrvin's Personal Protector, as well as from the Royal Guard training he had received. Instantly, a silk blanket surrounded Gibb and was drawn up and woven shut before he could shout out in surprise.

The blanket had been crafted with power dampening spells as well as binding spells. Once placed upon someone it could only be removed by the one who had crafted the spells; in this case Princess Harmony had made the blanket.

Gareth vaporized out of the room taking Gibb with him. He shifted in a breeze until they went out the ceiling of the cavern. Once above the compound they returned to their rightful six inches.

His second in command followed him out, so he instructed, "Take this 'package' to the Queen. We will be along shortly."

Gareth collected two of his battalion members to join him in the holding cell. They assumed their normal six inch size and asked the Yellow Fairies to downsize so that they could carry them all in a few satchels. They became the size of lady bugs and entered the cases. Soon all filtered up to the plateau above the Troll compound. Each bag had a ward on it as well, so there was no possibility of escape. They Traveled to a holding pen prepared for them. Gibb postured in a deep bow before the Queen as she spewed forth her Power and Light; soon the new prisoners were groveling as well.

Gareth did not stay to witness the sentencing. He had already heard what Queen Laurel had in mind. She had counseled with Jasper, Aerrvin, Harmony, Culain and Gareth. They felt it was fair and just to cause them to swear an oath of true service, one which they would be unable to break, even if they wanted to, due to severe lack of oxygen should they consider doing anything contrary to the wishes of their Queen. The group did indeed swear an oath of fealty to both Queen Laurel and Princess Harmony. Princess Harmony sentenced them to service in her newly created Academy, dedicated to fabrication and the art of glass making.

In time, they came to be renowned as the greatest artisans in millennia. Gibb eventually admitted his wrongheadedness and was allowed to leave the galaxy with the promise of never returning. *Right good thing, I say!*

Gareth returned to the plateau with his battalion just as a few Elves recommended by Clay also appeared. "Mikhail, just in time. Please proceed." Gareth bowed daintily, being six inches next to a six-foot Elf, he could *only* be seen as dainty.

Mikhail and his four companions each began to weave a separate ward upon the entire compound. They had worked together for years, as was obvious to any who watched as they wove their wards so intricately one with another. It only took ten minutes and the Trolls were bound to their compound. They would not be able to leave unless one of these five Elves granted them permission. The spell was large, encompassing 100 acres, thus allowing the Trolls to continue their ranching of cattle and sheep. Someone would bring in supplies from time to time, but for now, the Trolls were effectively imprisoned. The Elves then went to each known Troll compound and did the same thing.

***

Aerrvin was overjoyed at the success of Gareth's operation. With luck and the same competent skill, each of the other Holds that Morvayne had set up would soon be closed to Morvayne's meddling and the world would be safe from their evil designs.

Mara could sentence them at her leisure once she gained

the crown and a few years of experience. Of course, not all of Morvayne's Holds had been visited by Mara and her chronicler, Ivy. Breeze had gone in Mara's place to a few. Aerrvin was still not sure of Breeze. He understood that Mara trusted her, but perhaps that had more to do with her desire for an older sister-like figure, someone to replace her lack of Aunts. Breeze also made Aerrvin uncomfortable simply because she looked so much like Mara.

"Ah, well. At least I get to see what Mara will look like in 900 years. I am the luckiest Fairy alive!" He swooped a few loop de loops, which is easier to do as a Fairy, than a hawk, but he maintained his avian form and opening a tiny bend of light he Traveled to the tree bordering Morvayne's Vashon Island property. Mara was thinking of him.

"Yes!"

***

Mara wondered how Aerrvin's chores were going. Clay had informed her of the rescue operation. Hopefully Aerrvin kept his distance from the fighting. She imagined Aerrvin and his companions in battle with Trolls.

"Ivan? Do you think they were successful?"

Ivan was watching the fish as they gathered in the corner where Morvayne was feeding them from the other room. He looked over at her concerned face. "Of course, not a problem really. We do not generally have to go to war with them, but when we do it really is quite simple and usually bloodless. The Trolls cannot compete against Elves or even Fairies, they are strong physically, but their wits are slow."

"Didn't seem like the Yellow Fairies were very effective in not getting eaten."

Ivan rolled his eyes and replied, "They were entrapped

with the help of an incredible wily Elf. Trust me, Trolls rarely best us."

Suddenly Mara smiled. "He just arrived out back! I knew he would be safe." She fought the urge to run outside and instead thought happy thoughts toward Aerrvin, even as she felt his loving concern coming to her.

Elwood and Hannah saw Aerrvin arrive. After giving him a thumbs up signal, they came inside to join Mara and Ivan on the sofa.

"We have an hour before dinner, would you like to visit Aerrvin for a moment? He is settling down in a tree right now," Hannah said as she sat next to Mara.

"Sure, that sounds great. Do I have to go to my room? Never mind, Morvayne would just walk in uninvited. I might as well do as I please wherever I am." Mara's belligerence made the others smile.

Elwood chuckled deeply in his broad chest. "Do as you please, Your Highness. He is barely a threat any longer." He nodded towards Morvayne on the opposite side of the aquarium.

Mara lay her head in Hannah's lap and felt soothed as Hannah smoothed her hair away from her face. Mara was soon in her old bedroom, opening the window for Aerrvin. She longed for the day when he would always be real. His ocean scent eluded her for now.

"I have missed you so much!" she said as they embraced.

He was dressed as he had been on the first day she had seen him. Khakis and a t-shirt. "What's up with the clothes?"

"Just thought I would remind you how I appeared when first you set eyes on me," he replied impishly.

"Well, thank you, I like it!" Mara replied, trying to be

demure and failing. Instead she caressed his face and submitted to his nuzzling of her neck. She had started out in her nightgown, but had switched to her cut offs and happy-faced flower t-shirt.

"Let's take a walk on the beach!" Mara exclaimed, surprising Aerrvin with her boldness at taking control of the situation.

Suddenly her room became a beach off of southern California, a place she had visited often with her Mother when staying at her Grandparents. Aerrvin lost his shirt and was now in board shorts and barefooted.

"I like how you think." He smiled as only he could, his violet-grey eyes twinkled merrily.

They walked hand in hand along the shore allowing the waves to catch them from time to time.

"So I take it all went well at the Troll compound?" Mara queried.

"It did. Your servant Ivy was a great help. She should be returning soon, through the Brownie portal, if she has not already. Gareth is amazing. I had been fearful myself at first; I do not know what I would do without him," Aerrvin said openly.

Mara felt his fear as he briefly relived it. She paused to hug Aerrvin. "I have never felt so close to so many people before. It really is as if I were truly half-dead and certainly sleeping all these years. It feels wonderful to be so wide awake and *alive!*" She shouted the last word joyfully.

"Race me to those rocks." She nodded to an outcropping a few hundred feet away. Taking off she fairly flew towards them; perhaps she did, she could not tell. Aerrvin matched her step for step. It seemed as though they moved in slow motion while the rocks zoomed in upon them. Soon they were there and they stopped short of falling into a tide pool.

"It's a tie!" Aerrvin said as he hugged her to him. "Mara, I can hardly stand this separation. Do you plan to be done with this charade on your Birth Day?"

They snuggled down to enjoy the sun and the light breeze from the ocean. "Yes, I will be crowned shortly after taking the oath. Clay has a plan for trapping Morvayne. I don't know the details of it though. I don't see how to get the information about Arianna and my dad. We still do not know if Arianna is really with him. Also…" Mara twiddled with the necklace around her neck. "I still have not learned anymore about this key. I guess I will be able to ask Gwennara when I see her."

She trembled suddenly at the thought of meeting her eldest living progenitor and the former Queen of all the Realms.

Aerrvin held her tighter. "She is not so formidable as all that.

Mara nodded, "Yes, but Brand looks like my dad. Gwennara is…beautiful beyond words. I am sure of it, and her power must be significant. Judging by the way people react to me."

Aerrvin created cushions to lounge against; he pulled Mara to a reclining position beside him. He smiled an almost pitying smile, shaking his head he said, "Mara, Mara, you have no clue. You are truly the most Powerful and Brightest being any of us have ever seen. Not even Gwennara matches you in Brightness, not now that she has passed on her Power to you. But even in her fullest Glory and strength, she did not surpass your Glory. I have been in her presence twice when she was moved to show forth all of her Light. Believe me, it was awe-inspiring. Once—she had been provoked by a renegade band of Water Sprites, probably the same ones who helped Morvayne. Anyway this was one hundred and ten years ago, I think. They had decided to dam up a river to keep the water for themselves, thus causing all kinds of problems for those living downstream, especially the Nyads. Gwennara was not pleased and commanded a return to the natural waterways.

They obeyed and tried to appease Gwennara as best they could. Hmmm…an enmity grew up between her and Water Sprites because of that situation. No, do not get upset, Mara! She does not hate your Mother, nor you. I was just saying, politically, it has been contentious for her."

Mara mumbled onto his chest, which she just then noticed was bare. "I guess I can see her point if they were always being a pain to her." Mara sat up briefly to look at Aerrvin—his golden hair fluttered gently away from his face; his smooth muscles were as well defined as Clay's. Truly a feast to be savored. She only had a few minutes left so she asked, "What was the other occasion?"

Aerrvin felt her approval and could not help but swell his chest in pride. Mara resumed her former position allowing him to stroke her soft curls as he spoke above her head. "The only other time I saw her full Power, was when she celebrated her one-thousandth Birth Day. All were invited. I was of course not able to get too close, but being Royalty we were at least in the main garden with her when she revealed her Light and Power. My parents spoke with her, but children were not introduced. It was so magnificent and glorious, but I speak true, Mara, you are—and I am not saying this just because I love you. Look at me, Mara. *You* have the potential to be the greatest Queen we have *ever* had. Your Power and influence can literally change the world!"

Mara blushed, sending sparkles out into the wind. "You sound like Morvayne. He says much the same only his plans are not so great."

Aerrvin smiled gently as he stroked her cheek lightly. "I know, but tis true. Come, let's dance our way back to your room."

They did not make it all the way back before Hannah knocked at her Dream. "Sorry, Sweetie, time's up."

Mara kissed Aerrvin as though memorizing the shape of his lips and smiled shyly. "See you soon."

Aerrvin regretted the loss, but then retreated to his own Dream to continue on where they had left off. He had nothing better to do for the next two days.

***

Mara awoke to find Morvayne waiting for her. She sat up, self-consciously straightening her shirt. "Is it dinner time already?"

"Not quite, but I want to leave in one hour. You might want to go get all dolled up." He leered in what should have been a charming way, but only served to give her a shudder as opposed to a tingle.

Mara smiled anyway and complied by practicing her gliding walk. Thinking tranquil thoughts, she hoped she did not look absurd, like a child trying to be like mommy. She giggled to herself at the top of the stairs. "What am I thinking!" she said to herself, "My whole life is absurd!"

George roused from his Dream and peered out from his makeshift glen beneath the lamp table.

"Pardon? Your Highness?"

Mara shut the door and sat down on the sofa. "George! What are you doing up and about? I thought you had all kinds of places to explore."

"May I?" George indicated he would like to upsize his form. "Of course! You needn't have to ask. It's just me, plain old Mara."

George proceeded and then sat in the recliner. "That is better. Elves are always far too imposing to me in my natural state. I do have a thousand Dreams to explore, but my thoughts kept returning to you. I am grateful for this second chance at life. How grateful could I be if I chose to hide from your disastrous fate? I want to help you."

Mara blinked back tears. "Oh, George, that is so sweet. I do not know what you can do. I have learned a new trick from Brand the Bright that I can teach you. It is called Vaporization, once mastered Morvayne's wards cannot keep you."

Mara proceeded to explain and then demonstrate the technique. "So work on it and you will be free. You seem to have gained renewed vigor, George. How is that done? Do you just tell your body how to look or does using your Light renew your vitality somehow?"

George chuckled, his voice was clear and free from the nagging cough he used to have. "A little of both I guess. I can transform my looks, just like I can become a bird or a lizard. I can make myself be as young as I would like to look. I am not ready to look as young as my years as a Fairy would have me be. So I am allowing my Power and Light to repair the damage that living as a Human caused. I don't think I will ever choose to look younger than 40 though, I tend to gain greater respect with some signs of age."

George twinkled his eyes at her, causing her to laugh happily as she recalled all the flirting he liked to do. "Ah, George, I am so happy to have you as a friend. I hope you will be part of my household once I get one."

George nodded, but before he could speak Mara said, "Oh! I better get ready for dinner. If you manage to leave, contact Aerrvin or Queen Gwennara if you cannot find him. They can tell you how you can help. Thank you, George." Mara kissed him on each cheek, blessing him with success and happiness. He blushed, dropping pinky-red dust and she was startled.

"Oh, I didn't mean that. But since I did—how do I collect it? And where does everyone get their pretty vials from?"

George chuckled again. "You just imagine the jar like anything else. You can use whatever powers you have to collect. Have you not yet tried using wind or attractant spells?"

Mara shrugged, "The wind obeys me, somewhat." She tried to collect it with the wind, but it splashed the Dust all over her. "That didn't work!" Mara said giving George a mock scowl as he chortled at her mishap. "What is an attractant spell?"

"It is what I use, but you don't have enough time to learn it right now. Have you tried simply wishing it to do as you desire?" George hoped she had that ability as he knew Queens were generally blessed with the Power of Compulsion more strongly than others.

"That sounds too simple. Dust in the bottle!" Mara commanded as she held out a beautiful cut crystal vial. At her command the Dust was suddenly not all over her and the couch; it zoomed into the bottle almost quicker than her eyes could follow. She laughed in delight as George clapped and then bowed.

"By your leave, My Lady. I must practice this new technique."

"Yes, of course, George, and thank you for my lesson. I learn something new every day."

Mara went to her room to get ready for a night in downtown Seattle. She felt out of touch with fashion. She sighed as she looked in the mirror. "Not that I have ever been in touch with the styles of the day anyway. She wished all her clothes away and stood there in her Dragon shed slip. "I need some advice!" she said to the air.

Ivy projected her voice so Mara could hear her; she was still a tiny ladybug, just sitting on the baseboard. "My lady, I can advise you."

"Who are you? Show yourself." Mara demanded.

She really did hate having beings all about her. A lithe little Brownie appeared near the mirror. She was dressed in tawny pants, nearly leggings, and a cocoa colored tunic. Her golden hair was pulled back in a French braid which hung to the small of her back. "My name is Ivy, I have been away helping Gareth secure your kingdom. My, what fun that was! Sorry, My Lady, I am one of your two Chroniclers. We take turns; one month on, one month off. So I missed what you did today, sorry about that. Nothing overly important I hope. But you can replay it for me once we go to the Void together. Well, say something!" Ivy stopped to take a breath.

"I am delighted with you little Ivy. Oh, no I did not name you Little Ivy. Ivy, you are delightful. Aerrvin mentioned you today. I forgot to even ask about you. But now I want to know, how can you stay quiet for a month at a time?" Mara smiled at the hardship it must be.

"You have no idea how long I have been waiting to tell you that very thing. But, once you are asleep I talk to Sylvie and Beau or who ever happens to be about," Ivy said with exaggeration at her hardship.

"Honestly, I have wanted to style you since forever; so if you wouldn't mind, please adorn yourself with a simple black silk. I will make the adjustments."

Mara had no idea how Brownies did things. It was an education in itself, watching Ivy as she pulled and tucked, sewed and adjusted, until she had the dress exactly as she wanted it, all while maintaining her six-and-a-quarter-inch self. Then she busied herself with styling Mara's hair.

The dress was delightfully simple, yet beautiful as it showcased Mara's slim figure. Ivy had created cute capped sleeves, which had the slightest puff to them. The neckline was a wide scoop neck, allowing her tanned chest to be the canvas upon which the beautiful pendant shone. Gazing at the necklace reminded Mara that she could now remove it. Not wanting to risk Morvayne having access to it she removed it and then placed it on again. Testing it to be sure it was once again firmly locked in place.

"We can never be too careful." She smiled lightly at Ivy. "And this dress is beautiful. I love it, I just wish I were going out on the town with Aerrvin instead."

Ivy finished Mara's hair. Mara did not know how she did it but Ivy had managed to smooth her hair better than any hair product Mara had ever tried. "It is so silky smooth, Ivy, I love it."

"I always did Tigerlily's hair for her; she loved it this way too," Ivy said wistfully.

"What? I thought her hair was naturally straight? How old are you anyway?" Mara asked.

"I am five hundred years old next month on the 27th.

Tigerlily had my mother, great is her memory, do her hair before me. It stays straight through several washings, however if you want your natural curls back, I can undo it with a simple rinse.

"Sorry, but I cannot reveal the ingredients; trade secrets you know." Ivy was the sprightliest Brownie Mara had ever met.

"I do love it, but Aerrvin said he loves my curls. We will have to do this only every once in a while. Maybe, once he feels how luxuriant it is, he will change his mind." Mara watched Ivy change herself into a tiny black bug, and attach herself to the underside of the hem. Looking at her reflection one last time, Mara went downstairs.

As usual, she was last to arrive. Silent awe greeted her.

Love, compassion and desire all mingled as her newly formed family greeted her. Hannah broke the silence first.

"Your Highness, you look stunning."

Breeze had smoothed her already straight hair as well, it was a bit shorter than Mara's but they looked almost identical, certainly like sisters. Morvayne had been holding her hand.

Seeing Mara looking exactly like his lost love put him in a trance. Breeze easily removed her hand and went to Mara.

"I approve your look as well. It would be vain to tell you how absolutely perfect you look, now wouldn't it?" Her laugh resounded like tinkling glass.

Mara smiled in response, but began to be concerned as Morvayne continued to gaze without speaking.

"Jasmine, I love your dress! I had one like it a while back; it looks great with your pale skin and dark hair. Purple is a favorite color of mine," Mara gushed, holding back her questions about why Jasmine and Clay had returned.

The mention of purple brought Morvayne out of his daze. "Yes, *purple* for fabric is lovely. Mara, words cannot express the wondrous visage before my eyes. Clay, do you see her as I do?"

Morvayne had reached out a hand to Clay. Clay rested his arm around Morvayne's shoulders as he replied. "Yes, a sight I never thought to see outside of my Dreams."

Ivan and Elwood were equally enthralled with Mara's recreation of Tigerlily. Mara could hardly take it any longer.

"Stop it! Surely Tigerlily did not have a dress like this! Look at it, it's indecent for the times she lived in."

Elwood grinned and said, "Maybe among the Humans, but add leggings like so, and you have a perfect night life party ensemble." Mara looked down to see she was wearing silver and black leggings, which actually looked like spider webs all over her legs. "Actually her dress would have been slightly shorter as well. Elwood started to shorten her dress when Clay stopped him, sensing Mara's horror at wearing anything shorter.

"Among Human's she would have worn it like this:" Clay added as he caused a velvet skirt to fall away from her empire waist. "Either way she was quite bewitching." He returned her dress to the way Ivy had made it. "Do you wish to keep the leggings? They still work depending on where Morvayne is taking us."

Clay swiveled back to look at Morvayne.

"What? Oh, no we are not going to a grunge bar or other super trendy places. Just your ordinary classy social club. Nude legs are fine." Morvayne said as he leered again, making Mara consider keeping the leggings.

"No—I will stick with the original outfit, thank you. Those were cool leggings though; I will have to wear them soon." She tried to be casual as her legs were revealed. It was not as though she were indecent, it was just the fact that she was being gawked at while her clothing was going on and off.

Clay offered her his arm as Ivan took the other. Clay's calming influence allowed her to gain control and hear what Morvayne had to say next.

24
Hope Dies

Morvayne was in total awe of Mara's transformation. Really only her hair had been changed, and yes the dress was cut in the same fashion as several of Tigerlily's dresses. But the remarkable thing, which he was sure only he could discern, was her carriage. She seemed far more confident than she had when first he met her, and then those first few days at the Palazzo; she had been so moody and tearful. Yes, Clay was a remarkable asset to his plans. Ivan appeared to be having a positive effect as well.

Now if I could only get her to latch on to Elwood. He has ever been far more gregarious than the rest. Perhaps more like Daisy and her flamboyance. Too bad she chose to leave the leggings behind; they were more suited to Elwood's wild personality. Maybe I should allow Daisy to return now as well? He tucked that thought away as Mara stood before him, flanked by her two Attendants. She exuded love for them. How they managed to garner those feelings so quickly was amazing. Yet she had professed a love for him as well, *I must not lose sight of that fact.* Something about his personality put her off. Morvayne resolved to ease up and observe how the others handled her. One could always learn new tricks.

"Mara, I want you to relax tonight. We will have no training or dignitaries to meet, just a few friends out on the town. I hope you have noticed? I no longer have you bound by any wards," he said, as though he had granted it.

Mara acted as though it was an honor. "Thank you, Morvayne. I appreciate the trust you have placed on me. Shall we go? I'm starving!"

Everyone laughed at her rustic wording. Morvayne arranged for a stretch limo to pick them up. It afforded them the ability to all ride together and enjoy the fellowship of good friends once again.

Morvayne brought forth a bottle, causing Mara to cringe. "I realize you all choose not to drink often, so I have procured this bottle of Rose Elixir. Mara, this is not nearly as powerful as the Honeysuckle, but it is certainly delightful. Will you celebrate this night with me and my dearest friends?" He looked about noticing that all were waiting upon Mara's decision before accepting his offer.

Mara looked him squarely in the eyes and asked, "What are we celebrating, Morvayne? I was under the impression that this elixir was reserved for momentous occasions."

Morvayne much preferred this bold woman to the sniveling frightened girl of days gone by. He tempered his smile as he had often seen Clay do.

"I will not be able to attend your Birth Day tomorrow night; please think of this as my gift to you," he felt her heart melt. Surprised that he had affected her so profoundly, he wanted to grab her and hold her close, but he allowed Clay to offer her a comforting hand.

Mara was surprised at her reaction to Morvayne's statement, a tear actually threatened to fall. Blinking the moisture from her eyes she replied sincerely, "Thank you, Morvayne, I never expected such a gift from you. I will treasure it, always." This time a tear did escape.

Morvayne had no clue as to why she was so touched.

Mara felt sorrow for Clay and her other companions at the impending conflict they would have to perpetrate against their Hold Mate. Evidently, he had not made any recent contact with any of the Holds, which Mikhail had shut down. Morvayne really was happy. Mara determined to make it a joyful evening for all.

"Very well, a single glass, if that is not too much?" She looked to Breeze and Hannah. They agreed it was acceptable. Mara spent the forty-five minute drive sipping her drink and enjoying the flavor, body, and aroma of the Rose Elixir, as well as snuggling up next to Hannah, enjoying her light citrusy scent. She had never noticed it before, but Hannah smelled like the lemon trees on her Grandfather's property in California.

Why she kept thinking of him, she could not figure out. She barely visited maybe every three years. Mara allowed her mind to wander as she found she could single out each person's scent and then combine them all, creating a story in itself: Clay's rich, earthy scent, Ivan's woodsy aroma. Breeze smelled similar to Aerrvin's ocean scent, yet lighter and more brisk somehow. Jasmine was obviously named after her scent, sweet and flowery.

Elwood presented a new scent; she had not been that close to him before. He was warm and spicy like cinnamon and nutmeg. Lastly, she identified Morvayne, that sweet-yet-bitter after scent still unnerved her. *It must be the wine, which has ruined his whole person, including his scent,* she concluded.

Dinner was pleasant. They had a private room, which was mirrored on three walls, and the fourth had clear blue glass facing out to the main part of the restaurant. It was a Moroccan themed eatery, so they reclined on pillows as they enjoyed each course. Afterwards, they watched the belly dancers and then left to find social dancing elsewhere.

***

Morvayne was curious to see how many people he could

get Mara to love, so he drew Clay aside and asked him to guide Elwood into catching Mara's attention. He found that she was so like Tigerlily in that arena as well. *Actually, it became a fault, as Tigerlily allowed her affections for Humanity to overcome her good sense.* Morvayne tamped down bad thoughts; he truly meant to give Mara a gift to be grateful for.

He blinked in surprise as he thought, *I actually love this girl!*

With a new sense of wonder he watched as she laughed in delight at some small thing Hannah had said. Never had he thought he could truly fall in love again. Oh, he still wanted the Power and Glory that she would offer; it was simply a bonus, as he saw it, to actually love the one he planned to marry. He moderated his smile and personal charm, noting that she was truly drawn to Clay and Ivan's more laid-back personalities.

"Mara, may I have this dance?" Morvayne asked, keeping all demands inside.

She smiled sweetly and nodded. She was at it again, growing melancholy. "Mara, I have noticed your moodiness has altered. You no longer exude fear and hate. I am thankful for that, but I sense overwhelming sadness when you think of me. I do not understand your concern. It touches me, but I would like to know what it is that causes your sorrow."

Mara knew this was coming; she could not control her emotions well enough. She flared briefly as she let a little Light from one pocket loose. She really did need to learn to make that neighbor boy in her head be in charge of her pockets of Light.

But then again it was kind of fun to just let lose without having to ask. She knew her emotions were still going up and down and sideways as Morvayne waited for her response.

"I think it is for loss."

"Loss? Whose loss?" Morvayne asked as solicitously as he

could.

She glanced at him, trying to imagine him as young and carefree, someone Aunt Lily could have loved. Tears welled up. "Sorry, I just feel bad for everyone. You, Clay . . . me. We have experienced loss of someone we hold dear. I feel it most when I am near you."

"Ah." Morvayne nodded and then spun Mara away and back into a tight embrace before resuming a normal dance pattern. He thought that he understood now. She was sad at leaving Aerrvin. She had empathy for Clay and his own personal loss. *She is an empath!* He thought. *I will have to keep her away from Humans in the future, no sense in her feeling their loss as well.*

"Well, Buttercup, you need not have pity for me much longer. My life has taken a turn for the better; thanks goes entirely to you." The tune ended and Morvayne lead her to Elwood. "I fear I do not like pop music as much as traditional. Elwood would you care to escort Mara to the dance floor?"

"I would love to."

Taking her hand, he danced towards the center of the mob. He had to speak up for her to hear. "Now this is more like it!"

He definitely knew how to dance. Soon they had a space around them as other couples had moved back to get a better view. Mara was uncomfortable at first, but she found that she could match his moves almost in sync. She assumed that to the Human eye they would not even be able to tell. They stayed on the dance floor for the next three songs. The last one was once again a slow song. Elwood was as skilled as every Elf and Fairy she had ever met. She was almost breathless, but mostly energized as he pulled her close.

She breathed in his scent deeply; it reminded her of Jill's pumpkin bread, she smiled up at him and said, "You make me hungry!"

He lowered his lids halfway and replied, "I have heard that one before."

Like Clay, Elwood was much taller than Mara, yet he was also broader than the typical Fair One. Elwood had to lean down to sniff at her neck as he said, "Your scent is like sunshine, so warm and golden."

Mara was delighted to get a description rather than being told it was intoxicating. "Thank you, Elwood! I think you are the first person to describe my scent. I can't really smell myself you know, and no one else has told me how I smell besides wonderful, blah, blah, blah."

Elwood laughed deeply which Mara could feel reverberating beneath her hand and cheek as she was too short to dance cheek-to-cheek with one as tall as he.

He asked, "Besides making you hungry, how would you describe mine? Not everyone can perceive the scent in the same way, you know."

"No, I didn't. But I guess that explains why my scent drives Clay out of his mind and it only causes others to enjoy being near. Different chemistry for different people, I guess. Anyway, sorry for rambling, Elwood. You smell like pumpkin pie spices, more specifically like pumpkin bread."

"See? That is very instructive for me, some say I smell like cinnamon toast. Some only smell the pumpkin. One or two have only smelled nutmeg. But you, my little Princess, have captured all of it with your pretty little nose." He playfully ran his finger down her nose. She looked up at him and smiled, he was like the best big brother she never had. He gazed back and then kissed her atop her head. "You are so sweet. I have missed being near you."

Mara wanted to kiss him in return, but with everyone

watching she suddenly felt too shy. Elwood chuckled as he felt her emotions as well as her temperature.

Clay had been watching closely and could not stand being parted from her any longer. He was glad that they were renewing a friendship, which they had enjoyed when she was a toddler, yet he nursed a small jealous streak that wanted her for his very own. With Jasmine in his arms, he danced near and, as soon as the song ended, he asked if they cared to switch partners. He was gratified at Mara's sincere smile and acceptance at trading places. He probably should not have accepted the Elixir at all, knowing what it would do, but really, who can resist it once offered? Mara withdrew some of her scent as they danced.

"Please don't!" he begged hungrily.

"Clay, why do you like to torture yourself so?" Mara asked shakily. She felt his calming influence immediately. "It hurts me to see you so needy. Knowing what you desire and not being the one you truly want."

Clay was shocked at what he was doing. "Mara, forgive me." He stopped dancing and started to guide her back to their table. Having all of his desires awakened by Mara's own awakening and then renewing his relationship with Arianna only served to bind him more fully to the Dust to which he was completely addicted.

"No, Clay. I still want to dance." She stopped walking, waiting for him to resume dancing. He ceded to her desire.

"Mara, I am sorry, but I must inhale if I am to be near you." He buried his face in her hair as it fell over her neck tickling her; she giggled. Mara apologized for the giggling. "Sorry, that usually doesn't happen. Elwood said everyone perceives our scents differently; he said I smell like sunshine. What do you smell?" Mara was truly curious. She also wondered how others perceived Aerrvin.

Clay was now mellowed, having received a nostril full of Dust from when she had glowed briefly at Morvayne. He fluidly danced her about the floor, keeping perfect timing. "Beautiful question, Mara. Yes, you certainly have a bright note of sunshine, all golden and pure. But more than that, you smell like a meadow in full bloom at midday. With the flowers fully opened revealing all they have to offer to any passing insect wishing to partake of their bounteous nectar and pollen." He paused to inhale once more. With a sigh he resumed his detailed description. "The sunshine at noon is so hot and pleasant as it draws forth the scent from the flowers, creating an intoxicating, heady scent. Have you never visited a meadow at noon?"

"No, I guess not, but it sounds wonderful. I think I will try it soon." She smiled at him as she firmly tamped away all the rest of her scent. "I think there is enough residue upon my person, besides you have vials of it somewhere. You can breathe it in when you have a spare minute."

He knew she was being reasonable, but he still hated to have her tighten up so severely. It was his own fault for being so obvious. He used to have greater control. *Maybe being crazy is genetic,* he thought, *I should convince Mara to release me as soon as Morvayne is sentenced to his everlasting punishment.*

Mara interrupted his thought with another crazy thought of her own. "Clay? Do Elves ever party in the streets like the Fairies do? Aerrvin used to take me out in the neighborhoods; the street musicians are so much fun! I miss that already and it was only a few weeks ago that he introduced it to me."

Clay laughed with pity as he shook his head, "Mara, Mara, you are the quirkiest Elf I have ever met! As a general rule the Elves do not practice street music, but we do occasionally downsize to enjoy a night of singing and dancing with the Fairies. Elves think highly of themselves and take pride in being at the height of fashion in music, art, or otherwise. You do not know this, but one third of all musicians and actors in Hollywood, and elsewhere, are Fair Ones and ninety percent of those are Elves. They are of course neutral in this war with Morvayne. Seeing as how they depend on the adulation of Humans, which most despise, they find they are in a bit of a quandary.

"They wish to take over the arts industry completely, thus doing their part to overcome the Human encroachment, yet they need enough Humans living to give them the worship they crave. Truly you have a large job before you once you become Queen. I ask your forgiveness, but Queen Gwennara has been too passive these last few hundred years."

"I see. That explains a lot. I guess it would not be wise to ask Morvayne if we can ditch this place to find some Fairies playing jigs in the street." She smiled broadly, hoping to get him to respond in kind.

He tried to maintain his serious demeanor, but looking at her bright eyes and toothy smile, he eventually cracked and added his broad grin to hers. Kissing her atop her head he commented, "I think you are better at collecting kisses than you are at collecting Dust."

The room eventually thinned out as the night wore on. It was time to return home. But Mara did not know where home was anymore. Morvayne agreed it was time to leave. He called his friends over and they chatted amiably as they filed out to the waiting limo. *Should I wait until morning?* Mara did not know. Clay had never said what she should do. She knew she could not keep Morvayne from feeling her sorrow no matter how hard she tried.

Her mood affected everyone else. They became quiet and cautious as they waited to see what she would do. Morvayne finally addressed her. "Mara, I thought you enjoyed this evening, you were laughing and coy. I am finding you to be quite puzzling and your mood is infectious. What else can I do to ease your sorrow?"

Mara did not know what she would do, but suddenly she felt an inner strength well up as she thought of releasing all of her Light and demanding his compliance. The interior of the car was too degrading of a place to make him grovel, so she refrained in favor of his house.

"I wish you to swear your allegiance to me," she said instead.

Morvayne felt a compulsion to agree, but he managed to resist through sheer will. "Mara, I have told you that I will swear myself to you once you are crowned Queen of all the Realms. That is all I can swear to right now." He was nervous for the first time as beads of sweat and Dust formed like dew upon his brow. "I can tell you this truth, I have fallen in love with you tonight."

Mara was stunned, as were her companions. She had not thought Morvayne capable of pure emotions any longer. "I . . . I am flattered, Morvayne. Thank you for the lovely evening, as I said before, I will treasure it always."

She snuggled up to Hannah and went into the Void and waited to see who would follow. Clay soon arrived followed by Jasmine.

"Sorry, I can't seem to control my emotions!" She began crying in earnest. Jasmine held her as Clay soothed her back.

"Mara," Clay said calmly. "We have prepared for this day for years. I know it is all new to you and I appreciate your empathy. Morvayne has been almost sane these past two days and it has been a gift I will treasure, greater than anyone else ever could. But we must not forget, he has just killed over five hundred thousand people with his tsunami and hundreds from his deal with the Trolls. Not to mention the twenty plus Yellow Fairies eaten like candy. It is sickening." Mara felt his shudder through his hand on her back. "You must face the truth and pass judgment. I fear he will try to flee should he learn of the work we have accomplished today. Use all of your Power and Light; it will be strong enough, I assure you."

Aerrvin knocked at her Dream and entered whe Mara waved him in through the window. Having straightened her posture, she allowed Aerrvin to dry her tears with his breeze.

"I can do this!" she said resolutely. She opened all of her pockets of Light as a trial run. Her three companions bowed.

Aerrvin gasped. Even his eyes were lowered. "My Love, your power has grown, surely you can do anything."

Mara quickly put all of her Light away. "Are you sure that this was not just a wish of my Dream?"

Jasmine laughed, brushing her wispy dark hair behind her shouders, she enthused, "If it were possible to Dream greater power, we all would stay forever in our Dreams. No, what you manifest here is reflected in the waking world. Never have the Realms had one as Bright as you. I foresee a millennial reign unlike any we have seen before, My Lady." Jasmine bowed gracefully, reminding Mara that she still wanted to work on her graciousness.

"So much to learn! Very well. Will you be able to bind him, Clay?" Mara asked.

"You will bind him. Ivan and I will then Transport him to a stasis chamber, if that is your desire. Everything is entirely in your hands. We are here to advise and counsel, but you are she to whom the Queen has entrusted her Power. Today, you are free to cause that he should be no more. After you have taken the Oath you will be restrained from that, perhaps you should consider that option." Clay worked his jaw in irritation. None else would have suggested it, especially in his presence, so he felt it was his duty to inform her. However much it sickened him, it would solve many of their concerns.

Mara was appalled at the thought. "Clay! I could never cause one to cease to exist. Not even the most vilest of creatures, at least not in cold blood. Were I being attacked surely I would defend myself. But now that I know I have the upper hand I will be fair and just—as I have pledged." She left Aerrvin's embrace to seek comfort from Clay, as well as to lend it.

Aerrvin stifled his jealousy. *Clay is going to be a permanent fixture in this marriage. Might as well get used to it,* he thought.

Hannah signaled it was time to rouse themselves. They were parked in front of the house. Mara had a firm hold on her emotions and Morvayne was at peace as he helped her exit the limo.

Once inside, Mara stood in the main room flanked by five of her six attendants. Breeze was unaware of the impending judgment so she stood as puzzled as Morvayne as Mara began to reveal her Light.

Mara saw that the Brownies, who had snuck in to serve her, as well as George, and Hans, were bowed as low as everyone else.

She realized that it was up to her to speak first. "Breeze, you have sworn to serve me, you are excused."

"Yes, My lady. Thank you. I would like to witness the proceedings, if I may?" Breeze said in her airy voice.

"Very well. But stand behind me. Morvayne, I have learned of your depravity and cannot wait another minute to place a judgment upon you. Stand up!" Mara commanded.

Morvayne stood weakly, but he was unable to look at her.

"Tell me your crimes!" Mara demanded; why she wished to hear them she did not know, but it seemed a proper thing to do. It so happened that it was a part of the Queen's Court to recite one's crimes.

Morvayne had no doubt that Mara had received the Queen's Power even without being crowned upon the Crystal Throne. He could not see them now in his blindness, but he could recall the image of his former Hold Mates gathered around Mara. Had they influenced her? Or had she drawn them to her with her compulsive nature? *It is not fair! Clay always rises to the top, he will not gain access to Arianna.* Morvayne swore to himself that he would accept any sentence, but never would he allow Clay his most cherished desire.

Morvayne began with his childhood and continued through the years. Mara had not thought it would be like this. But it was a full disclosure to her question. She was not tired and could stand there for hours, and she did. Then he got to a part about deceiving Arianna by Transforming himself into Clay. Mara was appalled and Clay issued a strangled cough.

Mara asked, "Wait, Morvayne, you are the cause of Arianna's refusal to meet with Clay? Why?"

Morvayne enjoyed this part, he wanted to hurt Clay for being the favored son. "It never seemed fair that he should gain happiness if I could not. Tigerlily enjoyed my company, but she refused to become serious. When I saw Clay's success, it hurt my pride. I will admit I used Arianna for a little pleasure and then I influenced Clay to break her heart."

Clay could not control his anger further, ignoring the Brightness of Mara's Glory he charged as he growled in fury. Morvayne had no time to stop Clay's attack. He was still wearing the ring, which should have protected him from attacks in the first place. Yet, Clay was on top of him, pounding his face repeatedly.

Mara screamed, "Stop!" and suddenly Clay and Morvayne both were bound, unable to move a muscle.

"Ivan take him away. I need to rest before I hear anymore."

"My lady, can you lower your Light? I can barely move," Ivan said

Mara tucked away one pocket, too afraid to put the rest away. She released Clay once Morvayne was taken away by Elwood and Ivan. Clay lay huddled on the floor exhausted and weeping, his fingers were a bloodied mix of both his and Morvayne's blood. It was more than Mara could bear and she swooned, barely being caught by Hannah, who easily set her on the couch. Jasmine and Breeze healed Clay's wounds and sat with him murmuring words of comfort. Mara's Brightness eased, allowing all to move freely.

Hans sat next to Mara, offering tea and a cool cloth. "My Lady, that was more drama than I have seen on Broadway! What a way to win your freedom; it was magnificent! Pity I do not get to hear the rest of his trial. Clay has every right to what he did; please do not judge him harshly."

Mara sat up accepting the proffered tea. "I have no intention of passing any judgment against Clay, I know he had cause. Thank you, Hans," she nodded gratefully, for the tea as well as his concern.

Hans bowed as he spilled Dust in embarrassment. He had not meant to advise the future Queen. "My apologies, Your Highness. I did not mean to speak out of place."

Mara felt he was being a nuisance as she wanted to attend to Clay, but she felt restrained by good manners and duty. "Hans, I am not nearly as formidable as you make me out to be. I understand your concern. Promise to serve me always, and I will allow you to be one of my chefs when I put my Household together."

She called forth his Dust and placed it in a beautiful vial. Opening a tiny window, she set it on a shelf with her very small, but growing collection. She smiled sadly as Hans promised to serve her forever with a flourish worthy of any actor she had ever seen; he bowed and retreated from her sight. No doubt still watching the proceedings in order to regale friends and posterity of the visions and sights he beheld on the momentous day before the Queen's coronation.

Mara felt overwhelmed with the weight of responsibility which was settling upon her. She wanted to go stay at Ironwood Estates, but did not want to intrude in the middle of the night. Later, she realized that most of the household would have been up and about, but at the time she was still thinking in Human timeframes and etiquette.

"Is there somewhere we can go? I cannot stay here another night."

Daisy and Aerrvin had been let in to witness the trial. "We can go to my nest in the woods," Aerrvin offered.

Mara accepted and they all downsized before stepping through the tiny beam of light that Aerrvin created. Even George came along. Mara and Jasmine each held onto Clay, who had stopped crying but was numb and unspeaking. Hannah went to check on Ivan and Elwood in the spaceship and to inform them of their location.

Mara had never visited a natural nest before. She would have delighted in a tour had it been happier times. The nest was really a hollow tree with several levels. Aerrvin's private nest was easiest to identify as it was filled with a variety of textures, most of them silky, smooth or soft. Mara offered a private smile to Aerrvin as they passed by on their way to the communal nest in the center of the tree. He gave her hand a squeeze in return.

George was more concerned with Clay than Mara would have thought. He caught Mara's attention. "May I speak with you privately?"

Mara walked a little distance away from the group. "What

is it, George?"

"I have been studying this topic recently; I fear that Clay is going to Fade. He is receding into his mind. If you wish to save him you must catch him before it is too late. True he could stay that way for years, but it will be easier to bring him back if he never crosses over the line."

Mara waved Breeze and Jasmine over, repeating George's assessment. "What can be done? Do we all go or only one; who should go?"

Aerrvin offered his educated opinion, "It works best if it is someone very close to him, any of you should be acceptable, not counting Breeze of course." Aerrvin nodded to her by way of apology. "But, you also need the skill of knowing where to go. "

Hannah appraised Aerrvin with appreciation. "You seem to have studied this quite a bit; none of us have taken the time to understand the workings of the mind as much as Clay has. Not even Elwood or Ivan. Clay has been like a brother to each of us, I hate to admit it, but Mara is truly the best candidate along with you, Aerrvin. You should go and try to bring him back."

Elwood and Ivan walked in just then. "Morvayne is securely placed in stasis, you may continue his hearing in the Void when you have the time to attend to it. How is Clay?" Ivan asked as he bent down to sit with him.

Clay reclined on a pile of fluff, his face at peace. Mara had never seen him look so sweet and vulnerable. "Morvayne can wait a hundred years for all I care. We need to reach Clay before he jumps so far we cannot find him. What do we do?"

"Well first we can all enter and let him know we care. But then those he has no interest in speaking to will have to leave. We will have to play it by ear. Do you know of anyone he might have been close to who might be able to garner his attention better then we?" Aerrvin said.

His authority with the Elves impressed Mara. She found it amazing that she was betrothed to a King of the Fairies, but now she saw that she was honored to be crowned Queen, and to have such a worthy Fair One as her King Consort. *Double kingdoms!* It was mind boggling.

Jasmine answered, "There are none but us, which is why he claims no land, nor name, nor title. Though in truth he is Lord ap Stewart of Scotland."

"Very well, let us enter the Void," Mara said as she chose a spot next to Clay. Aerrvin lay above them with his head touching both Mara's and Clay's. Taking Aerrvin's lead the rest of Clay's friends lay head to head, creating a radiant circle of life as they stepped into the Void.

Meeting at the crossroad within the Void, Mara was taken aback by their numbers. The place had always been so open and spacious when there was only two or three visitors. Jasmine lead them down the southern hall. How she knew which hall to search Mara did not know. But as they got closer, Mara found that she could feel Clay's essence pulling her on towards the proper door.

"I am going to have to develop my skills in this emotion sensing stuff, that is certain." Aerrvin gave her a weak smile as Jasmine tapped at the door, a secret knock that she evidently shared with Clay unbeknownst to her fellow Hold Mates.

They waited and finally Clay allowed the door to open. He sat in a meadow filled with blossoms in full bloom. The warm Scottish summer sun shone down, filling the meadow with a heady floral scent. Mara instantly recognized the parallels and breathed in deeply, having never smelled her own scent. Clay looked up and smiled weakly at her. He greeted each of his friends warmly as though to say goodbye. He seemed to be at peace, yet he was determined to go. "Thank you for coming, it means so much to me to have all of you here. You too, Aerrvin. I know that Mara is in good hands with you."

"Shut up!" Mara shouted as tears spilled from her eyes. "You cannot go anywhere. I need you!"

"I love you too, Mara, but I have no hope left. Arianna could never trust me, not now."

He sat back down and closed his eyes. "You may leave me now, I have much in the way of contemplation to achieve before I go."

"I am not going anywhere and you can't make me." Mara sat down opposite him and waited.

After a while she said to the rest, "You may leave us, see what you can learn about Arianna's location."

Clay's eyes flew open. "No! Do not bring her to me. I could not bear the shame."

Mara searched his face and emotions. He truly feared meeting her in his shame. "Go and find her, question Morvayne if you can. Clay, I will not bring her if you do not wish it. But we will rescue her anyway. I don't understand. Please talk to me!"

"Aerrvin, can you give us some space?"

The Dream was expansive, not at all what Clay had claimed when he stated that he preferred to keep his Dreams tight and enclosed. Aerrvin became a hawk and flew up into the sky.

Clay sat there, aware of Mara's scent far stronger than any flower he had created in this meadow. He was mortified and could not bear to live. Yet, she refused to leave, and Aerrvin would not leave without her. Hours had passed by already.

Finally he spoke. Willing his eyes to remain shut. "Mara, you are ruining my concentration."

"Good," she replied. "Open your eyes. No sense in being rude."

Clay opened his eyes and saw Mara sitting there dressed in her copy of Tigerlily's reception gown. The one Tigerlily wore on the day of her Presentation to the Realms after her graduation from the Academy of the Arts and Social Sciences. Mara even had the tiara arranged with her hair woven through it exactly like Tigerlily.

He groaned. "Oh, Mara, what are you doing to me? You torture me with your presence and your likeness. Please, leave me in peace."

He looked deeply into her soul, willing her to understand.

"Clay, I feel your pain, but I need to understand. If you can convince me that I am better off without you, then I will leave. You have my word. Please, tell me what it is that has you so shamed. Morvayne was wrong to do as he did. Your anger was justified in my eyes. I do not fault you at all."

Mara scooted over to sit beside him, creating pillows as he was wont to do, then she pulled him back to lie beside her as she snuggled under his arm.

Breathing in her scent deeply, he steeled himself as he prepared to bare his soul.

25
Heartache

Aerrvin tired of flying in circles. He had already caught two mice and brushed by the lake. Now he sat in a tree a few hundred feet away from where Mara sat snuggled up with Clay. She was coaxing, and firmly confident, yet still filled with sorrow and puzzlement. Clay would have to explain the peculiarities of Elven etiquette before she understood his mortification. Aerrvin thought he understood, but then again perhaps there was still more to the story than had been revealed.

Clay brushed his lips across her silken hair as he kissed her temple, being careful to keep his face from being scratched with her crown. "Really, Mara, the tiara is dangerous so close to my face." Instantly it was gone and her silken straight hair spilled down across his chest. "I fear your understanding is limited, it will take time to explain why I cannot face Arianna, nor you, nor any of my dear companions."

"I can wait. Even if it means missing my birthday. I am to receive my fathers' journals and a letter I have been waiting for all these years." She allowed her tears to fall easily, she had been crying already; no sense in holding back now.

"No, Mara, do not do this. The world needs you, your twenty-first birthday is meant to be the most joyous occasion, a celebration and recognition of the end of your infancy and growing into your young adult responsibilities."

Mara sat up and smacked him on the chest. "How can it be joyous without you?! Clay, please be reasonable. Tell me your reasons and be complete. I will just have to learn time travel if I must and arrive just in time for my Oath. There. Now tell me, please!" Mara commanded as she released all of her Light for emphasis, then she quickly put it all away, except for the hankie, of course.

Clay began, "Mara, Mara," he paused and sighed. "Visiting the Land of Dreams can be dangerous, because it makes one think that what has been experienced in a particularly good Dream should be recreated in reality. I foolishly lived several Dreams involving Tigerlily and Arianna. I was equally in love with both of them. In reality I had a hard time choosing which one to pursue. I was young and not in full control of my abilities and Powers. If Arianna was not near me I could be totally in love with Tigerlily, but if Arianna showed up, my attention shifted like a breeze, certainly when it blew her scent my way." He inhaled automatically.

"Arianna thought it great fun to toy with me, as well as tease Tigerlily by taking away what Tigerlily thought was hers. Tigerlily did the same. When we allowed Morvayne to join us it seemed a good solution; Tigerlily liked Morvayne as well as me and it left me free to gain Arianna's trust." Clay paused to breathe in deeply as he hugged her to him. Mara still did not understand, so she simply waited for him to continue.

"We pledged ourselves to each other, not a public wedding, but true enough in the world of Fair Ones. Then I saw her go running off into the woods with Morvayne." His voice grew thick with sorrow and rage. "I did not see it then, but know it now, that was when Morvayne had Transformed himself to look like me. Not much to change really, from that distance I could not see that he had changed at all. Arianna and I had agreed to spend time together sailing to America. But seeing this betrayal I considered seeking comfort with Tigerlily." Clay sat up and searched Mara's eyes to see how she judged him.

"I do not condemn you Clay, it was still Morvayne's doing." Mara said, pain and sorrow echoed on her face.

"There is more. I returned to Arianna and pretended that nothing had happened, yet I behaved cruelly until I drove her away. The pain was torture as I craved her scent. Yet, I could not bear what she had done. What I thought she had done, not then anyway. Morvayne was forgiven, somewhat. I never asked him about it, but I assumed it was her doing. Her vow was with me. Not long after, I found forgiveness and sought to win her back, but she had found a new life and had married a Human. Now I know she has forgiven for me, she said so when last we met. But Mara, I am so ashamed I cannot bear to face her. I broke her heart with cruelty, she never forsook me until after I drove her away. Surely, you can see why I must Fade?"

"No! I don't. I guess I do not get this Elven logic yet. Clay, I need you. You promised to serve me until I released you. How can you break your promise?"

Clay barked a humorless laugh. "Precisely my point Mara, I am not trustworthy. Neither you nor Arianna can trust me. Tigerlily and I made our peace together, and we remained dearest friends, but I fear that my defects are genetic; I may be too much like Morvayne. I cannot allow myself to be a threat to you."

"No, I don't believe it! Morvayne poisoned his mind with wine. You said so yourself. Your story is tragic, but understandable. How is it different from Morvayne sharing his Honeysuckle Dew with me? Teach me how to Travel back in time. I will stay until you have taught me all you were meant to teach."

She sat up, expectantly awaiting a lesson. She had changed her attire to a sundress like the ones she wore in Italy. And then created a wicker chair with a soft cushion to sit in.

"I can only sit on the ground for so long before my muscles ache," she explained. She was aware that it was now one o'clock in the afternoon. "Just a minute, can I contact Sylvie from here?"

Clay grudgingly created a matching chair and sat down. "Yes, just step into the Void and go to her Dream as usual."

Mara did as directed and felt lost momentarily. She was stepping out of a Dream, not her body. She had to remind herself of where her body was, in Aerrvin's Nest.

"This gets easier with time I hope." She located Sylvie's Dream and tapped politely at her window. Sylvie's room was much like Mara's, she noted.

"Mara, are you free?" Sylvie asked as soon as Mara entered the room. Mara hugged her and affirmed that she was. "Morvayne is bound, awaiting judgment. But Clay is despondent at something Morvayne told him and is trying to commit suicide!"

"What? That is not like him. Where is he?" Sylvie asked worriedly.

"Well, maybe not suicide, exactly. He is in the Third Level of the Void and is preparing to Fade. That is pretty much the same thing: Leaving this world. Anyway, Sylvie, could you please let my family know that I intend to be at my Oath Taking Ceremony? I may be a bit late as I am the only one, along with Aerrvin, whom Clay has allowed to stay. I can't let him go and have promised to stay until he agrees to continue as my Protector. I don't know how stubborn he is, so please extend my apologies to one and all."

"Of course, Your Highness, we all wish you the best of luck. We would sorely miss Clay were he to choose this path. Please let him know we are sending good thoughts his way." Sylvie bowed and shooed Mara away to her task.

Mara entered the Void once more. This was the first time she had gone to the Third Level alone. It felt a little scary, why she did not know; she felt as though unseen eyes were watching her. She took the Southern hallway and felt Clay and Aerrvin's presence guide her to the correct door. With a shock she realized that Morvayne was right next door. She tapped at his door and entered, he was not at liberty to lock his door.

Ivan had a special binding technique, which was superior to Morvayne's. It kept Morvayne from Fleeing into the Land of Dreams permanently, he could visit, but could not stay. The binding spell also prevented him from locking the door or leaving altogether. He was however, able to Dream as he chose. Mara entered to find him sitting in a pleasant yet, dark cave.

"Morvayne, I need your help. I have not yet come to ask for the rest of your crimes as I do not have time. Clay is distraught, and I need him as my Protector."

"Clay is distraught." Morvayne mimicked. "What do I care? It has always been Clay is so talented, or look how well Clay is doing. Mara you tricked me. I thought you loved me, I felt your love. Yet you revile me. How is that possible?" He looked at her with a bereft look, soon replaced by scorn.

"Morvayne, I love you, because I love Clay, he loves you and I felt compassion for him. I love you for what you could have been, for your potential. I have learned about Dreams and the many different paths we could be taking daily, but most importantly the crossroads where a choice can drastically change history as it was meant to be. I think you crossed the line with Arianna, and it ate at your soul. Because of your actions you caused Tigerlily to eventually distrust you and that had the various chain reactions, which have been your life of crime and evil. After I am through with you, I think I will visit an otherwhen, a time before your transgression. I wish to experience you as the man you could have been. I wish to have happy memories of you and Clay like the last two nights, only better." Mara let a single tear slip. "Please tell me something that I can do or say to help Clay. I love him and need him with me."

"I am touched by your desire to see me in a better light, but I have no desire to help Clay while I sit here trapped awaiting sentencing. How you plan to enforce the sentence without the full authority of the Crystal Throne, I have no clue," Morvayne replied.

"Gwennara is safe with Brand, Morvayne. It appears your plot was futile from the start. I will insist on your cooperation in revealing the location of my Father and Arianna. Assuming they are together, but right now Clay is ashamed to meet the princess." Mara paused but received silence. "Very well, since you choose to *not* be helpful you shall sit here and stew for a while. I have much to attend to. Be thinking on which alternate reality you would like to choose, as that may very well be your sentence."

"I see you have been taught more than I expected. I will begin sampling Dreams not heretofore encountered. Perhaps I *will* find the Dream I am looking for. Tell Clay I said, sleep well." Morvayne smirked as Mara shook her head in disgust.

Upon her return, Mara found Aerrvin and Clay in earnest discussion. "Hello, did you miss me?" Mara said sweetly in her soft, whispery voice.

Aerrvin nodded and Clay could not keep his mouth from twitching as he shook his head. "Mara, you bring life to this old Elven soul."

"Good! And no more talk of being old. Gwennara and Brand are—how old? Twelve hundred or something, right? They are fit for a pleasant retirement; in Human years they look no older than fifty at most. Well, I have not seen Gwennara, but judging from Brand they are in their prime. I admit, I thought that one hundred and ninety was my limit, but I have to confess, were I not engaged to the fairest Fairy ever, I would be hard pressed to turn you down based on your age."

Clay laughed his first real laugh, it seemed like it had been forever since the previous night's dancing had cheered him. "Aerrvin did you see that? Your fiancé just made a pass at me! That Elven nature is starting to take hold, along with the Water Sprite and Fairy tendencies." Clay gave Aerrvin a look filled with mock warnings.

Aerrvin smiled at both of them. "I saw. She will need to be taught a few lessons in propriety, but I do believe she will make a fine Queen twice over." He eyed her hungrily before turning his attention back to Clay. "Do you wish more privacy or may I stay?"

Clay sighed, "No, stay, it appears my life is an open book."

Mara noted the huge pile of feathers they were on and plopped perfectly between them, well except for the elbow to Clay's ribs and a small kick on Aerrvin's shin. "See? I need you both for practicing all of my most important skills on. Clay are you ready to return to the land of the living?"

Clay and Aerrvin each took a deep whiff; evidently she had released a good bit of scent into her clothing while she had been speaking with Morvayne. "See? It is sunshine and blossoms," Clay said over her head, completely ignoring her.

"Yes, I can smell the sunshine, but the floral scent I get is lavender and rose. Not your random mix of wildflowers." Aerrvin responded amiably.

"Hello! I am sitting right here. Is it proper to discuss the Queen's scent in her presence?"

"Depends on who is doing the discussing," Aerrvin said, "and besides you are not quite Queen."

He chuckled richly as Mara pounced on him, trying to find

his most ticklish spots. He was far too ticklish to lay still for her though.

"Clay, hold him down for me. Isn't this in your job description? Defending me against attacks?" Mara asked breathlessly.

Clay had assumed his reserved attitude, but he smiled good-naturedly and held Aerrvin's shoulders down. "If your future husband and lifetime Protector cannot discuss your finer qualities who can?" he asked.

Mara successfully tortured Aerrvin and then turned to Clay. "Really, Clay? You will stay with me forever? Aerrvin, what did you say to him?" Mara climbed off of Aerrvin and hugged Clay.

"Nothing really, we just talked." Aerrvin said. Mara could see it now, men and their own little secrets!

"Fine, keep your confidences. Just so long as I get my way." Mara smiled at Aerrvin and Clay mischievously. "Can you still teach me time travel?" Mara asked Clay.

"No, not today. I would not want to risk you taking a wrong turn on such an important day. Remember, you are not supposed to even be here until after you take the Oath." He indicated the meadow within the room.

Mara hung her head, but accepted his words as true. She also wanted to visit that Dream concerning a joyful marriage between them which he had told her of, but it was not the right time to ask about it.

"Well, we still have five hours until dinner at the Estate. What can we do while we wait?"

"Let me return to my companions and reassure them that I will maintain my role as their Hold Master and as your Protector. Then we will all return here and share parts of our life with you. You can start with viewing Aerrvin's first few weeks at the Academy. That should be eye opening for you," Clay offered knowingly.

Aerrvin eyed Clay questioningly. "You were there?"

"Aye, a very senior Professor too. Though you never bothered taking any of my classes. I had occasion enough to observe you and your antics." Clay smiled softly, giving the uncomfortable Fairy a twitch of his brow as he opened the door and excused himself.

As soon as they were alone they embraced. After a good long kiss Mara asked, "Well, are you going to share your experiences with me or not?"

"I'd rather continue as we were, but I suppose a sample of my ingenuity would be beneficial. As Queen you will not attend the Academy; the Academy will come to you. Nevertheless, you will still be required to pass certain exams. Watch this," Aerrvin said as he clasped her hand and invited her to lay beside him on the pile of fluff.

Viewing his life, Mara felt amazed and delighted at Aerrvin's mischievous behavior. Had he been her son, she would have been vexed more than delighted. Aerrvin played pranks on his assigned Nest Mate the first day on campus. They were fairly harmless, yet would have been humiliating to Mara had he tried them on her.

The first exam on the third day of school required the students to find a companion who could perform at their very own level—without speaking, while also blindfolded. They were placed in a large arena filled with sand. There were about one hundred students in the class. Occasionally, an object would be placed in the path of Aerrvin, but instead of stopping to go around it he used the wind to move it out of his path. Though seeing it through Aerrvin's eyes, she saw actual Wind Sprites obeying his desire.

In a relatively short amount of time he joined hands with Gareth. They were each other's favorite cousin and had managed to each make sure that they were in the same classes. Having spent some time together as youngest of younglings, they had somewhat cheated the game because they already knew each other. Yet the inquiry afterwards revealed that they were equally gifted and suited to be Nest Mates along with Jaera, Seanna and Talitha. They soon saw that the real purpose in the exercise was to help the students find suitable Nest Mates, as they would be together for as long as they chose to remain at the Academy. Aerrvin and Gareth managed to be equally good at causing mischief, as were the three female Fairies in their troupe.

One particularly glaring offense caused them to be bound for a month before being returned to class. Fortunately, Mara did not have to endure the month-long incarceration as the rest of her Attendants pinged on the door before entering. Aerrvin returned the room to Clay's meadow.

"Why would you have even thought of putting pebbles in Master Groban's dinner-party fare in the first place? And exploding ones at that? Did you see that Clay was indeed one of the guests at the party?" Mara asked with great wonder expressed on her wide-eyed face.

Aerrvin grinned as only he could and replied, "I did indeed recognize him this time. Did you see the look on his face as he got splattered!" Aerrvin chuckled richly. "Gareth and I would read far and wide from the most rarest of books in the libraries to find unused spells and the like." He stopped talking as Clay sat down wearing his own smirk.

"I trust you did not know, that it was my suggestion that you be bound for that month, as well as forced to endure the driest histories ever taught." Clay asked as he placed a brotherly arm across Aerrvin's shoulders.

Aerrvin sounded his mirth and thanked Clay for the lessons. "Actually those lessons have served me well and have helped me get out of countless other situations which I managed to find myself in over the years. Let us see you at *your* youngest ages in the academy. I dare say you were not always so controlled and calm, were you?"

"Not hardly," Clay admitted with a glance at Breeze.

Breeze giggled at her own remembrances of the young Clay. "By all means, Clay, share your youth with us, it should be priceless to see it from your point of view."

Finding comfortable places as the pile of fluff grew to accommodate their numbers, Clay felt he needed to explain the circumstances before the viewing took place. Clearing his throat he began, "I had been my parent's one and only child; they had recently brought my sister into the world and were doting on her in an insufferable manner. Or so it felt to me."

"Clay? I never knew you had a sister! Where is she?" Mara asked in delight.

Clay's face clouded slightly, "Long gone, I am sorry to say. Now don't get upset, it is a part of my life. Many have come and gone in my 901 years of existence."

"Wait, you said you were 900 hundred; were you just rounding? When is your date of birth? Tell me!" Mara demanded glaring at everyone.

Clay took her hand to calm her. "It was June 7th. I had a quiet remembrance. Do not trouble yourself over it. Mara, my 900th was celebration enough to last the century." He smiled at his friends, remembering the fun they had allowed themselves, limited as it was considering their duties.

"I would have liked to have known," Mara pouted. "From now on, everyone tells me when they have a birthday or other important occasion to celebrate. Okay?" She tried to soften her command as she heard her own demanding voice. "Sorry, Clay, you may continue your explanation." She smiled sweetly, trying to ensure no one was mad at her; they weren't.

"As I was saying, I was put out by my parent's adoration of Clarissa. She was eight years old and absolutely delightful. How could a gangly twenty-one year old compete with that? Normally, as you know, we Fair Ones put at least forty to fifty years between children to help soften the jealousy, so this closeness was particularly embarrassing to me. I did not want to go to the Academy that year, but it was tradition to leave one week after taking the Oath. My parents insisted on taking me there in person, as they did not trust me to arrive on my own."

***

The school was larger than the castle in which Clay had grown up in. Scotland has several small castles still inhabited by descendants, or the newly rich of the eighties. The home Clay grew up in had been built by his very own ancestors along with the neighboring Human clan in the area. He felt overwhelmed by the largeness of the school. But he tried to exude a calm exterior. Having been the center of attention for so long, it was very trying as one student after another stopped to welcome him and then proceed to be delighted with Clarissa. He was relieved when he was finally shown his room and assigned a roommate.

"Hello, my name is Morthe," said the large-mouthed Ogre. "I guess we are to be roommates, until we get reassigned at any rates" Ogre's had a penchant for rhyming, Morthe just happened to be poor at it.

Clay smiled, relieved that he did not immediately turn away to sweep up little Clarissa as so many others had. "Hello, my name is Lord Clay ap Stewart of Scotland. I am pleased to meet you."

Clay turned to hug his parent's good-bye. "Thank you for seeing me off to school. I will see you at Christmas, perhaps," he offered jokingly, as he was sure they would want him to visit sooner.

His mother smiled and hugged him warmly. "Very well, Christmas it is. Take care and keep out of trouble." She took Clarissa by the hand and then had her give her big brother a hug. Despite his humiliation, he loved the child, as all young are precious.

"Will you miss me?" he asked.

She squirmed and replied, "Maybe." But softened her rudeness with a kiss.

He bid farewell to his father and then lay down on his bed.

The room was fairly large compared to other student's rooms, owing to the fact that he was landed gentry and Morthe was large in stature and needed more space. The Ogre and Clay were like-minded and equally tempered, meaning that they wanted peace and quiet, but had yet to learn to control their tempers.

Three days later and Clay was still being referred to as the Elf with the adorable sister. Clay kept it all in, but finally allowed his wrath to explode when Morthe unwittingly set him off. They were in Earth Sciences learning the properties of various soils.

"Hey, Clay," Morthe said as they set about classifying the soils assigned to them. "This soil is so fine and pale it reminds me of Clarissa's hair."

Clay was unable to control his emotions as he caused all of the soil in the lab to swirl about until Morthe was thoroughly covered in dirt. The whole class cheered at his display of Power, yet the teacher was not nearly so approving. Nor was Morthe; he caused a swarm of gnats to land on Clay. Class was dismissed except for the still fuming Clay and the rumbling Morthe.

The professor was amused, as shown by the twinkle in his eye, but he was not about to allow such behavior to go unpunished. With a wave of his hand he removed the gnats from the room.

"Would you care to elaborate on the purpose of your display?" He looked at each in turn, not sure who had started the commotion.

Morthe made his excuses and accused Clay of rashness. Clay accepted the tirade and then exclaimed, "I do not wish to hear my sister's name mentioned ever again! It is not fair that she should intrude upon my life and experiences. I cannot understand my parents and I wish–I wish–ah! I don't know what I want, Morthe, I am sorry." Clay caused all of the dirt to sort back into the individual piles from which they had come, leaving Morthe as clean as he had been before the incident.

Morthe was amazed at Clay's skill and forgave him with conditions. "Promise you will teach me how to do that, please?"

Clay nodded and smiled at his newfound friend. The professor sent them to the school board to rehearse their crimes and receive a punishment. They had to sit outside of the office for two hours as the board discussed a fitting chastisement. Clay and Morthe spent the time really getting to know each other and learning what each felt to be their strongest and weakest abilities.

Being called in individually Clay did not learn what Morthe was punished with until later.

"Clay, we are impressed with your Brightness and skill. You shall be required to meet with Master Shane every day at sunrise until lunch. You will do as he asks without question. Is that understood?"

Clay nodded meekly; everyone had heard of Master Shane

and feared to anger him, as his punishments were swift and humiliating. Master Shane taught Mental Prowess as well as Biology. Both were classes Clay was interested in, but his fear of Master Shane had prevented him from signing up for those classes that first quarter. He thought to wait a few years and then begin his studies with the dreaded Professor. It proved to be a fortuitous assignment as Clay became Master Shane's star pupil.

***

Released from the Dream, most simply smiled while Ivan and Aerrvin chuckled. Their respect for Clay overcame any desire to ridicule him for his lack of control. "Impressive, Clay!" Aerrvin said. Ivan nodded in agreement.

"Who'd a thunk it?!" Mara said, cringing as her mother's strange saying leapt from her mouth. Having earned smiles from everyone, she quickly asked another question. "Did you ever have a good relationship with your sister?"

Clay took Mara's hand in his and replied, "The best."

Mara knew he was not up to sharing more, so she took heart in the hopes of having a great time with her little sisters. "I guess now that my sisters are aware of who they are, I might be able to have a long and happy adult life with them. I admit I was jealous of them at first as well. Ah, siblings." She shook her head trying not to think of Morvayne. "Hannah, it's your turn!"

26
An End to Childhood

Back in the Nest, Mara expressed how much she had enjoyed becoming better acquainted with her newly acquired best friends forever. "Thanks for sharing yourselves with me; that was wonderful. Well, we have one hour before dinner. Aerrvin, may I use one of your guest suites at the O'Shea Mansion? I hate to beg, but I don't have a home anymore." She gave him a forlorn expression as she waited for his response.

"Mara, I thought you would never ask! I would love for you to move in with me!" Aerrvin grinned mischievously, knowing she would balk at the suggestion. Before she could voice her objections he kissed her as he drew a line of Light in the air and stepped into his room of white and mirrors. Her companions entered with her.

Gareth and Jaera came running in as soon as they felt their arrival. "Mara!" they exclaimed and then bowled her over with their hugs, being careful to not really allow her to land on the ground. Gareth danced her around the room inches from the ground and then released her to hug Aerrvin.

"You will have to give us a complete accounting sometime. I am sure it has been horrific and amazing. We are so glad you are safely home. You too, Clay." Gareth hugged Clay as tightly as he had hugged Aerrvin, receiving an equally intense hug in return.

Mara was amazed that Clay accepted Gareth so easily. *Must*

be my Human upbringing; these Fair Ones are so much more loving than I am used to, she mused.

"I am in need of a shower and a few moments to collect myself before dinner. Aerrvin, which rooms will be mine and my friends."

"The choice is yours, Your Highness." He bowed politely, and not too deeply so as to not embarrass her.

"In that case, I should like to have the royal purple apartment if you and Clay could share the other room with the floating bed?" She looked expectantly from Aerrvin to Clay, not sure that they would agree to her desire to be near each of them.

Almost as one they bowed and replied, "As you wish."

"I wish, but stop being so formal. I can hardly stand it! Ah!" she exclaimed breathily.

"No problem, Mara. The kittens are far too active now to get a good rest with them. You will have to visit them soon. Be that as it may, I can create a nest anywhere and be as comfy as I could desire." Aerrvin ran his finger from her ear down her neck and wriggled his eyebrows suggestively as his eyes twinkled merrily.

As hard as she tried, she could not keep from blushing. "One of these days Aerrvin . . ." she threatened. "Now what about everyone else? I am sure they don't want to keep popping back to their individual residences every time they need a shower or a nap."

Jaera volunteered to share her rooms with Hannah, Jasmine, Daisy and Breeze; and while Gareth willingly offered up his rooms, Ivan and Elwood opted to take the decidedly manly rooms found at the top of the stairs.

"I personally don't mind the kittens, so I will be with them most of the time anyway. Unless I am with Gareth," Jaera said, as she climbed onto his back. He dutifully carried her out and helped her get the guests settled in.

Aerrvin showed Mara all of the amenities of the bathroom before leaving her to her ablutions. Then he returned to his sitting room where Clay sat meditating. He sat with him in silence for ten minutes, truly a short span of time. Clay became aware of his presence and asked, "May I see my room? I was not here when Mara received her tour."

Aerrvin showed him the floating bed and was pleased to see Clay give a nod of approval. "Truly beautiful, Aerrvin; your sense of aesthetics is impeccable." He looked about and realized there was only one bathroom for the two bedrooms to share.

Aerrvin apologized, "Sorry, if you would like, you can bathe in the pond. Or you can wait for Mara to exit. She has to get dressed so she can't loll around in the tub all day."

Clay smiled gratefully. "The pond and waterfall sounds inviting. Thank you." Clay left to go for a dip.

Mara took another ten minutes and emerged from the bathroom with a billow of steam, wrapped in a terrycloth bathrobe. "Whew! I guess I made it a bit too hot. It feels nice out here. Where is Clay?" Mara asked. Realizing she was alone with her intended, she suddenly felt awkward and shy.

"He went to swim in the pond. Do you have a clue as to what you would like to wear?" Aerrvin said as he contemplated all the designs he had dreamed up for her thus far.

Mara went up to him. "No, I assumed you would know what would be best. Oh! Where is Sylvie? And did we leave Hans at Morvayne's house?" Mara started to make a Window to return when Aerrvin interrupted her.

"Calm, Mara, Hans and George both slept in my Nest last night. They stayed below. But I took the liberty to ask them to visit with your mother and inform her of all that has happened; they will be at the Oath Ceremony and party afterwards. Ironwood wants to keep the dinner itself small. And. Jill is cooking like she said she would."

Mara crumpled into Aerrvin's arms as she recalled all she had been through in the past month or so. Jill was her link to Humanity, not counting genetics, one of the few persons who knew her as she had been. Aerrvin held her, sensing her need to expunge all her pent up emotions before she had to pull herself together once again. He dried her hair with Mirri's help, finding joy watching each tendril become large wavy curls. She still had some of the straightening properties in it so it did not become as springy as normal, but he preferred even a little bounce to none at all.

"Mara, we have twenty minutes left. Sweet pea, how about a little cheer, hmmm?" Aerrvin changed his clothes into his favorite deep blue leggings topped by a silvery white spider silk shirt drenched in lace at his cuffs and attached cravat. He wore a blue, silver, and gold brocade long-vest, more like a tunic. The tunic-vest was belted by a golden knife belt which held his knives, gifts given to him by his father not so very long ago, but which seemed a lifetime or more gone past.

Mara was instantly delighted with his attire. She chose not to say she found it funny that such a studly guy would dress so fantastical. So she emptied her thoughts and laughed with joy.

"Can I match?"

Aerrvin felt her fleeting mirth at his expense, but he was used to it. Most everyone responded similarly, but he had no intentions of changing his style, ever. Besides, Clay just told him his style was impeccable.

"I have two dresses for you to choose from." Being in the white on white room with its wall of mirrors, it was not hard to position her in front of a mirror. "First, I was considering this one."

Mara looked at her reflection, one minute she was standing there like a puffy white marshmallow and the next she was wearing a slinky silver gown, which puddled at her feet and trailed behind, shimmering as she moved. It was slashed on one side with deep blue, matching the blue Aerrvin wore. It was similar to the first silver dress he had designed, yet he had modified it to make it match him with the blue slash of color. "No gold in it, had I added gold, I think it would have looked gaudy."

Mara looked askance at him in his silver and gold. But she smiled and said, "I guess yours works because it is all broken up into that leaf pattern." Referring to her dress she admitted, "I like it, but it is a bit low in front. And don't I have to walk around in front of people? I think I might trip." She shortened it and raised the neckline, effectively making it look like a homemade prom dress.

She sighed as Aerrvin shook his head in dismay at what she had done to his creation. "Sorry. What else have you got?"

"Promise not to alter it first," Aerrvin said, standing with his arms folded and lips pursed. "The first dress was a representation of you becoming a woman. Many choose to dress thusly to celebrate the grand event. This next dress is to represent your last day of childhood. Since you never really got to experience a true Elven childhood, I think it would be proper that you get to dress like a youngling for a day, or at least for dinner." He smiled as only he could and asked again, "Promise?"

"I will not alter it, I promise. I do not promise to wear it!" Mara waggled her finger at him causing him to snap at her fingers playfully.

"Very well."

Right before her eyes Mara became every girl's dream fairy

princess. Even her hair had been curled to lay in perfect waves as it fell silky and dark about her bare Dust covered shoulders. Her cheeks sparkled with pearlescent Dust placed precisely so to catch the light as she turned this way and that. Her legs were clothed in lacy silvery-white stockings matching Aerrvin's shirt. She had on pinky-golden slippers that laced halfway up her shins. Her dress was two layers, the under dress was the same pinky-gold as the slippers and the over dress, actually the skirt portion, was made with a very open weave of the finest spider silk—dyed the deepest midnight blue, matching Aerrvin precisely. Looking closely she saw that the lacy pattern was the same leafy-vine pattern sewn into his long-vest. The dress was form fitting on top with an empire waist allowing the silk to fall gracefully away from her hips. It barely came mid-thigh in a tattered lacy handkerchief fashion. Truthfully it revealed more than the first dress had, but Mara loved it and would not have changed a thing. Aerrvin applied a sheer fabric shawl about her shoulder's which looked like tulle, but was utterly smooth and softer than the softest down.

She was dumbstruck. Never had she ever imagined she could look as lovely as she did at that moment. She noticed that the shawl had an illusion of wings attached; as she turned this way and that the eye barely registered seeing a glimmer of wing.

Mara suddenly wanted to see herself as other's saw her. She had never considered viewing herself in the mirror at full Brightness.

Alas, perhaps it was not the best room to try the experiment!

As soon as she opened all of her pockets, the Light reflected tenfold off of the countless mirrors and crystals causing even her own self to fall to the ground in awe. "Oh!" she exclaimed. Aerrvin chuckled richly, but was otherwise unable to offer assistance.

***

Clay enjoyed the pounding of the waterfall and racing with the fish. Eventually he climbed out to dry in the breeze and check in mentally to monitor Mara's mood. She had been delighted, melancholy, and mischievous, even almost mocking—covered quickly by joy. Truly, she was capable of switching emotions faster than any Fair One he had ever met. To top it off it was infectious. She also had the gift of empathy and compulsion. While deliberate compulsion spells are frowned upon, natural ability is what it is. Clay donned his evening attire and started upstairs in order to escort the future Queen to her big event. Just as he reached the door his companions also arrived and suddenly Mara was struck with great awe and pleasure. He assumed it would be inappropriate to walk in on her with her fiancé, so he waited.

Each of his companions stood outside the door beaming at her pleasure. "We will probably never know!" Daisy said with a wicked grin on her face.

The,n even more suddenly, her awe grew ten times greater, as did her panic. Clay tried to open the door and found it was locked. Thinking quickly, he vaporized and slid under the door. On the other side he started to coalesce. But realizing what the situation was, he stopped halfway and tried to see if he could unlock the door in his partial state. He spoke and found that his voice was muted, but Mara was able to hear him. "Mara, please put away your Light."

Shocked into obedience she complied. Then she stayed prostrate upon the ground. Clay reformed and opened the door, the others had not realized that he had unlocked it. Gareth rushed past and helped Aerrvin up. "What happened? Aerrvin? Was there an attack?" Gareth asked.

Aerrvin shook his head ruefully. "Not unless you count Mara revealing her Light to herself an attack. She wanted to see herself as I saw her in her Glory. Unfortunately all the mirrors arranged precisely to reflect light was more than a being could handle. Leave it to Mara to knock her own person out with her Brightness!"

He chuckled as he went to Clay's side as he helped the future Queen to stand. Her dress was made for wild flights through starry nights, so it was none the worse for wear. She looked every bit as lovely with her disheveled hair as she had before.

Nevertheless he smoothed her hair with a breeze and kissed her soundly before berating her. "Next time give me some warning. I could have told you it was not the right room to view your full Light in."

Clay kissed her on top of her head and added, "Your attire is completely appropriate, Mara. You *are* still a youngling as far as magic goes. Please consult before acting. That is lesson number one. Are you okay?"

Mara surveyed the room and saw all the concern among her dearest friends. "I am fine. I had no idea it could be so overwhelming. Should I hold some back at my revealing, or is it required to open your whole Light to the world?"

"Great question, Mara!" Ivan responded. "I love it when you think things through. It will certainly cause all to bow as it should. But it will be dark and none will be reflected back to you. It will be safe to reveal all, as is proper. It is not a rule, but as far as I know no one has ever wanted to hold back. Being as vain as we are we want to show everyone all that we can on our Birth Day." He smiled crookedly looking at everyone just to verify if the rest were nodding and smiling in agreement.

Jaera whooped and said, "Then let's party!"

Opening a portal to Ironwood Estates, Gareth and Jaera went first, followed by Elwood, Jasmine, Daisy and Hannah. Then Ivan and Breeze went through, allowing Mara and Aerrvin to arrive last with Clay to follow up as her rear guard. They did not Travel to the interior as that was rude and not possible anyway with all the wards in place. But they did arrive right on the front entryway.

Gareth had already knocked and soon they were in, reuniting friends and family. Amanda and Mara's sisters were there, as well as her stepfather and stepbrother. *In case you were wondering, let it be known that Brentwood's command to Mara's Attendants to stay away from Amanda was set in advance to end on the eve of Mara's birth.*

Brentwood had been optimistic, in the hopes that Mara would celebrate in the Elven way.

Mara was not even glowing and they were struck with awe.

Amanda responded first, "Mara you are more stunning than I ever thought possible! Only the moment of your birth was more amazing than this." She wept as Mara came and hugged her.

"Shh. Mom, I am safe now. Morvayne will not cause me any more trouble. Tonight we get to celebrate, for real."

Sarah and Becky were amazed and asked why they didn't get to wear fairy dresses too.

Aerrvin brought forth smaller lacy shawls for each of them, gaining delighted hugs and kisses. They were dressed in adorable party dresses and appeared fairy-like anyway as their Water Sprite abilities grew with increased contact and belief. They sprouted their own wings without realizing it. Simply seeing Mara with them sparked desire and they suddenly had them. Rick and Ricky simply stared at everyone as though in a dream.

Ironwood drew the crowd into the main gathering hall and had Mara sit in a prominent seat. "As Birthday girl, you get to sit while your guests are introduced to you. It is not always done this way, but I am doing it this way because it feels right."

Mara was then formally introduced to all of those present including those who came with her, as well as her family. Then she was introduced once again to Morthe, Balmoral and Master Groban. Ironwood had said it was to be a small gathering, so she was surprised when he said there were more. Aerrvin's parents were introduced as well as Harmony and Culain. She had nearly forgotten about Brand and Gwennara, but suddenly remembered moments before they entered the room. She did not know what effect seeing someone who looked like Bentwood would do to her mother, but she knew it got her every time.

Unable to remain seated, Mara rose and greeted them halfway, first hugging Brand and then kneeling at Gwennara's feet. She noticed that the rest had bowed as well, it being it their first time seeing her since her return from captivity. At least that was how Mara reasoned it out. In truth they respected Gwennara for her great age and service as Queen, but all acknowledged that Mara was the rightful heir and since she bowed they were obliged. Rick and Ricky simply did as they saw others do, lost as they were to protocol.

Gwennara reached out and raised Mara up. "Daughter, how I have longed for this day." Gwennara hugged Mara with as much love as Mara could have ever hoped to be able to receive. Joy was felt by all, yet not a soul had a dry eye.

Rick had thought that Brand was indeed Brentwood, the likeness was so close, but hearing him being introduced he relaxed until he saw Amanda's response. She burst into tears and asked to be let out of the room. Clay guided her out and calmed her with his touch.

Still the tears fell as she said, "I never knew. I didn't wanted to believe it." She looked at Rick as he came to hold her. "It's okay, I will be fine. I just did not want to create a scene in there."

"Nonsense!" said a lilting voice. Amanda turned to find that the former King and Queen had come to see her. "Family should never be ashamed of each other. Come here."

Amanda went and felt Gwennara's love. It gentled and stilled her soul. "You have beautiful daughters, Amanda. Do you know your birth name?"

Amanda spluttered in shock, "What? No, how could I?"

"It is a talent of mine, not really very useful, but it is mine nevertheless to use as I see fit. Would you like to know your name, and that of your birth mother?" asked Gwennara, not really addressing the question.

Tears threatened again, but Gwennara sent more comfort her way as she continued to hold Amanda's hand.

"Yes, I should like that very much."

Mara had joined them along with Aerrvin. Most of the guests stayed in the main room as Balmoral began to direct his orchestra. Ironwood listened in from the door, preventing more guests from peering in.

Gwennara beckoned Brand to come and stand near her. "Brand has told me that Water Sprite runs strongly in Mara. Would you allow him to check your heritage as well?"

Amanda nodded; avoiding looking at him directly, she held out her hand. Brand took it and gave her a firm pat. "I am sorry for your loss, Amanda, sorry for the pain I cause. You are seventy-five percent Water Sprite and a mixture of Mermaid, Nyad, and Human make up the rest." Brand took Gwennara's other hand and they stood in a circle while Gwennara closed her eyes in concentration.

It took only moments before she opened her eyes and pronounced. "Your mother was a Nyad with a portion of Mermaid and Water Sprite in her genes. That explains a great deal about her leaving you. Nyads are very particular about who can live in their community. Meaning that your father was a Water

Sprite with a portion of Human in him. Nyads do not care to mix with Humans, except to tease, of course. When you failed to show a spark as an infant your mother must have feared that you would be shunned as Human, so she gave you your name and left you for Humans to take care of." Gwennara smiled gently and continued. "Your name at birth was Estelle. You were born at night beneath the starry sky with eyes that shone like the stars. Your birth mother hales from southern California; a strange place for a colony of Nyads to set up, as water is oftens sparse there, but that is where they are. Her name is Sachiel, it means Water Angel. Someday when you are ready, you can seek her out. I am sure she longs to know of your life and happiness. Any proper mother would."

Amanda felt peace; simply having that bit of information gave her comfort. She had a family! She understood how Mara felt about having living ancestors. Including distant cousins who looked like her. Breeze was so similar that Amanda had nearly hugged her first when entering the room.

"Thank you, how do I . . . address you?" Amanda asked more timidly than she was used to be being.

Gwennara patted her hand one last time and replied, "You may address us as Brand and Gwen, or Gwennara if you prefer. I have had enough Your Highness and My Lady speech to last me another thousand years should I choose to stay that long."

"Well, thank you Gwen, that was so kind and helpful. I think dinner is about ready. We should go back in." Amanda saw the small crowd she had attracted and apologized. "Mara, sorry, it's the eve of your big day. I want you to be the star." She smiled and took Mara by the arm and returned to hear the conclusion of Balmoral's before-dinner show.

Ironwood welcomed everyone formally and presented Jill to describe their dinner. Mara ran up and hugged her and stood beside her as she told everyone about the forthcoming meal.

"First let me say this is the largest sit down dinner I have prepared and it has been wonderful working with Ironwood's staff." Jill stood straighter and said, "We will start with a light won ton soup served with sushi on the side. The next course will consist of soba noodles and a variety of garden vegetables as well as your choice of lobster or crab." She paused to allow for the oohs and aahs to wind down. "You will then receive a lemon sorbet to cleanse your palate, followed by a delicate white layer cake served with a refreshing strawberry, rhubarb and orange compote. I promise you will love it, even though it is *not* chocolate!"

The last was specifically spoken to Mara, as she knew well Mara preferred chocolate over fruit.

Dinner was wonderful. Mara sat on the end, just as she had the last time she ate at the Estate; this time her mother sat to her right, with the rest of the family seated one after the other down the line.

Jaera managed to be seated next to Sarah, and Gareth was directly across from Becky. To her left sat Clay followed by Hannah, Aerrvin and then Gareth. Gwennara was not seated next to Brand as he wanted to sit across from the little girls as well. So Gwennara sat next to Ironwood at the head of the table and she had Aerrvin's parents and sister Harmony as well as Culain to keep her company.

Mara was delighted when Dougie came in from the kitchen and sat in the empty seat next to Brand. That made the table 12 seats long, twenty-five dinner guests! Mara never thought she could ever have so many people care about her. Before dessert was served, Ironwood directed a servant pour everyone a glass of Rose Elixir in the most beautiful hand blown glasses she had ever seen. Mara suspected they were from Harmony.

"I should like to offer a toast in honor of my dearest granddaughter, Mara Lilyana Jamis. To wonders and knowledge with the Brightest of futures." He clinked his glass with Gwennara and all followed suit, sipping with delight the coveted Elixir.

Amanda diligently ensured that her daughters were safe to drink it and indeed they were, though they were also given much smaller glasses. Rick and Ricky sipped cautiously not knowing what to expect. They needn't have feared, to them it was simply a sweet rose water, pleasant, but not exciting. For some Humans who may have Fair Ones in their distant genetic ancestry they can sometimes experience a slight improvement in focus, but it would last only a few minutes at most.

Mara basked in the attention, glowing from joy rather than Power. Jill joined them for dessert, with Mara scooting over to allow a stool to be brought up next to her.

"Jill, this was the best dinner I have ever had. Thank you for everything. Did they say you could stay for the whole night? I never asked if Humans were allowed to attend." Mara turned to Clay to inquire.

Answering before she could repeat, he said, "If she would like to stay it can be arranged for her eyes to be opened allowing her to see your full Glory and Light. This includes you, Rick, and Ricky as well."

Ricky surprised Mara with his acceptance and enthusiasm. "I wouldn't miss it for the world! In fact, I think—I think my life has taken a turn for the better!"

Amanda and Rick looked at him inquiringly. Rick asked, "What was wrong with the old life?"

"Nothing, Dad, I just felt kind of bored and obligated to be the football star. You know?"

"I thought you liked football! What was so boring about living in Sequim?" Rick kept his tone down, but he was unable to keep his facial features smooth.

"Dad! Chill! I like fishing and boating and football. I love the store and working there too. But it was just so—ordinary. I guess I secretly dreamed of adventure and excitement coming my way, and Mara has provided it." He looked over at her and smiled the nicest brotherly smile he had ever given her. "Thanks, Mara, this has been the best graduation present ever! I hope it never ends."

Mara brushed a tear away and replied, "I don't think it will. What about your girlfriend?" Mara noticed he was constantly glancing at one Elf or another, but especially Daisy which was hard since she was way down on his side of the table.

"We knew that we would probably find other people to date at college; she is going to college in Oregon so graduation was really our last night together. We are still friends. If things work that way fine, but if not, that's fine too!" He grinned as he realized how shallow he sounded. "I know what you are thinking: She's better off without me."

Rick shook his head. "No, I was actually thinking, 'Smart kid!' Good for you for having dreams and all. No sense getting engaged at such a young age, better that you have a career first. Right?" Rick looked at his nearby table companions. They all nodded agreement before being interrupted by Ironwood.

"If we are all finished eating, we can return to the main room for dancing until the appointed hour."

Balmoral played waltzes and minuets and even some big band music, providing everyone an opportunity to dance to something they could enjoy. Mara danced with everyone, as did Amanda and each of the little girls.

"It is hard to tell who is more popular! Me, Becky, or Sarah," said Mara as she stood with Clay, Aerrvin and Harmony.

Aerrvin recalled Clay's jealousy and replied. "Yeah, little sisters can put a crick in any party!"

Clay smiled, but shook his head. "We get jealous, but we love them dearly."

Harmony was just about to spout off when Aerrvin drug her out to the dance floor. Mara watched with amusement as Aerrvin did some fast-talking, then some silly antics until Harmony was laughing, and enjoying being with her brother.

"Why is it that the Fair Ones love children so much?" Mara asked as Clay escorted her once more out to the dance floor.

"Many reasons. We love their innocence and faith. Being near children actually energizes our Power. That is one thing we have not been able to learn how to replicate or discern how it is done. Mind you, most do not go near children merely to use them for a recharging station. Truly we love them and cannot get enough joy and happiness from them. Looking at your sisters tonight, I can see how everyone felt about meeting my sister," he smiled sadly. "Some revelations only come with age."

Mara was confused. She knew she had read about it, but she had to ask anyway. "Why don't the Faire have more children then?"

"Always questions, Mara. You are lucky that I enjoyed my years as a professor. I am quite sure that you are aware that we Fair Ones are not able to have as many children as we would like. It is a genetic anomaly built in by the Creator. Humans are his Chosen People and he means for them to be the caretakers of the world. Were we able to produce the numbers that Humans are capable of, we would have created a paradise on earth eons ago. This world was created for Humans to work out their salvation and earn a judgment according to their deeds. True, all will gain a new life in the hereafter, but they will be rewarded to varying degrees of Glory and Power based on the life they live here. This is why we are not supposed to interfere too much with the Human population, as you will learn after taking the Oath."

Mara pondered a moment and then asked slyly, "So how hard do Fair Ones try to circumvent their lack of success?"

Clay grinned and replied dryly, "Not very hard at all actually. We do not have the same drive built in that Humans and animals in general have. We are given to meditation and exploration of minutiae as you have been learning." He leaned down to inhale from behind her ear, brushing her cheek with a kiss. "We prefer getting Dusted to procreation any day." He saw her indignation as well as felt her heating up, so he quickly added, "Not that making babies can't be enjoyable too. I am just being truthful, Mara. You asked and I am your appointed mentor. Have you been tempted beyond your control with Aerrvin?"

Mara thought he was getting too personal, but he *was* trying to teach her a lesson on a topic she had brought up. "No, of course not! I am a proper Christian girl and you know it." She wanted to slap him, but he kept a firm grasp on her hands.

"I can tell you that it is the same for most Fair Ones. I would wager that you have shared your Light with him on more than one occasion. Yes?" He asked breathing deeply once more.

This time she managed to get her hand free and slapped him on his chest. "Stop that! If I had known that enjoying my Dust was better than, than intimacy, I would never had allowed it."

Clay chuckled and drew her closer. He whispered in her ear. "Really?"

She relaxed and admitted that she enjoyed Clay's reaction as well as Aerrvin's and everyone else who cowered before her Light and then hastened to do her bidding. "Okay, maybe I would have. So, it is not a sin or forbidden. Right?"

"Not at all." Clay replied, exaggerating one more huffing breath in her hair.

"Hey! Hey! Hey! Lay off the Dust, Clay!" Aerrvin hissed as he danced up to them with Breeze. "Time for you to take a real breather."

Not a sin, true, but still guarded jealously.

Mara joyfully accepted Aerrvin's reprimand as he danced her to the opposite side of the room. "What was that all about? He took three deep breaths within two minutes. He is addicted I know, but you shouldn't encourage him so."

"I am honored that you took note. I was not counting the minutes. How many minutes since we last danced and you breathed in my scent?" Mara asked coyly.

Aerrvin stopped being jealous and replied. "Too many." Then he bent and replaced Clay's lingering kiss with his own. "So what were you discussing that caused you to glow, thus allowing him to inhale?"

"Oh! I had not noticed that I had glowed at all. How embarrassing," she glowed a bit more, noticing this time as the Dust fell in a swirl when Aerrvin spun her around and back. "I had asked about the Fair One's lack of children and he proceeded to teach me the facts of life, mainly that you prefer Dust to any other . . . um, excitement."

Aerrvin chuckled richly and brought her up close just as Clay had done. "Mara you are truly a marvel. I do glory in your Light and bask in your glow as I have said. I do not doubt that I will enjoy further excitement as well," he flashed his quirky smile, causing her to laugh.

"Good, that is all I needed to know," Mara replied. "Do you really wish me to limit Clay to brief snorts of Dust?"

Clay coughed out a laugh as he had danced near. "Mara,

please use more delicate language. I am not a cocaine addict, nor your charity case. I will respect Aerrvin's wishes regarding your private space."

Mara was chastened. She had not meant to offend. Aerrvin looked at her empathetically, sensing her desire to be of compassionate service to Clay. "Mara, Clay; you have my permission to be discreet. No more exaggerated huffing as you were doing. It shames me to have no control over my intended." He looked downcast momentarily, and then beamed a crooked smile at them. "No hard feelings, right, Clay?" He let go of Mara to embrace Clay.

"None at all," Clay replied, returning the hug and adding a kiss to Aerrvin's forehead. "I like you, Purple!"

Aerrvin enjoyed letting his Purple self out, so he grew purple wings and danced Mara about the room a few inches off the ground. One dance was all he could do without tiring too much. They found a small table to sit at and created a platter of bread and cheese to renew their energy. Mara began to feel nervous as she realized that it was only ten minutes until the moment of her birth.

"Here comes Grandpa, Aerrvin, what am I supposed to do? No one has told me anything!" She looked so desperate and adorable Aerrvin couldn't help shrugging, thereby causing her further angst.

He was enjoying her plight when Ironwood gripped his shoulder and asked, "Are you teasing my Mara?"

"Sorry, sir, she wished to know what she should do. I just thought she looked adorable. It is time then?"

"That it is. Mara?" Ironwood held out his arm to escort her to one of his many lovely gardens.

27
I Promise

They went through two rooms to get to the back portico. It seemed like the longest and shortest walk of Mara's life. "Grandpa, what am I to do and say?"

"Be at peace, Mara. I just went through the Oath Ceremony and it was glorious. You will know what to say when the time comes. First though, is your Birth Day moment of revelation, in other words you are to reveal all of your Light just as you did at birth," he chuckled. "You glowed the entire day! Such a sweet baby you were. Here we are."

Mara had been so intent on learning all that she could, that she had not noticed that the yard was literally filled shoulder to shoulder with Elves, Fairies and other beings she had yet to identify. The trees sparkled with literal Fairy Lights.

Looking at the faces closer calmed her, as she saw the love and encouragement in her newfound friends and family. Her sisters were as wide-awake as ever and thrilled beyond measure to view this special occasion. Seeing their joy and knowing that they would grow up with the truth did not fill her with self-serving pity, rather she rejoiced at the freedom they were afforded because of her own awakening. Mara was led to an open gazebo, placing her above those who had come to witness. Jill, Rick and Ricky were the only Humans and Mara could see that their eyes had been opened as promised. They were simply in awe at the numbers and sparkling nature of those who soon would be Mara's subjects. *Two minutes! What am I to do?*

Amanda stood and took Mara's hand both to reassure as well as to gain courage. "Mara is my firstborn daughter. The day of her birth is a cherished memory." She smiled over at her daughter, rejoicing in the fact that she could once again fully see her aura and more. "Her light as a newborn was glorious and Bright. Brentwood said she was the most precious sight he had ever seen. He had looked forward to this day and I sorrow at his not being able to be here. Mara, I am sorry for my mistakes, please forgive me and accept this gift from your father as though I had desired to give it to you as well. I now wish to give you my full support." Amanda placed the letter and journal from her father on a long table prepared for gifts. And then she handed a ring to Mara. "To be used during the ceremony," she whispered.

If it wasn't quiet before it certainly was now. Mara could feel the seconds counting down within her mind and body as though she were being born anew. A pressure gently swept over her from her head to her toes, urging her to reveal her Brightness and Glory to the waiting crowd.

By now she knew what to expect, but she was nevertheless surprised at the suddenness of the response as well as the gasp as if with one voice. It felt so good to glow that she stood there a full minute, showering those nearest her with her Dust. She saw Clay and Aerrvin peeking up; they were closest to her emotionally and capable of witnessing without fear. Eventually Amanda forced her head up; a stream of tears flowed as she marveled at what she had brought into the world.

Mara packed away most of her Light, leaving one pocket free as she bid the audience to rise. "Please rise; thank you for being here to witness my celebration and Oath. I have never felt so loved before."

The time arrived for the next important step in Mara's life.

Normally the father of the initiate performs the ceremony. Mara was amazed that Ironwood would have the Oath memorized already, having just taken it himself. But then she remembered the teaching techniques used on her while in captivity; everything taught was right there, ready to be used as needed. Ironwood was calm and sure as he announced the Oath in a clear rich voice.

"Mara Lilyana ap Jamis. You stand before me this day to pledge your soul to the Light. Do you promise with all your being to live true to the teachings you have received so far?"

Mara found it easy to answer. "Yes."

"Do you promise to allow your Light and Glory to be used to beautify and edify the world in which you live? To protect and give joy to those around you?" Ironwood intoned.

"Yes," Mara answered in her whispery voice.

"My daughter, do you swear by your everlasting soul to never use your Powers to cause harm, or death unless in self-defense? If so please reveal your Light and swear by your faith in the One True God that you will uphold all goodly practices as taught to you throughout your young life thus far."

Mara felt a glorious release as she opened up her Light and answered, "I do swear by my unwavering faith in the One True God that I will never use my Powers or influence to cause harm or death to any being unless in self-defense. I will uphold all of the goodly practices I have been taught."

She was surprised and gratified to feel a loving presence give her a warm embrace and then retreat.

Realizing who or what it could have been, she stood there allowing the tears to course down her cheeks. Her mind raced as she thought of Morvayne and his followers. *How could they turn away from this?* She reflected on her promises for five minutes before putting away her Light.

Breeze brought forth a cool cloth to cleanse her face.

"That was beautiful, Mara. I am so glad to have been a part of it," Breeze said as she took back the cloth and discarded it elsewhere.

Mara smiled her thanks and addressed the crowd once more, "Again, I thank you for wishing to attend the twenty-first celebration of the day of my birth. Please, feel free to place your gifts here. She signaled the table and found that a chair had been placed behind her. She asked for more so that Gwennara, Brand, Laurel and Jasper could also sit with her and Aerrvin. She did not think that her Mother and Rick would feel comfortable receiving the bows that would surely be extended for the next hour or so. She barely registered that Balmoral had brought his orchestra outside as she began the task of receiving her gifts. The Brownies and Fairies were first, filling baskets at Mara's feet with miniature articles of clothing, delightful feathers, and other gifts of nature. Mara had not thought it possible to be so pleased to receive such simple gifts, yet she was as delighted with them as she would have been to receive a pair of cute shoes. And she received a good number of those as well, especially from those who lived in her home!

Because they were too fearful to speak, the procession of gifts went smoothly and more swiftly than Mara would have thought. She had not consciously kept count, but when she thought about it, she realized that the Yellow Fairy before her was the four hundredth being to present a gift.

"When you consider how many miniaturized beings can fit into so large a space as this, it is amazing to realize the numbers." Mara had meant to think, but had lapsed into speaking her mind.

Gwennara responded musically, "Once, on my one thousandth Birth Day, I had a party in a similarly sized courtyard. Everyone down sized so that when the accounting was done it was truly amazing to learn that over two thousand had attended. I judge that there are only eight hundred or so here. Still remarkable for an Oath Taking Ceremony."

Brand chided Gwennara, "Now Gwenna, you know very well that they are here to see the Crystal Throne and coronation of our sweetest descendant ever." He grinned at Mara, moving her emotions as he had the same mannerisms as her father.

"What is a common number for that?" she asked without thinking.

"When I received the Crown it was a joyous occasion and May Day as well. Celebrations went on throughout the world in my honor. My parents had a restricted guest list, which included five hundred of their most trusted supporters. I recognize most of these guest as loyal friends. You can trust them to love you as well as they have loved me." Gwennara nodded regally to a particularly fair Elf who came forward first among the Elves to present gifts.

"Queen Aegle," Gwennara said, rising and then bowing. Mara hastened to follow suit as the rest on the platform also acknowledged the Mother of the Graces.

The beauty bid them sit, except for Mara. "This has been a delight, Mara. I am honored to be she who will lead Clay to find your father. Gwennara, if your daughter is there she will be found and returned to your bosom as well." Turning back to Mara she said, "Yes, I can see you are my daughter through your mother. She has grown in ability since I saw her just a few days gone by." She waved to Becky and Sarah, gesturing for them to come near. Placing a hand on each shoulder she asked, "and are these your dear sisters?"

Mara smiled at each of them as they glowed their tiny Lights. "Yes, these are my dearest sisters in all the world."

"With your permission, and Amanda's, I should like to bless them as my gift to you." She turned to get Amanda's approval. Gaining it, she kissed each child and said, "May you find the treasure and joy each of you deserve."

After meeting one so great, the rest of the guests, though notable, were met in a blur of time. Though in truth, only another hour and a half went by, making it half past three o'clock in the morning.

Midsummer is noted for being the longest day in the year and having the shortest night. Therefore, it was known by all that the sun would be rising soon. Two separate bonfires flared up as the revelers resumed the yearly ritual of rejoicing in the long days of summer and harvest and sorrowing at the shortened days ahead. Mostly it was another occasion to party, and Fair Ones wrote the book. Mara looked out and considered donning her "adult attire" which Aerrvin had created for her, but taking a second look at the fantastical crowd, she changed her mind.

Looking at the golden-haired pretty boy standing next to her, she whispered, "Hey, Aerrvin, it's my birthday! Will you dance with me?"

A Quick Reference Guide to the Fair Realms

In Order of Power and Importance

(Not an exhaustive list.)

Dragons–Chose to serve neither good nor evil. Therefore, they are free to serve either on a whim and are consequently revered as capricious beings.

Elves–Serve good. The Queen of all the Realms is precisely that. She rules and judges all magical beings. Elves can transform into anything.

Goblins–Serve evil. Live below the surface of the earth and are cousins as well as enemies to Brownies, Gnomes, and Dwarves.

Brownies–Serve good. Live below the homes of Elves and Humans. They are a servant class but are revered for all the good they do.

Fairies–Serve good. Wings are not physical appendages, rather they are holographic in nature and represent the qualities of each particular Fairy.

Red = Poetic. Orange = Loyal and temperamental. Yellow = Studious and often perfectionistic. Green = Wild and carefree. Blue = Sincere and great strategists. Purple = Playful. Silver = Nobility. Gold = Royalty. White = Singular focus and a need to withdraw. Black = An absence of conscience, only two have ever been recorded. Other winged beings are all related to Fairies but rank lower, some of these are **Aeries, Sprites, Nyads,** and **Dryads.**

Mermaids–Serve good. Limited powers, but they can still transform.

Others who chose evil include: **Kraken, Trolls,** and **Ogres.**

Characters in Books One and Two

Mara Lilyana Jamis is a twenty-year-old photography major, kidnapped just before she was about to graduate. After recently accepting the truth about her Elven heritage, she became vulnerable to enemy attacks.

Aerrvin ap Rosewin is a Fairy Prince sent to America by his parents to prevent squabbling between him and his sister **Harmony**, who is to become the new Fairy Queen when her mother steps down from the Rose Crown. Aerrvin has been given the Americas to create his own Kingdom.

Bronwyn of Clan MacIntash is a Brownie Chronicler. He is married to **Button**, and their children are **Gingham, Seamus,** and **Calico**. Seamus is a Chronicler in training and more often than not accompanies Aerrvin on his travels and exploits. Brownies are a servant class, serving either a location or an individual.

Jill Beckett is Mara's renter/roommate. Jill is a chef. She watches out for Mara like a big sister; they are best friends.

Amanda Powers is Mara's mother. She remarried when Mara was young and moved from Seattle to Sequim, Washington, where Mara's stepfather owns and operates an electronics store. She very strictly frowns upon the mention of, and belief in, magic.

Rick Powers Mara's stepfather. Father of **Ricky Powers,** Mara's eighteen-year-old step-brother, as well as the father of Mara's half-sisters, **Sarah** and **Becky**.

Ironwood ap Jamis is a wealthy professor and Mara's grandfather whom she loves but rarely sees. Father of **Brentwood Jamis,** Mara's father who was lost at sea.

Gareth ap Rosewin is Aerrvin's cousin and bodyguard, chief of security and most importantly Aerrvin's Nest Mate and best friend. Fairies prefer to sleep in nests, so those with whom they sleep and choose as lifelong companions are called *Nest Mates*.

Jaera the Green is another Nest Mate and best friend of Gareth and Aerrvin. They had two other female Nest Mates, but they do not go to Seattle for the adventures which follow.

Laurel ap Rose Fairy Queen of the Rose Crown and Aerrvin's mother.

Jasper ap Rosewin Consort to Queen Laurel and Aerrvin's father.

Pastor Mike is Mara's pastor and also psychologist to whom she turns when she fears she is going mad.

John and Sarianne are very minor characters who are the youth pastors at Mara's church.

Dougie of Clan Byrne is the geek neighbor who lives across the street from Mara and Jill. Also a Brownie.

Sylvie of Clan Dunkirk is a Brownie. Her family has served the house Mara lives in since it was built in the 1800s. Her parents are **Duncan** and **Juniper**.

Gwennara Wallace is the Elven Queen of all the Realms and mother of the three princesses **Daffodil, Tigerlily**, and **Arianna.**

Brand the Bright is a Fairy. More importantly Brand is King Consort to Queen Gwennara, and father of the three princesses.

Morthe is an Ogre friend of both Ironwood and Clay.

Balmoral is a famed musician among the Fairies and all the magical Realms; he resides in Tacoma, Washington, living quietly while tending a library for the Fair Ones. He is quite old for a Fairy, well over 900 years of age.

Lorelei is Ironwood's second wife; she's a very shy Elf and is a naturalist, with a preference for study over interaction.

Rowan is Lorelei's sister.

Johann and Sasha are husband and wife, they are Fairies, and are the parents of rare twins named **Berry** and **Bright**.

Meriel is a Sea Dragon with three young Dragons at home in her cave. Dragons are neutral as far as good and evil, so they are best approached with caution.

Mirri Sihee is Aerrvin's constant companion; she is an Aerie or Wind Sprite. Mara has yet to acknowledge seeing her.

Morvayne ap Stewart has chosen to serve evil. As an Elf, he ranks higher than Fairies, Brownies etc. He has had a major upset in his life, causing him to hate and despise Humans. He desires to cleanse the world of two-thirds of its Humanity.

He is confident that the remaining people will come to worship and adore him as the King of the world. He chose Mara as his bride long before she ever learned about him and the world of the Faire.

Clay of Glennferry is Mara's Personal Protector and Attendant. He is a Hold Master, meaning he requested his friends to pledge fealty to him, and in return, he offered them a home for life. Mara comes to depend on Clay, and he commits to serving her as long as she needs him. He is excessively pale and thin. The other five Attendants are –

Hannah Thistlewite: second in command of the Queen's guard. She has blonde, billowy hair and wears Dragon armor.

Daisy du Lac: best friend of Princess Arianna. She has red hair and a fiery attitude to match.

Jasmine ap Weaver: fairly reclusive, yet loving. She has dark brown, nearly black hair, and looks like Audrey Hepburn.

Ivan Andiluv: owns a spaceship inherited from his parents. He grew up in space and was too shy to start school at the traditional age of twenty-one, so he is slightly older than his companions. He has red hair and keeps it short, an oddity among Fair Ones.

Elwood (The Mighty) Kildare is Mara's final Attendant among her appointed six. He is large for an Elf; most Elves are slight, but Elwood is broad and well-muscled. He has dark brown hair and an affinity with trees and Dryads.

Additional Minor Characters include:

Breeze Fairlane: second cousin to the three princesses, granddaughter of Queen Gwennara's brother. Currently third in line to the throne.

Kiana: a Water Sprite and expert masseuse who lives and works in the resort near Morvayne's palazzo in Italy.

Ivy: a Brownie who shares duties as one of two of Mara's Chroniclers, she generally hides herself as a ladybug.

Tessa: an Italian house servant who works for Morvayne, along with a cook and a grounds keeper.

George: A Fairy whom Mara first met when she still worked at the retirement home as a Human. She and Aerrvin helped him find his way back into the world of the Faire.

Hans: Morvayne's Yellow Fairy servant and cook assigned to take care of the house on Vashon Island.

And a Troll King, and a Water Lord, and a daughter of Zeus and . . . and . . . and . . .

ABOUT THE AUTHOR

M. Kari Barr has been accused of being a Fairy in disguise. In truth, she is a lover of fantasy and books in general. As the mother of eight children, and having nine grandchildren, Kari has an affinity for all things make-believe. Growing up with a storyteller for a mother adds dimension to her experience, as does living in a log home…on top of a hill…surrounded by trees…in the middle of miles and miles of wheat fields. Says she, "Solitude is lovely."

Tales of Destiny is her debut series with imaginative interpretations of old myths, legends, and folklore.

Visit her website intangience.net

All of the Books in the Tales of Destiny Series

Once Again

And Again

(Sorry for the delay)

Of Love and Loss

(Release date 2020)

Triumph

(Release date 2020 fingers crossed!)

Future Books in the Series

Clay and Arianna: A Prequel

(It's written!)

Arthur and Lilyaura: The Conclusion

Other Books by M. Kari Barr

Thinktacular Thoughts

They Came From the Sea

Rain on Me ~ Poetic Frenzy

Arcadium Autum Emporium ~ Tales of the Gatekeeper

Dawns of Exordium ~ An Anthology